lia James lives in L[illegible] [illegible]aceful
[illegible]rdant countryside and [illegible] wi[illegible] [illegible]ornwall.
[illegible]e also loves the Mediterranean—so rich in myth
[illegible]d history, with its sunbaked landscapes and olive
[illegible]oves, ancient ruins and azure seas. 'The perfect
[illegible]ting for romance!' she says. 'Rivalled only by the
[illegible]sh tropical heat of the Caribbean—palms swaying
[illegible]y a silver sand beach lapped by turquoise water…
[illegible]hat more could lovers want?'

Clare Connelly was raised in small-town Australia
[illegible]ong a family of avid readers. She spent much
[illegible] her childhood up a tree, Mills & Boon book in
[illegible]nd. Clare is married to her own real-life hero,
[illegible] they live in a bungalow near the sea with their
[illegible] children. She is frequently found staring into
[illegible]e—a surefire sign that she's in the world of
[illegible] characters. She has a penchant for French food
[illegible] ice-cold champagne, and Mills & Boon novels
[illegible]tinue to be her favourite ever books. Writing for
[illegible]dern is a long-held dream. Clare can be contacted
[illegible] clareconnelly.com or at her Facebook page.

Also by Julia James

Heiress's Pregnancy Scandal
Billionaire's Mediterranean Proposal
Irresistible Bargain with the Greek
The Greek's Duty-Bound Royal Bride
The Greek's Penniless Cinderella
Cinderella in the Boss's Palazzo

Also by Clare Connelly

My Forbidden Royal Fling
Crowned for His Desert Twins

A Billion-Dollar Singapore Christmas miniseries

An Heir Claimed by Christmas

No Strings Christmas
(Available from Mills & Boon Dare)

Signed, Sealed...Seduced collection

Cinderella's Night in Venice

Discover more at millsandboon.co.uk.

CINDERELLA'S BABY CONFESSION

JULIA JAMES

VOWS ON THE VIRGIN'S TERMS

CLARE CONNELLY

MILLS & BOON

First Published in Great Britain 2021
by Mills & Boon, an imprint of HarperCollins*Publishers* Ltd,
1 London Bridge Street, London, SE1 9GF

www.harpercollins.co.uk

HarperCollins*Publishers*
1st Floor, Watermarque Building,
Ringsend Road, Dublin 4, Ireland

ISBN: 978-0-263-28273-3

12/21

MIX
Paper from
responsible sources
FSC C007454

This book is produced from independently certified FSC™ paper
to ensure responsible forest management.
For more information visit www.harpercollins.co.uk/green.

Printed and Bound in Spain using 100% Renewable Electricity
at CPI Black Print, Barcelona

CINDERELLA'S BABY CONFESSION

JULIA JAMES

MILLS & BOON

For my long-suffering editors, JW and CT—
they'll know why!

PROLOGUE

ALYS STARED AT the little white stick in her hand, blue line clearly visible. The blue line telling her that she was pregnant.

Pregnant.

The word tolled in her head, and she tightened her hand on the edge of the basin in the bathroom, as if to give herself strength.

How am I going to cope?

She dragged her gaze up to her reflection in the mirror over the basin. Her face was white with shock, eyes distended. Thoughts started to race through her head, urgent and fearful.

I can't be pregnant! I can't! Because I can't afford to be! Not now!

She felt a stab of fear claw at her. Downstairs on the kitchen table the letter that had fallen onto the doormat the previous morning still sat, its dread message stark in her head. She took a ragged breath, still staring at her stricken reflection.

Dear God, hadn't the last four years been hard enough? Ever since that nightmare day just before her finals, when she'd been phoned by one of her mother's colleagues to tell her that her mother was in the A&E department of the very hospital she worked in as a nurse. That she was being taken into emergency surgery after having been knocked down by a hit-and-run driver. That she might not survive surgery…

It was a phone call that had changed her mother's life—and hers.

Her mother had been made bedridden, almost entirely helpless, and had needed twenty-four-seven care—care that her daughter had given dedicatedly, devotedly, until complications from her horrendous injuries had finally led to her protracted death little more than six months ago.

Alys shut her eyes, head bowed, as if bearing too great a weight.

She had loved her mother, had willingly devoted herself to her care—but, oh, it had been hard! Hard to give up her own life, her own dreams, to care for her frail, broken-bodied mother—the mother who had devoted her life to the care of others suddenly needing total care herself. There had been times when Alys had longed to escape, to seize life with her own hands—but she had known she couldn't abandon her mother…

And when the end had come it had devastated her. Her mother, the only person in the world who had existed for her, who had loved her, was gone…

I've got no one—no one at all.

The bleak words that had been echoing in her head since her mother had died echoed again now.

Then without conscious thought she let the white stick with its fateful blue stripe fall into the basin. Let her hand drop and fold across the still completely slender curve of her midriff. She felt emotion well up within her. Her fingers splayed out, encompassing. Protective. Cherishing.

She *did* have someone—someone to love and be loved by. Invisible, intangible, beneath her splayed fingers. And suddenly, out of nowhere, it was not just a blue line on a stick, changing her life for ever, but something hugely, powerfully real.

My baby.

Emotion poured through her.

Whatever it takes, I'll do it! My baby will be safe and loved! I'll make a good home for it—somehow...

But she knew, with a hollow feeling inside her, just what that 'whatever it takes' would have to be.

And then memory came, vivid and unforgettable…

CHAPTER ONE

THE MUSIC FROM the DJ's deck pounded as Alys danced unenthusiastically with whoever it was she was dancing with—a friend of Suze, who was a friend of Maisey, whom Alys knew from uni days.

Maisey had urged her to come and stay with her in London for a weekend break—a break from the grim reality of probate, mortgage arrears and piercing grief—to come to this party tonight.

'It's some kind of flash bash at a luxury West End hotel that Suze has got invites for through her modelling contacts. It'll do you good! After all you've been through, a fabulous party is just what you need, hon!'

But now, having let Maisey lend her an outfit, do her hair and face, Alys was not so sure. Maybe she'd been out of circulation for too long, or maybe this kind of party was just not her thing. But she could feel male eyes on her, taking in the short tight dress, the wildly flowing long blonde hair, her eyes huge with make-up, her mouth made a rich scarlet with lipstick. And instead of enjoying herself she just wanted to cut and run, feeling totally out of it.

When the track finally ended, she headed back towards the cocktail lounge, intent on finding Suze, or Maisey, to tell them she was leaving. Her gaze threaded the room, searching for them…

And stopped dead.

As did the breath in her lungs.

Nikos stood by the bar, martini glass in hand, surveying the crowded room with displeasure. His mood was not good. He'd flown in from Brussels late that afternoon, having had to give Irinia her *congé* over lunch. It wasn't convenient to part with her—he had no replacement lined up as yet—but her increasingly blatant hints as to how their relationship could progress to their becoming engaged had passed the limit of his endurance. So he'd wished her well in her glittering career at one of Europe's international banks, and told her marriage was not on his agenda.

His dark eyes were shadowed in his strongly planed face. It hadn't always been so. Ten years ago he'd been engaged, desperate to marry. He'd been a gullible, trusting, eager-to-love twenty-two-year-old who'd naively believed the woman he'd fallen for loved him only for himself…

His sensual mouth twisted. It had been his father who'd saved him from making the worst mistake of his life. He could hear his words now.

'I had to threaten to disinherit you to get you to realise that Miriam Kapoulou only wanted to marry you so that Drakis money could stop her father going bankrupt!'

Miriam handing back his ring had proved his father right. As ever. He heard his father's words again.

'I won't let what happened to me happen to you! No gold-digging harpy will get her claws into you—whatever tricks she pulls!'

Nikos dragged his mind away. He'd grown up with the sorry saga of his own existence drummed into him all his life. Grown up with his father's perpetually resentful gaze on him…

Wishing to hell that I was any woman's son but the one who trapped him into marriage.

No, he wouldn't let his mood worsen by going over ground that was as painful as it was tediously familiar. He'd spent his boyhood trying to dispel that resentful gaze, spent his adulthood proving that he was a true Drakis. Doing what a Drakis did best in life. Making money.

And he was good at it—even his father had to acknowledge that. Deals came naturally to him and he could negotiate down to the wire. Thanks to his efforts, the Drakis coffers were overflowing. It was how he spent his life—on the move, with little time for leisure or relaxing. And when he did relax, it was not at hectic parties like this.

He was only here because he'd been expecting to meet up with a City acquaintance who'd seen him checking in and casually invited him along this evening to a party he was hosting—something to do with the fashion industry, it would seem, given the preponderance of over-made-up model-types and fashionistas swanning around extravagantly.

Nikos's gaze swept over them disparagingly. Too many of them were here to pull, he suspected cynically—as were, concomitantly, the males as well, of course. Well, he wasn't going to be one of them. Not tonight. Not his style.

He surveyed the room, impatient to spot his City acquaintance and sound him out briefly, decide whether to follow up any potentially lucrative ventures with him.

And out of nowhere all thoughts of *Not tonight. Not my style* evaporated totally.

Alys stood, her gaze fastened as though pulled by a magnet to the man sitting at the bar on the far side of the crowded cocktail lounge. Tall, lean-bodied, dark-haired, thirtyish, with a tanned skin tone that spoke of Mediterranean climes and sculpted features that somehow made her think that she had never, in all her life, ever seen a man so lethally good-looking…

And he was looking right at her.

It was electrifying.

Unconsciously, she felt her lips part, her pulse quicken, as her eyes met his gaze across the room. Then, distractingly, her former dance partner was helping himself to her wrist.

'Hey, babe, come on back!'

She turned, trying to tug herself free. 'No! Thank you—no!'

She got no further. Another voice—deep, accented and commanding—interjected. 'She said no.'

Alys's head spun round. It was the man from the bar, suddenly there, eyeballing her wannabe dance partner.

The restraining hand dropped from her wrist. 'OK, pal, I didn't know she was with you.'

'Well, now you do,' came the dismissive reply.

Alys felt her elbow lightly cupped, and then the man whose lethal good looks had stopped her totally in her tracks was guiding her towards the bar. She tried to pull her ragged thoughts together and failed totally. Instead, she let herself be helped onto a bar stool as the man settled himself back on his in a lithe movement.

'You look like you could do with a drink,' he said to her.

There was amusement in his voice now, the note of implacable command gone. She looked across at him, conscious that her heart was thumping, her pulse throbbing. Dear God, he really was the most fantastic-looking man she had seen in her life…

It was the eyes—incredibly dark, long-lashed, looking at her with a glint of amusement in them—and also something much more. Something that told Alys, with an instinct as old as time, that he had not just intervened out of masculine chivalry.

That something else had motivated him.

That he was liking what he was seeing…liking it *a lot*…

She felt heat flare in her cheeks again, beneath the make-up Maisey had cheerfully slapped on her, and was grateful it was helping to subdue the colouring of her face under his gaze.

'So what would you like to drink?'

The accented voice came again, and she was glad of the enquiry.

'Um…a Sea Breeze?' she heard herself say, her voice somehow breathy, which it never normally was. But her breathing was too rapid, too shallow, her pulse-rate too hectic, for it to be anything else.

I was going to leave. Find Maisey and head off. And instead—

Instead she was perched on a bar stool, while a man who was like no other she'd ever set eyes on in her life was coolly presenting her with a just-mixed Sea Breeze, lifting his martini glass to her.

'Yammas,' he murmured.

Joltingly, her fingers closed around the icy column of her own glass, her scarlet-painted nails vivid against it, matching the cranberry-red of her cocktail.

'Yammas?' she heard herself say, glancing up at him.

A half-smile tugged at his mouth—one that did yet more damage to Alys's frail hold on normality.

'Greek for cheers,' he replied, and took a mouthful of his martini.

His eyes washed over her almost casually, as if mentally assessing her. Cataloguing her features.

Alys was burningly conscious of what he was seeing. Her mane of artfully tussled blonde hair rippled over her shoulders, her eyes were deep with shadow, lashes thick with mascara, mouth lush with lipstick. The dress Maisey had smoothed over her was tight, almost a size too small, and her breasts were crushed beneath it, exposing a curve of decolletage that she'd never exposed even in her uni days. The hem she was suddenly so conscious of was riding on her thighs, moulding them and the curve of her hip.

Instinctively she crossed her legs, hoping it would make the dress less tight. All it achieved, she realised, with a little frisson, was making that dark gaze flicker to her legs…

'Greek?' she heard herself say, as if that might draw the too-attentive flicker away from the short hem.

It succeeded, and his gaze returned to her face, veiled slightly beneath lashes that were surely too long for a mere male…

She saw him relax his stance, lay a casually placed forearm on the surface of the bar as he took another ruminative mouthful of his martini. Then he placed his glass back on the bar, holding out his hand instead.

'Nikos,' he said. 'Nikos Drakis.'

Giving his name made his accent more pronounced. There was something about the way he said it that for a second made Alys think he was expecting some response to his name. But what it was she had no idea.

'Alys,' she said, sliding her hand into his. 'Alys Fairford.'

It was the briefest contact, but she felt her cheeks flare again, her eyes going to him, meeting his. Mingling.

'Good to meet you, Alys. The evening was looking very tedious. But now…'

The low murmured voice was still infused with that faint amusement…and something more.

Something that banished, as if they had never existed, the four long, anguished years she had spent looking after her mother, locked away from the world, turning her back on anything else, denying herself everything the world might offer, feeling her youth slipping by…

Something that made her want, with a fierce longing, all that she had been denied. All that she was not going to deny any longer, with this incredible man looking at her the way he was, with those dark, irresistible eyes, as no man had ever looked at her before.

And the certainty was suddenly searing within her.

She was not going to deny it tonight.

There was a voice trying to make itself heard inside Nikos's head. Demanding what the hell he was thinking of, picking up one of this gilded flock of party girls thronging the place.

Responding to whatever it was that had drawn him to his feet, to remove her from the oaf pestering her, had been an impulse he couldn't explain. Didn't want to. He wanted only to let his eyes run over her, from that silken mane of artfully tousled hair, to the short hem of her dress, exposing those long slender legs.

Yet there was something about her that was more than her looks…

Maybe it was in the eyes. They were blue-grey and widened now, fastening on him with something in them that just for a moment gave him pause, that was somehow at odds with the rest of the packaging. Not that he objected to the packaging. Not in the least…

He resumed his full-on appreciation of her stunning physical charms. Male response as old as time started to purr within him as he went back to appreciating all that was on display. Though blatantly picking up an unknown female like the way he was doing now was not his habit, for a woman like this one he'd make an exception…

Unwelcome memory flickered in him. The all too familiar saga of his father's resentment-fuelled youth, and the woman who had so fatefully—so disastrously—caught his eye.

Nikos shook it from him. He wouldn't be making the same mistake his father had. Forewarned was forearmed.

He made himself relax, take another mouthful of his martini. This knock-out female had walked into his vision, so why not enjoy it? Enjoy the evening and, if she were like-minded, the night ahead too…

Would she be like-minded?

Dressed as she was, she looked as if he might have little doubt of it, and yet once again he felt that sense of contradiction, difference. He put it down to the wide-eyed expression with which she was so openly gazing at him. As if she just could not stop looking.

She dropped her gaze back to her cocktail tumbler, two spots of colour suddenly burning in her cheeks beneath a layer of make-up. That, too, didn't quite go with the glitzy packaging…

He set down his martini glass with a click. Time to make the next move. He smiled across at her. Warm and inviting. Gaze lambent. Lids half drooping.

'Have dinner with me, Alys,' he said.

The hotel restaurant was quiet, and Alys was glad of it. After the crowded cocktail lounge and the thudding dance floor, the hushed ambience of the Michelin-starred restaurant was welcome.

Am I really here?

That sense of dazed disbelief that had washed over her ever since she'd set eyes on the man who was now wining and dining her came over her again. But it was a disbelief that was becoming more and more real with every moment. Her other self, so long buried, so long suppressed, was riding higher and higher. A sense of recklessness—of being unleashed, of seizing everything that life had denied her for four long years—was taking her over. And she was welcoming it, embracing it, with every passing moment in the company of this fabulous man.

Is this really happening?

But the exquisite gourmet meal was deliciously real enough, and the way Nikos's dark, long-lashed gaze flickered over her was even more real, making her shiver inside with a response that came from deep within her.

They were conversing, and she was grateful she was able

to carry on even a semblance of ordinary conversation when she could feel a shivering sense of awareness all through her, when her blood seemed to be throbbing in her veins and she could not stop it—did not want to.

She lifted a forkful of rich *canard au cassis*, asking him about his travels. He'd told her he was on the move constantly as part of his business, which seemed to be something about high finance and global investments—things she knew nothing about. But the question she asked was about the places in the world he'd been to—places she would never get to, and even if she did it would only ever be as a budget holiday traveller.

'The places I go to are less exciting than you'd think, Alys,' he was saying now. 'Brussels, Frankfurt, Geneva—all just places where business is done. So are places like New York, Shanghai and Sydney when you've been there more times than you can remember—and when you mostly just see the airport, a hotel and someone else's office! I don't get much time off.'

She paused in eating, looking across at him. He sounded jaded—almost…bitter?

'So why work so much?' she asked.

A thin smile was her reply. 'Contrary to popular opinion, money doesn't grow on trees.'

Alys frowned. 'But if you have enough for your needs, why go on making more?'

He picked up his wine glass, sitting back and looking at her with a slightly strange look in his eyes. 'How much money would you say you need, Alys?'

She blinked. 'Well, enough to pay the bills and a bit over, I suppose.' She gave a small shrug. 'I'm the wrong person to ask, really. I've always had to live modestly.' Even as she spoke she felt a twinge of guilt at eating a meal that she could never afford on her own… She bit her lip, feeling awkward. 'I'm sorry. Here I am, having this absolutely gorgeous gourmet meal…' Her voice trailed off.

The strange look in his eyes vanished, and his gaze was warming instead. 'You're more than welcome, Alys. After all, I did invite you, didn't I?'

She nodded, feeling better about it. But not entirely. Maybe it had been a mistake to accept his invitation to dinner…knowing what had motivated it. She reached for her wine, then hesitated. It was likely from a hideously expensive bottle.

She felt the lightest of touches at her wrist. 'Alys, I have said—you're my guest. Enjoy!'

Her eyes met his. In his there was only warmth. She felt the tension leave her. All the same, she wanted to move on to a safer topic.

She took a sip of her wine, then set the glass back on the table. 'So, if all you ever see of those fantastic countries you fly to is the airport, a hotel and offices, what about your own homeland?' Her voice warmed. 'I've never been to Greece—is it as beautiful as it looks? All those Aegean islands!'

'I don't travel about in Greece much. I'm based in Athens. There's a family villa on one of the islands, but I can't remember when I was last there.'

'Oh, that's a shame!' she said spontaneously. She directed a little smile at him. 'You should definitely promise yourself a visit soon. Take some time off! Chillax!'

'In the right company, that might sound appealing…'

His voice was distinctly husky, and Alys felt her cheeks warm. She reached for her wine again and then went on eating. A sudden, disturbingly intimate vision assailed her, of her and Nikos basking on the beach outside a beautiful Greek villa…

She was glad when he moved the subject on. 'So what about you, Alys? Are you a Londoner?'

She shook her head. 'I'm staying with an old uni friend at the moment. Home is in the Midlands. A rather dull dormitory town near Birmingham—though there is lovely countryside around. And it's not too far from Stratford-upon-Avon.'

That was safer territory, and she was glad when he followed up on it, talking about Shakespeare. Her voice warmed with enthusiasm as she recalled productions seen in her student days, which led on to him talking about classical Greek theatre.

She joined in readily, finding him both knowledgeable and easy to talk to. It was heady, knowing that she could talk so easily to someone whose incredible looks could make her melt inside—as if she had known him for much longer than a bare hour or two. He was putting her at her ease, and she was aware of that, yet she couldn't help but respond to it.

At some point she became aware he was eyeing her curiously. 'You realise I'd thought you were something in the fashion industry?' he said. 'With your looks, maybe a model?'

She felt herself colouring again slightly. 'Oh, no, I'm not tall enough—or thin enough!'

He lifted his wine glass, taking a leisurely mouthful, resting his eyes on her. 'I wouldn't change a thing about you, Alys,' he replied.

And that husky sound was there in his voice again.

As was the colour in her cheeks.

And the quickening of her heartbeat when he looked at her like that, with those incredibly dark deep eyes of his…

He tilted his wine glass to her. 'To you, Alys—and to our evening together…'

His eyes held hers and she could not let hers drop—could not do anything except fall into his expressive gaze, which was telling her burningly, clearly, just why she was with him…

Then he was speaking again.

'I only regret that I have to fly out tomorrow,' he said, and the huskiness was gone now, leaving something brisker in his voice instead. 'Geneva. I'm only passing through London briefly.'

He met her eyes, and Alys got the impression he was

conveying something to her. For a moment she didn't know what. Then she did. It made her flush, and reach for her wine glass. She said nothing, and a moment later he had gone on to make some remark comparing Geneva to Zurich, drawing more questions from her about both, and the conversation moved on in the same easy fashion as before.

Yet all the time another conversation was running. She knew it, felt it—did not reject it. And when, at the end of their leisurely, exquisite meal, it finally surfaced, she did not reject it then either.

He sat back, idly cupping the bowl of his empty wine glass, resting his half-hooded gaze on her, giving nothing away—giving *everything* away.

'Shall we have coffee upstairs?' he murmured.

He paused, and the expression in his eyes told her that the question he was asking her was more than those words.

'What do you say, Alys?'

She could feel her heart beating beneath the tight contours of her dress. Feel the supreme consciousness of the moment.

This won't come again. If I say no now he'll smile, and accept my answer, and see me into a taxi. He'll thank me for the evening...and it will all be over...

And she couldn't bear this amazing, intoxicating encounter with this fabulous man to be over—not yet.

She heard her own voice speak. Give him the answer that he wanted—that she did too.

'Why not?' she replied.

And felt her heart beat more strongly than ever.

CHAPTER TWO

CAREFULLY, NIKOS LEVERED himself out of bed, then stood looking down at the slender, still-sleeping figure half covered by the bedclothes, pale hair drifting across the pillows. A frown drew his brows together. She looked so different from the way she'd looked the evening before.

At some point in the night she must have retired to the en suite bathroom and removed her layers of make-up, because her face was quite clear of it—as were her eyes. No longer heavily shadowed, her eyelids were almost translucent, and her lashes, without lashings of mascara, spiked delicately on her cheek.

His frown deepened. She looked younger. More…innocent.

He discarded the word. Discarded, too, the memories that pricked at him now of the way she'd gone into his arms, with passion flaring in her eyes, her lips receiving his, opening to him as he'd drawn her enticing body against his.

And yet for all her readiness to return his ardency there had been that last-minute hesitation as he had led her into the suite's bedroom. He'd kissed her again, consumingly and deeply, sweeping her up into his arms to lower her down upon the bed, peeling her too-tight dress from her, eager to feast on the lissom body beneath that had been tempting him all evening and which he could no longer resist.

Could that hesitation have been shyness? Or had she merely been being coy?

At the time he hadn't cared—his arousal had been full and he'd wanted only to sate it, and to bring her to the pleasure he knew he could arouse in her. Memory flared again, hot and humid. And he had brought it to her time and time again.

Now, as he looked down at her, he felt arousal stir again. There had been something about his possession of her, hers of him… She'd clutched him to her, her fingertips indenting on his shoulders, her slender thighs holding his fast as her spine had arched beneath him, and her face had lit like a living flame as her body pulsed and throbbed around him, enclosing him in a union of the flesh that had been…

Like nothing I have known.

Again, that frown flickered in his eyes, as if seeking questions he did not wish to answer, only to suppress.

He clenched his jaw with a fierce imposition of necessary self-control, and had to suppress the overpowering urge to lower himself beside her once more, to turn her sleeping form to his and wake her in the way that he so wanted to…

He turned away—forced himself to do so. There was no time for anything more than what he had had already. His morning schedule was full, and then, as he had deliberately warned her, he was flying out to Geneva.

He strode into the bathroom, decisively shutting the door. She'd come out of nowhere, for one night only, and whether his impulse to keep her with him for the night had been rash or irresistible, it was, without a doubt, now over.

Alys stirred, waking slowly from sleep. Nikos was kissing her. But not as he had kissed in the long, endless night… This was brief, not lingering. A token kiss, no more than that.

She opened her eyes and saw him straightening away from her, standing by the bed, fully dressed, as he had been the night before, in a business suit. He was freshly showered and shaved, with a faint hint of expensive aftershave about him, and the morning light was glinting on gold cufflinks.

He smiled down at her, but it was not the intimate, sensual smile of their lovemaking. It was a smile that hinted of regret and dismissal—no more than that. Making it clear to her that their time together, so brief, was now over.

'I have to leave,' he told her. 'There's no rush for you,' he went on. 'Take all the time you want. Order breakfast, obviously—it's on the suite's tab.' He paused, still looking down at her. 'I want you to know,' he went on, and now she could hear the faintest huskiness in his deep voice, 'how very memorable our night together was.'

For an instant so brief it almost seemed not to exist, he seemed to hesitate. Then it was gone. He smiled again, but his eyes were still veiled. All intimacy vanished.

'Look after yourself, Alys,' he said.

Then he was turning away, walking out of the bedroom. A moment later she heard the suite door open and close again. Then there was silence. She was alone.

Alone with only golden memories of a night that would never—could never—come again in her life. A night that would change her life for ever.

Three months later

Nikos gazed out of the window over the wide Atlantic far below, stretching out his legs in the spacious first-class seat as the plane headed east. It would land at Schiphol in the morning, the familiar red-eye, and there in the Netherlands he'd change planes and head south, back to Athens, ready to debrief his father on another lucrative business venture accomplished, boosting Drakis profits yet higher.

His father would be pleased.

'You're proving yourself a true Drakis!'

He could already hear his father's approbation. And something else. Something that always edged his father's voice when he spoke to him. Something that always grated.

Deliberately, he flicked his thoughts away, lifting the glass of pre-dinner champagne to his mouth. His negotiations in Chicago had been tough, requiring focussed concentration and days of late-night working. What he wanted now, he knew, was some R&R.

And he knew just who with…

The fantastic blonde who'd beguiled him that night in London when he'd finished with Irinia.

He frowned. He'd tried telling himself it had been a one-off indulgence—an impulse he couldn't explain and didn't need to. Yet since that night he hadn't been able to put her out of his mind. Or his memory.

She flickered there now, just as beguilingly as if she were actually with him. The memory of her velvet mouth opening to his, the sweet ripeness of her breasts cupped in his hand, her body arching to receive his…

He set down his champagne glass with a click. This wasn't the place for such memories. But they filled his head all the same.

He hadn't given her any indication that they would have any more than a single night together. After all, unlike Irinia, she didn't come from his world. He had picked her up at a party, seduced her that very evening, never intending it to be any more than a passing fancy.

But why shouldn't I make it more?

They'd been good together—*very* good.

Memorable—that was what he'd said to her that morning when he'd left her lying in his bed.

So why deny himself something that had been that good? He'd wanted her from the first moment he'd set eyes on her.

And I still do.

He reached for his champagne again, decision made. He

wouldn't go straight back to Athens after all. He'd divert via London.

Find Alys.

Make her his once more.

Sunshine bathed the little garden beyond the kitchen window, but Alys could not appreciate it. She'd received a second official notification—more starkly worded than the first—informing her that unless payment of her mortgage arrears were received, court proceedings would start imminently.

Foreclosure.

The grim word tolled in her head and real fear clutched at her. This modest semi had been her home since her schooldays, when her mother had finally saved enough money to put down a deposit, start paying a mortgage instead of rent. She had managed to raise her single-handedly, somehow juggling a baby, a child, then a teenager, with the non-stop demands of being a hospital nurse.

How much of her mother had she actually seen during her childhood?

Not enough.

That was the brutality of it.

I don't want that for my baby.

But what she did want—desperately—was a safe home, first and foremost.

Fear clutched at her again. To be threatened with losing her home now, of all times, with a baby on the way…

The mortgage company had allowed the arrears to build up after her mother's accident, switching to interest-only repayments, which had just been manageable with her mother's incapacity benefit and Alys's carer's allowance, and a great deal of punishing, penny-pinching budgeting. But after her mother's death payment of the backdated monthly repayments had been demanded.

Alys had begged for more time and got a job—nothing fancy, just something in the nearby supermarket—before making a start on the mountain of arrears. But now repayment in full was being demanded. Foreclosure was threatened.

Alys looked out through the window over the sunlit garden, which was mocking her with its brightness.

There was only one way to get the kind of money she needed in time—only one hope.

She bit her lip, her expression stark. The letter she'd sent—so difficult to write, so essential—had been posted to the hotel in London, with a request to forward it.

But would it be forwarded?

And, even if it was, how would Nikos respond?

She simply had no idea.

Nikos walked across the hotel lobby, heading for the concierge desk. Concierges knew everything that went on at a hotel, and he was the man most likely to be able to track down the woman who had been at a hotel function several months ago.

'Ah, Mr Drakis—how good to see you again. What can we do for you this evening?'

The familiar greeting of the concierge was reassuring. But, on the point of making his enquiry, Nikos saw the man take something out of a drawer in his desk, hold it out to him.

'We were about to forward this on to you, sir,' the concierge said.

Nikos frowned, glancing at the envelope. He took it, noting the thin, cheap paper and the handwritten address—his name, care of the hotel. It had a UK stamp on it, but the postmark was blurred. His frown deepened and automatically he turned away, ripping open the envelope, impatient to dispose of whatever it held so that he could put his enquiry to the concierge.

But as his eyes scanned the handwritten contents that enquiry became totally and absolutely unnecessary… As did all his plans for the woman who had beguiled him that single memorable night. And who had just exploded a bomb in his life.

Alys finished her last piece of toast and put her plate in the sink. She needed to get going…head down to the supermarket for her shift. Her mood was bleak. The morning's post had been and gone, and there was still nothing from Nikos.

What if he just doesn't want to know?

After all, it would hardly be welcome news, would it?

Her expression changed, became haunted by a familiar ghost. One that had been with her all her childhood.

Her mother's words rang in her ears.

'I never told him—he wouldn't have wanted to know, believe me…'

A pang smote her—an old grief, a sense of loss for the father she had never known, who had never known about her. She took a breath, her hand going to her midriff. At least *her* baby would never have to bear hearing *her* say, *I never told him…*

Then her burst of defiance collapsed. She might have written to tell Nikos that she was going to have his baby—but that didn't mean he intended acknowledging it. Let alone helping her financially.

The stab of too-familiar fear came again, at the threat of foreclosure hanging over her head, and even as it did so she heard the front door bell ring. It was a courier, holding out an envelope to her.

'Needs to be signed for,' the courier announced, and proffered an electronic pen and pad.

She closed the door after signing, ripping open the envelope anxiously. Was this the possession order she was dreading?

Please, no.

But the single sheet of paper was not from the mortgage company.

It was from Nikos.

And as she read it relief flooded through her.

The plane was starting its descent. Out of the window Alys could see the coast of Greece, so familiar from maps, with the narrow isthmus of Corinth leading out from the mountainous mainland into the bulge of the Peloponnese.

Memory plucked at her of how she'd asked questions of Nikos about his homeland that night she'd had dinner with him—the night he'd swept her into his bed. The night that had brought her here, now, flying out after using the plane ticket Nikos had provided, having dug out her passport, unused since student days, filled with relief that he was not rejecting the news that she was pregnant from their single night together.

Because why else would he have sent for her?

She felt the plane dip, drop height, and pressed her hand down on the arm of the seat, feeling her stomach drop too. Would Nikos be there, at the airport, waiting to greet her as she came out at Arrivals?

Thoughts raced through her head—thoughts that should not be there, that had no place there. They swept her back to that night when he had only had to smile at her, only had to let his lidded gaze wash over her to make her feel she was melting honey…

She wiped away such tempting memories with a shake of her head. She had not come here to see Nikos again as a lover—that single night they'd shared was all he'd wanted of her. She had to accept that. After all, he'd made no mention of seeing her again, of their encounter being anything more than what it had been. She'd never heard from him since—only now, in response to the letter she had sent him telling him about the baby. The baby that, thankfully, it seemed he was prepared to acknowledge.

Neither of us intended this to happen, but now it has surely we can sort out something between us...

She felt anxiety nip at her again. Whatever the eventual outcome of what she and Nikos agreed to, surely he would not want to see her made homeless?

As for anything more—would he want any involvement other than financial? She must not hope too much. Must not impose the forlorn hopes of her own fatherless childhood on him…

With a change in engine note and ailerons lowering, the plane glided down towards the runway that seemed to race up to meet the wheels. There was the bump of contact, the roar of reverse thrust—and she had arrived in Athens.

To whatever awaited her here.

Her fate, and that of the baby she carried.

Nikos glanced at his watch. The plane would have landed now, and Alys would be en route to the city in the car he'd sent for her, taking her to the hotel he'd booked her into. Nowhere fashionable—the last thing he wanted was anyone seeing him with her, starting gossip. His expression hardened. There would be gossip aplenty before long. Unless…

No, he would not give space to such pointless thoughts. He would deal with the situation as it developed, on the basis of fact, not speculation.

Forcibly, he dropped his eyes to the complex document he was perusing, which set out the intricate terms and conditions of the latest deal his father had assigned him to. After this one was complete there would be another one for him to land. And then another. It was his life—deal-making.

A true Drakis! Those words were what his father would praise him with.

His mouth twisted in bitter irony. Soon he would be striking a different kind of deal. One he would have no choice but to strike.

Unless…

That word again! He dismissed it, as he had before, forcing his gaze to focus on the fine print in front of him on the wide mahogany desk in his palatial office in the splendid edifice that had been Drakis HQ for over a hundred years—a historic heritage which, so his father constantly informed him, he was fortunate to possess. To strive to be worthy of…

Father to son for over a hundred years.

Even a son like himself—

He pulled his mind away. What point to dwell on what had been drummed into him all his life? None. Except that now, irony of bitter ironies—

No! With a clenching of his fist he silenced his jibing thoughts. By sheer willpower he focussed finally on the document in front of him. Time enough tomorrow to face what must be faced.

Alys was standing to one side of the lobby in the hotel she had been delivered to by the civil but unforthcoming driver who had held up her name as she'd emerged into Arrivals and ushered her into a sleek, expensive-looking car with tinted windows, that had purred quietly as it made its way from the airport into the city.

She had craned her neck, trying to take in her surroundings, burningly conscious that her stomach was still hollow, that she was truly here in Greece.

Summoned by Nikos Drakis.

Of whom there had been no sign—at the hotel or thereafter. Only a message, relayed to her by the receptionist, to say that she would be called for the following morning at eleven o'clock.

She had been given her room key, and her small suitcase had been removed by a bellhop who had escorted her to a room in this modern but quite anonymous hotel. She'd felt her spirits, determinedly buoyed up during the flight, sink right down. Tiredness had swept over her, for the day had been long, and stressful—the coach journey to London, then the tube out to Heathrow and the four-hour flight to Athens.

Now, the next day, waiting in the lobby a few minutes before eleven, her back and shoulders stiff, she saw the same driver who had brought her from the airport walking into the lobby. He came up to her, bidding her follow him. She did so, clutching her handbag, and he opened the rear passenger door of an even sleeker, more expensive-looking car than yesterday's, which was waiting at the kerb.

She climbed inside the spacious interior.

Nikos was there on the far side, his face unsmiling.

CHAPTER THREE

NIKOS'S EYES WENT to her. His first thought was that he barely recognised her. She couldn't have looked more different from the way she had that night in London. Her hair was drawn back into a tight French pleat, she had not a scrap of make-up on, and her plain shirt dress in pale brown obviously came from a chain store.

His gaze dropped automatically to her midriff. Absolutely nothing showed.

Memory—completely illogical, completely inappropriate—suddenly pierced Nikos's armour-plated thoughts.

A memory of how he'd first set eyes on her, paused in the cocktail lounge, drawing his gaze towards her for reasons he still could not explain to himself. His eyes lingering on her...how incredibly, irresistibly enticing she'd looked...

His already thin lips thinned even more.

Well, I damn well should have resisted her!

But it was too late for regrets.

Far too late.

Alys sat back in the deep, soft leather seat. Her mouth had gone dry and she could think of nothing to say. Thoughts of what she might have been expecting from Nikos—hoping for—had disappeared.

Then Nikos spoke. Just saying her name.

She swallowed, then gave an awkward half-nod, wondering how best to respond to that unsmiling face.

'Thank you for inviting me here,' she got out. It seemed the only thing to say.

'What else did you expect?' Nikos's voice was as dry as it was accented. He nodded at her. 'You will need to do up your seat belt,' he informed her.

Thankful for something to occupy her, she fumbled with the belt, finally getting it slotted into place. She was burningly aware that, despite his unnerving, unsmiling gaze, he was having exactly the same impact on her as the first time she'd set eyes on him—he had the same lethal good looks, the same potent air of cosmopolitan elegance in his superbly tailored light grey business suit, the same hint of expensive-smelling aftershave, familiar from spending that one and only night in his arms.

But she must not think of that—not now. The car was moving off into the traffic, and she glanced out through the car's window.

'Where…where are we going?' She tried to make her voice sound normal, but knew it wasn't.

'To get you checked out,' came the reply.

The accented voice was cool, completely unlike the warmth that had been in it at their first encounter.

Our only encounter.

'Checked out?' Her gaze swivelled back to Nikos.

'A medical check-up at an obstetrics clinic.'

'Oh. I had a check-up last week. At my GP surgery, with the midwife—'

'This will be far more thorough,' Nikos cut across her. 'With a consultant obstetrician.'

She fell silent. Her thoughts were in tumult. She hadn't known what to expect when she met Nikos again, how he would react. Well, now she knew. And she could feel her heart sink.

Impulsively, she spoke again. 'Nikos, I know this has come as a shock to you. It did to me. I never expected—'

She broke off. For a moment he simply held her gaze, his own totally unreadable. She turned away again, looking out of her tinted window, dismay spiking through her.

I shouldn't have come! I should never have written that letter to him telling him about the baby—

She cut herself off mid-flow, her lips pressing tightly. It was too late for regrets—and anyway, she thought silently, she couldn't afford to regret telling him. The threatening letter from the mortgage company weighed like lead in the base of her handbag.

She heard Nikos start to say something, but as she turned her head she realised it wasn't to her. He'd taken out his phone and was making a phone call. It was in Greek, and she was glad of it, turning her head away again, tension racking her.

The tension stayed for the rest of the car journey, until the car pulled up outside a modern building, and the driver got out, opening her door. Nikos got out as well, and led the way inside, striding up to the reception desk and speaking tersely in Greek.

A nurse came hurrying forward and approached Alys, who was lingering by the door. 'Please come this way,' the nurse addressed Alys.

Alys half looked at Nikos, but he had settled himself down in the waiting area, was picking up a newspaper…ignoring her. Numbly, she followed the nurse, and was shown into a spacious consulting room.

'Ah, Miss Fairford—how very good to meet you!'

The urbane, dark-suited consultant behind the wide desk got to his feet, gesturing for her to be seated, and resumed his own seat, opening up the folder placed in front of him by the nurse, who then stood back, hands folded neatly, clearly 'in attendance'.

The obstetrician introduced himself, his English only slightly accented, and then smiled benignly. 'Now, before we proceed to the examination, may I just check the details so far? Is this your first pregnancy? Yes…good. And how many weeks would you say? I see. Any discomfort of any kind so far? No? Good…good. No medical issues? You've been seen by your own doctor, of course, and heard nothing but good? Excellent! Now, allow me to place you in the care of my nurse, and then we'll make ourselves absolutely certain that everything is proceeding exactly as it should.'

He smiled again, as warm and reassuring as only a very expensive medical consultant could be, and then left her with the nurse to supervise her undressing.

It was quite some time before she was ready to emerge again from the consulting room. Nikos had been right. It had been a very thorough check-up indeed.

And if there had been the slightest flicker in the consultant's eyes when she'd confirmed that she knew exactly how far her pregnancy had progressed, that there could be no ambiguity about the date of conception, she had refused to allow herself to blush.

Nikos Drakis was there that night with me!

And one night was all it had taken.

'Please come this way, Miss Fairford.'

The nurse was speaking again, and Alys was shown into a small, but comfortably appointed waiting room, with easy chairs, magazines on the table, washroom facilities and a complicated-looking coffee machine.

'Allow me to make you a coffee,' the nurse said brightly.

Alys nodded, wondering what was going to happen next. She had given the consultant her permission to talk to Nikos, answer any questions he might have, so presumably he was doing that now. She sipped her decaff, a troubled look on her face. Feeling very alone. And very far from home.

Nikos lowered himself into the chair in front of the obstetrician's desk.

'Well?' His demand was terse.

'Definitely pregnant. And, yes, she is as advanced as would be expected after what you have told me,' came the answer, smoothly spoken, professional and medically authoritative.

Nikos's expression did not change. Nor did he speak, only went on listening as the consultant briefed him, finishing by indicating the expected due date of Alys's eventual delivery shortly after Christmas.

The words echoed in Nikos's ears.

And then I will become a father...the father of a child...

Emotion scythed through him. Many emotions, all tumultous, had been doing so ever since that fateful moment when he had ripped open that cheap, thin envelope the hotel concierge had handed him. Yet none had had anything like the intensity of the one that possessed him now.

But he set it aside. He had no room for it yet, could not, must not, acknowledge it. Because there was another question he had to ask—could not, must not, avoid.

A question on which would hang the future of his life—and not just his own. A question he did not want to ask but must.

He eyeballed the consultant, looking back at him with his professionally bland expression, and put the question to him.

'All finished?'

The nurse had come in again, and was glancing at the half-drunk cup of coffee on the table by Alys.

'Mr Drakis is waiting for you in reception,' she informed her with a polite smile.

Thankful, Alys got to her feet, picking up her handbag, following the nurse out of the room. Nikos's tall, severely suited figure struck her immediately as he stood up, clearly indeed waiting for her, with the same unsmiling expression on his face as before. He asked no questions of her, nor said anything, only ushered her from the clinic and back into the car that was waiting by the entrance.

Alys felt her own expression tighten, mirroring his as she resumed her seat. Could this brusque, unsmiling man really be the same man who had melted her with his desiring gaze, swept her into his arms, his bed…who had been sensual, seductive and, oh, so passionate towards her? Had that night really happened? It seemed almost unbelievable.

She felt emotion tug at her—a sense of desolation. This was not how she'd imagined it would be. Not by a million miles. Whatever she had hoped for, this was not it…

Then he was speaking, and she made herself pay attention as the car moved off.

'I'll drop you back at your hotel,' Nikos was saying, his voice as inexpressive as his face, his glance unrevealing. 'I suggest you rest in the afternoon. Tonight…' An edge had crept into his voice—Alys could hear it. 'Tonight we must talk. I'll send a car for you at eight. Please be ready in time,' he finished.

Alys said nothing. A moment later he'd got his phone out again and seemed to be checking emails. She left him to it, turned to look out of her window but saw nothing, her thoughts bleak.

Out of nowhere, a sudden urge to tell Nikos to drive her to the airport—to send her back to England—almost overcame her. To tell him that *she* would deal with everything from now on, that he could absolve himself of all responsibility as to the reason she was here at all!

Then emotion twisted inside her, like a wire tightening around her guts, as she remembered the letter in her handbag.

She fought for composure. Nikos had said they would talk tonight. OK, so talk they would.

This is not just my baby! It's his too. So he has responsibilities as well as me!

Responsibilities that surely meant she had every right to ask him—a wealthy man, after all!—for the financial help she so urgently needed.

She felt her hands tighten over her handbag again.

He can't turn me down! Surely he can't.

That was the hope she had to cling to. However much she didn't want to.

Nikos was back in his office, attempting to work. But it was impossible. His mind was far too full. The arrival of his father, just walking in, was the last thing he needed.

'You were going to give me a progress report on the New York deal—where is it?' his father demanded, not bothering with pleasantries.

'You'll get it—but not right now,' Nikos rejoined. He was in no mood for his father's browbeating.

'Later is no use,' his father barked back. 'Haven't I drummed into you that time is always of the essence? You have to close—and fast—every time. Don't ever let the other party have time to manoeuvre, rethink, get ideas, find alternative partners. As my son, you should know that by now!'

Dark eyes lanced Nikos, the expression in them one that had been familiar for so, so long.

Bitterness rose in Nikos's throat.

Always the same! The barbs—the resentment. The constant reminders about the son I 'should' be...

It had been that way all his life.

He hauled his mind away. He must not let it go there—not with his father standing right there in front of his desk, frowning in displeasure.

The stab of bitterness came again in Nikos's throat.

Because I can never, never be the son he wants—not with the mother I had.

He felt emotions swirl within him, dark and turbid. But they were not about himself. In his head he heard the obstetric consultant confirming Alys's pregnancy, and felt those turbulent emotions swirl inside him again, darker now. Memory bit—how he had warned himself, that fateful evening he'd first set eyes on her, to make sure he didn't go down the same dangerous path his own father had. How he'd arrogantly dismissed his own warning to himself.

Well, he was paying for it now, all right.

But I have to ensure that only I pay for it! Not—

He stilled his thoughts, crushing down the fierce emotions that went with them. His father was talking at him still, moving on, wanting reports on other deals in the pipeline, on fresh prospects on the Drakis agenda. An agenda that never got any shorter, that always had to be fulfilled, that kept Nikos globetrotting constantly. Because that was what being a Drakis was all about. As he constantly had to prove…

Teeth gritted, Nikos gave his father the updates he demanded, and it was a good hour later before he had his office to himself again. He glanced at his watch. No point trying to focus on business any longer. There was only one focus for him now.

The evening ahead.

And the woman he was going to have to spend it with.

And why.

Because it's the most important deal I'll ever make in my life.

And he could not—*could not*—afford to lose.

His eyes glittered darkly as he threw himself back in his leather chair. But why should he lose? He held the trump card—the one that would win every time. The one that, tonight, she would feel the full force of. Feel the full lure of.

Drakis money.

He stared blindly out across his spacious, thickly carpeted office, climate-controlled against the increasing heat of Athens as spring gave way to summer.

Tonight I will show her what can be hers.

Alys was asleep. Delayed exhaustion had wiped her out after she'd tried to consume the sandwich lunch delivered to her by room service, but now a knock at her door was rousing her. It was the bellhop, handing her a wide, flat, white-lacquered cardboard box, embellished with large gold lettering in Greek script she couldn't read.

Blinkingly, she took it, putting it down on her bed. A gilt envelope was tucked into the satin ribbon tying up the box, with a card inside it.

For you to wear tonight—Nikos

She lifted the glazed lid of the box, peeling aside the silver tissue paper to reveal a dress. A cocktail frock in slub silk, pale green, in a tailored, knee-length shift style, with darted bodice. It was sleeveless, with a round neckline, and very slightly fuller at the waist.

As she held it up, Alys's face lit with sheer pleasure at so beautiful a garment. A designer number, obviously, and it was impossible not to feel delight at holding it up to view.

And temptation too. She was honest enough to acknowledge it. When, in her life, had such a dress ever been within her reach? Never—that was the answer.

But for the mother of Nikos Drakis's child...?

The thought hovered in the air, tantalising and taunting. If she had not spent time with him today, seen him unsmiling, businesslike, the hopes that she had been harbouring might not have been wiped from her. Hopes for something even as modest as coming to a civil, amicable agreement between them. If she had only recalled how he'd been in London that magical evening, she would have still been filled with unquestioning delight at so beautiful a dress.

A sense of longing rose up in her. To make that unforgettable evening come again, to put on this beautiful, expensive dress for Nikos, to make herself as beautiful as she could for him, to see again that look in his eyes, desiring her...

She crushed it down, as pointless as it was impossible. Most likely, she thought bleakly, he'd only sent the dress because he didn't want to be seen dining with a woman in a cheap outfit like the one she'd worn today.

For a moment she was filled with an impulse to pack it away in its box again. Then she paused, her expression steeling. Maybe wearing an expensive dress like this, the indifferent offering of a rich man, would serve to remind her of just how rich he was—and how urgently, desperately, for her baby's sake, she needed him to be.

Nikos reached for the cocktail that had been placed in front of him as he'd taken his seat in the restaurant—one of Athens's most exclusive—and took a mouthful of the strong, astringent martini, feeling he could do with its shot to the system. Beneath his habitual impassiveness he could still feel that hard, heavy stone inside him. The one that had been there since his world had imploded. Since he'd read Alys's letter, telling him she was pregnant.

History repeating itself. First my father—now me.

Bitterness, on so many counts, was acid in his throat.

His phone pinged and he glanced down at it. His driver, informing him that he'd dropped Alys off. So she would be here imminently.

His eyes went to the restaurant entrance and she was there—being ushered unctuously towards him. Nikos's eyes fastened on her, and as they did so he knew, with a plunging hollowness inside him, that sending her that dress had been a mistake. A big mistake.

The emotions he'd had no intention of giving admittance to surged uncontrollably.

Thee mou, *but she looks incredible!*

He could not tear his eyes from her as she approached. If he'd been unable to resist her when she'd been looking so blatantly over-the-top and enticing that first fateful evening, now she was looking just…

Perfection. Absolute perfection. This is the way she should always look!

The image was flawless. The dress was ideal for her, flattering her fair colouring, and the ultra-chic simplicity of its design only enhanced the fullness of her natural beauty—a beauty subtly enhanced by the make-up widening her eyes, shaping her mouth, heightening her cheekbones. But nothing was overdone, like at that party, and nothing was unnecessarily slapped on. Her hair was not loose in wild abandon, as it had been that night, nor tightly pulled back as it had been this morning. Now it was loosely, gracefully coiled, wound around itself at the nape of her neck, accentuating the fine-boned contours of her face, the slender extent of her throat, exposing her tender earlobes.

He felt the visceral response of his body, and for a few abandoned moments let himself simply drink her in. Other male heads had turned as she'd crossed the restaurant floor, and he knew exactly why.

No wonder I could not resist her that night! No wonder I threw caution to the winds and made her mine!

His expression altered. Yes, he had—he had, indeed. And now there was going to be a price to pay for it. Who better than himself to know that?

All my life.

It was like a douche of cold water in his veins.

His eyes hardened, veiling, and he got to his feet.

'Alys.' He kept his voice punctiliously civil, stayed standing until she was seated before resuming his own chair. His reaction to her was back under control, and his gaze flicked over her assessingly. But not just in respect of her beauty, however breathtaking. She was looking outwardly composed, but he could see a pulse beating at her throat. She was not as calm as she obviously wanted him to think.

He heard her murmur his name, then busy herself with her napkin. Waiters were there, placing menus in front of them, and the customary rituals of bringing iced water and bread rolls gave him time to dispense with the last echoes of his response to her. There was no place for it now. None.

The dress is to impress her—not me.

That was its purpose. Not to remind him of her fantastic beauty, or the impact it could have on him.

Yet for all his reminders he heard himself say, as the waiting staff finally took themselves off, 'The dress suits you.'

Had there been a trace of admiration in his voice? He strove to keep it nothing more than civil.

'Yes. Thank you for thinking of it,' Alys answered him, in the same unexceptional tones.

He saw her glance around, take in the elegance of her surroundings, including the other diners. Then her gaze came back to him, and he thought he saw something change in her eyes, but it was swiftly concealed.

It had been there for only a fraction of a second, but that was all that it had taken. Even less than the time it reached him. He slammed shut on it. It had no place here. Not now.

Waiters were hovering attentively, proffering menus, asking Alys what she would like to drink. She asked for orange juice and soda. Nikos found himself remembering how she'd ordered a Sea Breeze in London. But remembering anything about that fateful night was irrelevant. Only what he had to achieve now was of any purpose.

The most important deal of his life—

He flipped open his menu. 'Tell me, what might you like to eat tonight? This restaurant is noted for its soufflés. Does that appeal? Savoury as well as sweet.' He made his tone of voice civil. For now.

She glanced up from her menu. 'Whatever you think best.'

He could hear constraint still in her voice. There had been none that night he'd swept her off with him.

What if I could do that tonight?

The thought was in his head before he could stop it. Block it. Bringing in its wake more tumbling thoughts, just as out of place.

I intended to pick up with her again—have more time with her. So why not?

Again he slammed down hard on his thoughts. Whatever he'd once intended had vanished the moment he'd read her letter. Now there was only one priority. And it was *not* the way she looked right now and what it was doing to him.

His eyes went to her, focussing on the only important thing about her now. She did not look pregnant—had the obstetrician not confirmed it, he would not have believed it. And yet…

Is there something about her that is not just the elegance of her dress, her natural beauty?

He wanted to rest his eyes on her but did not permit himself. He had an agenda for tonight—and he would stick to it. And it did *not* entail memories that no longer had any use. Or intentions that were long gone and could not come back. The present was all that mattered. Succeeding in his purpose.

The waiter was there again, setting down her juice, taking their food order before disappearing again. Nikos turned down the wine menu—he wanted a completely clear head… one martini was enough. He took another mouthful, then set down his glass.

Time to open the dealing.

'So, Alys,' he said, and his eyes rested on her with deliberate unreadability, 'let's talk. Just what is it that you want?'

CHAPTER FOUR

ALYS STILLED. So here it was, then. The purpose of her presence here—the reason she had come to Greece, had contacted Nikos at all. She lifted her chin, steeling herself to say what she had to say. She would make it clear to him, however difficult it was.

However much I wish it wasn't like this—that you were like you were in London. Not this cold, unsmiling stranger, so obviously unwelcoming of my presence here, and the reason for it.

She took a breath, making herself look right at him, unflinchingly. 'Nikos, I don't have to be a mind-reader to pick up that you are not exactly ecstatic about this,' she said, straight out. 'But I would remind you that it takes two to make a baby.' Her eyes met his, not letting them go. 'You were there as well. I thought we practised safe sex, but evidently not safe enough. The realisation that I was pregnant came as a shock to me, believe me—as much of a shock as it obviously has to you.'

She spoke calmly, but without backing down. Without accusation or apology. Trying as best she could not to let the impact of seeing him again deflect her. She tried to stamp out her reaction. It would avail her nothing—only get in the way of what had to happen now. They needed to find some kind of agreement between them, for the sake of the baby she carried.

Why can't I just blank him? Oh, why can't I just be indifferent to him?

A mixture of resentment and futility filled her at how impossible that was.

She sought to infuse her voice with resolve. 'Whether we like it or not, Nikos, we have to deal with the situation.'

'Ah, yes, "the situation".' Nikos's voice echoed hers flatly. 'And just how do you we propose we do that?'

She searched his face, but there was nothing there. Nothing at all. She felt her heart sink again. But she couldn't give in—she had to keep going.

'Nikos,' she tried again, 'I'm really trying to make allowances for the fact that you are still coming to terms with me being pregnant. To keep remembering that I've had a lot longer than you to do so. But I can only assume you have *some* interest in the matter, or why bring me here to Athens? Why take me to see that obstetrician this morning if you don't intend to have anything to do with this baby?'

His expression did not change.

'That was simply to confirm that you are, indeed, pregnant.'

Alys stared. 'I'm past the first trimester, Nikos! This isn't something I'm imagining, believe me!'

She saw his mouth twist. 'But it is something you might have been lying about,' he said.

There was no emotion in his voice, nor in his face, and his eyes rested on her without expression. But there was a world of meaning in his words alone. Meaning that slammed into her as if a brick had hit her.

Two spots of colour flared in her cheeks. 'Well, now you know I'm not,' she got out tightly.

Disbelief filled her that he could think such a thing, but there was no opportunity to say more. Two waiters were sailing up to them, depositing their savoury first-course soufflés in front of them with a theatrical flourish. Alys could only be grateful for the interruption.

Is that really what he thinks of me? That I might have been lying to him?

Somewhere inside her she felt wounded—and it hurt. She fought for composure again, making herself pick up her spoon and start on the delicious-smelling soufflé.

Memory caught at her of how she'd relished eating the gourmet meal she'd shared with Nikos that one and only night with him. The night that had resulted in her being here now. The reason she was here. The *only* reason, she reminded herself bleakly. She felt the same wave of desolation sweep over her now as she had felt at the clinic.

I'm just a nuisance to him—he couldn't make it more obvious! He resents that I'm pregnant—wasn't even willing to believe it without proof! Well, if that's his attitude I can be likewise!

She put the spoon aside, her soufflé demolished. Then she lifted her head and looked across the table. Nikos still had that closed, remote look about him, and had already finished his soufflé. Alys took a breath. Directed her gaze right at him. This was not how she'd imagined it would be, but it was the way it was and she had no option but to deal with it. So she would be blunt—as blunt as he had been.

'You ask me what I want, Nikos. Well, I'll tell you. I'm in debt, and with a baby coming I have no way of paying it off.' She took a breath, knowing she must explain about the threat of foreclosure, of losing her home, the home she needed for her baby.

But she got no chance to tell him that.

'How much?' His voice cut across hers.

She swallowed. 'Twelve thousand pounds.' She'd added three months' extra repayments, to put her back in credit, to give herself a margin. 'And I… I need it right away.'

Her eyes were stuck on him, not daring to look away. Yet she could tell nothing about his reaction. She watched him, her anxiety mounting, hating it that she'd had to say it the way she had.

'And you would like me to settle that debt, would you not?' There was nothing in his voice—only expressionless enquiry.

Alys nodded. What else could she do?

'And so I will,' he answered.

His expression was still unreadable, but relief at what he'd said flooded through Alys. It was going to be all right! She wasn't going to lose her home! She and her baby were safe!

She opened her mouth to speak, splutter out her thanks, but he was holding a hand up, silencing her. His eyes rested on her face. Expressionless. Implacable.

'When,' Nikos said, 'we are married.'

Nikos heard himself speak, but it seemed to be coming from very far away. From somewhere he did not want to be. From somewhere he would be forced to be now, for all his life.

Just as my father was.

Savage emotion filled him—but what was the use of that?

'Married?'

The single word fell from Alys's lips.

The incredulity in her voice was genuine. Well, it might well be so. After all, it was probably something she'd never thought she could possibly achieve out of her fertility lottery win. A prize beyond her wildest dreams that made the paltry sum she wanted from him—only the beginning of her demands, that much was obvious!—nothing more than chickenfeed.

'Did you think it would be otherwise?' he returned.

She was still staring at him, and for some reason it annoyed him. Angered him.

'You cannot be serious?' he heard her say in hollow tones.

This time, as well as the incredulity he'd heard before, there was another note he had not. It annoyed him in the same way her staring at him annoyed him.

He levelled his gaze at her. 'No child of mine will be born a bastard,' he said.

He saw her flinch, saw colour flush her cheeks.

'Don't say that word! It's foul! And these days no one cares if parents are married!'

'*I* care,' he said. He knew there was steel in his voice. Adamantine steel. 'And because of that we will marry, Alys.'

He made his expression change. Made his voice lose the steeliness. Time for the next stage in this deal he had to bring to completion. And no deal he'd ever struck had been this critical—this essential for him to win.

'Don't look like that, Alys. There's no necessity for it. You will find being my wife very pleasant.' He changed his voice again. 'Indeed, exceptionally so.'

He reached inside his jacket, retrieved a small box.

'A small token, up-front,' he said, 'of all that you will enjoy as Kyria Drakis.'

His voice was dry…as dry as desert sand filled with the bones of the dead.

He flicked open the box.

Alys stared. Shock was still slicing through her and she was still not believing she could have heard him say what he had. To *marry* him?

Her gaze was glazed as she saw him flick open the lid of the satin box with long, powerful fingers. Fingers that were now sliding the open jewellery box towards her across the damask tablecloth.

'You should wear them now,' he was saying in that dry-as-a-desert voice, his eyes never leaving hers. 'They will suit your hairstyle tonight.'

She dropped her gaze. It seemed as heavy as lead, suddenly. Light from the candles on the tables caught the iridescence of pearl earrings, nestled against the silk of the box's lining.

Nikos was talking still. 'You see?' he was saying now, and his words seemed to be coming from a long way away. 'You see how very pleasant it will be for you to be Kyria Drakis? Jewellery such as this, designer dresses, couture gowns, chauffeur-driven limousines—a life of luxury awaits you, with everything you could dream of wanting all yours.'

There was something wrong with his voice. Something that cut like a knife to the very quick of her. She made no move to take the earrings, nor to push them back or touch them in any way. Yet she could feel, somewhere inside her head, words forming.

How beautiful they are! How exquisite! And they could be mine...

Her eyes were on him now, and she felt breathless suddenly. The smooth black of his dinner jacket sat perfectly across his broad shoulders and she looked at the tilt of his head, his dark, lidded eyes resting on her, the set of his sculpted mouth… The lethal combination of his looks and that seductive air of wealth, power and command. The leashed sensuality in the way he was looking at her now, holding her breathless gaze.

He could be mine...

Memory drowned her—of his skilled, effortless seduction of her that night she had gone to him. It could be hers again. *He* could be hers again.

Though her gaze never shifted from him, she could see in her peripheral vision the rest of the restaurant: its damask-covered tables, candlelight glinting on silverware and crystal glasses, and the jewellery of the expensive women dining here on gourmet food, drinking their vintage wine, living a life inconceivably distant from her own reality.

But it could be my reality... I could say goodbye to my old life. For ever.

The vision hovered like a tantalising dream within her reach.

Never again to be fearful of what bills and threats the day's post might bring…never to scrimp and save and search for budget items in the supermarket, snapping up food reduced for quick sale…never to walk to save the bus fare… never to shop for clothes in charity shops again.

To live instead a life not just of comfort and ease but wealth and luxury. And with Nikos.

Nikos! Nikos and me—like we were in London, but for always!

And why not? After all, what was there for her in England? Her mother was gone—she had nothing there to keep her! So why not think about what he had just said to her? Think about staying out here, in Greece. With him.

His wife. With his baby.

They would be making a family together—the kind of family she herself had never known…

For a moment so powerful it was unbearable, she let the image hang in her head. Then it crashed to the floor. The Nikos she had known in London, who had effortlessly seduced her into his arms, did not exist. Only this hard-faced, hostile man who couldn't be making it more obvious how unwelcome her pregnancy was.

Her eyes dropped to the earrings as she heard him telling her again how 'pleasant' life would be for her as his wife—as if that would be her only reason for marrying him.

He was still speaking but his face was shuttered, unreadable, his voice brisk and remote, businesslike, and his completely unemotional, expressionless gaze was levelled at her. Alys felt her throat tighten, tension stiffen her as she listened to him. She could do nothing but listen, even as her dismay at what was coming from him mounted.

More than dismay.

Worse than dismay.

'The marriage will take place as soon as possible,' he was saying, announcing it as if he was running through a prearranged list. 'However, before that can be so, there is unavoidable paperwork to complete. You will need to send for your birth certificate—give me the details and I will see to it. I have already had an…an *appropriate*—' she heard a twist in his voice, an extra hardness '—pre-nuptial agreement drawn up for you to sign. The wedding ceremony itself will be civil only, privately conducted, with only ourselves and the requisite witnesses. Beforehand you will sign a non-disclosure agreement, again already drawn up by my lawyers, so that anything that passes between us will never be spoken of to the press or anyone else. Once we are married you will at all times conduct yourself in a manner befitting the wife of a Drakis. You will also sign a legal agreement giving me full custody of our child in the event of any divorce or of you giving me grounds for divorce such as adultery. The child will be a Greek citizen, and you will not be allowed to remove him or her from Greece for any reason without my express consent—all this will be legally binding. You will, for the duration of the marriage, be given an allowance adequate for your position as my wife, but you will not be permitted to run up any more debt, as seems to be your habit.'

She was hearing what he was saying—how could she not hear the ugly litany of conditions under which he would deign to marry her? And the even uglier assumptions that so obviously underlaid them. This was not about marriage—it was about control. Control of her, of her baby…

As if I'm an enemy—not the mother of his child!

It was repellent—repulsive.

She opened her mouth to speak, to stop what he was saying, to protest, but with every word that came from him her throat was tightening, as if a garotte was strangling her into forced silence, acquiescence.

When he reached the jibe about debt she flushed. She leant forward, desperate to speak. She had asked for that money because she wanted a roof over her head for her and for her baby—*his* baby! Not because she had been extravagant, or profligate! She wanted to explain, to justify herself—defend herself against what he was throwing at her.

Urgency filled her. She opened her mouth to speak, but he was not done yet.

'All of this, however,' he went on, in the same uninterruptible, blank-faced way, 'is entirely contingent upon the results of the test you will be having tomorrow morning, before we proceed any further with the wedding arrangements.'

Alys's expression changed, and her protest against what he'd announced—all the hostile conditions of how marriage to him would be and the ugly assumptions he was making about her—died on her lips.

'Test?' The single word fell from her. What he was saying to her was unreal.

Dismay was total within her. Mocking what she'd so stupidly, pathetically imagined only a handful of minutes ago.

Making a family together.

He was answering her question, but now his manner was not brisk and impersonal, as it had been when he was outlining the terms and conditions under which she, a lowly one-night stand who'd had the temerity to get herself pregnant by him, would become his wife. Because surely she could only possibly be interested in his money—why else would she have got in touch with him, come out here to Athens? And now, for the sake of the baby she so regrettably carried, she would have to become his wife—become Kyria Nikos Drakis, an honour she did not deserve—simply to legitimise a child he did not want and would never want *her* to be the mother of…

The garotte around her throat was still strangling her. But now, as he spoke on, she felt something like the blade of a knife sliding in under her ribcage. The final, deadly thrust of all he had dealt her.

'The test, Alys.' His voice was stark. 'The obstetrician this morning assured me it is perfectly safe, both for mother and baby—nothing more than a blood test for you, completely non-invasive, for which you are booked tomorrow morning.'

'I don't understand…' It was all she could get out, her voice hollow. She stared at him. What test could he mean?

And then Nikos's words were enlightening her.

'The test will show whether the child you are carrying, in your pregnancy that was confirmed this morning, is in fact mine.' He paused. His eyes were on her, yet completely empty. 'You do not imagine I will marry you without that assurance, do you, Alys?'

His words fell into the space between them. The space that was a chasm.

She was white—as white as bone. 'Who else's could it be, Nikos?'

She saw him shrug. A gesture of supreme indifference.

'How should I know or care into whose bed you fell before you fell into mine, or indeed after…?'

The garotte around her throat was tightening. 'How can you *think* that?'

His eyes rested on her, as empty as his voice.

'Alys, you were in my bed within hours of seeing me for the first time in your life. For all I know you make a habit of that every night—'

He got no further. The scrape of her chair silenced him. She propelled herself to her feet, incapable of enduring any more. Her whole body seemed to be shaking…her mind was in white-out. Then she was walking towards the restaurant exit on legs that nearly buckled under her. A hysterical laugh wanted to burst from her—or something did. Something that was choking her, that she needed to expel.

He caught up with her before she could walk out, seizing her arm. 'Do *not* make a scene. I will not permit it!'

She could hear rage in his voice—as if, dear God, *he* had cause for anger.

His hand clamped around her arm, he led her out into the lobby, where he turned on her. 'This test *will* take place, Alys, protest all you want!' His hand dropped from her. 'Now, do you intend coming back to the table to finish your meal, or will you flounce off like a drama queen? There's still more to discuss. If you want me to pay your debts for you, you'll need to give me your bank account details and so forth. Of course that will have to await the outcome of the DNA test tomorrow, but—'

She stepped away from him, her face completely blank. Schooled into being so with the last threads of her self-control.

'I'd like to go back to the hotel, please.'

She heard her own voice speak, say all that she could cope with now. Inside her head a vortex had opened up and was sucking her down into it. Down, down, down.

For a moment Nikos just studied her, his own face still completely unreadable, as blank as hers was. Then he spoke, his voice clipped. 'Very well. I will make allowances for your condition. I can see you are in no state to continue this discussion or to finish your meal. I'll call for the car. But, Alys, do not imagine this is going to allow you to evade the test I require. Be ready for eleven tomorrow morning. The test will take place at the same clinic we attended this morning.'

She didn't bother to answer, or even to acknowledge what he'd said. Only turned and left the restaurant. With the vortex inside her swallowing her whole.

CHAPTER FIVE

NIKOS WALKED OUT onto the balcony of his apartment. The night was warm, but he felt cold. His expression was as dark as the night beyond. His mood darker.

So it was set in motion—what had to happen. What there was no possibility of avoiding.

Unless—

Unless the test tomorrow shows me another outcome.

Even as he made himself think it, emotion knifed in him. Yet he did not know from which direction it had struck.

There was only one rational emotion to feel, surely, if the test tomorrow told him he was not, after all, responsible for Alys's pregnancy.

Relief—that was all that he should feel. Relief that he would not be a father after all, that the baby was not his—

Yet why did the thought of it pierce like talons in his flesh?

He pushed it aside. It was not a negative result that had to be dealt with, but its opposite. Just as his own father had had to.

He felt emotion churn within him, demanding admittance, but he would not allow it. Clenching his hands instead, thrusting them deep into his pockets, he stood, legs apart, gazing blindly out over the city of his birth. A birth his father had never wanted…had deplored all his life and still did—with every barbed reproach, every challenge designed to enforce the fact that he had to prove, endlessly, that he was worthy of being a Drakis. Yet he was perpetually resented for being one. For having been forced upon his father.

He could hear his father's bitterly familiar refrain—one he'd grown up with.

'"There will be no Drakis bastards!" That's what my own father held over me! Forcing me to marry! Ruining my life for me!'

It mocked him now, thinking of the very word he'd spoken that evening over dinner. More than mocked him. The emotion he would not allow admittance to pressed again. He thrust it back. There was no place for it. No place for anything other than doing what he had already done, doing what he must yet do.

He stared out over the city, brilliant with lights, at the Parthenon on the Acropolis, floodlit to the stars above, his hands numbed in their clenched fists.

Feeling nothing.

The safest thing to feel.

It was an admonition he continued to level at himself the next morning as, steely-faced, he walked into the hotel he'd booked Alys into. Alys…the woman who had rocked his senses so disastrously in the impulsive, reckless passion of a single night, who now might or might not be carrying his child. And if she were, then he would do the only thing that must be done.

But he found her not waiting for him, ready to be collected, as she'd been yesterday. He strode, annoyed, to the desk, to have her telephoned. Only to hear, in apologetic tones, that Miss Fairford was no longer at the hotel.

That she'd checked out two hours earlier.

After asking for the quickest way to the airport.

Alys stood in the security queue, willing it to move faster, her tension sky-high. She would not feel safe until she was through Departures and in her seat on the plane—bought at the airport, as cheaply as she could. Which wasn't cheap at all in her precariously overstretched budget.

She wanted to give a hysterical laugh. She had come here hoping above all that the crushing debt hanging over her, jeopardising her and her precious baby's future, might be lifted from her—only for now to be even deeper in debt, to the tune of the price of a flight back to London.

And when I get there I'll have to face what I've desperately tried to avoid. Losing my house, my home, my baby's home…

Because her one hope to save it had gone, and now she must sell it in time to meet the arrears payment deadline or lose it to foreclosure.

But she dared not think of that—not yet, not now. Dared not give vent to any emotion at all—not a single one. Lest they rip her to pieces.

She could feel them twisting like fanged snakes inside her, tightening and tugging and knotting, as they had been all night. She'd lain there sleepless, tormented, desperate for morning so that she could do what she was doing now.

Fleeing from the nightmare she had walked into.

Because *anything*—even losing her home—was better than what she now knew Nikos had planned for her.

A grotesque mockery of a marriage! With him despising me even as he forces himself to marry me! Wishing to God he didn't have to! Thinking I've trapped him! Hating me for it!

But she must not let herself play and replay, over and over again, as she had all through her hideous, sleepless night, what he had said to her, how he had shown what he thought of her.

All she must do now was urge the queue forward, try to push it on with her exhausted mind, one hand clenching the handle of her carry-on suitcase, the other clutching, with aching fingers, her precious passport and boarding pass.

And now she was nearly there, inching her way forward towards Departures, with only a few people left ahead of her now. She focussed on them, trying to distract herself from the seething emotions writhing within her. It wasn't good to be so upset and agitated…it wasn't good for her baby…

I've got to keep calm—I've got to!

But it was impossible. Deep within she felt her insides clutch, her throat constrict. Her face puckered. Her eyes stung like acid.

She blinked rapidly, hating it that she was so close to the edge, so near to plunging over…

The four people ahead of her were now only three, now only two…decreasing with glacial slowness. Her hand was numb with the tightness of her grip on her ready-opened passport. Only one more person in front of her now—

'Alys.'

The voice behind her, the sound of her name, cut through the airport's hubbub.

She spun round, stomach plunging.

Nikos.

Striding towards her, black fury in his face.

Oh, no. No, no…

Terror seized her like a wolf savaging her throat. Paralysing her.

'Alys.'

Her name came again. His voice was more demanding now. Harder. Harsher. Angrier.

Her elbow was seized, immobilising her.

'What the *hell* are you playing at?'

Nikos was looming over her, so much taller than she was, overpowering her with his presence.

Words broke from her. Protest. Vehement and vital.

'Let me go! *Let me go!* I'm going home! Back to England!'

His face darkened. '*What?* Don't be absurd!'

She shook herself free, wrenching back from him. With a fragment of her mind she was aware that the queue was moving forward again. It would be her turn next. And she *must* get through.

But Nikos had seized her elbow again, his grip like iron, his face black with fury.

'You're going nowhere! Do you understand me? You're coming back! Do you hear me? I won't have this!'

She could feel him pulling her away, out of the queue, could see the rage in his face, his eyes.

She broke.

Broke as if she had been snapped in half.

She was shouting back at him. Face contorting. Fury fuelled to flashover. 'No, *I* won't have it, Nikos! *I* won't! I won't have anything to do with you! I wish to God I'd never come here!'

Her voice was rising dangerously, desperately. Emotion was storming through her—uncontrollable, unstoppable. She felt his grip tighten on her, and with a cry of rage she flung it off.

'Don't touch me! Don't come near me! Get away from me!'

People were turning, looking at them, stepping back. But she didn't care—she didn't care about anything. She was way past that.

Now he was trying to catch at her hand, but she knocked him away, feeling her passport and boarding pass become dislodged from her grip as she did so. With a cry of distress she stooped down to pick them up, abandoning her grip on her carry-on. She had to have them. She couldn't get into Departures without them. And she had to get through, had to get away from this vile, foul man…

Her cry of distress came again. Higher now. More frantic. She was scrabbling on the ground, desperate to seize up her passport, her boarding pass. But she couldn't hold them, her fingers were clawing uselessly, hands flailing, and she couldn't see. She could only cry out again, yelling at him to get away from her, her voice rising in desperate urgency.

'Alys!'

There was something different in his voice now. It was not

demanding any more, but alarmed. And now he was stooping down beside her, retrieving the scattered passport and boarding pass, straightening, taking her up with him, grabbing hold of her pull-along, trying to place an arm around her waist, to draw her away.

Away from the sanctuary she was trying to reach in Departures, where she would be safe from him. Out of the queue she mustn't lose her place in.

'Let me go!' Her voice was high and thin, and she was trying to snatch back her passport and boarding pass, pummelling frantically at his chest, anywhere she could reach, almost insane with desperation. 'I'm not going back with you. You can't make me! You can take your bloody paternity tests and marriage proposals and you can *choke* on them! I wouldn't marry you if you crawled on your belly to me!'

Her rising voice was shaking like a leaf in a storm, ripped from her throat, which was constricting so much that she couldn't breathe, couldn't talk, couldn't do anything at all but flail at him with her hands.

'So just get off me! Do you hear me? Get off me and go to hell, Nikos Drakis. And take your stinking money with you! You're the last man on God's earth I'd want for my baby's father!'

The words were spewing from her as her fists thumped uselessly against him. Because he would not let her go. And now there were people running up to her, footsteps and agitated voices, all speaking in Greek. Still her hands were pummelling at him, but he would not leave her—would not do anything except give orders in that stentorian voice of his, though it was speaking in Greek now.

She felt an arm come around her waist, but it wasn't his because he was stepping away from her, and then a woman's voice was speaking to her, saying words that she could not understand, and she was being drawn away, gently but insistently, across the concourse into a room that opened off it. She was led to a couch of some kind, pressed down upon it, and now she wasn't yelling any longer, only shaking...

And then someone else was looming over her. A man in a white coat, with a stethoscope around his neck, and he was talking to her. This time she heard—understood—what he was saying to her, speaking in accented English.

'I am the airport doctor—for emergencies, you understand—and you are here in the medical room. And you must be calm, because this agitation is not good for you—nor for your baby. So please, take slower breaths. You are hyperventilating and your pulse is racing, and this is not good. You are safe here...quite safe.' He was chafing her hand gently, looking down at her reassuringly. 'You must sit here quietly, for a little while, and my nurse is making you a cup of tea, and that will help to calm you too.'

He went on talking quietly to her, encouraging her to slow her breathing, and she could feel it easing, feel her hectic heart rate slowing. The nurse brought a mug of tea over, a tisane, and Alys took it numbly, sipping it slowly as the doctor directed. Little by little she felt the storm of emotion subside within her, her shaking cease, her throat untighten as she drank her tea.

When she had finished it, the doctor spoke again, his voice still calm and reassuring.

'And now you need to rest for a little while. Rest completely.'

He was lifting her legs onto the couch, and she was tilted back, sinking against its contours into the cushions behind her. He was taking the empty mug from her and her eyelids were fluttering. They were heavy, and she did not want to see the world...she wanted to shut it away.

Her breathing slowed and sleep came, blessed sleep, after her endless sleepless night, the tumult of her emotions, the desperate race to the airport, the hideous storm of adrenaline that had rushed over her just now. It all drained away into stricken exhaustion, and she was finally released from a consciousness she could no longer bear.

Nikos sat in the plastic armchair in the medical room Alys had been taken to by the female security guard who had come running up as she had stormed and flailed at him. He sat motionless, watching her lie so still and pale on the couch, her chest rising and falling in exhausted sleep.

The doctor had gone, after instructing a nurse to fetch him again as needed, and the nurse had covered Alys with a light blanket before busying herself with paperwork at the desk nearby.

Nikos's eyes rested on Alys. She looked as if a gust of wind might blow her away. He went on watching her, still in shock from what had just happened. Her fury, her incandescent rage at him—her outrage!—had been so real, so blazing…

It had shaken him to the core.

He sat completely still, but behind his expressionless face his mind was racing.

Is that truly how she feels?

But how could he doubt it? He'd been on the receiving end of it—seen it in her eyes, in her face, heard it in her voice. Total and absolute meltdown…

A sombre furrow creased his brow. There had been more than anger in the words she'd hurled at him, in the fists pummelling at his chest. She had seemed almost…distraught—as if everything had become too much for her to bear. Her face had contorted not just with fury, but with distress—as if a moment longer and she'd have been in uncontrollable floods of tears…

As if I'd pushed her beyond her limits, wounded her, hurt her…

The thought, unwelcome, and unwanted, hung in his head. He did not want to credit it…to believe it. He fought against it. He *knew* what she was! A woman he'd rashly fallen into bed with, after succumbing to the overpowering desire of a moment, who now was intent on doing to him what his own mother had done to his father.

His expression darkened.

What Miriam intended to do to me—to make use of the Drakis millions, shamelessly exploit my devotion to her.

His mouth set. Hadn't Alys openly admitted last night that she had debts? And was that not the reason she'd comc out here? Because she wanted him to pay them off for her?

But then why bolt this morning? Why unleash her fury on me when I told her she could have all the luxuries of being my wife?

Grimly, he realised he knew the answer to that.

It was when I said I would insist on a paternity test—that was what sent her flying!

He felt his jaw tighten, aching with the tension that was racking his body, as he tried to make sense of what he could not make any sense of at all.

Had it been his demand for a paternity test before they married that had made her flee, lest the truth exploded all her hopes of getting any money at all from him?

But what she hurled at me was not that she knew she could not get what she wanted from me! She threw back in my face everything I'm prepared to do for her! As if it were poison to her! As if I am poison to her—

His hands clenched on his knees, his gaze searching her face. His eyes rested on her as if seeing her for the first time.

And into his head came a memory. A memory that had nothing to do with the jolt of lightning-force electricity that had arced between them when he'd first seen her across that crowded cocktail lounge all those months ago in London. Nothing to do with the way his eyes had fastened on her last night as she'd approached the restaurant table wearing that dress that had made her look so stunningly beautiful that every male head in the place had turned instinctively towards her.

No, this was a different memory.

The way she looked the morning I left her lying in my bed—her face bare of make-up, her hair flowing across the pillow—so very lovely that I wanted to reach down and kiss her softly, possessively, make her mine again, knowing I must not... The regret I felt as I left her...

His gaze flickered over her again now, taking in something more than her fragile stricken beauty. Taking in, for the first time, the way her hand was resting over the blanket draped across her, her fingers gently cupping her abdomen. As if shielding the baby she carried invisibly within.

He felt emotions clench inside him. Emotions he dared not confront or admit to. Questions flickered inside his head as he gazed at her.

What do I do now? What should I do? I thought I had her sussed. I thought it was obvious what had happened to me—I'd been caught in the same benighted honeytrap that was sprung on my father! I thought that meant I knew exactly what I had to do.

But now only one thing was certain.

He took a deep and silent breath, feeling at last some of the unanswerable conflicts in his mind distil into resolution. He did not know the truth about her—could not know...not yet—but one thing he did know with searing certainty. She must not flee him again.

So I have to find another way forward. I have to keep her here. But how? And where?

Not in Athens—somewhere quiet and remote and private.

His mind raced, searching for a solution that would work.

And where it came from he did not know, but suddenly it was there in his head. That fragment of his mentioning on that long-ago evening he'd spent with her in London his family villa in the Aegean, Villa Drakis.

His eyes lit. Yes, he would take her there! It was quiet, remote and private—just what he needed. Relief filled him at how perfect a solution it would provide. It was hardly used any more—he hadn't been for years, and his father had never cared for it. It stood there empty but for the maintenance staff. Ideal for his purpose.

He felt some of his tension subside. Now all he had to do, when she awoke, was persuade Alys to agree.

And once they were there…

His face grew sombre, and there was a darker look in his eyes now.

Then I find another way to achieve what I need to.

Alys was stirring. Light was pressing on her eyelids, pushing her back into the world. As her eyes flickered open she saw Nikos sitting opposite her. She opened her mouth to gasp in protest, but no sound came out. Then the nurse was standing up, coming across to her, picking up her hand to take her pulse, releasing it with a smile.

'Much slower,' she announced reassuringly.

Alys sat up, her body heavy and lethargic. She didn't want Nikos Drakis there. Didn't want him anywhere near her ever again.

But he was leaning forward, speaking to her. 'Alys, please…we have to talk.'

She made herself look at him. There was something different about him. He was less arrogant. Less hard… And his tone of voice wasn't the way it had been when he'd accosted her in the Departures queue, the way it had been since the moment she'd arrived here in Athens.

Alys frowned. He sounded almost diffident. Her frown deepened. Nikos Drakis didn't *do* diffident. He did orders and high-handed diktats and contemptuous insults.

And I'm done with all of those!

She shook her head. 'No, we don't have to talk at all. All I have to do is get my flight—or the next one, I don't care which—and go home.'

He reached out a hand towards her, as if to stay her. 'Don't go,' he said. Then he let his hand drop and turned to the nurse, speaking in English to her. 'Will you allow us a few minutes, if you please?'

The nurse hesitated, glancing at Alys, but when she made no objection, conceded, 'Very well—but there must be no more agitation.'

Nikos nodded, giving her his assurance. And as the nurse left, he turned back to Alys. There was something else different about him now that she'd not seen before. Hesitation.

'Alys…' His eyes rested on her and there was something different about them too, she realised. 'Please hear me out.'

His tone was guarded, and she could see he was watching for her reaction. She eyed him warily. She might as well let him get on with whatever he was going to say, and then she would pick up her bag and get the hell out of here…find a flight she could get on and get Nikos Drakis out of her life for good—the way he had to be now that she knew just what he thought of her.

She felt something bitter twist inside her, tightening her expression as she looked at him, her face stony. He seemed to pause, to look for what he wanted to say, which she did not wish to hear anyway, and then he spoke.

'I am sorry that you were so upset,' he began. 'I… I want to make amends.'

Amends? Her mouth twisted in derision, the word mocking her.

'I don't want it to be like this between us,' Nikos said.

His eyes held hers. Hers flashed angrily. 'How the hell else can it be?' she demanded, derision still in the twist of her mouth. 'After what you've said to me?'

'Alys, I—'

Emotion started to knife in her again, and she would not let him finish. 'You don't even think the baby is yours! You want me to have some slut-shaming paternity test to rule out all the other men I must obviously have slept with as well as you!'

His mouth set. 'That was crass of me,' he answered. 'And I apologise.'

Alys looked at him, the stab of emotion dying away as swiftly as it had arisen. She had no energy for any more emotion. And her chest had tightened again, though she did not want it to. And here he was, telling her he was apologising.

She felt her throat constrict and wondered why. It was as if tears were threatening. But why should that be? He had no power to *hurt* her—only people who meant something to her could hurt her—and what did Nikos Drakis mean to her? Nothing—less than nothing!

Acid welled in her mouth, souring it, and she heard him speak again in that strange, different voice he was using. The voice that went with the frowning, troubled look on his face, the tension in his brow, his stark cheekbones.

'Alys, hear me out. I haven't handled this well. You're upset, and I understand that, but I want things to be different.'

She saw him draw breath, and then he continued, his eyes never leaving her face, though she kept herself expressionless—because she could not, *would* not, do anything more.

'So what I propose is this. That we leave Athens and go somewhere where there is peace and quiet and rest for you.' He paused. 'You may recall I mentioned that evening we spent together in London that my family has a villa on one of the Aegean islands. It is beautiful, and very peaceful, and I think it will do you good. We will stay for as long as it takes. It will help you…adjust. It will help us both do so.'

His eyes were meeting hers, but what was in them Alys didn't know. All she knew was what was in herself.

'You want me,' she said slowly, incredulously, 'to let you take me to some island—I have no idea where—and lock me away in a villa…? You really think I'm going to agree to that? To go with you? To *trust* you?'

'*No*—I give you my word. You may leave at any time, Alys. But I hope,' he said, his eyes never leaving hers, 'that you will not wish to leave—that you find peace there…and a respite that is good for you, for your baby.'

He paused, and something shifted in his eyes. Was it a veiling or a hesitation? She didn't know—knew only that she was hearing him speak and that his words were holding her as if she were in a bubble, suspended in the air.

'Yesterday, Alys…'

He was speaking again, and it seemed those dark, deep eyes that had so entranced her so long ago were probing hers, as if seeking answers she did not want to give.

'Yesterday you mentioned you had debts.' His expression changed minutely. 'Last night I said they must wait, but…' He took another breath, his gaze intent. 'Allow me to pay them right now. To put your mind at rest. To show my…my good faith.'

She stared at him. 'Why?' she said. Her voice was thin. Tiredness was dragging her down. And confusion too.

Nikos Drakis…talking to me of 'good faith'?

'I have said—to show my good faith,' he repeated. 'And in return you'll agree to come to my villa, as I have asked of you.'

He slid his phone out of his jacket pocket. 'Tell me what your bank details are and I will have the sum of twelve thousand pounds—that's what you said last night?—transferred right now.'

He was holding her eyes, but she could not hold his in return. She shut her eyes against him. Thoughts, hectic and heavy, clattered against the edges of her mind, demanding entry. She was too tired to stop them.

He says he'll pay it straight away! Right now! Twelve thousand pounds! It's what you're desperate for! Just take it!

Her eyes screwed tighter. She would sooner eat broken glass than take his money now!

Then you're a fool! You're thinking of yourself, of your own pride! He's the father of your child, however foul his accusations that he might not be! Twelve thousand pounds is chickenfeed to him! But to you it's the lifeline you desperately need.

Fear stabbed at her. She knew just what would happen if she failed to find that money—she would lose her home. The home she needed for her baby.

'Alys…'

Nikos's voice was in her ears again, making her open her eyes, look at him.

'Give me your bank account details so I can make the transfer. Right now.'

There was insistence in his voice, but she felt herself looking around, wondering belatedly what had happened to her luggage. Her carry-on was propped in the corner, and on top of it was her handbag.

Nikos saw her looking and reached for it, handing it to her. Hardly knowing what she was doing, she opened it with nerveless, fumbling fingers. The fatal letter threatening foreclosure lay at the bottom of her bag, but she did not take it out, only clumsily unfolded it enough to make out the account details and the sort code, given by the mortgage company, into which she must make the payment of her arrears. Chest tight, she read it out to Nikos, and he keyed it into his phone.

It was done in moments, and he slid the phone away, looking back at her. 'It's gone through,' he said.

And now there was yet another note in his voice she could not recognise, and something in his eyes that shifted minutely and then was gone. But she was still trying to take in the reality of what had just happened—that in a few swift keystrokes he'd lifted the terrifying threat hanging over her head.

He got to his feet. 'I'm going to arrange our transport to the island. Sit quietly till I return. I'll call the nurse back.'

She watched him walk out of the medical room and heard him say something in Greek—to the nurse, presumably, who promptly came back in, coming up to Alys and asking how she was, bringing her a glass of water to drink.

Numbly, she complied, then sat back, eyes closed. Wanting to feel relief that the threat that had been hanging over her for so long had vanished. Yet feeling nothing. Knowing, somewhere in the exhausted recesses of her mind, that 'nothing' was all she could cope with right now.

As to what would come next—she could not even go there…

CHAPTER SIX

THE PRIVATE AIRCRAFT that he'd chartered at short notice from Athens was touching down on the short island runway, taxiing towards the private section of the small airport. A handful of minutes later Nikos was vaulting down the extended steps, slowly followed by Alys, who was looking about her, saying nothing. She'd barely spoken on the flight, seeming to close in on herself. He'd let her be, making no demands on her.

He picked up Alys's carry-on case and guided her towards an SUV waiting nearby, summoned there by his phone call from Athens to Spiros, who looked after the Villa Drakis.

He opened the front passenger door before loading her case into the boot. She'd got in, and he did too, to see keys waiting in the ignition for him.

He gunned the engine. 'It's about a forty-minute drive to the villa,' he said, heading out across the tarmac to the perimeter gate.

Alys made no answer to his remark, and Nikos was glad of her silence. It gave him space for his own thoughts. He'd got her here—now he had to plan what happened next.

One goal was paramount.

I've got to stop her hostility towards me. Defuse it. I need her to co-operate—to want to co-operate.

But he could afford to make no more mistakes.

At least he'd succeeded in persuading her to come here with him.

Yes, by paying off her debts! Exactly what she wanted of you!

He felt a pull of acid cynicism at how readily she'd let him do so, then sought to quell it. He'd made the offer to pay, said it was to show his good faith.

And maybe that's what I have to keep on doing. Showing good faith.

His glance went to her. She'd closed her eyes, resting her head back. Her face was in repose, but strain was still visible in it…the marks of that raging meltdown at the airport. It had shaken his conviction that he knew exactly why she had come out to Greece at his invitation, exactly what her goal was.

But then she should have bitten my hand off for the chance to marry me! Not just wanted a paltry few thousand to pay off her debts!

It didn't make sense. *She* didn't make sense.

His eyes went back to the road ahead. He was taking the coastal route that hugged the rocky contours of the island, heading to the northern promontory on which Villa Drakis sat in remote seclusion—ideal for a member of the Greek plutocracy who did not wish to be bothered by tourists or the hoi polloi.

From time to time his glance went to her, and thoughts threaded in and out of his consciousness as he drove, glad that he could look at her without her being conscious of it. It seemed almost impossible to believe that she was here, sitting beside him, just because of one searing night together…

Why did it happen, that night with her? What was it about her that made me unable to resist her?

Memory took him back to seeing her at the entrance to that cocktail lounge, to his eyes fastening on her as if it had been impossible to do otherwise.

Her wild and wanton hair, her huge eyes, lush mouth, fantastic figure had been fully on display to him—the whole irresistible package.

But it wasn't that alone that drew me to her. Made me reach for her...

Made him act so out of character that he'd helped himself to her that very night, throwing caution to the winds, acting on an impulse so strong he had not denied it to himself. Denied *her* to himself…

And when I took her in my arms and she melted into me she was not as I thought she would be, expected her to be! Ardent, oh, yes, but not...

Not experienced.

Not a virgin, true, but there had been a shyness to her as he laid bare her naked loveliness, her pale cheeks colouring as he'd explored the intimacies of her body with leisurely caresses…

He shifted in his driver's seat, exerting torque on the steering wheel as the road snaked around a narrowing bend. He glanced at her again as he came out of the bend, flickering over her.

It hadn't been wise to remember their night together in such detail. And nor was it wise, now, to remember that flight across the Atlantic when he'd made the decision to have more than one single night with her—to seek her out.

And now she is here, beside me, heading to the villa with me. Where I will have her all to myself...

He gave a shake of his head. He was bringing her here only to stop her bolting back to England before he had the answers he *had* to have.

His glance went to her yet again, his eyes caressing the delicate contours of her soft cheeks, the tender swell of her lips, the smoky lashes dark against her pale skin…

How very lovely she was.

He felt temptation lick at him, move within him. Making him think thoughts that he should resist.

Wasn't the situation complicated enough, as it was?

And yet…

One night with her was not enough after all—I wanted more. And now—

Now she was here with him, at his side, heading to his villa. And while she was there…

His thoughts moved, taking form and shape. Making sense…

In my arms she will not oppose me...will not seek to leave me...

The thought hovered, tantalising and so tempting…

And after all, if the baby is indeed mine, then...

Then there could be only one outcome. Just as he had spelled out to her last night.

And this time she would not *want* to turn him down.

Alys sat with her eyes closed as the SUV headed forward. Had she been mad, letting Nikos bring her to some island she'd never heard of, to his private villa there? He'd said she would be free to leave whenever she wanted. That she had his word. Was his word worth anything? She didn't know. She didn't know anything about him.

Except that he thinks I'd be fine with foisting another man's baby on him and ecstatic at the thought of having all his stinking money to spend as his wife.

Anger, as familiar as it was bitter, twisted inside her. But what did she care what he thought of her?

What I care about is that he's paid off my mortgage arrears so I won't lose my home.

It would be a penny-pinching life—just as her own mother had experienced—but she would manage. As for Nikos… he could go to hell. She would take not a penny from him in maintenance.

To think she had hoped that his financial support would enable her to dedicate herself to her baby, as her own mother had not been able to.

But better that than what Nikos offered me! A toxic marriage, with him hating that he has to endure it.

No, even if she was doomed to repeat exactly the kind of life her own mother had had, it would still be better than the one Nikos wanted to impose on her.

The sound of Nikos saying her name roused her from her embittered thoughts.

'Alys—we've arrived.'

She opened her eyes. They had pulled up on a gravelled forecourt, with garaging to one side. In front was the wall of a white building that had only narrow windows in it, and a central door which was now opening. A figure was emerging, coming up to Nikos as he got out of the car, addressing him in Greek.

Nikos lifted a hand in greeting, then came around to Alys's door to open it for her. She climbed out, not taking the hand Nikos was holding out to her.

'Alys, this is Spiros, who looks after everything here,' Nikos announced.

She nodded, and got an effusive smile in return as the man went around to the boot to extract her small suitcase.

She let Nikos usher her forward, carefully keeping her distance from him. She could feel her heart beating in her chest, which felt tight as a drum. As she stepped through the doorway she found herself on a small landing, from which a flight of wide stone stairs led down to a circular, atrium-style hall, off which were set doors at intervals.

She headed down the stairs, holding the banister as the steps curved round. At the foot, a maid was holding open a door, smiling in a welcoming fashion. Spiros nipped past her, carrying her suitcase. Alys followed him into a room.

Her gaze swept around. It was a beautifully appointed bedroom, in creams and blues, with louvred blinds on the floor-to-ceiling windows, creating a cool shade emphasised by the air con.

The maid was busy starting to unpack, but Alys stayed her. 'It's fine—I'll do it.'

The maid smiled and left her to it, closing the bedroom

door behind her. Still feeling numb, all emotions tamped down, Alys headed into the en suite bathroom. It was as beautifully appointed as the bedroom, with a huge walk-in shower with both rainfall and jetted shower heads, a marble-topped vanity unit inset with a massive basin, with a whole array of expensive-looking toiletries lined up beside it and piles of fluffy white towels on the shelving.

The room was making her feel weary, and grimy, longing to freshen up. Hardly realising what she was doing, she started to strip off. Moments later she was standing under the pounding shower, letting the pummelling water wash all thought from her.

Nikos walked into the master bedroom, sliding back the capacious fitted wardrobe in the dressing area, looking for something more comfortable than the business suit he was wearing. There was probably something left here from whenever he'd last visited. When *had* he last visited? he wondered. He tried to think and failed. Years, definitely. But then, of course, he got so little time off to go anywhere that wasn't work-related.

He sifted through some assorted beachwear and casualwear, chucking a selection on the bed before shrugging out of his jacket, extracting his phone as he did so. He'd made use of his time on the flight over by contacting his PA, updating her on a few urgent matters, then coolly instructing her to cancel all his appointments—home and abroad—indefinitely.

His father would kick off, but he didn't care. He had a far more important matter to attend to, and he didn't want work calls distracting him. His mouth thinned. If his father was that fussed, he could deal with them himself, for once.

He tossed his phone into the top drawer of his bedside table. From now on it would not be a priority.

Alys stepped out of the shower, wrapping herself in a huge fleecy bath sheet, twisting her newly washed hair into a towel turban, padding back into the bedroom on bare feet. She felt...*revived.* She sank down on the soft bed, lying back. The heat from the shower and the dim light in the shaded room, together with the cumulative sleep debt from her sleepless night, all made her feel drowsy. She felt her eyelids grow heavy...

It was a soft knock on the door that roused her. One of the maids was there, telling her in accented English that Kyrios Drakis awaited her on the terrace, if she cared to join him.

Alys stood up, murmuring her thanks, and the maid disappeared again, leaving Alys to extract fresh undies from her suitcase and try and decide what to wear. She had packed for Athens—not luxury villas in the Aegean.

In the end she selected a denim skirt and a loose white top, slipping her bare feet into the flats she'd worn to the airport. Her thoughts flickered. Had Nikos not intercepted her before she'd got to Departures she'd be back in England now.

Instead...

She took a breath. Yes, well, she was here now. To what purpose she had no idea. Nor did she care.

You and me, my darling baby—we're all that matters. No one else.

Least of all Nikos. He could go to hell and stay there.

Face set, she left the bedroom and walked across the central atrium. Double doors had been flung open, opposite the foot of the stairs, and she made for them. Deep gold light filled the room beyond—a lavishly appointed lounge set with white sofas and floor rugs—and she stepped inside.

Immediately she made for the bifold doors drawn aside almost the entire length of the external wall. It was impossible to do otherwise. She stepped out onto a broad terrace that opened directly off the lounge. The rich gold light that had drawn her was drenching the world. It was the sun, lowering to the right of her, bathing the vista in its rays.

And such a vista it was—a sweeping semicircle of azure sea extending around a low promontory that projected out beyond the terraced gardens that tumbled down to beaches on either side. She could do nothing but stare, drinking in the breathtaking panorama.

'We get both sunrise and sunset here. Right now, it's sunset…'

Nikos's voice to her left made her turn. He was strolling towards her from further along the terrace. Against her will, Alys felt her breath catch. He was bathed in the golden light from the lowering sun, which was turning his skin to bronze, and his dark hair glinted with gold, etching his features. He was no longer in the sombre business suit that made him look so remote, so austere—so forbidding. He'd changed into buff-coloured chinos and a pale blue cotton shirt open at the collar, cuffs turned back, showing sinewed forearms dusted with gold.

He looked incredible…

She swallowed, unable to tear her eyes away, feeling her pulse surge. Helpless to stop it.

'Pretty good, isn't it? The sunset…'

He was speaking again, and Alys made herself breathe, forcing back control. She was not here to be struck breathless by the sight of Nikos Drakis. That was no part of the reason she was here. *None.* Never again…

She swallowed. 'Yes,' she said, because she had to say something.

He smiled. 'I'd forgotten how spectacular the view is from here,' he said. His eyes met hers. 'This is a good place, Alys. I'm glad you've come.'

There was something different in his voice. Something that had not been there before. Something she did not want to hear. Something that she wanted to block.

She made no reply, and he spoke again.

'Let me get you something to drink. What would you like?' He gestured to a drinks trolley nearby. 'There's a variety of juices to choose from.' He reeled them off for her.

'Pomegranate, please,' Alys said. Her voice was clipped, doggedly neutral.

She watched him cross to the trolley, half fill a tumbler with ice, then top it up with dark red juice. He handed it to her, poured a beer for himself and raised his glass.

'Yammas,' he said.

Memory stung her. That was what he'd said in London, when they'd shared cocktails together. Before sharing so much more…

She dragged her eyes away, walking towards the stone balustrade at the edge of the terrace and looking over at the gardens plunging down the steep drop in a series of terraced beds, verdant with glossy-leaved greenery and festooned with swathes of vivid bougainvillea. She lifted her gaze to the setting sun, now turning to bronze, pooling on the horizon with the sea that was also turned to bronze as the two touched together. Thoughts jumbled in her head—memories that she didn't want, that had no place any more. She banished them ruthlessly, closing in on herself again.

She became aware that Nikos had also come up to the balustrade, positioning himself a little way away from her. But he said nothing, only stood as she was standing, watching the sun set over the encircling sea. In the bushes, lush with bougainvillea, heavy with the scent of jasmine as the evening came on, the ceaseless chorus of the cicadas seemed to intensify.

It was easy to stand there, even with Nikos so close, and pay attention to the incredible display Nature was putting on before her eyes as, imperceptibly, the sun slowly pooled into the waiting water, spreading out its last crimson glow before, almost with a sigh, it was swallowed up.

Dusk gathered, and she could no longer see the colour of the flowers. She saw only the dim white of the jasmine, and caught its heady night scent in her nostrils.

She saw Nikos lever himself away from the balustrade, drain his beer. Behind them, she was aware of maids turning on lights in the lounge, placing candles and a freestanding lamp on a table further along the terrace—set, Alys realised, for dinner.

Nikos put his empty glass down on the drinks trolley. 'Shall we?' he asked, indicating the table.

She didn't answer, only walked towards it. Still closed in on herself, knowing it was the only way she could cope right now.

The warm night air embraced her like a soft shawl as Nikos pulled a chair out for her, and she sat herself down as he took the one opposite. Spiros emerged onto the terrace, with a young manservant behind him carrying a large and laden tray.

She heard Nikos exchange what she assumed were pleasantries with the young man as he deposited a platter of *mezze* between them, while Spiros placed a bottle of opened wine beside Nikos. He murmured his thanks and dismissed them.

He looked across at Alys. 'I hope this is to your liking… dining al fresco?' he enquired solicitously.

Alys nodded. A sense of unreality was unfolding over her. Last night Nikos had treated her as if she were a promiscuous, gold-digging tramp. And now…

Now it's as if I'm a welcome guest—to be treated with courtesy and solicitude.

The difference was bizarre. And tasted bitter in her throat.

Wariness filled her.

He was lifting up the wine bottle, speaking again. 'Will you have any wine at all, Alys?' Again, as before, there was nothing but courteous enquiry in his voice.

She shook her head, reaching for the jug of iced water on the table to top up her pomegranate juice. Then Nikos was indicating the platter of *mezze*, telling her what each delicacy was, placing a selection on her plate.

She began to eat, making herself not look at Nikos, though she was aware of him all the time, because she almost could not stop herself. She was aware of how he helped himself to more from the platter, how he lifted his wine glass to wash it down, how the soft light from the table lamp cast a glow over him, like *chiaroscuro* across his planed features, throwing them into relief.

Tormentingly aware.

He made light conversation. Nothing that demanded any reply from her. Telling her about the villa, that there was a swimming pool lower down, and a beach on either side, walks to the tip of the promontory beyond. That the larger beach to the left-hand side had a quay and a small boathouse, containing a dinghy and a motorboat.

She listened because there was nothing else to do. Her sense of unreality was paramount. She was actually here, in this luxurious villa, on this sea-girt island in the Aegean, dining with a man she had fled from only this morning…

Wariness flickered in her again.

Yes, with a few careless keystrokes he had lifted from her the crushing burden that had been hanging over her head, that she had been so desperate to dispel, and yet it had happened only because she had agreed to come here with him.

But why?

Was it just to renew that nightmare demand he'd made of her about the paternity test? The demand that had shown her just what he thought of her? But her answer would be the same—total refusal. How could it be otherwise?

She gave up trying to think, simply folded her numbed wariness around her, like a cloak. Closing in on herself. Unable and unwilling to let any emotions in or out. It seemed the safest and the least tormenting thing to do.

Mezze demolished, Nikos pressed a buzzer beside his plate. Moments later Spiros and the young manservant were back, whisking away the empty plates, depositing new ones along with grilled fish, herbed potatoes, green beans and salads. Then they disappeared again.

As before, she ate steadily, trying not to look at Nikos, trying to shut him out of her consciousness. He was doggedly continuing his monologue about the villa, talking to her in a polite voice that he might use to any welcome guest, seemingly immune to the fact that she was not replying to him as he moved on to telling her about the island and the places of interest on it, then this whole region of the Aegean, and the chain of which this island was a part.

Memory stabbed at her of having dinner with him that unforgettable night they'd met, and how she'd been the very opposite of the way she was being now. Not closed and silent and unsmiling, but she'd opened up to him, drinking him in, face lit, eyes glowing, still half disbelieving that she really was with this incredible man who could melt her with a glance from his long-lashed dark eyes…a glance that had told her of his desire for her and how he wanted the evening to end…

Her jaw tightened, bringing her back to now.

Well, it's ended here, hasn't it? This is where that evening has brought you—to this. Pregnant by a man who doesn't even believe your baby is his, and thinks you're just trying to get your hands on his precious money.

Bitterness filled her and she felt her throat constrict. It had become painful to swallow. Impossible. She set down her fork, fish unfinished.

He paused, looking across at her. She did not wait for him to speak again, to say anything more, but spoke instead.

'Why am I here, Nikos?'

Her question was direct, and it came not from any conscious decision to speak, yet the words hung between them.

For a moment he did not answer, first reaching for his wine, taking a draught of the ruby liquid glowing in the light of the candles in their sheltering glass holders.

She felt the moment lengthen, knowing her voice had been low and strained. But how could it be anything else? Just hours earlier she had been clawing at him, pummelling him, yelling at him in gasping rage and fury. Yet now they were sharing dinner together under a starry sky, above the quiet lapping of the Aegean Sea, with the low, ceaseless murmur of the cicadas all around.

He set back his wine glass, looked across at her. 'To give you time,' he said. His voice, too, was low. 'Time…' he drew a breath '…to be less angry with me.'

Her expression altered. 'Why should that even be possible?' she answered. There was a bitterness in her voice she could hear herself. 'After what you've accused me of!'

He drew breath again. 'What if I said to you…' he spoke slowly, picking his words with care, and she was aware of it, could see it in the way he looked at her, as carefully as he was speaking to her '…that in Athens last night I got it wrong?'

She did not answer, only waited. And after a moment he went on, still in that careful voice, with that watchful regard, seeing how she would react, she knew.

'And that now,' he said, his eyes never leaving her, 'I am trying to get it right.'

The candle flickered in the night air and she was not sure she could read him. There might be something that she could not see.

'You mean,' she said, knowing that her mouth had twisted, her voice too, 'you no longer think I'm some kind of scheming gold-digger, trying to get her hands on your precious money and scamming you with a baby that isn't even yours!'

She did not bother to hide the expression in her eyes. She saw his face tense.

'I told you. I got it wrong last night. And I'm sorry for it. Which is why—' he took an incised breath '—I want to start over.' He paused, eyes holding hers. Then, 'Alys, we have to get to know each other. We spent one night with each other, but we're still strangers in all other respects, and that is what has to change. For you, for me—for the baby.'

He paused again, and she could see something move in his eyes, but still did not know what.

'Our baby,' he said.

The words fell into the space between them. She wanted

to challenge him, to demand whether he believed that—believed what he'd just admitted.

But why would he say it if he doesn't believe it, doesn't acknowledge what I know to be true?

'Give me a chance, Alys.' He was speaking again, his eyes still holding hers across the table, candlelight flickering in their dark depths. 'A chance to mend the mistake I made last night. To get it right instead of wrong. Will you let me do that?'

She did not answer. Could not. Painful thoughts contorted in her head. Last night she'd wanted only to flee Nikos for ever. But now…?

Confusion filled her, and wariness, and uncertainty, and above all an inability to give voice to any answer at all.

It seemed he did not need one. She saw his expression flicker in the candlelight.

'I'll take your silence as consent,' he said. There was dryness in his voice, and wryness.

But she could not answer even that. She was beyond it. Beyond everything. Instead, she picked up her fork, resumed eating her dinner.

After a moment, so did Nikos.

CHAPTER SEVEN

NIKOS LAY IN his bed, staring up the ceiling fan circling slowly.

Had he said the right thing? Had she believed him? It was impossible to tell. Impossible to read her. He would just have to trust that he had convinced her. But at least he was further on than he had been at the airport, with her about to bolt back to England.

Hasten slowly...

Sometimes that was the way forward in a deal. Not to rush the other party. To give them time to feel comfortable.

And that's what she needs to feel.

The way she'd obviously felt with him in London. And he with her.

I need to recapture that—make it real for her again.

He would start tomorrow. Hastening slowly. Getting her exactly where he wanted her to be. *Needed* her to be. Using all the skill he possessed to achieve it.

Alys had retired as soon as they'd finished dinner, and although she hadn't thought she would sleep easily, with so much in her head, she'd slept deeply and peacefully, waking to sunshine slanting thinly through the louvred shutters. She'd dressed quickly in cotton trousers and a short-sleeved shirt, before stepping out onto the bedroom's balcony—

which, she now realised, was an extension of the terrace, curving around the entire frontage of the villa.

The morning sun on the sea was dazzling, dancing on tiny wavelets, almost too bright to bear. The air was warm, and sweet with the scent of flowers. Vivid crimson bougainvillea tumbled down the walls, over the balustrade, down the steep garden. Beyond the garden, on the promontory, thin cypresses pierced the azure sky.

She gazed out over it, all so wonderfully beautiful about her. And out of nowhere she felt her spirits lift.

I am here, in this fantastic luxury villa, and for whatever reason I am here I might as well enjoy it!

After all, it would not come again. Soon she would be back in England, finding a job to last until she had her baby, keeping her costs as low as possible while she continued to pay the mortgage—now blessedly not in arrears, with that crushing fear lifted from her. Perhaps she could get a job that would allow her some maternity leave...and she must try and find a childminder too. Because although she had not wanted to be a working mother, now she must be.

Her expression hardened. Whatever her confused thoughts and feelings about what Nikos had said to her last night, she must still be wary. She had let him pay off her arrears, removing the worst of her fears for the future, but that did not mean she would or should let herself be dependent on him for the future of herself and her baby.

Who knows? He might change his mind about me yet again?

That jaundiced, cynical thought was in her head and she would not banish it. Nor let down her guard just because of a few well-spun lines from him about starting over and making amends for what he'd said to her in Athens.

Not yet.

And maybe not ever.

She walked further along the terrace until she reached the section where they had dined, in front of the wide reception room. Nikos was already at the table, now set for breakfast.

He got to his feet, courteously coming around to pull back her chair for her. She nodded briefly, sitting down. She was hungry, and the scent of fresh-baked rolls curled around her.

Nikos resumed his place. 'How are you this morning?' he asked. 'You slept well, I hope?'

Alys nodded again, reaching for a roll and a dish of pale butter.

'May I pour you some coffee?' Nikos offered. 'Or perhaps orange juice first?'

'No coffee, thank you, but orange juice will be lovely,' she said, and he poured it for her as she buttered her roll, then followed it with a spoonful of golden honey.

She focussed on what she was doing, not on Nikos. It was safer that way. And not because she was still closed in on herself, still infinitely wary of what was going on. But because looking at Nikos would mean taking in his physical impact all over again.

He looked different again now, in a pair of cut-off denims and a white tee that moulded his powerful torso in ways she should not, *must* not pay attention to.

She swallowed, helping herself to more orange juice, which refreshed her, so when Nikos, glancing across at her, asked in that careful voice he was using whether she would object to a quiet day at the villa, she felt she could only nod assent.

She kept it at that, starting to eat her honeyed roll, savouring the softness of the fresh bread, the richness of the butter, the sweetness of the honey.

The sun was warm on the back of her head, her neck and shoulders, and she looked around her at the glorious, sun-drenched vista, feeling a sense of blessing from the sheer beauty of the place.

'It's good here, isn't it?' Nikos's voice sounded, quiet against the backdrop of the cicada's ceaseless chorus. 'You can see why I thought it would be the right place for us.'

Her eyes went to him. 'There is no "us", Nikos. There is a baby, but there is no "us".'

There was a tightening in her throat as she spoke. The sense of blessing had vanished. Replaced by all that was between them. All that made his 'us' impossible.

He nodded slowly. 'I won't pressurise you, Alys. What I said is what I meant—that we should simply spend time here. Get used to each other. Get to know each other.'

She looked at him, then dropped her eyes, saying nothing in response, only continuing with her breakfast, looking out over the vista to give herself something to do—and because it was so beautiful to look at.

After a while, Nikos spoke again. In that same courteous, solicitous tone. 'So, after breakfast, would you like to spend the morning by the pool?'

'I didn't bring any swimwear,' Alys heard herself answer.

'No matter—some is always kept here for houseguests. The maids can bring you a selection to choose from.'

'Oh. Well. Thank you.' Her answer felt awkward, but he did not appear to notice.

'Good,' he said. Then frowned. 'You must ensure you have sufficient sun cream, though—protect your pale skin.'

As he spoke, a memory flickered in her head of how he'd laughed as they'd lain entwined in each other's arms, that one single night they'd had, at how her skin was so pale against his Mediterranean tan. She pushed the memory away. There was no place for it here.

He was telling her that the maids would also bring her a selection of sun creams, as well as the swimwear.

'Do you swim?' Nikos asked.

She nodded, glancing down at the stepped pathway winding through the terraced gardens. At the bottom she could see the swimming pool, glistening under the sunshine. It looked dazzlingly inviting…

It looked even more so when, wearing a royal blue one-piece swimsuit whose simplicity did not disguise the fact that it was a very expensive item, as were the blue-patterned wrap that went with it and the blue bead-encrusted flip-flops on her feet, she emerged onto the pool deck. It was semicircular, with the oval pool at its centre, a pool house to one side and a low retaining wall smothered in yet more bougainvillea.

As at breakfast, Nikos was already there. Clearly ready for a morning swim.

Alys felt her stomach hollow. He was propped up on a lounger. Dark green board shorts snaked around his hips and his bronzed torso was bare. Memory flared—memory she did not want, could not stop.

Running my fingertips across his chest, grazing them over every contour, feeling every honed muscle beneath my touch, revelling in it, glorying in it—

She felt colour run up into her cheeks and turned away to drop down on the lounger set a little way away from Nikos's.

'Did you put sun cream on?'

His voice made her turn towards him. He was wearing sunglasses and she could not see his eyes.

'Yes.' She nodded. 'I've brought the bottle down. And I hope you don't mind… I found some magazines—'

She spoke awkwardly, not actually wanting to talk, but feeling she ought to, because she'd helped herself to the magazines. They weren't magazines she would have chosen, but they were in English, and presumably they must have more than fashion pages in them.

'There are some English language books on the lounge bookshelves as well,' he replied. He held up a paperback with a lurid cover showing two men shooting at each other, and a speeding car in the background. 'I found one for myself.' He gave a half-smile. 'Action adventure—haven't read anything like this in years!'

She didn't smile back, only settled herself on the lounger, feeling the heat of the sun beating down on her. She got her own sunglasses out of the bag and put them on. It gave her some protection. And not just from the brightness of the Aegean sun.

From Nikos.

She shut her eyes, lying back, thoughts racing. Could she cope with this? Could she really cope with lying here, sunbathing next to Nikos at his luxury villa, going along with what he'd asked of her, and yet all the time being so burningly conscious of him, of how it had been that very first time she'd set eyes on him…

She made herself relax, felt the heat soaking into her, heard cicadas chorusing all round, the sound of Nikos turning a page from time to time, the low lap of the sea on the beaches below.

It was very peaceful. And slowly, very slowly, she began to feel the peace of it too. Without being conscious of it she slid her hand across her abdomen, resting it lightly where, safe and secret within, her precious baby lay. She felt her breathing slow right down, let the chorus of the cicadas fade away, and under the somnolent heat of the sun slipped into drowsing slumber.

Nikos heard her breathing change. Through his dark glasses he glanced towards her. He felt his breath catch. She'd let the beach wrap fall back and now she lay there, arms and shoulders bare, long legs exposed, her still-slender figure moulded by the one-piece. Across her lower abdomen her hand was resting, splayed out. A timeless gesture of protection for an unborn child.

His throat tightened.

How beautiful she looked! Like a sleeping expectant Madonna—mother and child-to-be…

He felt emotion well in him, new and strange. Confusing and conflicted.

For a long, timeless moment he watched her…the slow rise and fall of her breasts, the grace of her body, the beauty of her face…

Then he looked away, back to his book.

But he was paying no attention to it.

Alys rested her hands on the sun-warmed stone of the balustrade edging the terrace, watching the sun turning the world to gold just as she had twenty-four hours ago.

And just as *he* had twenty-four hours ago, Nikos was strolling up to her, a tumbler of pomegranate juice in one hand, a beer glass for himself in the other. He handed the former to her and she took a sip, her eyes going back to the gold-lit vista all around.

'So, has it been a good day, do you think?'

Nikos's enquiry was quietly spoken and she glanced at him. Nodded slowly.

'I'm glad,' he said. He paused. Then, 'So, do you think you prefer the beach to the pool, or the other way around?'

His enquiry was polite, and Alys heard herself answer, because a nod would not work to answer his question. 'They're both beautiful. The whole place is beautiful,' she said, her voice low.

She let her gaze slip out towards the panorama. Down below, to her right-hand side, she could get a glimpse through the greenery of the small curve of sand and shingle that was the tiny beach they'd gone down to that afternoon. Lunch had been served on the pool deck, a light al fresco affair of fresh bread and cheeses, charcuterie and sweet tomatoes, and sweeter peaches.

Easy to consume, and easy for Nikos to make his unfailing one-sided conversation over. Just as he was doing now, making some remark about sea swimming. He'd done just that after they'd settled on the beach, and she'd watched him run lithely into the lapping water, arch his incredible body and launch himself into the deeper water, then swim vigorously away from the shore in a strong, powerful freestyle, splashing up diamonds in the sunshine as he ploughed forward.

He'd returned some time later, hair slicked back, those same diamonds glancing off his body as he'd reached for a towel, padding himself dry. He'd been grinning, visibly exhilarated, and then he had thrown himself down to dry off completely in the sun.

Alys had looked out to sea again, because that had been

easier than looking at his near-naked body bringing memories she must not have…

She felt her stomach hollow again, her eyes going to Nikos in chinos and an open-necked shirt with turned-back cuffs, his hair freshly washed and feathering at the nape of his neck. He was freshly shaved too, it seemed, judging by his pristine jawline.

Wariness prickled in her veins. She should steel herself against him, warn herself that he might turn on her again, as he had in Athens…

And yet all day long Nikos had done nothing except treat her as if she were made of porcelain, endlessly solicitous, painstakingly courteous. He was still doing that now, asking her if, tomorrow, she might like to try going out on the water.

'There's a choice of sail or motor,' he said. 'Which would you prefer?'

'I've never tried either,' she answered.

'Then we'll see what the wind conditions are like tomorrow. Too light, and the dinghy won't get us anywhere. Too brisk, and it could get a bit bumpy.'

There was a sound behind them and he turned. It was one of the maids, lighting the candles on the table, which was set for dinner again. As she left, Nikos thanked her.

Alys could hear the word *efharisto*, and something more, and she saw how the girl flushed with pleasure and hurried off. A tiny, brief vignette, and yet her gaze flickered. It showed that she herself was not the only female whose head would turn at Nikos's glance, warm to his smile.

They took their places at the table, with dusk melting into night, and somehow, despite all her wariness, all her holding back from him, and perhaps because of the day they'd spent in each other's company, Alys found herself replying in the face of Nikos's continued punctilious politeness towards her.

Just little things—a question that came to her from something he'd said about tourism on the island…an observation of her own. Not much, and not often, but she did it all the same.

The food was once again delicious, served by Spiros and the young manservant—Spiros's nephew Andreas, Nikos told her with a smile. Alys smilingly praised the food—chicken tonight, in a light, lemony sauce, with delicate rice and grilled courgettes, following on from a layered seafood terrine in a lobster bisque.

She ate with a will—not just because the sun and sea air seemed to have given her an appetite, but to make the most of this brief spell of indolent and pampered luxury.

Make the most of being here with Nikos.

She froze, her fork motionless in mid-air. Where had that come from? That totally out of place, irrelevant and untrue thought?

Her eyes went across to him as he tucked into the delicious dish. Something kicked through her—something about the angle of his head, the way his shirt collar framed his sinewed neck, the way his long, strong fingers pressed the blade of the knife into the tender chicken breast…something about the way his thick, dark lashes dipped down over his deep brown eyes as he ate…something that she was suddenly aware was quickening her pulse, making her feel her heart thud in her chest, emotion build within her.

Just from looking at him.

Being with him…

'Alys?'

She heard her name spoken, a note of concern in it.

'Are you all right?'

She nodded—a hasty gesture. 'Yes, thank you. It was nothing.'

Because 'nothing' is all I can ever allow myself to feel about Nikos. Even if he does now believe my baby is his, that does not mean there can be anything between us. If he has any concern it will be about the baby. Not about me.

His next words, when he spoke, echoed just that. She

could hear the same note of concern in his voice—but it was not for her.

'The obstetrician told me you were progressing well—that you had no health problems, had reported none and he could see none.' He was frowning slightly as he spoke, his eyes searching her face. 'But I wondered just now, when you stopped eating, if maybe—'

She drew a breath. 'I'm fine,' she said. 'Completely healthy.'

His eyes were still on her. 'You hardly show yet,' he said.

'I'm not as slim as I was,' she answered.

Then, immediately, she wished she had said nothing in response. Nikos's gaze was now flickering over her.

Out of the meagre wardrobe she'd brought with her to Greece she was wearing the knee-length denim skirt again, but a different top this time—one that, she realised now, with a flush, had become tighter since the previous summer. It moulded her breasts, outlining them. Was he seeing that?

She hunched forward to minimise the effect. She must change the subject…think of something innocuous to say. But Nikos spoke first.

'You look,' he said slowly, 'radiant.'

Her eyes went to his. There was something in them that made her reel.

'They say pregnant women have a glow about them, and in you I can absolutely see why.'

She swallowed. 'I caught the sun today, that's all,' she said. She reached for her iced water, needing its chill.

He shook his head. 'It's more than that,' he said, in the same slow manner, as if he were realising it for the first time. 'You're more beautiful than ever, Alys.'

There was a huskiness in his voice, colour in his cheeks…

'Don't!'

The word came automatically to her. Negating what he was saying. She took a mouthful of water, cold to her throat.

He gave a slow shake of his head. 'You make it very hard, Alys,' he said.

She could feel the heat beating up into her cheeks, the quickening of her heart rate. She wanted it to stop. Wanted this whole moment to stop—just stop.

She looked away, felt a churning inside her. Then, to her relief, he began saying something else. Something about taking the motorboat out the next day, where they might visit in it. She was glad—and grateful. She answered him in kind, getting past the impossible moment that was now thankfully gone.

Because I can't have it! It's got no place between us. Not any more!

She heard herself ask something about how fast the motorboat could travel…could it reach the other islands in the group clustering in this part of the Aegean? The subject was so much more bearable than what he had tried to talk about.

Before long they had finished their main course, and Spiros and Andreas were there again, bestowing upon them a creamy peach bavarois that slipped down her throat like balm, followed by coffee served Greek-style for Nikos and a herbal tea for herself.

Not wanting to go anywhere near what he had said earlier, she asked him about Greek coffee, hearing in return how it was derived from the way the Turks had introduced it, which led on to the time of the Ottoman occupation, and the long, dark centuries of conquest and occupation by the Sultan's forces.

He spoke with passion and feeling, regaling her with the history she knew only dimly herself.

'That must go very deep into the modern Greek psyche,' she heard herself saying, looking across at him.

A thought struck her, making her wonder. *Will my baby share that too?*

Her eyes rested on Nikos. His face was animated by what he was telling her.

Will he—or she—look like him as well? Share those dark, devastating looks of his?

She silenced the questions. What would it matter? Her baby would grow up without Nikos in its life. Grow up without a father. As she had had to.

Unless...

Did it have to be like that? She had been forced to think so, resign herself to it, after he'd revealed his ugly condemnation of her. Now, though, he had told her he accepted her baby as his—did the rest of his condemnation of her still hold?

Does he still think all I want is his money?

After all, hadn't she justified his low opinion of her by letting him pay off her mortgage arrears as she had? She could tell herself all she liked that any court would impose maintenance demands on him, but how did that avoid his accusation that she wanted to profit from her pregnancy?

So would she want him in her baby's life, thinking that of her?

Surely there could be only one sane answer to that.

In her head, as she sat listening to Nikos telling her the tale of the struggle for Greek independence, she heard the echo of her own voice at breakfast.

'There is no "us", Nikos.'

It went on echoing.

CHAPTER EIGHT

NIKOS OPENED THE throttle of the sleek motorboat and it thrust forward with a powerful roar of the outboard engine. He gave a laugh—a carefree sound. He couldn't even remember the last time he'd taken a motorboat out like this, and certainly not here at the Villa Drakis, where he hadn't been for years.

He felt himself frown. Had his life really been restricted to endless business trips abroad to do endless deals to make ever more money for the Drakis coffers? Only snatching brief time off to spend a weekend every now and then with the likes of sophisticated females like Irinia, wining and dining them in Michelin-starred restaurants in snatches before flying off yet again, or heading back to Athens to report to his father, set up yet another potential money-making deal, and then be off again?

He shook his mind free of such thoughts, focussing on the here and now—on what was now essential to him: putting everything else about his life totally aside and focussing on the woman who was so totally unlike all the Irinias of this world—who was changing everything in his life.

Changing it for ever.

And I have to get it right! Far too much is at stake.

And surely now, after his initial near-catastrophic miscalculation, he was beginning to do so? Though it was slow going with Alys, she was finally progressing beyond mere nods and monosyllables. He was on the right track with her. Yesterday had been good—today would be better.

Bringing her here to the villa had been exactly the right thing to do. Slowly, but inexorably, she was responding to his new treatment of her, letting go of the hostility that his previous harshness had engendered.

And it must not come back. That's essential!

It was more than essential.

Because I don't want to feel hostile to her either.

He heard an echo of his words to her over dinner last night. *'You look radiant.'*

He turned to look at Alys now, sitting by the gunwale, her hair streaming like a flag in the wind, her face in profile lifted to the sun and the wind. How beautiful she was…

He dragged his gaze back to the sea. They were heading parallel to the rocky shoreline of the promontory, and before long had cleared it to starboard and made a wide, circling manoeuvre out to sea.

He pointed to the rounded tip of the promontory, turning to Alys from the wheel. 'Can you see? Right at the very tip there's a cove, a sandy beach. You can only reach it by sea. That's where we're heading.'

He steered towards it, reducing speed as the water became shallower and calmer, became turquoise. Moments later he was cutting the engine, lifting the motor out of the water, dropping anchor.

'Time for our picnic,' he said. He knew his voice was cheerful, enthusiastic, still infused with the sense of being carefree that had come over him as he'd let rip with the motorboat.

He hefted up the wicker picnic basket and chill box and jumped down into the shallow water, splashing to shore and depositing his burdens in the shade of a large rock. Then he came back for Alys. She was standing up, beach bag and towels in hand, about to jump into the ankle-deep water.

Instead of letting her do so, Nikos reached out his hands,

put them around her waist, swinging her down. She was as light as a feather, but he could feel her whole body stiffen before he lowered her onto the sand, feeling the warmth of her body in his hands.

She went to the picnic things, busying herself deliberately, or so he fancied, then getting a towel, flapping it down on the sand, placing her beach bag on it to weigh it down. She was wearing the one-piece suit again, with a tee shirt over it today—stronger protection against the midday sun than a flimsy wrap.

'We'll rehydrate, then catch a swim before lunch,' Nikos declared.

He hunkered down to click open the chill box and extract a plastic bottle of mineral water, cold to the touch. He handed it to Alys, taking another one for himself. Then he straightened, unscrewing the top and taking a good few gulps, making sure she did as well.

'OK, let's hit the water.'

He waited for her and, as she stepped gingerly over the hot sand, took her hand to help her. He felt her try to yank it back, but would not let her.

'I don't want you stumbling,' he told her.

It was strange to hold her hand, however briefly. Strange and very good.

When they gained the lapping edge of the sea she extricated her hand. His felt empty suddenly.

'Leave your tee shirt on,' he recommended. 'You can burn just as badly in the water. In you go.'

Carefully, she waded in beside him, going as deep as her waist. She seemed to hesitate a moment, then she pushed off into a gentle breaststroke, her tee shirt billowing out above her shoulders as she did so.

He came up beside her. 'Nice?' he asked.

She nodded.

'It won't get deep till you're quite far out.' He gave her

another smile. 'I'm going to work up an appetite!' he said lightly, and plunged in with a duck dive.

He surfaced ten metres out, after dolphin kicks under water. Then he took off in an energetic freestyle. As it had the day before, it exhilarated him. He headed straight out, felt the swell increase with the depth of the water, and turned to head back inshore. Alys was now sitting in the shallows, the wet tee shirt clinging to her body. Outlining her breasts. Her crested nipples.

He stopped short. Arousal, out of nowhere, surged in him. Thank God he was still over his waist in water. He fought for control. But it took an effort he could barely make. Did not want to make.

Because what he wanted was to—

No. He slammed the brakes down. Hard. With gritted teeth, he ground out his maxim to himself.

Hasten slowly—with the whole emphasis on slowly, dammit!

He was barely two days out from bringing her here. And no way was she ready yet.

But I have to get her there. Have to get her to exactly where I want her...need her...to be.

He drew a breath, conscious that his heart was pounding—and not just from the exertion of his vigorous swim. He slicked his hands through his hair, wading towards her, water splashing around his thighs.

She'd knotted her hair loosely on top of her head, but fronds had tendrilled around her face. Sunshine kissed her skin, flushed from yesterday's sunbathing, like a honeyed peach.

Emotion caught at him—or something did. Something that was not the urgent arousal that had surged in him so overpoweringly just now. Something else. Something that was more like what he'd felt yesterday, watching her sleeping by the pool, a recumbent Madonna, dreaming of the child she was to bear. Something that seemed to join the two together—the erotic charge of the first with the wonder of the second. Something that met and melded with them both.

He hunkered down beside her, his breathing easing now, his elevated heart rate recovering from his exertions, holding out a hand to her.

'I'm starving. Let's see what's in the picnic box.'

She curled her legs under her to propel herself upright. Nikos kept his hand out. There was a moment's hesitancy, then she put her hand in his, to let him draw her effortlessly to her feet.

He wanted to punch the air in triumph. But he did not push the moment, letting her go and heading across to the shade of the rock, throwing himself down on the towel and flipping open the cool box. Getting out the water bottles, he handed one to Alys as she came up, then lowered herself cross-legged to her own towel. As she started to drink thirstily her hand moved across her lower stomach—the same gesture she'd made yesterday by the pool. It was becoming familiar to him. More than familiar…

Emotions flickered in him like a faulty electrical circuit that was uncertain of the connections it needed to make it flow properly.

He slugged down the rest of the water, then reached for a beer, making inroads on that too, before undoing the wicker picnic basket. It was brim-full of goodies, and his stomach growled.

'Dig in,' he invited, starting to spread out the feast: cold chicken, cold salmon, prawns and crayfish, cheeses and hams and ready-mixed salads, fresh rolls and butter and salad dressing, a meltingly flaky filo pastry pie and tomatoes the size of apples.

Eating was messy and informal. Nikos lounged back on one elbow, and Alys stayed in her flexible legs-crossed position as they worked their way through the repast. Nikos kept up a flow of easy-going conversation, as he had become used to, making all the running, getting only occasional replies from Alys.

He'd never had to make the running when it came to women—they never held out against him, were always eager for his attentions. As Alys had been that first night together.

Yet now…

To get even the suggestion of a smile out of her was an achievement. That wariness, that withdrawal into herself, keeping him at bay, was still paramount. Oh, she was lowering her guard against him, but he could take nothing for granted. Nothing.

A thought came to him—one that struck him out of nowhere.

What if I hadn't left her that morning in London?

He stilled a moment, letting it sink into him. What if he'd cancelled those damn appointments in the City? Never flown off to Geneva that day to talk to yet another bunch of private bankers? If, instead, he'd taken off with Alys, fresh from his bed, to somewhere much, much more enticing. The Caribbean, the Maldives, the Seychelles…

Just her and me taking off together. Being together like we are here, now. Carefree, enjoying ourselves. Enjoying life, enjoying being with each other...

It was a powerful thought. One he could not dismiss. Did not wish to…

His eyes rested on her. She was eating one of the giant tomatoes and a thread of juice was running down her chin. He wanted to lean forward and lick it away, move his lips up to her mouth, open it to his…

He reached for a slice of the filo pie, to distract himself from thoughts that could bear no fruit. Not yet…

Picnic finished, he watched her pack the remains away, make use of the scented handwipes provided, then he settled himself back on his towel, reminding Alys she needed to top up her sunblock. He folded his arms under his head, watching her do just as he'd told her, liking the way her hands smoothed down over her long legs in wide, sensual strokes. Wanting to do it for her…

Then she was done, lying back as he was doing, the tee shirt, quite dry now, protecting her torso.

He gazed upwards into the cerulean sky, avoiding the sun. Thoughts circled in his head. That first night here, at dinner, he'd said 'our baby'. He'd said it because he'd known she needed to hear it or she would make it impossible for him to achieve what he must achieve with her.

But hadn't he needed to hear it too?

Do I really believe that she fell from my bed into another man's, or came to my bed from another man's? Do I truly believe that of her?

Yes, he had seen her and swept her into his bed in a single night, but did that mean she made a habit of such things? He himself did not—so why should he think it of her?

And, for all the way she'd been glitzed to the nines, when he'd taken her to bed she had not been some highly experienced sexual sophisticate at all—ardent, yes, but with a sweetness and eagerness that had captivated him. And in the morning, watching her sleeping, he had seen an innocence about her that had told him their night together had been as rare for her as it had for him…

He levered himself up on his elbow to look down on her as she lay, eyes closed, breathing gently. Whether she was asleep or not he did not know. All he knew was that she had looked just like that as he'd gazed down on her sleeping figure that morning in London, when he'd left her. And she was filling him with the same desire… A desire that surely could only prove one thing…

How could I desire her believing she carries another man's child? It would be impossible.

Yet desire was what he felt now—strong and insistent. Just as he had in that moment of arousal as he'd watched her, lolling in the water, her nipples cresting beneath the wet fabric of her tee shirt. It was his own body telling him the truth about her…

About myself…

As if she'd sensed him gazing down at her, she opened her eyes, meeting his. For an instant, a moment of time so brief it might not have existed, something moved in their depths—and then it was gone. Shuttered out.

'What is it? Why do you look at me like that?'

There was defensiveness in her voice—he could hear it. He did not want it there. Needed to banish it.

He spoke slowly, almost haltingly. 'I was remembering how I looked down at you that morning in London, asleep in bed, knowing I had to leave you.' He paused. 'Not wanting to.' His expression changed, shadowed. 'I thought I had to leave you. That it was the only prudent thing to do. Thought that what we'd had was…' he took a heavy breath '…a one-off encounter. That I should walk away and leave it like that. But—'

He stopped, his eyes switching to the azure sea, to the far horizon where it merged with the sky. It was impossible to tell which was which. Impossible to know where the boundary was.

Like the boundary between that night with Alys and the reality of my life, where work dominates and only women like Irinia give me any respite.

His gaze dropped down again, meeting her eyes, still shuttered as they were to him. He knew he needed to tell her this. Wanted to tell her.

'I came back for you—I came back to London to find you.'

The words fell from him before he could stop them, consider them…decide whether they were the right words to say. He didn't care. He wanted to say them. Wanted Alys to hear them.

'I realised I didn't want just one night with you. So I came back to find you. I went to the hotel and then—' He broke off.

There was a moment's silence.

'Then the concierge gave you the letter I'd left for you.' Alys's voice supplied the answer. It was expressionless.

He took another breath. 'Yes. And then…' He paused again, feeling that breath tight in his lungs. 'Then it all went wrong,' he said. 'But now…' His expression changed again. 'Now all I want is to get it right. Not just because of the baby. But between *us*, Alys.'

Alys sat on the gunwale of the motorboat, as she had that morning on the trip out. Nikos was going more slowly now, gently bobbing across water that was turning to gold with the lowering sun. Her eyes went to him. His hair was wind-ruffled, eyes masked by his sunglasses, his bronzed, leanly muscled torso lit with the golden sun.

His words to her, as she'd lain there on the beach, with him gazing down on her, burned in her mind. *'All I want is to get it right...between us,'* he'd said.

Then her own words to him of the night before slammed over them. *'There is no "us", Nikos.'*

She heard them both, playing and replaying in her head. Impossible to reconcile. Her eyes lifted to the approaching shoreline, to the white villa above the bougainvillea-laced terraced gardens, landscaped into the steep slope.

Just imagine living here.

She yanked the thought away. No, that was not possible—not permissible. She was simply passing through, that was all.

Yet she felt a pang for all that. She could grow to love this place…

What if there were an 'us' between Nikos and me?

The thought was in her head, taking form and shape. Becoming reality. Bringing others in its wake.

He said he came back to London to find me... What if I had not left that letter for him, or if I had never conceived that night...?

She pulled her thoughts away. It had not happened like that. It had happened the way it had, and that was why she was here now—for no other reason. Not because there was any 'us' between her and Nikos.

There was only a baby yoking them together, and everything about the future was still…uncertain.

That was all she must remember.

Yet once the boat was docked and moored, as she and Nikos made their slow ascent up the steps to the terrace, she heard his words in her head again.

'I came back for you…'

And she felt a strange and hopeless ache form inside her…

CHAPTER NINE

DINNER THAT EVENING, after their second full day with each other at the villa, seemed easier. Conversation seemed easier. Just being with Nikos seemed easier.

He drew no attention to it, and Alys was glad. That made it easier too: easier to respond to what he was saying, to make replies, ask questions, almost to have a conversation with him.

She didn't want to examine it, or analyse it, or question it. All she wanted was to let it be as it was: feeling easier.

There was the same atmosphere at breakfast the next day too. As she took one of an array of freshly baked rolls, reaching for the butter and honey, Nikos smiled across at her.

'How about if I show you something of the island today? We could take off after breakfast, if you like, and maybe have lunch in town if that appeals?'

She nodded, but it was not to avoid replying verbally. 'Thank you—that would be nice,' she said.

Was there less constraint in her voice? She thought there was. It seemed to be part of this 'easier' that she was so conscious of.

Easier not to perpetually be on her guard against him, to be wary of him, withdrawing into herself, speaking as little as she could. Easier to acquiesce, to let his solicitousness continue, to reply rather than only nod when he spoke to her, to be complaisant and agree to his suggestions—like she was now, about going out. Because, after all, why not?

He smiled, nodding in return. 'Good,' he said, and reached for the coffee pot.

They set off late morning—breakfast had been leisurely—and the high wheel base of the SUV afforded a good view over the countryside and coastline. Conscious that she had seen nothing of either on the drive from the airport, her eyes doggedly shut throughout, her mind too battered and exhausted to pay attention to anything, Alys looked about her now with interest.

The hilly, rugged interior of the island was mostly dry, with olive groves on the lower slopes and maquis interspersed with tall cypress trees. Nikos chatted casually, telling her about what they were seeing, pointing to a radio and communications mast on one of the rocky peaks. Modern windmills were also noticeable in places, reducing the island's dependence, he told her, on imported power. They passed through some coastal fishing villages, then gained the outskirts of the island's small capital.

'What would you like to see first?' Nikos enquired. 'There's an old harbour, but it's a bit touristy as I recall. The marina beyond the ferry dock is more upmarket, and more modern.'

'Could we start at the harbour?' Alys asked. 'Touristy' was, after all, more her natural *milieu*—not a marina stuffed with private yachts.

It wasn't Nikos's, though, that was obvious.

He parked the massive SUV half on the pavement of a side street, and it looked out of place amidst the run-of-the-mill hire cars belonging to the tourists and those owned by the locals. So did Nikos himself.

She glanced at him. Though he was casually dressed, in chinos and an open-necked shirt, he didn't look like a tourist. He looked…

Expensive. Those casual clothes he wears with such effortless elegance cost a fortune, and his sunglasses likewise, and the thin, exclusive-looking gold watch around his wrist! Everything about him just says money. Wealth.

It was a disturbing thought, somehow. Disturbing in its implications.

I shouldn't wonder that he's so suspicious of me, thinking that I've told him about the baby, claimed it's his, because I want to get some of his wealth for myself?

After all, what if she *were* what he had accused her of being, doing what he was accusing her of trying to do? She rallied her thoughts, fighting them off.

Did he still think that?

He believes the baby is his. That, surely, has to be a start.

Her face shadowed. The start of what?

Nikos had talked of 'us', but there was no 'us', nor could there be.

Weariness washed through her, and a deep, deep reluctance to wade back into such turbid, toxic waters.

She looked about her, focussing on the busy scene, taking pleasure in it and putting aside—for now, at least—the impossibility of her situation and the tangle of sharing a child with a man like Nikos Drakis. The situation was fraught with doubts and demands, mistrust and hostility, but now it seemed this tentative, fragile, careful almost-truce was allowing them to be civil to each other, to learn not to be strangers…

As she walked beside him, their pace unhurried, they must look, she realised, just like any other couple strolling along.

'I came back to London to find you,' he had said to her on the beach in that secret cove yesterday. *'I wanted more than one night with you.'*

She felt emotion clench inside her. If that were true, and if she had not fallen pregnant, had never needed to leave that fateful letter for him, would she now be with him? The two of them together as lovers?

The thought pierced her—but what was the use of thinking it? It hadn't happened that way. And even if it had it would not have lasted. It would have been only an affair and then he would have moved on, back to his own world, a world of money and wealth a million miles removed from her own reality.

She felt again the strange ache that had come out of nowhere yesterday, as she thought of might-have-beens that never had been and then set them aside. What else was to be done with them? They had no place in her life.

They were approaching the harbour, which was typical of a thousand others dotted around the Aegean coastline, familiar from travel programmes and postcards. Fishing boats and tourist expedition boats bobbed at their moorings and the quayside was lined with tavernas, their shaded seating areas overlooking the water, their kitchens across the cobbled roadway. The air was filled with appetising smells, and breakfast suddenly seemed a long time ago.

'Can we have lunch here?' she heard herself ask Nikos.

She saw him glance dismissively down the row of tavernas.

'There'll be better fare at the marina restaurants,' he answered.

But she did not want to sit in some sleek, expensive restaurant, feeling out of place, knowing she was only there because she was the one-night stand of a rich man who'd ended up pregnant by him.

'Here looks more fun,' she countered. 'How about this one?'

It looked cheerful, with blue-checked paper tablecloths and a striped awning, and it was already filling up with customers.

Nikos was looking at her. 'Would you really prefer here to the marina?' he asked.

She nodded. 'This is me, Nikos. My world. And…' she looked at him straight '… I'm quite happy with it.'

Without waiting for a response, nor wanting him to insist on the upmarket marina, she turned to the waiter allocating tables.

'For two?' she asked, pointing to herself and Nikos, then at a table right by the water. 'That one?' she said hopefully.

She sat down happily, feeling comfortable there, and flicked open the menu the waiter had hurriedly handed her.

'Tourist fare,' said Nikos, hardly glancing at his.

A tiny smile hovered at her mouth. 'You'll survive,' she said dryly.

A reluctant laugh broke from him, and he raised a hand in surrender. 'You win,' he said. And then his eyes were on her, even though she couldn't see them through the designer shades covering them. 'It's worth it just to see you smile...'

For a second, she looked at him. She couldn't see his eyes yet she knew she was holding his, and he hers. Something seemed to be holding them together...

Then the waiter was there again, to take their drinks order, and Nikos was ordering beer for himself, asking what juices were available for Alys, relaying them to her in English. She chose a fizzy apple juice and mineral water and the waiter scurried off, just as another one deposited a woven basket of roughly sliced hunks of bread with a few butter pats down on the paper tablecloth.

She looked at her menu, felt herself start to relax, to feel at home here in this tourists' taverna, hearing the mix of languages around her. Maybe it was because everyone around her was relaxed as well—here on holiday, intent on enjoying themselves.

The waiter was back with their drinks, ready to take their food order, and then he disappeared again. Alys sipped her fizzy apple juice, and Nikos took a ruminative mouthful of his beer. It seemed to be a signal to himself to resign himself to his fate in eating at so lowly an eatery, and Alys saw him sit back, stretch out his long legs, take another mouthful of beer before setting it back down again.

She wanted to let her gaze linger on him but would not allow herself to do so. Instead, she gazed out over the harbour.

'Where does the ferry go to?' she asked, just for something to say, seeing the large ship nosing away from the wide quay beyond the harbour wall.

'It will call at the other islands in this group and circle back round. It will make connections with other ferry routes that would eventually take you back to Athens. All of Greece is connectable by sea—sometimes more so than by land.'

Alys looked at him. 'Do you ever use the ferries?' she asked.

He shook his head. 'The Drakis yacht is moored at Piraeus—the port of Athens.'

He paused, and Alys knew he was looking at her from behind his expensive sunglasses.

'I could have it brought here, if you want, Alys.'

She shook her head. 'No yachts, Nikos,' she said quietly.

'And no upmarket restaurant at the marina either?' he replied. 'Just this tourist taverna instead?'

'Yes,' she answered, and looked away again, out over the harbour at the water dazzling in the sunshine. Making her blink. Or something was.

There was a sudden touch, as light as it was brief, on her hand lying on the paper tablecloth. 'I'm sorry, that was unfair of me. Unkind.'

Nikos's voice was low, and its tone was different from the way he'd spoken before. Alys swallowed.

'But understandable,' she said. She looked across at him, half glad she couldn't see his eyes, half wishing she could. But not really wanting to see what was probably in them.

She gave a sigh. 'I can't prove to you that I am not what you assumed I was that horrible night in Athens, Nikos,' she said. 'And nor do I see any need to do so.' Her voice was edged. 'It was you who brought me here, remember. I would have returned to England, never to trouble you again—'

'No.'

The word was strongly spoken, and sharply too.

Alys tensed. 'I'll be going back anyway, Nikos, when

you've decided you've had enough of me being here.' She kept her eyes on him, though she still could not see his. 'I'm glad you've accepted that the baby is yours,' she said steadily, 'but it doesn't change anything. I'm going to be living in England, and I won't be making any financial demands of you at all. You can put funds aside for college fees or whatever later on, if you want to—but for myself I need nothing. You've paid off my debts, and for that I am truly grateful, but from now on I neither need nor want any of your money.'

She saw his expression tighten.

'You cannot possibly mean that,' he said slowly.

She gave a half-shrug. 'Why not? My mother raised me single-handed, so I can do likewise with my child. There'll be some state support to begin with, and then, like my mother, I'll use a mix of childcare and flexible working around the school calendar when the time comes.'

He frowned. 'What happened to your father?' His question was abrupt.

Alys gave another shrug. 'He wasn't around. He—he didn't know about me.' She looked away, out over the harbour. The bright sunshine dazzling on the water made her blink again.

She heard Nikos speaking, but did not look back at him.

'So because you grew up without a father you think that's OK for our baby too, do you?'

Was there challenge in his voice? Criticism? She didn't know or care. She gave yet another shrug but did not answer. Suddenly, she could not…

To her relief—because it *was* relief, surely?—the arrival of the waiter, as harassed as ever, allowed her to look back. He was depositing large plates of food hurriedly down on their table, and Nikos was absently thanking him before he scurried off again.

Alys picked up her fork, took her chicken souvlaki off the skewer and got stuck in. Eating was preferable to talking if the subject was going to be a difficult one. So she'd better stick to easy ones.

'This is good,' she said, taking another mouthful.

She didn't want Nikos resuming a subject she had no intention of discussing with him. Yet his words echoed in her head, and her own unspoken retort too.

No, I don't think it's OK. But it's not as bad as having a father who thinks the mother of his child is an avaricious gold-digger, hell-bent on getting her hands on all his money courtesy of her baby!

But what use was there in telling him that? He could think what he liked of her.

Defiantly, she went on eating.

Without enthusiasm, Nikos started on his tourist fare. But the pork was surprisingly tasty, the fried potatoes crisp, the beans in their tomato sauce peppery, and it was all washed down well by his beer. With a better will than he'd expected, he worked his way to a clear plate, mopping the remaining juices with a couple of hunks of fresh bread.

He made no attempt at conversation while he ate, but his mind was occupied. His own words echoed.

She can't possibly be genuine in her ridiculous assertion of not taking any child maintenance from me! Is it just some line she's trotting out for my benefit? But if so, what benefit? Why say it at all?

Maybe it was just virtue signalling.

But to what purpose? She didn't need to be virtuous to extract generous financial support from him!

Not that that was going to happen.

More words echoed in his head, from that ugly scene in Athens that evening.

'No child of mine will be born a bastard.'

He felt his fingers grip tightly onto his knife and fork and forced them to relax. Alys would not be returning to

England, and she would not be raising his child as a working single mother.

He had very different plans for her.

His gaze went to her, his mood improving automatically. Even dressed as she was, in cheap clothes, without a scrap of make-up, and with her hair simply drawn back into a ponytail, she still looked breathtakingly beautiful.

Radiant.

The word he'd used to describe her over dinner came again, as true now as then, washing away the tension that had flared between them as they'd ventured into difficult waters. It had been his fault, he acknowledged, baiting her with that line about having the Drakis yacht sailed over, tempting her with yet more of the wealth he could offer her…

He would make amends…lighten the atmosphere.

She was just finishing off her own meal, and as she pushed her empty plate aside, dabbing her mouth with her paper serviette, he reached for an uneaten hunk of bread.

'Watch,' he told her.

Their table was right by the water's edge, and near them there was a strip of water between two fishing boats, bobbing either side. Darting about in the clear water were small silvery fishes. He made sure Alys could see them too, then crumbled the bread into the water.

He heard her give a gasp and laughed. The placid-looking fishes had turned into a seething ball of feeding frenzy, devouring the crumbs.

'I used to do that when I was very young,' he heard himself say. 'It never failed to delight me.'

'Was that with your mother?' Alys asked. There was curiosity in her voice.

'No, a nursemaid.' He kept his voice casual. He frowned. 'I think that particular one was called Maria. Or maybe it was Tonia. They changed pretty often.'

He was aware that Alys was looking at him. Aware that he was cursing himself for having opened such a subject.

'Did your own mother not look after you at all?'

It was an enquiry that was very carefully voiced.

'No,' he said. He didn't want to say any more.

He saw that Alys was frowning, and he wanted to change the subject, but she had started to speak again.

'Did she work?' she asked. 'I mean, not out of financial necessity, but to have a career?'

His mouth twisted. He could not stop it. 'Her "career" was spending money,' he said shortly.

He could feel Alys's gaze on him. Didn't want it to be.

He reached for his beer, drained it. 'Then she took off for California, to continue doing so with her divorce settlement,' he said.

His grip on the empty beer glass tightened. Why the hell was he telling her this? He could see Alys open her mouth, about to say something, but he didn't want to hear it. He turned to summon the waiter imperiously, ignoring the fact that the man was laden down with full plates for other customers and indicating to him that he wanted the bill.

It came promptly, but Nikos could not be bothered to wait either for a credit card swipe or change, and simply put down an excess amount in notes and got to his feet. Alys did likewise.

'What would you like to do now?' Nikos asked as they made their way back onto the street. Alys was pausing, he saw, to nod and say *efharisto* to the harassed waiter, who smiled gratefully in return. Or perhaps he just smiled because what man would *not* smile back at so beautiful a woman?

Instinctively Nikos felt his hand reach for her elbow, guiding her across the roadway to the pavement beyond. A mark of possession, he knew. Primitive, but undeniable.

She carries my child—of course I feel possessive.

He paused when she did, looking about her.

'Could we just explore a little?' she asked. 'Wander around a bit?'

'Of course,' he agreed smoothly. After all, this entire enterprise was about making Alys feel comfortable about being here with him. 'How about up that street?' he suggested, pointing to a narrow cobbled lane lined with souvenir shops. It looked quaint in a touristy sort of way.

They strolled along, threading their way amongst other tourists doing likewise, with Alys pausing frequently to look at the wares set out on displays outside the shops. At one point she examined some ceramic jugs and bowls, glazed in the brilliant blue that was always to be found in such places, with the name of the town and the island on the base. Nikos could see she looked tempted, and was about to offer to buy one of each for her, but she replaced them and moved on.

'Didn't you like them?' he heard himself asking.

'Yes, but they're souvenirs,' she answered.

Nikos frowned faintly. 'So?'

She gave a shrug. 'I'm not exactly on holiday, Nikos,' she said, her voice dry.

Then she pointed across the narrow street towards a shop whose window displayed beachwear. Its doorway was hung with flounced skirts and patterned sundresses, and racks of sandals were set on the pavement.

'Actually, what I do need is some more clothes. Not much—just a couple of things more suitable for here than what I brought with me from England for Athens.'

Nikos glanced dismissively at the shop she was pointing at. 'There are some boutiques in the marina,' he said. 'You'll do much better there.'

She shook her head. 'This place is fine, Nikos.'

She made her way across, and he followed reluctantly. Pausing only to skim the shoes and grab a pair of plastic flip-flops, she disappeared inside, busying herself riffling through the packed racks of clothes, extracting some items swiftly. She looked through a pile of tee shirts, helping herself to a couple, picked up a pair of pale blue cotton shorts, then seized a yellow cotton peasant-style skirt with embroidery around the hem, and a flower-sprigged top in light green.

She took them to the till, but Nikos tried to get there before her, silently extracting his credit card. The cashier was already placing Alys's purchases into a pair of carrier bags, taking the debit card that Alys was holding out to her.

'Allow me,' he said. Though his voice was smooth, he could hear an underlying edge in it. Knew why it was there.

Alys ignored him, keying in her pin, then removing her card, tucking it back into her handbag, thanking the cashier and taking the carrier bags.

Slowly, Nikos put his credit card away. Followed her out of the shop.

On the pavement, Alys turned. Chin lifted. 'Keep your money for yourself, Nikos. I don't want it. You bought me lunch, and I'm having your free hospitality at the villa—but I won't let you pay for my clothes.'

She walked off.

He strode after her, taking her arm. 'I did not mean—' he began.

'Yes, you did.'

Her contradiction was flat. Spots of colour were in her cheeks, anger in her voice. For a moment they simply eyeballed each other, then Nikos lifted his hand away.

Was this more virtue signalling on her part, like insisting on having lunch at that cheap tourist place? Well, it was his turn to insist on something now—and he would tell her so.

'OK, so I did,' he conceded. 'But even if you won't let me buy your clothes, there is one thing I insist you let me do...' Calmly he helped himself to her carrier bags. 'I'll carry these for you,' he told her.

For a moment—just a moment—those angry spots of colour stayed in Alys's cheeks. Then they vanished. She gave a reluctant half-laugh.

It was all Nikos needed.

It was the first laugh, however reluctant, he'd got out of her yet. That had to be worth something.

He felt his mood improve. The moment of conflict had passed.

'Let's get a drink,' he said amiably. 'And, just to show my respect for you, I'll let you buy.'

Carrier bags swinging in either hand, he set off up the road, Alys beside him.

Somehow, it felt good.

CHAPTER TEN

ALYS GAZED ABOUT HER. The top of the narrow street had opened out into the town's central square—'The *agora*... the old marketplace,' Nikos had informed her—which was dominated by a handsome church with the characteristic Orthodox dome.

There were several cafés at the edge of the square and Alys let Nikos choose one, grateful to sit down under a shady awning in the afternoon heat.

Had it made a difference, she wondered, insisting to Nikos that she pay for her own clothes? She hadn't been keen on spending her scarce money, but she really did need to supplement her wardrobe at the villa—and anyway there would be summers in England too, where such light garments would be fine.

Nikos gave their order to the waitress, who glided off. Alys was not unaware of her lingering glance at Nikos as he pushed his sunglasses up on his head and stretched out his long legs. Other female eyes belonging to the café's customers were coming his way. She was well aware of that too.

For a second so brief she hardly noticed it she felt a pang of possessiveness go through her. Then, dismayed, she caught herself. She had no claim on Nikos—none whatsoever. Carrying his baby conferred upon her nothing of the sort.

One day he'll marry some posh female from his own

world—someone as rich as he is, so he won't have to fret that she's only interested in his money.

She tried to conjure up a feeling of caustic cynicism at the thought, but instead only that illogical out-of-place pang came again. She looked away out over the *agora*, blinking at the sun, dazzling on the white walls of the church…

Their drinks arrived—orange juice for herself, and a very Greek dark, thick black coffee for Nikos, together with iced water. They drank companionably enough, with Alys mostly people-watching, taking in the scene. She asked Nikos a few questions about the church and he answered what he knew, looking up more information on his phone for her, telling her which saint it was dedicated to and when it had been built.

'I know almost nothing about the Greek Orthodox Church,' Alys heard herself musing. 'The priests have long beards and there are icons… And Easter is a different time to ours, mostly. I've never understood why.'

Nikos explained it to her, how the Orthodox church used the the older Julian calendar and the Latin churches the newer Gregorian calendar. Alys still wasn't sure she understood fully, but as they finished their drinks Nikos said, 'Would you like to see inside the church?'

Alys nodded and they got up, with Alys digging in her purse for the euros she needed to cover the drinks and a tip. Nikos, true to his earlier promise to let her pay, made no attempt to override her, and she felt she had won a small victory.

But did it amount to anything at all? Preferring a cheap tourist restaurant to a flash marina one, paying for her own clothes and buying Nikos a coffee might not be enough to convince him she was not after the Drakis money…

But I've made it clear I don't want child maintenance, that I can cope now he's paid my debts.

He hadn't contested her, she realised. Did that mean he'd accepted that she had no intention of leeching off him?

She didn't know. All she knew was that being with him

was getting easier, less constrained, and she was less endlessly wary. Her guard was lowering, her reserve dissipating. She could hold a normal conversation with him now—talk about innocuous things, as they were doing now.

Nikos was holding open the heavy church door for her and she stepped inside. It was cool and dimly lit, rich with the scent of incense. Candles were set before gilded icons, and rich Byzantine murals glowed like jewels.

In a low voice, Nikos explained what she was seeing as she gazed about her.

This will be as much my baby's heritage as the parish churches of England.

Her eyes went to the baptismal font. Would Nikos want their baby christened? Well, if he did, there were Greek Orthodox churches in the UK, she thought defiantly. Yet for all her defiance, she felt, in this centuries-old church, the weight of tradition to which her baby would be heir.

Do I have a right to keep him or her from that?

Her chin lifted. All she'd said to Nikos was that she didn't want his money—not that she didn't want him to have anything to do with their son or daughter... But if he did want to play a part, have some kind of access to their child, what form would that take?

Her eyes went to him. It was he who'd insisted they stop being strangers, accept they were going to be parents together. Yes, he'd treated her like dirt to start with, insulted her unforgivably in his initial assumptions about her, but if he was setting them aside now—as he did seem to be doing—then wasn't he right to have brought her here? So that they could slowly, carefully accustom themselves not just to each other, but to shared parenthood?

But how shared?

The memory of what he'd said to her at that nightmare dinner in Athens sounded in her head.

'No child of mine will be born a bastard.'

He had told her, dictated to her as if she were the lowest of the low, that he would marry her to legitimise their baby—however much he clearly loathed the idea. Loathed the fact that she was pregnant, landing him with an unwanted child by an unwanted woman.

But he doesn't look at me with loathing any longer...

She felt her emotions well and shift within her, disturbing her certainties, her own assumptions that Nikos would far rather she had *not* got pregnant from their brief single night together.

'Seen enough?' Nikos was asking her now, and she nodded again, letting him show her out of the church.

The heat of the afternoon hit her as they stepped back into the *agora.*

'What would you like to do now?' he asked solicitously.

A wave of tiredness swept over her, and a longing for air conditioning. 'Would you think me very feeble if I said I'd like to go back to the villa now?' she asked.

He slid his dark glasses over his eyes now they were in the bright sunshine again. 'Alys, believe me, you are the very last woman on earth I would describe as feeble,' he said.

His voice was dry, but there was a wry humour in it that made her glance at him uncertainly. She wished she could still see his eyes—then was glad she could not.

Without her realising what he was about to do, he slid her hand into his. 'Come on, let's get you back to the car,' he said, and the humour was still in his voice. 'And if you come over feeble let me know—I'll carry you there!' he finished lightly.

Her carrier bags swung from his other hand as he started to walk forward, taking a quieter street than the one they'd come up, leading her back down to the seafront.

She went with him meekly, letting him keep her hand, because it was quite nice to be able to lean some of her weight on him as they headed down the paved road, uneven in places, with cars parked on either side. Alys realised it was the street he'd parked the SUV in and saw it, still huge and gleaming and expensive-looking beside the other vehicles, but right now a welcome sight.

'In you go,' Nikos said, opening the passenger door for her, and hefting her inside, placing her carrier bags in the footwell, then closing the door and moving around to his side, swinging himself into his seat.

He gunned the engine, carefully extricating the vehicle from the tight space, and Alys sat back in relief as the air con got going.

Nikos glanced at her as they gained the road out of town. 'Time for home,' he said. 'And maybe a cooling dip in the pool before drinks. Sound good?'

He cocked an enquiring eyebrow at her, a smile playing around his mouth.

Alys nodded. 'Yes,' she said. Because it did sound good.

Nikos was accelerating, his eyes on the road, and Alys let her own eyes linger on his profile. She was feeling things she should not feel.

But did, all the same.

Nikos relaxed back in his chair at the dinner table, idly twirling his wine glass in his hand, letting his eyes rest on the woman sitting opposite. Alys, her hair freshly washed after their dip in the pool, waving in delicate tendrils over her shoulders, was wearing one of her newly purchased outfits: the yellow gypsy-style skirt and the pretty flower-sprigged green top.

And with all the judgementalism in the world he could not condemn it. Cheap it might be, but her natural beauty was such that she could make any outfit look as if it had cost a million…

He took another leisurely mouthful of his wine, savouring the bouquet. 'This really is very good,' he observed, setting down the glass and resuming eating. The rich lamb was tender and succulent, and he ate with a will. The island air seemed to give him an extra appetite. Or something did…

His eyes went back to Alys, lingering on her. He felt desire rise within him and let it do so. Soon, maybe, he would be able to indulge it. But not quite yet. She was much less guarded with him now, and their outing today had moved them forward significantly, but she was not ready for him yet. He had made one heavy miscalculation with her already—he could not risk another. Not when she was still so determined to return to England…

Her words over lunch, telling him she would be a single mother, rang in his head, unwelcome, showing him just how far he still had to go.

He took another mouthful of the wine to distract him. It was, as Spiros had promised him, standing up well to the rich lamb.

'I'm only sorry you can't share it with me,' he said to Alys now, watching her sip at her iced pomegranate juice. 'Spiros persuaded me to try it. It's local, and I suspect the grower is one of his relatives.' There was a wry glint in his eye. 'Spiros is probably hoping I might like it and decide to invest in the winery.'

'Will you?' Alys asked.

He shook his head. 'Probably not.'

She looked at him. 'Why not? You were saying on our drive this morning that the island could do with more inward investment, reducing reliance on tourism. So why not from you?'

'Something like an individual winery is too small-scale for Drakis,' he replied. 'And wine itself is a risky business. Too many uncertainties—the weather, the harvest, changing consumer tastes…'

As he spoke, he knew he was echoing his father's views. He went on echoing them.

'Drakis investments are all very carefully planned, Alys, and on a scale you are probably incapable of comprehending. Risk has to be extremely carefully managed and minimised. Contained. By whatever means necessary.'

His eyes rested on her. *By whatever means necessary indeed...* And not just with financial risk. With risk that was far more important to contain. He felt himself tense, shuttered his eyes. So much depended on what he was doing now, here at the villa…

And if I get it wrong...

No, he would not be getting it wrong! He would be getting it right—totally right. And every day she spent here with him was proving that.

But Alys was talking to him, replying to him, and he made himself pay attention.

'Well, you could risk a bit on a vineyard, couldn't you?' she was saying. 'Wouldn't it be peanuts for you? So why not?' There was an encouraging note in her voice. 'After all, Spiros does a superb job of running this place for you, and however well paid he is, why not do something for him in return? At the very least,' she finished, 'if you like the wine so much you could buy a shedload of it off his relative!'

Nikos gave a laugh. 'OK!' he said, and held up his hand in a yielding gesture. 'I'll buy a good few cases and then maybe I'll think about investing in his expansion plans.'

Alys smiled at him warmly. It was a warmth that made him glad he'd made the reply he had.

'You see,' she said, 'you can be something more than a ruthless rainmaker—or whatever it is people like you are called—pulling money-spinning deals out of thin air!'

He gave another laugh, but he knew it was edged this time.

'It's not quite thin air, Alys,' he said. 'There's a hell of a lot of work involved in every one of them. I don't get much time off.'

She frowned. 'That's so stupid,' she said. 'What's the point of all your money if you don't get time to enjoy it?'

'It doesn't make itself,' he answered. Again, he heard his father's voice in his head as he spoke. Always another deal to set up, to see through to completion, to collect the profits on. And then another…

The way to be a true Drakis…

'Making money is what I do,' he spelt out.

Proving myself a worthy son, despite the disaster of my birth in the first place.

'Haven't you got enough by now? How much more do you want?' he heard her persist.

He wished she wouldn't.

He reached for his wine, took a hefty mouthful. She was speaking again, and there was something different in her voice now.

'You're so incredibly privileged, Nikos,' she was saying. He saw her gesture with her hand, indicating their surroundings. 'This fabulous villa, your lavish lifestyle, never having to worry about mundane things like paying bills… So why not enjoy it?' She was looking at him now. 'You said that you couldn't remember when you were last here. That's so sad! Such a waste!'

She looked away, and in the soft light from the candles and the table lamp her expression seemed to change.

'None of us know how long we've got on this earth, Nikos. We have to make the most of what we have while we have it. Life can change in an instant…devastatingly—'

She broke off. Nikos looked at her. 'That sounds personal,' he said slowly.

She swallowed. He saw her hand go in that increasingly familiar gesture to just below her midriff. He thought she might be about to say something, but she only blinked, looking away, out over the night-dark vista. The chorus of cicadas sounded louder in his ears, the heady scent of jasmine catching his senses.

'Look, there's a crescent moon!' he heard Alys exclaim, pointing behind him. 'Just visible.'

He craned his neck. 'New tonight,' he observed. 'You should make a wish,' he added, looking back at her with a half-smile.

His gaze clashed with hers and for a moment, an instant, they held.

Then she dropped her eyes, shaking her head. 'Wishes are dangerous things, Nikos,' she said.

Her voice was low, and he could hear, once more, a note of constraint in it. She moved to pick up her knife and fork again, to resume eating, but he reached out his hand, touched her wrist. The briefest touch.

'Not always, Alys,' he said.

Her eyes flew to his, and for an instant that was not so brief, they held his.

He gave a slow, intimate smile. 'Sometimes,' he said, and his eyes never let hers go for a moment, 'we do get what we wish for. And everything comes right.' His smile deepened, his eyes still holding hers. 'Everything…'

Alys stared at her reflection in the mirror behind the vanity unit in her en suite bathroom. She should get undressed, brush her teeth, go to bed, get a good night's sleep. But she could not. Her eyes were wide, and huge, gazing at herself. In her head, those words of Nikos's at dinner played like a refrain she could not unhear. Did not want to unhear.

'Sometimes we do get what we wish for. And everything comes right. Everything...'

She felt her breath catch in her throat.

What's happening to me?

Her reflected gaze stared back at her, giving her no answer. But she did not need one. She knew what was happening to her.

But I can't let it. We had one night together, that's all—one single night, nothing more.

Her expression changed.

But he came back to find you—he did want more!

She pressed her hands down on the surface of the vanity unit, whitening the tips of her fingers with the pressure of it.

OK, so we might have had an affair—but that would have been all! Nothing to keep us together.

Yet again her expression changed.

But now there is something to keep us together. A baby that links us for ever...

She gave a low cry in her throat and turned away, hearing her own voice again now in her head.

'Wishes are dangerous things, Nikos.'

She went back into her bedroom. The luxury of it was familiar to her now. So was being waited on hand and foot by Spiros and his staff, not having to lift a finger for herself. Nikos all solicitude towards her…

Nikos was familiar to her…

They'd been here only a handful of days, and yet she knew that all the wariness she'd arrived with was all but gone already. He was so unutterably different now from the way he had been in Athens it was almost impossible to think he had ever spoken to her so hideously, treated her so contemptuously, made such ugly, harsh assumptions about her, such accusations…

It's like it never was. Like the way it was when we met the way we did. Drawn together...unable to resist each other.

With another cry stifled in her throat, she paced restlessly around the room. Then she halted, remembering more of what Nikos had said that evening. Talking of risk. For him, it was business risk. But for her—

Her expression grew troubled.

He talked about minimising risk, containing it. And isn't that what I have to do too? Isn't that why I don't want him looking at me the way he does sometimes? Why I don't want him taking my hand, or lifting me out of a boat or—?

She resumed her pacing, as if it could bring release from her tormenting thoughts. But that, she found, was not possible.

Nor was it possible the following day.

Seeing Nikos at breakfast seemed harder than before, yet

for a completely different reason. Did a slight colour run up her cheeks as she took her place, wearing one of her new tee shirts and the new blue shorts, knowing that the expression in his eyes was telling her he was liking what he was seeing.

'So, what kind of day would you like today?' Nikos was asking, his tone genial. 'Another outing, or something more lazy?'

Alys poured herself some orange juice—freshly squeezed, she knew, not from a carton. It tasted delicious, and she also knew, with an inner sigh, that she was getting used to all this luxury. Dangerously used to it...

'Could we do lazy?' she asked.

'Of course we could,' Nikos said. 'Breakfast, pool, lunch, beach, drinks, dinner. Sound OK?'

She made a wry face. 'How could it not?' she answered. She looked about her and gave a sigh.

'Why the sigh?'

Was there concern in his voice? She looked back at him. 'Because this is all just so beautiful,' she said, putting her thoughts into words. She looked at him across the table. 'I meant what I said last night, you know. You should make the very most of having a place like this.' She gave him a humorous smile. 'Promise me you'll come here every summer from now on. For at least a fortnight! Take time off from work—force yourself to have a holiday!'

He gave a laugh, and it tugged at a memory of how his laugh had been so ready that first dinner they'd shared together in London.

Are we getting like that again, little by little?

She pulled back mentally. She must not wish for what it was dangerous to wish for...

But it was hard not to. Increasingly hard.

The lazy day passed just as she had asked—with extreme leisure. Down at the poolside she opened one of the English language books she'd found, as Nikos had said, on the bookshelf in the beautifully appointed lounge, with its picture windows opening to the terrace. It was, of all things, Jane Austen's *Emma*, and she found herself happily absorbed in the familiar tale.

Nikos seemed to have finished his original action adventure paperback, and was now on to a legal drama, full of corrupt politicians and twists and turns of plot. He had no idea yet how they would turn out, he informed her as they compared reading matter.

'I can't remember how many times I've read *Emma*,' she mused. 'That's the joy of Austen—something new every time, and what's familiar so delightful anyway. And every time I read a new lit crit of any of her novels there's something fresh to discover.'

He looked across at her from his lounger. '"Lit crit"? That sounds quite heavy duty.'

'I did English Literature at university,' she answered. She swallowed. 'I never finished, though.'

'You dropped out?' Was there disapproval in his voice.

'Ycs,' shc said. 'Just bcforc Finals. Maybc onc day... Well, perhaps I can repeat my third year, claw back a degree. It would help, I know, when it comes to getting a better paid job.'

He was still looking at her, a frown on his face. 'Why did you drop out?'

She didn't want to talk about it. Wished she'd never mentioned it. 'Life changed,' she said shortly.

She turned a page, making it obvious she was reading. She was conscious of his head still turned towards her, but she would say no more. It was too raw. Too painful.

But Nikos was speaking again. 'Is that when you ran up those debts?' he asked, and there was an edge in his voice now.

She did not look at him. 'Yes,' she said. 'Things got... difficult.'

'Were you living it up in London? Spending more than

you could afford? It's easy to do if you hang out with the wrong people in the wrong places…places they can afford, but you can't…'

He paused, and she knew he was still looking at her.

'Like the party I met you at.'

She set down *Emma* and looked across at him, stung by the implicit accusation he was making. Her voice was flat as she riposted, 'I was only at that party because I was spending the weekend with an old uni friend who lives in London and whose flatmate works in the fashion industry. She wangled us all an invite to that flash bash that night. My friend lent me a dress—a size too small for me, as I'm sure you could tell pretty instantly. I didn't like the party the minute I got there, and I was about to cut and run when—' She broke off. 'You know the rest. You were there.'

'Yes,' he acknowledged, and now that edge was no longer in his voice. 'And I was about to "cut and run" as well—I only turned up because I knew the guy hosting it through a business contact and I wanted to catch him about something. He proved elusive, so I was about to leave myself. Until…' He gave a half-laugh. 'Well, you know the rest too.' He paused. 'And now here we are…' he said slowly.

'Yes,' she said, and swallowed.

She picked up *Emma* again, immersing herself so she didn't have to think about all the complications in her life. Only one thing in it was simple. Her free hand went to her abdomen, curving around it. Whatever happened—whatever it turned out to be, this messy, difficult, complicated situation with Nikos—her baby, she vowed, would be safe.

Whatever I have to do.

Nikos lay back in the warm pool water, floating buoyantly in the ultimate form of relaxation. Alys was still reading *Emma*, lying back on her lounger.

His thoughts played through his head. There were contradictions in what she'd just told him. She'd been to university, yet dropped out. Run up debts, yet not from a hard-partying lifestyle, so she claimed. Yesterday she'd said she didn't want any maintenance from him for the baby, talked about being a working mother, refused to let him pay for those cheap clothes she'd bought. So…virtue signalling to impress him, or genuinely meant?

He gave a mental shrug. Did it matter? It wasn't going to alter what was going to happen. His plans for her were not derailable.

And yet…

I don't want her to be what I don't want her to be.

It was a convoluted thought, but it made sense to him.

I'm glad that when I took her to bed she was the way she was. Glad that I couldn't get that night out of my head—glad that I wanted to go back to find her...claim her again.

His thoughts flickered in his head like that faulty electrical circuit again, trying to make the connections that would let the current flow smoothly, powerfully.

And when she went into that meltdown at the airport... maybe I was glad of that too.

He frowned. Glad that she had wanted to bolt back to England?

Glad of why she wanted to—because she felt I'd accused her unfairly, made assumptions about why she'd got in touch with me, about what she wanted from me.

And he was going on being glad. For many, many reasons.

Glad that she's now warming to me, that I'm winning her round. Glad, too, even if it was just virtue signalling, that she didn't want me to buy her clothes or take her shopping at the marina.

He opened his eyes, turning his head in the water towards where she was lying, one hand still curved protectively where her baby lay beneath.

Glad, above all, for that…

His eyes lingered on her, moved up to her face. Her eyes were moving as she read, tender lips slightly parted, the warm flush of heat on her cheeks, the honeying tan of the sun on her skin.

Despite the cool water he felt arousal stir.

With a contraction of his abs he flipped over, diving down to the bottom of the pool. Cooling his ardour.

At least for now.

CHAPTER ELEVEN

'WE'VE HAD TWO lazy days in a row,' Nikos announced, glancing across the breakfast table at Alys, 'so today it's out and about. Tell me—how's your head for heights?'

She looked at him cautiously. 'No abseiling down from the radio tower on the top of that mountain,' she adjured him.

He gave a laugh. 'Nothing like that,' he promised.

She was intrigued, but he would not be drawn.

She found out soon enough—after breakfast. Nikos led her up the staircase to the villa's front door, stepped out. Alys looked around. No car had been parked up for them, and the area was deserted.

'What—?' she began, but Nikos put a finger against her lips.

'Listen,' he said.

And then she heard it. The staccato stutter of a helicopter approaching.

A moment later it was soaring over the cypress trees encircling the wide gravelled area, sending the branches into a frenzy of whipping as it hovered a moment and then swooped down to land. The noise was deafening, even when the pilot cut the engine to idle.

Nikos took her hand. 'Come on!' he shouted. 'And duck when I do!'

She did, and he ran forward with her, lifting her inside as the pilot opened the passenger door for them. She took her seat, Nikos beside her, but still couldn't hear a thing until he handed her a pair of headphones, donning another pair himself.

Instantly he was audible and the noisy engine was not. 'Fancy a bird's-eye view of the island?' he asked, and grinned.

The pilot lifted off, and Alys gave a gasp as they crowned the trees, seeing the villa drop away below as the helicopter gyred around, heading out to sea.

It was incredible, it was amazing, and Alys loved every single moment of it. They circled the island, dipping sometimes almost to wave level, churning up the surface of the sea, then soared upwards again, heading inland to skim the peaks of the rocky interior before speeding out to sea again. Alys stared, enchanted, as far below sailing craft and motorboats and the ferry to the neighbouring islands were turned to miniature toys.

Eventually they had seen everything, and Nikos instructed the pilot to take them down. But they did not land at the villa. They were lowered down onto a helipad by the marina, a massive 'H' denoting just where the chopper should deposit them.

As he helped her out, guiding her to the edge of the helipad as the pilot took off again, Alys turned to him. Her eyes were shining.

'That was *fabulous*, Nikos! Thank you!'

He gave a laugh, clearly pleased with her open delight. 'We'll go back home the same way,' he promised her. 'But first…'

He was looking at her with a glint in his eye. Was it a challenge? She wasn't quite sure. But when he spoke she became sure.

'Now it's time for part two of today's mystery treat,' he announced. 'And, Alys, please…' the glint wasn't in his eye now, he wore a different expression, more serious '…accept this from me.'

She looked at him uncertainly. 'Accept what?' she asked.

He didn't answer immediately, but walked her away from the helipad, down to where the marina proper opened up. An array of sleek, expensive-looking boats were moored in a neat line on one side of the wide concourse, and on the other side an array of equally sleek, expensive-looking restaurants and shops. He headed for one of them, and Alys realised it was a beauty salon.

'A pampering session,' he told her. 'To counter some of the sun and sea's wear and tear on you. It's very popular, so I'm told, for yachties when they dock.'

Mixed feelings filled Alys. She wanted to refuse to let Nikos spend what she knew perfectly well would be a hefty sum of money on her, for whatever treatments an obviously upmarket place like this offered its wealthy clients. But there was something in his expression that stayed her.

'Please,' he said. 'It's for you.'

Her expression flickered. Then, 'Thank you,' she said.

She didn't say more than that. There seemed to be a bit of a lump in her throat, and she blinked.

Then Nikos was taking her elbow, guiding her into the salon before she had a chance to change her mind and object.

Inside, the receptionist greeted them fulsomely, her smile encompassing them both. But Alys did not fail to recognise that she was being especially fulsome towards Nikos.

Because he's clearly Mr Rich? Or because he's making her knees turn to jelly by being probably the most fantastic-looking bloke she's set eyes on in her life?

She didn't have time to come up with an answer—it was probably both anyway—before two members of staff appeared from the back of the reception area and whisked her away.

There then followed nearly two hours of what most definitely deserved the description 'pampering'. She was given a body wrap, a face peel, a pedicure and a massage. And then, having showered and had a gown swathed about her, she was ushered into the hair salon section, where she had her hair done while her nails were manicured and lightly lacquered in clear varnish.

Finally she was shown back to the changing room, where the final touch of Nikos's lavish treat was waiting for her.

'Mr Drakis has had these delivered from the boutique next door,' she was informed brightly.

Alys stared at the dresses hanging from the rail. All three were beautiful. Floaty-looking sundresses in floral patterns in different hues. For a moment she stilled, her memory going back to how Nikos had had that beautiful designer cocktail dress delivered to her hotel room the night of that nightmare dinner in Athens.

Emotion knifed in her and she almost turned to the assistant to demand her own clothes back—the cheap shorts and tee shirt she'd bought herself. Then she took a breath. This wasn't a repeat of that dress in Athens.

We've moved on since then—things are better between us now.

That was what she had to believe—because it was true.

Slowly, she breathed out, turned to the assistant. 'Thank you,' she said.

The young woman smiled brightly. 'There is lingerie to go with them, and a choice of shoes. When you are ready, we will do your make-up.'

She smiled again, and whisked out of the room.

Nikos sat in the reception area, long legs stretched out as he leafed through a motoring magazine he'd brought with him from the premises next door. There was a sound from the rear of the area and he looked up. Alys was emerging.

Every muscle in his body clenched—and then slowly… infinitely slowly…relaxed.

Thee mou, she looked…

Breathtaking, enchanting, gorgeous, fabulous, fantastic... and just enchantingly beautiful!

All the dresses he'd chosen after she'd disappeared into the salon were exactly right. The sales assistant had helped him. But of the three he'd selected, the one she was wearing was his favourite. It was white, in ultra-fine cotton, with a print of delicate pale blue flowers across the bodice, deepening to a richer blue on the softly gathered calf-length skirt that showed off to perfection the turn of her slender ankles, themselves enhanced by the low-heeled, strappy sandals that exposed the elegant arch of her foot.

As for the rest of her…

Her hair had been washed and styled, trimmed a little, then blow-dried into a sleek, smooth fall over her shoulders, waving back from her face. Another wash of appreciation went through him. A face that had been subtly made up to give her already lightly tanned skin a peachy glow, with a little shadow to deepen her eyes, a touch of mascara to darken her lashes, a light lipstick to give her lips a sheen.

He got to his feet, his magazine tossed aside, and moved towards her, hands outstretched. 'You look…' he breathed '…absolutely wonderful!'

His eyes worked over her again, showing in their open gaze all his appreciation of what he was seeing.

A slight colour washed up her cheeks. 'Yes,' she said dryly, 'it's amazing what a very expensive round of pampering can do. And a very expensive frock.'

He shook his head. 'They need the base material to work on,' he told her. 'And you…' He took a breath. 'You have it in abundance.'

He lifted his hand to encompass the staff present.

'Ladies, thank you! You've made me a happy, happy man!' His smile was broad, his thanks to them well deserved. Then he turned back to Alys. 'Time for lunch,' he said.

He led the way out—he'd settled the bill already, not even glancing at it—and they emerged into the hot sun. He could feel his stomach growl, and hunger bite.

And not just for food.

But he set that other hunger aside. Time for that later…

For now… 'It's just along here,' he told Alys.

There were several restaurants to choose from, but he'd chosen the one with the best view of the marina. He wondered whether Alys was going to demur, or say she'd rather eat at one of the harbourside tavernas. But it seemed, since she had acquiesced gracefully to the pampering session, and the outfits he'd bought her, that she was going to do likewise now about lunching here at the marina.

He was appreciative of all the concessions on her part. His eyes went to her again as they took their seats. He was appreciative of so, so much…

She was studying her menu. 'Definitely *not* tourist fare,' she remarked dryly, but with a touch of humour.

Food orders taken—calamari for him, grilled fish for Alys, with a light starter of a courgette terrine for both of them—he sat back to taste his chilled Chablis as Alys sipped from her gently fizzing elderflower spritzer.

'So what did you do, Nikos, while I was being pampered to within an inch of my life?' Alys asked. 'Besides going shopping for expensive frocks for me?'

'Next door to the salon is a gym and a barber shop. I indulged in both. Cycled ten kilometres…did some weights—then got a massage and,' he added, smoothing an appreciative hand over his ultra-smooth jaw, 'the ultimate male indulgence: a professional cut-throat wet shave! Nothing to beat it. Oh, and the barber trimmed my hair as well—haven't you noticed?'

He cast a smiling challenging look at Alys, and saw colour run up her cheeks again.

'Yes, I did, actually,' she answered. 'You look very smart, Nikos,' she said, with deliberate approval.

Her eyes met his, and for all the note of humour in her voice she dropped her gaze again, colour still in her cheeks.

Satisfaction flowed through Nikos and his state of relaxation increased. This was good…this was *all* good.

And it went on being good.

The food was excellent—even if it was not, he mused with good-humoured irony, as hearty as the tourist fare at the taverna—his wine was excellent and his company for lunch was excellent. Not just to look at, breathtaking though it was every time his eyes went to Alys, but to enjoy in conversation. Conversation that was, as he was not slow to appreciate, as easy now as it had been in London, over dinner together that first night.

That only night.

And now it's back. Back for good.

He would permit no other possibility.

As they finally left the restaurant, strolling out onto the marina concourse, Nikos's eyes went to her figure. The breeze moulded the soft fabric of her frock to her body, and the contours of her full figure were clearly noticeable to him.

For a moment, while his eyes rested on the gentle swell exposed by the tautened fabric, his expression shadowed. Whatever Alys might proclaim or prefer, there was going to be only one outcome he would permit. And he would make very, very sure she wanted it too…

Alys stood half leaning on the balustrade edging the terrace beyond the dining table, where there was less light to occlude the stars and the newly risen moon, its crescent thicker now.

Her mood was strange. She was exquisitely conscious of Nikos standing next to her, though scrupulously not too close. For all that, she could still feel him close to her, and was aware of how she looked to him.

She was still wearing the dress he'd bought for her, now with the little lacy bolero—cashmere, she fancied wryly—that had been lying wrapped in tissue paper on the seat of the helicopter, along with her own clothes, when they'd finally emerged from the long and leisurely lunch that had gone on into mid-afternoon.

The flight back to the villa had been less swooping than

the one in the morning, instead taking them along a valley leading into the interior, where they had hovered over a Mycenaean-era archaeological site that was yet to be fully excavated, and so was best seen from the air.

Alys had been fascinated, listening to Nikos telling her what he had read up on it. Then they had headed back to the villa in time for Alys to freshen up before emerging onto the terrace for drinks and then dinner. She'd put her hair up into a loose chignon and touched up her make-up, knowing, with a tiny tremor of her hand as she carefully reapplied her mascara, just why she was doing so.

She had known it again as, seated opposite him across the dining table on the terrace, he'd raised his glass to her, the ruby wine winking in the candlelight as he'd murmured his tribute.

'To a perfect day,' he'd said. And then something in his voice had changed, deepened. 'And to your perfect beauty.'

She had accepted the tribute, no longer rejecting it. Something had run between them…something that she had necessarily held at bay, scarred as she was by his harsh, contemptuous condemnation of her.

But that was all gone now—as if it had never been. And if it was no longer there, then…

Then I do not have to hold him at bay, do not have to hold myself at bay, nor tell myself that I must not, should not...

Instead…

Instead she had done as she had been doing all day, and over dinner she had let her gaze mingle with his, let his gaze wash over her, telling her just what he had told her that very first night together…how much he desired her…

Like it was that very first evening.

Back then, she had given herself up with wonder and delight to what had happened between them.

But it was simple then. Desire was a flame burning between us, unable to be quenched, unwilling to be extinguished, for there was no reason to do so.

But now? Now it was not simple at all…

As she leant against the still-warm balustrade she felt her hand drop to where her tiny baby was growing, day by day. Complicating everything. Demanding, requiring, deserving only the best, the *very* best, for its little life…

Had Nikos seen her gesture? She did not know.

But a finger lifted to her cheek, drawing slowly down it. Eyes dipping to hers. 'Beautiful Alys…' he murmured.

That huskiness was in his voice, as it had been when he had toasted her beauty. His eyes held hers, and she was helpless to free herself.

'You do know…' he spoke again, his voice still husky '…that this has been waiting for us. This moment now. Nothing has changed that. Nothing can ever change it. From the first I have desired you…and I desire you still.' He took a slow breath, his eyes drowning hers. 'I always shall.' Something changed in his eyes—something infinitesimal. 'And now that you carry my child…'

She gazed up at him, feeling the line where his touch had been. She could feel her pulse start to beat faster, feel the breathlessness inside her.

'Nikos, I…'

There was a question in her voice, her eyes. She stepped away. The sliding doors into her bedroom were behind her, and she moved to slip them open. But her hand was caught by his, staying her.

'Alys…'

He said her name again—softly, sensually—and the huskiness accentuated his accent, sending weakness through her. She turned back, and he was dark against the night sky.

'Don't hold me away,' he said, his voice low. 'Not any longer. Not tonight…'

And then he was stepping towards her, past her, sliding open the glass door, drawing her within. Drawing her to him. Into his arms.

And now she could question no longer—could only know

what had always been between them, only do what she had day by day been yielding to, deny it all she could, resist it all she would…

She could do so no longer. And as his mouth lowered to hers, easing her lips open to his, his hands at her spine, making her pliant towards him, she gave a little sigh, her body folding to his, yielding to his…

It was bliss, it was wonder, and it was all the sweet, sensual pleasure that had ever been between them. He was teasing and tasting the honey of her mouth, opening it to his. Her hand was stealing to the strong column of his neck, moving around his muscled waist, and she was feeling, with a little shock as her hips pressed to his, just how powerfully his body was reacting to hers…

A moan broke from her and he drew back, holding her in the circle of his arms, gazing down at her. In his eyes desire blazed and burned.

'You do not know,' he said, 'how I have craved this moment.'

His eyes held hers and she could feel hers distending, feel the brand of his hands on her spine, holding her body to him, feel his desire for her. She could feel the blood surging in her veins, heat filling her as, his eyes never relinquishing their hold on hers, one of his hands dropped from her spine, came around her body and closed, slowly and possessively, over her breast.

It flowered beneath his touch, cresting and filling, and she gave another low, helpless moan as pleasure—oh, such sweet, honeyed pleasure—swirled within her. Her legs seemed to weaken, and she could feel his body harden against hers more powerfully yet.

Then he was kissing her again, his hand still cupping her breast, palming its crested peak. His other hand was moving up her spine—gliding, she realised dimly, inchoately, with one smooth movement the zip to her dress down. He eased it from her shoulders, never letting go her mouth, until the soft fabric fell to the ground, pooling at her feet.

For a moment he stood away from her, and she could only stand there with the lacy bra, the wisp of her panties all that shielded her nakedness from him. She felt her heart thudding in her chest, drumming in her ears.

His eyelids swept down. He was fastening his gaze on the swell of her abdomen. 'Like a sweetly ripening peach…'

His voice was low and he stepped towards her, one hand reaching to splay across her softly rounded body. Something moved in his eyes, and then he was sweeping her up into his arms, striding to the waiting bed, laying her down upon it.

To make her his again.

Completely his.

Only in the moment before his possession, as her body throbbed with her own desire, did he pause, gaze down at her, his face stark.

'I… I would not hurt you,' he said. 'Or—'

His hand splayed over her abdomen as protectively as the gesturc she made herself. She felt her heart swell.

She lifted her head, raising her mouth to his, brushing it softly. 'You never could, Nikos,' shc told him. 'Not now.'

For a moment their eyes held, and for a second she thought she saw his veil. Then it was gone, as if it were impossible it should ever have been.

Her hands came around his back, lightly resting there. Then slowly, deliberately, never letting go his eyes, she pulled him down to her. Yielding to him completely. And to her own desire.

And to so much more…

CHAPTER TWELVE

DIM LIGHT WAS dissolving the darkness of the night away. Her bedroom drapes undrawn, Alys lay in the circle of Nikos's arms, strong and warm around her. Sleep still meshed her, and her rousing to wakefulness was only temporary…enough only to let emotion fill her. Certainty possess her.

Her arms tightened around Nikos's waist as if she would never let him go.

And I never will. Not now!

The same emotion swept through her again, wondrous in its realisation, bringing a smile to the lips pressed against his chest, secret and blissful. Then drowsiness took her again and she felt the sweet ache of her body, her thighs mingling with his, the soft swell of where, secretly within, their baby nestled safely.

The smile stayed on her lips as she gave herself to sleep once more.

Safe in Nikos's arms...

Safe for ever...

Nikos was making a hearty breakfast. He needed it. He deserved it.

A sense of supreme accomplishment filled him from head to foot. Satisfaction in every cell in his body. Satisfaction on every count.

Mentally, as he reached for another fresh bread roll, generously slathering it with butter and honey, he ran through the reasons for his extraordinarily good mood on this bright, sun-drenched morning, with the Aegean sea girdling his vision, cicadas merrily striating away in the lush vegetation, the bougainvillea, vivid and vibrant, the honeysuckle and jasmine cascading all around, scenting the air with their rich fragrance, mingling with the aroma of freshly brewed coffee.

His reasons were not hard to find. And they all focussed on the woman sitting opposite him, gracefully pouring orange juice.

He felt emotion clench inside him. So much emotion. Relief, pure and unadulterated, that finally he could set aside all that had beset him from the moment his eyes had scanned that letter left for him at the concierge's desk in London, that had plunged him into a darkness he had been fighting to emerge from ever since.

And now he was clear of it! Completely and totally clear! Everything had come right.

His gaze went to her, the woman who would now never again threaten to bolt back to England, who would never hold any kind of malign power over him, would never oppose him again or resist him again…

Because now, finally, she had no more reason to want to do so. No reason at all.

She is mine completely now.

Alys lolled lazily, half in the warm shallow water lapping at her, half on the soft sand, as Nikos, emerging from his vigorous swim, hunkered down beside her to kiss her with a salty mouth.

'You taste of the sea.' She laughed.

'And you taste of honey,' he replied, kissing her again, then rolling back beside her, taking his weight, as she was doing, on his elbows.

'Glad we came back here?' he asked.

'Oh, yes!' she agreed warmly.

They had taken the motorboat out again, to the secret cove at the tip of the promontory. But this time how much more wonderful it was! She felt a glow go through her, emotions turning over and over inside her.

Nikos kissed her again, more lingeringly this time.

'You do realise, don't you, why I've brought you here?' he said, his expression revealing. 'Because there is absolutely no way this place can be overlooked. Which means…' his voice deepened '…that after lunch I intend to make mad, passionate love to you right here on the beach.' A wicked look entered his eyes, making Alys quiver with delight. 'I might even carry you off into the sea and make love to you all over again.'

Her eyes danced. 'Is it possible?' she asked. 'In the sea?'

The wicked look intensified. 'You'll just have to wait and find out,' he said, and kissed her again.

His kiss deepened but Alys drew back, a wicked look in her own eyes now.

'You said *after* lunch, Nikos! And don't you need to ensure you have enough energy for mad, passionate lovemaking?' she teased.

'True,' he allowed, and levered himself to his feet, drawing her up with him.

Her hand held his tightly. Was it really only so short a time ago when she had hesitated to let him do so? Hesitated to let there be any kind of physical contact with him, however mild or brief.

Because it was just too risky...

She felt the same emotion that had filled her when Nikos had kissed her flow through her again. The emotion that was always there now, like the warm, bright glow of the sun.

How unnecessary her fears had been! There had been no risk at all—none! All risk had vanished away, burnt off by the hot passion of Nikos's searing embraces. Making everything all right between them.

Because how could it not be right? Nikos had made it

right! In his arms, safe and cherished, it was all so obvious to her now.

I'm in love with him! Totally, completely in love!

Impossible to fight it, deny it, or fear it…

For there was nothing more to fight, or deny, or fear…

I love him—I carry his child—and we shall make our future together.

How could it be otherwise? Hadn't he declared that evening in Athens, when it had all gone so hideously wrong between them, that they must marry? Then, the way he'd said it, the way he'd thought of her, had only repelled and repulsed her, sending her fleeing. But now everything was different.

Now I want to marry him—can think of nothing that I long for more...loving him as I do...

She felt her heart turn over inside her, swelling and filling her with joy and wonder and delight. She laced her fingers in his, loving the feel of them, loving him beside her as they walked up the beach to where they'd set up camp, just as last time, under the shade of a sheltering rock.

As before, the kitchen at the villa had done them proud, and the wicker hamper was groaning with picnic treats. And after they'd eaten, just as he'd promised her he would, Nikos made love to her slowly, leisurely, taking his time, bringing her to a throbbing climax that made her cry out, unguarded in this remote, deserted spot, as her body convulsed around his, fusing with him in a shared pleasure so intense her hands clenched over his shoulders, her neck arching, as she cried out again when he surged within her.

Then later, strength restored, he made good on his second promise—hefting her gloriously naked, as was he, into his arms, and striding laughingly out into the sea. Where, Alys discovered, to her amazement and delight and intense, thrilling pleasure, that, yes, making love while cradled by the water's buoyant swell was indeed perfectly, blissfully possible.

As was making love in the shower of her en suite bathroom on their return to the villa...and before and after breakfast...and in the pool house...and in Nikos's own bed all night long in the blissful, passionate days that followed.

Day after day after day.

Night after night.

In a happiness so perfect that time stopped completely...

And yet...

She stood beside him now, languorous after dinner, leaning on the balustrade, lazily looking out into the warm night, watching the moon rise in the night sky. It had waxed to full, and waned to dark, and was now once again a new silvered crescent against the stars.

She might not feel the time passing, but it was all the same. Her body was telling her so—not just the cycle of the moon. Her pregnancy was advancing inexorably, her body was filling out, her baby growing within.

How long will we stay here?

Nikos had said nothing about leaving the villa, the island, nothing at all about what would happen when they did, as surely they must at some point? He had said nothing, she realised with a little frown, of their future at all. Like herself, he seemed content only to continue this lotus-eating lifestyle, with day merging into day, night into night, blissfully easy and idle, indulgent and lazy.

She wanted to ask him, yet also did not want to. Wanted to continue as they were, idle and leisured in this peaceful, beautiful place that had brought her her life's happiness.

And his?

She looked at him now, at his so familiar profile, feeling the little rush of love that always overcame her when she gazed at him.

I love him—but does he love me?

It was a question she did not want to ask, and even as she thought it she dismissed it. The way he was with her was enough for her—how could it not be? The Nikos who had been so coldly critical, hostile and contemptuous of her, laying down his diktats and demands, had gone completely. Here, at this beautiful villa, he'd become once more the man who had melted her like honey from the very first, with the heat of desire in his dark eyes… And now he was so much more than that.

A man so very dear to her.

A man I want to live my life with—make a family with.

And surely he must want that too! For why else would he have swept her into his arms, his bed, as he had?

She felt her heart turn over again as she lifted his hand from where it lay on the stone balustrade, pressing it against her mouth and then her cheek.

He turned to smile down at her. Was it the moonlight, the starlight, or the candlelight from the dinner table that made her think she saw something move in his eyes? She could not tell what it was and then it was gone. Replaced by a very, very familiar look.

'Enough moon-gazing,' he told her.

His dark eyes glinted in the way that always—every time—made her weak at the knees.

'Time for bed—'

He lowered his hand, keeping hers within his, to lead her indoors. And willingly…oh, so willingly… Alys went with him.

Nikos opened the door of the office suite that the villa housed and reluctantly stepped inside, conscious that Andreas and the maids would be setting out breakfast and that he'd left Alys getting dressed after their morning lovemaking.

He did not want to do this.

But I can't avoid it any longer.

He could not go on holding the world at bay, however much he longed to.

Steeling himself, he stepped inside, closed the door behind him, and settled himself down at the desk.

He turned on the computer. Sent the message he needed to send, that he could put off no longer…

'I have to go back to Athens.'

The words fell from Nikos as Alys looked at him across the breakfast table. She searched his face, hoping that the dismay his out-of-the-blue words had engendered in her was not showing in her own.

She tried to keep her tone nothing more than enquiring as she replied. 'Do…do I go too?'

'No, you can stay here for now. It won't take long…what I have to do in Athens.'

His words should have been reassuring, yet their effect on her was the opposite. She looked at him, with a troubled, questioning look in her eyes. Yet why should that be? She knew they could not stay here at the villa, cut off from the world in this blissful lotus-eating idyll for ever—that at some point he, at least, a man of business affairs, with all the responsibilities that pressed upon him, responsibilities that he had neglected for her sake, must reclaim them again. And besides, she and Nikos had to make their own plans and preparations for the future.

Plans to marry—for surely that will be what we'll do? Marry and make a family together.

Yet he had never made any mention of such a future for them—not since that nightmare night in Athens.

But everything is completely different now between us! Now, instead of the thought sending me fleeing, marrying him is all that I long for!

Another thought came to her, and she clung to it. Perhaps that was the reason for his sudden announcement that he must go to Athens. Perhaps it was to make the necessary arrangements for their marriage…

But then why not say so?

She felt unease pluck at her again, tried not to let it show in her voice. 'When do you leave?'

'Today. After breakfast. That will give me more time in Athens.' He made no mention of when he would return, only going on to say, 'You'll be fine here. Spiros will look after you, so just take it easy, OK?'

She gave a smile, forcing her voice to sound relaxed. 'It's impossible to do anything else here, Nikos!'

He laughed, and the familiar sound was reassuring, diluting her unease. But when, after they had breakfasted, she went with him to the SUV parked above the villa, her questioning unease returned in strength. Nikos had an air about him that was abstracted, preoccupied. Tense.

When will I see him again?

The question echoed in her head as she accompanied him to the car. Spiros was at the wheel, for he would bring the vehicle back from the airport.

Nikos turned to her, taking her face in his hands, lifting it to his. There was something in his face, his eyes, she had never seen before, and it troubled her. For a moment she thought he was going to speak, but then, with a dipping of his long lashes, he simply dropped a swift, fleeting kiss on her mouth and released her, climbing into the SUV.

Spiros gunned the engine and set off. She raised a hand as the vehicle left the gravelled forecourt.

But whether Nikos returned her salute or not she did not know. Her eyes were tearing up and she could not see.

She turned away, going back indoors. Feeling desolate.

And unaccountably, out of nowhere, fearful.

Athens was hot, crowded, oppressive. Sultry with heat as if a storm must break. Nikos's expression was grim as the airport taxi dropped him off at the opulent Drakis mansion in the exclusive suburb of Kifissia.

I have a storm of my own ready to break over me.

And break it did.

His father's rage was incandescent, as Nikos had known it would be. He let it pour over him as he stood in his father's study like a recalcitrant schoolboy, but he had come to know his father well enough over the years to know that until his temper was spent there would be no rational conversation possible.

So he simply stood there, stonily, while his father raged about his utter irresponsibility in disappearing as he had, abrogating all his duties, endangering half a dozen essential half-completed deals and abandoning delicate negotiations with parties both in Europe and the USA. Costing a fortune in lost business!

'So where the *hell* have you been? You just disappeared without trace—your imbecile of a PA had no idea! Only said you were not answering your phone or replying to messages! Outrageous! Absolutely outrageous!'

'I've been at the villa.' Nikos cut across his father, his voice as tight as a drawn bowstring.

Colour mounted dangerously in his father's face, and he looked ready to explode again, but Nikos leant forward, placing his hands flat on his father's desk.

'I have something to tell you. Something vitally important to me. And...' he took a deep breath '...something to ask of you.'

Alys was lying by the pool, the afternoon sun warm on her bare back, but uneasiness still filled her—as it had since she had bade Nikos farewell that morning. She tried to make herself relax, but it was impossible. Then, above the constant chorus of the cicadas all about in the vegetation around the pool deck, she heard a new noise.

Rhythmic, heavy. Getting closer.

She twisted her head, staring into the cerulean sky. It was a helicopter, approaching over the sea from the west. She levered herself up, watching it grow closer, distinctly heading towards the villa.

She felt her heart leap. Nikos—coming back already!

She pulled her tee shirt and shorts on over her swimsuit,

gathered her things, hurrying as best she could up the steep steps to the top terrace, hearing the helicopter make its descent to the forecourt. She wanted to be there to greet Nikos when he landed.

But as she finally gained the terrace, breathless, Spiros was hurrying forward out of the villa, his manner agitated, his customary cheerfulness quite absent.

Alarm filled her. 'Spiros, what is it? Has something happened?'

He beckoned her indoors. 'You must come,' he told her. 'At once!'

Nikos took his seat in the New York–bound plane, wishing he were doing no such thing. But he'd felt it impossible to refuse his father in this after his father's reaction to what he'd told him. He'd expected another explosion of rage—but it had been just the opposite.

He still could not credit it.

He'd also felt, because of that completely unexpected reaction from his father to what he'd had to tell him, that he was in no position to refuse his request.

'My boy, I understand completely! But, look, now that you have told me—and I am so very glad you have!—will you agree to what I say now? When you disappeared off grid as you did, the New York deal was so very nearly agreed—it is a pity to abandon it after all your preliminary work on it. So will you not go there now, get it over the line, and come back in a couple of days?' He'd clapped him genially on the back. 'What do you say?'

Nikos had said yes, though it was the last thing he'd wanted to do. But, given how supportive and understanding his father was being—not at all what he'd been anticipating—how could he have refused? As his father had said, he'd be back in a couple of days. And then—

But he would not allow himself to run on ahead. He would get this damn New York trip out of the way first.

He sat back, seat belt fastened, willing the plane to take off. The sooner he was in New York, the sooner he'd be back…

Alys followed Spiros across the atrium, flip-flops flapping noisily on the marble floor, her alarm increasing. Spiros had opened the door of a room on the far side that she had never been into.

'Please wait here,' he told her.

It was some kind of office, filled with high-tech kit, its window obscured by Venetian blinds. She heard footsteps sounding in the hall, and a voice—not Nikos's—addressing Spiros in Greek in stentorian tones. Then someone was walking into the office, shutting the door behind him with a snap.

Alys did a double take. The man was a middle-aged version of Nikos—but not quite. He was not as tall, and nowhere near as jaw-droppingly handsome, even allowing for the difference in age, and he was starting to run to fat, with greying hair and an ill-tempered look about him.

His eyes—like gimlets and starting to pouch—went to the visible evidence of her advancing pregnancy. She saw his expression harden. Then his gaze came back to her face, and she saw something twist in it.

'I am Nikos's father,' announced the man who looked so like Nikos—but not in a good way. 'And he has sent me here to sort out this mess once and for all.' He looked at her, and his expression was pitiless. 'It is all arranged. You are to return to Athens now.' Scorn bit in the dark eyes. 'The time has come for proof. No more prevarication! He has told me he needs to know—is the baby you are flaunting his?'

The blood drained from Alys's face, shock jagging through her as if she had just been punched. She heard the words he was barking out at her now.

'There will be a paternity test! Now—before you give birth. This time you will not refuse.'

She felt herself reel, clutch at the corner of the desk for

support, because the room seemed to be swirling around her, and her legs were starting to buckle.

'No…' The word scraped past Alys's throat, hoarse and harsh. 'No! I will not have any such test—I will not! Nikos never said… He would never… Not now…not when…'

Shock was making her incoherent. More than shock—a desperate rejection of what was being said to her. Everything she'd thought real was crashing down around her.

Not Nikos! No, not him—not wanting this!

He'd accepted that the baby was theirs—of course he had! How could it possibly be otherwise?

He cannot think that of me—not now! Not after all we have been to each other here.

She stared, her face white, still disbelieving what was impossible to believe.

Derision was etched across Nikos's father's face. 'Did you think he would not insist? My son is not the fool you take him for!'

'Where is he?' Alys cried, as the air was crushed from her lungs, blood drumming in her ears. 'Where is Nikos?'

She couldn't bear this—it was dreadful, hideous. She would not believe it…could not…

'On his way to New York,' came the harsh answer. 'On my advice. I told him I would deal with you. The maids are packing your things—go and make yourself decent! We leave for Athens immediately!'

Alys's eyes distended and her grip on the corner of the desk tightened. It was all that was keeping her upright.

'I won't go,' she said.

Shock, dismay, horror…all were swallowing her up.

'There can be only one reason for your refusal.' Nikos's father's voice was harsh, his eyes boring into hers like drills. 'And it shows him what he has feared from the start—that you know the baby in your belly is not his! So, do you still refuse to take the test that he demands? Answer me!'

The blood was pounding in her chest, and she felt as if

there was a garotte around her throat, but she managed to speak. To say all that was left for her to say.

'Yes…' she said faintly. 'I refuse.'

'Then you will be driven to the airport and a direct flight to England will be arranged—today. You will make no further attempt to contact my son. He has no further interest in you.' Nikos's father's voice twisted again—viciously. 'He will not have another man's bastard to raise.'

Alys heard no more. Could not bear to.

She turned and stumbled from the room.

CHAPTER THIRTEEN

NIKOS LET HIMSELF into his hotel room in Manhattan, a wave of jet lag and tiredness hitting him like a wall. On deplaning, after a flight spent going through the complex and intricate details of the proposal and planning his negotiating strategy, he'd gone straight into a dinner meeting with the other parties, which had been long and intensive.

More meetings were scheduled for the morning, but with luck he might hammer out a mutually acceptable agreement and be back at JFK for the flight home by the evening.

His face shadowed. Would it really be as simple as his father had promised?

He fished his phone out of his jacket pocket. Still no messages or voicemail. He frowned, disquieted. Suppressing an impulse to call, he reminded himself it was hardly dawn in Greece yet.

Another wave of jet lag and tiredness hit him. He would get some shut-eye first, then phone as soon as he awoke.

But when he did, and heard what the voice on the other end of the phone was telling him, all thought of the morning's meetings vanished. Within half an hour he was in the hotel's limo, heading back to JFK.

Driven by demons.

Alys let herself into her house, exhaustion—more than exhaustion—filling her. The journey back to the UK had been gruelling.

Andreas had driven her to the island's airport, where she'd had to wait for a flight. The only one direct to the UK had been to Manchester, leaving in the evening. She'd landed after midnight, and then waited at the airport for the first coach south to Birmingham. Then she'd got the bus to her home town and walked from the bus station.

Now she felt like a zombie, hardly able to put one foot in front of another.

She closed the front door behind her, treading on a heap of accumulated mail. Wearily she scooped it up, dumped it on the kitchen table. The house smelt stale and airless. She had not expected to be away so long. Nor to come back like this.

Destroyed.

What other word could there be? All her stupid, pathetic hopes had been ripped from her. Trampled into the ground.

Tears sprang into her eyes, burning like acid. She had not allowed herself to cry since fleeing the villa, knowing that if she started she would never stop. Even now she blinked them away, lugging her suitcase upstairs, then turning the immersion heater on so she could shower in a while, before going back downstairs to put the kettle on.

She sorted through the mail. Most was junk, but the one she wanted to see was there, and she tore it open, needing to see it in black and white.

Confirmation of the removal of any threat to instigate foreclosure proceedings and the information that her mortgage account was now three months in credit.

She shut her eyes, squeezing acid tears.

At least I saved my home.

Even if she dared not stay in it.

Cold snaked through her veins and her eyes flared open, going out over the small rear garden, its lawn overgrown, pot plants wilting. Another image overlayed it, vivid with bougainvillea, drenched in hot sunshine, girdled by the azure Aegean.

Then it was gone.

Anguish, raw and agonising, crushed her like a vice.

Gone for ever now.

She gave a choke, a cry that was the sound of her heart breaking.

And then the tears came…

Nikos was at his father's house again, striding in, handing his suitcase and his briefcase to the manservant, startled at his unexpected arrival.

'Where is my father?' Nikos's demand was grim. As grim as the expression in his face.

'Kyrios Drakis is at breakfast,' the manservant informed him.

Nikos strode past him, throwing open the doors to the palatial dining room. His father looked up from his place at the head of the table.

'Nikos?' he exclaimed. 'Why are you back so soon? You gave me no indication that—'

Nikos cut across him, slamming shut the doors behind him. This was not for the ears of staff or servants. Only for his father.

His eyes blazed with a cold, deadly light.

'What the *hell*,' he said, 'have you done?'

Alys was packing her suitcase. Not the small carry-on she'd taken to Greece, but a hefty one that would hold enough to see her through into winter. Her expression was set and she worked methodically, her mind racing through the things she still had to do before she could shut the front door and head to the coach station.

A set of house keys was already with the estate agent she'd signed up to put the house on the market. She would let them have a forwarding address once she was settled.

As to where that would be—that was the least of her worries. The only imperative was that it must be far enough away for Nikos never to find her…

Anguish stabbed her, as it had been doing ever since she'd fled his father, and tears were trying to sting her eyes. She blinked them away. There was no time for tears until she was safely out of the house—safely on a coach to anywhere she could think of.

Nikos's father sat back in his chair.

'What have I *done*?' he echoed. He lifted his hands. 'I have saved you—that's what I've done! Just as I did when Miriam Kapoulou so nearly trapped you. When you were so besotted with her, wet behind the ears! Well, I've done it again—saved you from another of her kind!' His face darkened. 'This time by using the exact same tactics that trapped *me*! I *vowed*, my son, that I would never let it happen to you! And now it won't.' There was triumph in his eyes. 'I've sent her packing—you are free of her!'

Nikos's expression was frozen. 'Free…?' There was a hollow ring to his voice.

'Yes, *free*!' his father repeated. 'She's gone back to England, tail between her legs—I told her that if she refused a paternity test it would be proof that she knew all along her brat was not yours! And she did refuse. Refused outright! So clearly you are *not* the father—and your fate will *not* be mine!'

An oath broke from Nikos. 'Of *course* I am the father!' His voice was twisted, bitterness ripping through it. 'And the fate you have tried to save me from is the only one I long for!' He looked at his father, face stark. 'She is the woman I love,' he said. 'And you have driven her away.'

There was desolation in his voice.

Alys peered out of the sitting room window over the wintry Yorkshire moorland. The holiday rental cottage was going cheap for the off season, but come the spring she would move out into the small but inexpensive flat she was buying in nearby Sheffield, now that the sale of her house had finally gone through.

By then she would be mother to the child who was now within a fortnight of being born. A child who would be as fatherless as she had been.

Better that than a man like Nikos for a father.

Familiar anguish filled her, as it had ever since her return to England, with her stupid, pathetic hopes and dreams in tatters. Her heart in pieces.

But what use was anguish or heartbreak? Only her baby mattered now, and she was all prepared for its arrival. Her hospital bag was packed and her little car—not much more than an old banger, which she'd bought locally—was parked outside the cottage. She'd already stopped working at the travel agency, which had taken her on during the busy high season in summer, after she'd fled her home, terrified that Nikos might come after her.

He must never find me! I could not bear it!

She gazed blindly out of the cottage window, memories crowding, each one an agony.

The hot sun bright on the blue sea...the pool sparkling in the sunshine...the brilliant crimson of the bougainvillea tumbling over the pristine white of the villa's walls...

And most agonising of all…

Nikos—oh, Nikos! Holding out his arms to me, taking my hand, laughing with me, kissing me, making love to me...

She tore her mind away, and it was as painful as if she were tearing her own flesh, turning away from the window.

Outside, unnoticed by her, caught as she was in her own inconsolable grief for what could never be, the first few flakes of snow drifted down out of the leaden sky. Then whirled down faster.

The SUV made its slow way along a lane that was narrowing between drystone walls as it climbed up to the open moor. The light was fading fast and snow was falling—light at first, then more heavily, whirled by the wind across the exposed landscape, thickening to become a blizzard.

His face increasingly grim, its driver pressed on relentlessly…nearing his destination.

Alys drew the thick curtains, then put more wood on the log burner. It was not comfortable to think that she was alone here in this isolated cottage in weather like this. But all she had to do, she told herself sternly, was hunker down and stay indoors. She had food, she had warmth, she had hot water and she would be fine—just fine.

She settled down on the sofa, flicking through TV channels idly. She came across a programme about moving to warmer climes, finding a holiday home in the Med…whitewashed houses and crimson bougainvillea and azure sea…

Just like her memories.

She changed channel abruptly. No point remembering. It was gone. And so was Nikos.

For ever.

She found an old film, reached for her mug of tea.

A noisy car chase on screen blanked out the sound of a car engine in the real world. But it was not sufficient, a few moments later, to blank out the sudden hard and heavy rapping on the front door of the cottage.

Who on earth...?

She got up, walking to the door in her ungainly fashion, unbolting it and hefting it open to admit a blast of icy wind.

And Nikos.

He strode in, snow whitening his hair and shoulders after just walking the short distance from the SUV pulled up outside the tiny front garden.

Alys had reared back, and his eyes went to her immediately, shock knifing through him. He had known her pregnancy would be advanced by now, but to see her so physically altered from what he remembered was a shock.

Shock was in her eyes too.

And disbelief.

And absolute rejection.

With the flat of his hand he shut the heavy front door, cutting out the freezing wind and snow, stepping towards her. She jerked away, clutching the frame of the door into the sitting room he could see beyond.

'Get out of here!' Her face was contorting. 'Go away! Leave me alone!'

He tried to speak.

'Alys, I—'

'Get out!' Her voice was a shriek now, high-pitched and frantic. Her face was as white as a sheet.

And then a cry broke from her. The look on her face was aghast. She froze, features distended, completely paralysed.

Alarm knifed in him. 'What—?'

She stared at him, that same dreadful, horrified expression on her face. Her eyes were round with disbelief. With terror.

'My waters have broken,' she said, in a voice that was completely blank.

He carried her out to the SUV. It was already almost invisible in the white-out, but he yanked open the passenger door, managing to place the towels he'd grabbed at her stricken direction on the seat. He slammed the door shut, before going back into the cottage to check that the wood burner was safely closed, to collect the hospital bag from her bedroom and lock the front door.

He got back into the SUV.

She was leaning back in her seat, eyes closed. For a second a memory stabbed of how he'd driven her, after her excoriating meltdown, from the island airport to the villa, and she had kept her eyes closed for the entire journey, shutting him out.

She was shutting him out again.

Emotion stabbed at him like a piercing dagger. But he had no time for that—not now. Now there was only one priority.

'Get the hospital on the phone…warn them we're on our way,' he told her.

He put the SUV into four-wheel drive—essential in these appalling conditions—and inched his way forward, hoping the snow drifts forming already would not be too high.

The journey down to the town in the dale below was a nightmare. He was barely able to see through the blizzard. He passed abandoned vehicles, a snow plough heading elsewhere, conscious all the time of Alys, face white, eyes closed.

And then her face contorted, her hands pressing over her distended abdomen, eyes flying open.

'Oh, God, that was a contraction! *Nikos—*'

Her voice was high-pitched. Terrified.

He reached for her hand. 'It will be OK,' he said. 'It will be OK. I'll get you there in time.'

He drove on, face set and grimmer still.

By the time he pulled up at the hospital her contractions were quickening. He leapt from the car, ran into the entrance lobby, yelling he knew not what. Then other people were running. Paramedics were coming out to the parked car, still with its hazard lights flashing, getting Alys out, lowering her onto a trolley, racing away with her.

He wanted to follow, but could not leave the SUV there, blocking the way. He went to park it, then ran back as fast as the driving snow would let him. Inside, he saw the signs to Maternity and vaulted up the stairs, nor bothering to wait for the lift. There was a reception desk at the entrance, and urgently he asked where Alys had been taken.

They would not tell him.

'She told us not to admit you,' the receptionist said. 'To ask you to leave.'

He made no answer, just numbly went to the waiting

area and sat down on a hard chair, his heart pounding, staring at nothing.

He would not leave. He would wait here.

For ever, if he had to.

Nothing else was possible for him.

CHAPTER FOURTEEN

ALYS WAS SITTING up in the hospital bed, the morning sunlight frail after the night's snowstorm. She was as weak as a kitten, her body aching, but what was that to her? Beside her, in a little crib, her baby slept.

Emotion poured through her, overwhelming her. Gratitude, profound and abject, filled her, because her baby was safe and well.

A knock came at the door, and a nurse put her head around it. 'You have a visitor!' she said brightly.

She didn't stop to check whether Alys wanted a visitor or not.

Nikos walked in.

Her face stiffened instantly. 'I don't want you here!'

She saw him pause by the door, shut it quietly, but firmly.

'And I don't want to *be* here either!' Alys forged on. 'You had no right to have me transferred to the private wing, to a room of my own! I would have been fine on the maternity ward!'

He ignored her protest, instead taking a chair and drawing it forward a little, sitting himself down upon it.

Her eyes went to him, baleful.

Defensive.

Because there was so much she had to defend herself from. From the past, and the present—and the future.

And she must defend herself, too, from something she was helpless to defend herself against.

He sat there, leaning forward slightly, his hands resting, upturned, on his strong thighs, his muscled torso moulded by a dark slate cashmere sweater, his eyes boring into her, darker yet.

Every centimetre of him was familiar to her—once precious to her.

But never again—dear God, never again!

She felt tears, hot and utterly unnecessary, prick behind her eyelids, but she would not admit to them. Would not admit to the buckling emotion convulsing through her, the longing filling her.

A longing that could never be slaked.

A love she could never have.

Not now. Not ever.

It mocked her with the poisoned tips of a whip that bit into her flesh, flailing her for her own blindness, her own stupidity, her own unforgivable folly in coming to trust him as she had, falling in love with him…

And all along—dear God—it was a ploy, a pretence, a charade on his part! Every word he spoke to me, every smile, every kiss and caress, a lie.

The pain lashed across her again—pain she must endure for the rest of her life…

But she would not let it show. She would *not*. She would never, *never* let him see how he had hurt her. Destroyed her…

'Alys…' his voice was low, and she had to strain to hear him '…we have to talk.'

She shook her head. 'No, we don't,' she answered him. 'And if you want me to thank you for getting me here in time—well, if you hadn't turned up like that I wouldn't have gone into labour because of the shock!'

A grave expression passed across his face. 'Do you think I don't know that?' he said heavily.

She saw his eyes slip from her down to the crib on the far side of the bed. There was a hungry look in his face. She wondered at it, then hardened her heart.

'It's not yours,' she told him. Her voice was flat. 'I fell into bed with another man the day after I slept with you. So you can keep your precious Drakis money, and not waste a penny of it raising another man's bastard!'

His face whitened, lines knifing around his mouth. 'Don't speak like that—' The words broke from him.

She snaked forward, her voice a vicious hiss, eyes venomous. 'Why not? It's what you said to me in Athens! And it's what your father said to me at the villa! When you sent him to do your dirty work for you!'

Nikos's eyes blazed with black fire at her accusation. 'I did not send him!' he ground out. 'Disbelieve anything you will about me, but believe this—I *did not* send him!'

She saw him shut his eyes, clench his hands. Then slowly, forcibly, he opened his hands, his eyes.

He was looking right at her.

'I have something I must tell you,' he said.

Tension was racking through Nikos as he started to speak, to say what he must. His voice was halting, but he made himself go on.

'When we ate at that taverna in the harbour, you asked about my mother. I didn't want to talk about her. I never have. She left for California when I was barely two years old—I have no memories of her and do not want any.' His voice changed, hardened. 'My father had quite enough of them to pass on to me. And I've heard them all my life.' His mouth pressed tightly. 'An endless litany that never stops.'

His gaze slid away. Away from the crib he could not see into on the far side of her bed. Away out of the window, looking over the hospital's busy car park. Away into the past. A past that was not his, but a past that had shaped him, warped him.

'My father met my mother when she was working as a hostess in a club on one of Greece's party islands—the kind of place my father liked to hang out at when he was young…

not just for the party atmosphere, free and easy after the strictures of his own upbringing, but because of women like my mother. Women who liked men with lots of money to spend on them, squander on them, before they moved on to someone else. But my mother didn't intend my father to move on to another woman. So she deliberately got herself pregnant. Yes—' he held up a hand '—I know. It takes two. But she lied to him about contraception, and he was…caught.'

His eyes came back to Alys. Her face was expressionless, but he could see something in the depths of her eyes that made him go on.

'Caught,' he said again, quite deliberately. And then he went on, incising each word, 'And he has continued, for his entire life, to think of himself that way.' And now he could not stop another note entering his voice—one that seemed to come from so deep down that it drew blood…his blood. 'Left to himself he would never have troubled to marry her just because she was pregnant—a nightclub hostess, marrying a Drakis! Unthinkable! But his own father was strait-laced. He insisted on the marriage, refused to tolerate any scandal, any Drakis bastards—' he had to force himself to say the word '—that might taint the family's pristine reputation. My father caved in—furious and reluctant, but not wanting to endanger his own inheritance.'

He looked away again, out through the window.

'All his life he has loathed my mother with a fury that time has not dimmed. Claiming she ruined his life, saddled him with me—' He broke off, still not looking back at Alys. 'And even though all the tests he insisted on proved I was his, I was still never the son he wanted… How could I be, with a mother like mine?'

He drew a breath, whipping his eyes back to Alys. She was sitting there very still, motionless. Eyes veiled.

'I've had to prove every single day of my life that I am a Drakis.' Each word was ground out like glass. 'Doing what a Drakis does—'

'Making money.' Alys's words fell into the gaping space between them. 'Keeping it safe from women like your mother. From women like me.'

He couldn't read her voice—there was no expression in it. He only nodded, his eyes slipping away again. Towards the crib he still could not see into.

'When I read your letter telling me you were pregnant,' he said, 'I—'

'Saw history repeating itself.' Alys cut across him. 'I get the picture, Nikos.' Her voice was tight—so tight it could have strangled him.

He fought for a breath, which razored in his throat when he saw the way she was looking at him. 'Not quite,' he said in a low voice.

He swallowed, and it was as if a stone was lodged there and he could not breathe past it. A stone that had lodged there a long, long time ago.

'You see, Alys, I do not see the world through the eyes of a man trapped into fathering a child he did not want by a woman he did not want. I see the world through the eyes of an unwanted child.' His eyes came back to her, open and unflinching. 'The unwanted child I was.' His fingers clenched again. 'Which is why, Alys, neither you nor I could ever be important in this. Only one human being is important.'

He would not let his gaze go to the crib—would *not*.

'Any child...*every* child...deserves parents who want them and are deserving of them. Deserves as decent a childhood as possible. In Athens, I wanted us to marry because I did not want any stigma—any taint, any doubt at all—to haunt the child you carried.' He swallowed, and still that stone blocking his throat would not shift. 'And I wanted an *in utero* DNA test because if we'd married first and had the test done after you gave birth, and it had showed...well, that the father was another man, it would have been a mess all round. You would have had no chance to contact the other man, maybe marry him, ensure the baby was legitimate—'

He stood up suddenly, striding to the window, whipping round to look at her. He must say what he had to say—the only important thing to say.

'It was the baby I had to protect, Alys—not me!'

She was looking at him, and he could not bear the way she was doing it.

'You could have told me that,' she said.

There was no emotion in her voice. It was completely empty, like her eyes, which were looking at him in the way he could not bear. But must.

'I couldn't take the risk,' he answered. 'It would have shown you I had a weak point…that I cared about the baby you carried. You could have used it as a weapon against me, as my mother used me to get a ring on her finger, and an eye-watering divorce settlement that has made her a rich woman. It's what made me so…so harsh towards you in Athens. I wanted you to be intimidated by me…cowed.'

He took another razoring breath.

'But it backfired on me. Sent you fleeing, and into that meltdown at the airport. I realised then…' and now his gaze at her was naked '…that I needed to change tactics.'

'By taking me to the villa.' Alys's fingers twisted in the coverlet. Her eyes dropped. 'Taking me to bed. Neutralising me.'

Her words dropped like stones.

'Yes.' The admission fell from him. As necessary now as his impulsive decision to take her to Villa Drakis had been necessary then. 'I had to stop you resisting me. I had to make you compliant.' A nerve was ticking in his cheek, but he could not stop it. 'I had to make you willing to stay with me while I—'

'Softened me up so I'd be willing to have that DNA test.'

Again, Alys's words cut across his. And still there was

no expression in her eyes, just her unblinking gaze that was impossible to meet. And yet he must.

And he must say what he said next.

'No.'

A single word, but it seemed to fill the room. Something moved in the depths of her eyes, but he did not know what it was. Knew only that he had to keep speaking.

'It was to give me time to make my mind up about you.'

He saw her fingers clench, entwined in the bedclothes, knuckles whitening.

Restlessly, he moved about the room, then turned.

'And I did,' he said. This time it was his voice, his eyes, that had no expression in them. 'Which is why…' he took a breath that could pass only with difficulty past that stone still lodged in his throat '…why I returned to Athens. There were things I needed to do. Including,' he said, 'talk to my father.'

'Oh, yes,' said Alys. 'Your father. Who wasted no time before rushing to the villa and sending me packing!'

Bitterness was in her voice now, open and scathing. It scored on Nikos's skin like acid.

'I did *not* send him!' he said again. 'I told him about the situation because I knew I could put it off no longer. I expected him to be furious…' He frowned. 'But he was amazingly forbearing.' His mouth tightened. 'You see, it was not just that he was thinking of his own disastrous marriage.' He took another heavy breath. 'He was thinking of the one I almost made myself.'

He shut his eyes for a moment, in that second seeing the past as vividly as if it had become the present, then opened them again.

'When I was twenty-two I fell for the daughter of one of his business acquaintances. I was besotted with her. She played me along, declaring she loved me—only me! Then my father disclosed to me that her father was close to bankruptcy and a Drakis son-in-law would be a lifeline for his family.' His voice hardened unconsciously. 'He told me that if I insisted on marrying her he would cast me out of the family, disinherit me, leave me penniless. Unlike my father, who buckled under *his* father's threat to disinherit him, I didn't care! I rushed to Miriam, certain she loved me as much as I loved her, certain she wouldn't care that I wouldn't be rich any longer.'

He frowned, as if speaking had become difficult.

'She walked out on me. The very next month married a man who was as old as her father but stinking rich. My father told me he'd taught me an invaluable lesson—told me that never again would I let myself fall in love with a woman who loved the Drakis riches more than me.'

He turned away. Walked back to the window to stare out of it sightlessly.

'So when I told him about you he rode to the rescue again. To save me from his own fate and from the fate that had so nearly engulfed me when I was still wet behind the ears. He was triumphant about it—about what he'd achieved while I'd been despatched off to New York on the pretext of finishing off a half-completed deal out there. Triumphant that he'd sent you packing, saved me from the clutches of yet another gold-digger after the Drakis money.'

He lifted his hand to fiddle with the blind cord, needing something to preoccupy him. Something to stop him thinking about what he would say next.

'But his triumph fell flat.' His voice was expressionless. 'I did not wish to be saved.'

Alys heard him and yet did not hear him. Her heart was thumping in her chest, and maybe it was that that made his words blur in her ears.

Nikos was turning around again, looking at her again. That familiar veiling was in his eyes, making them quite impossible to read. To dare to read…

'Since the moment I read your letter, telling me you were pregnant, I have had to face the fact that not only might the baby not be mine, but that you might be cut from the same cloth as my mother. Wanting only my money.'

Two spots of colour burned in Alys's cheeks.

'I did, Nikos. I did want your money.' She would not flinch from meeting his eyes. 'To pay off my debts, like I told you.'

'Why did you have debts, Alys? I tried to find out at the villa, but you would not tell me. So tell me now.'

His eyes were levelled at her. She gave a shrug. No point being evasive now. 'The mortgage on my house was in arrears. They were threatening foreclosure. I couldn't risk it—not with a baby on its way.'

'Why in arrears, Alys?'

His voice was persistent, his gaze still levelled at her. She swallowed. 'My mother was the victim of a hit-and-run accident that left her very badly injured. She couldn't work any longer, and I had to leave uni to be her carer. Money was incredibly tight, and that's how the arrears crept up. When she died last year the mortgage company wanted full repayment or they would issue proceedings for repossession. That's why I took your money, Nikos—'

She broke off, incapable of more. Emotion was heaving in her—unbearable, impossible. But she must not let it.

Her fingers twisted in the bedclothes again, whitening her knuckles. 'Look, just *go*, Nikos! I don't want you, I don't need you, and I don't need your money! I've sold my house, and there was enough equity to let me buy a one-bedroom flat. So I'll be fine, Nikos—just fine! I don't need any more of your money! So you can go and tell your precious father that he did, indeed, save you from a woman like your mother.'

She slumped back against the pillows, exhausted in body, and in mind, and in her stupid, battered broken heart.

'But my father didn't save me, Alys. He destroyed me.'

Nikos's voice was weary, drained of all emotion. Emotion that had had to be drained out of him, painfully and completely, in the months since his father had told him what he'd done.

Emotion he had no right to.

Would never have a right to.

Not any more.

He would tell her why. It might assuage her. Give her some satisfaction, however belated.

'You have every right to be angry with me, Alys. From the moment you told me about the baby I suspected you, accused you, condemned you and manipulated you—seduced you, lied to you. I treated you shamefully.'

He frowned.

'But these last months have been unendurable. You vanished, Alys. I could not reach you from New York, and when I phoned Spiros he told me my father had been and you had left the island. I confronted my father, and he told me what he'd done. I was desperate! But I could not find you… The estate agent handling the sale of your house would say nothing to me, and in the end I had to hire private investigators, who finally managed to track you down.'

'You shouldn't have bothered, Nikos,' he heard her say.

He flinched. The hostility in her voice was like a knife's stab. 'I had to,' he said. 'I had to find you! Find you and tell you—' He broke off. Was there any use in telling her? Was there any use in being here at all?

Except…

He felt his eyes go towards the far side of the bed, to the crib he could not see into.

'Tell you that I would give everything for my father not to have done what he did,' he said heavily—though to what purpose he did not know, for was she not lost to him for ever now, fleeing from him as she had, hiding from him, rejecting him? That stab came again, as if the blade was twisting in his guts. 'I would give everything not to have you believe I'm still the same man I was when you first came to Athens.'

Something moved in his face now, in his voice.

'Because I am not that man any longer! On the island, at the villa—yes, I wanted to make you mine, to win you over. Because I did not want you fleeing back to England again, taking our baby with you! A baby I *knew* was mine, for how else would I so desire you? But in those weeks I spent with you, Alys, I came to realise it was not just because of the baby—it was because of *you*. You, Alys. And I wanted you so, so much—just as I told you. Wanted more and more for there to be the *us* I told you I wanted! Those weeks I had with you at the villa…' He took a razored breath. 'They were the happiest of my life—'

He paused, gazing down at her. She had no expression on her face—none at all. But he knew he must keep speaking. He had sought her for months, and now had found her—he would say all that was within him. And then he would leave. Because she did not want him—would never want him.

He felt that knife twist in his guts again, pain convulsing him.

'That is why I knew I had to go to Athens,' he said. 'Knew I had to confront my father, and tell him…' he took another razored breath '…that I had fallen in love with you.' His face worked. 'I hoped he would accept it and welcome you as my beloved wife. Instead he destroyed all my hopes by driving you away as he did.'

He turned away, walking to the door—for there was no point staying any longer. No point at all.

Hand on the doorknob, he turned. 'I will leave you now, as you wish me to do. I will make arrangements for sufficient funds to be available for you so that you lack nothing as you raise your baby.' His voice thickened. 'The baby I make no claim to.'

For the last time he let his eyes go to the far side of her bed, to the crib he could not see into. There was a hunger inside him that could never be assuaged now. For his baby… for the woman he loved…

Her voice stayed him.

'I think you mean, Nikos, *our* baby.'

* * *

Alys saw him freeze, then slowly, very slowly, turn around. But it was hard to see him clearly. Silent tears were running down her cheeks and her vision was blurred with them.

'Come and see,' she said to him.

She watched him come haltingly, through her blurred vison, and go round to the crib side of the bed.

As if on cue, the tiny baby within stirred, securely wrapped and covered, one tiny starfish hand uncurling. Giving a tiny yawn, it opened its eyes. Gazing at Nikos with pale blue incomprehension.

'Say hello to our daughter, Nikos,' Alys said, and her voice was a whisper, because anything else was impossible.

'She's perfect… Our perfect, perfect baby.'

It was Nikos speaking, his voice husky, but it could have been her—for, as it happened, that was exactly her opinion of their baby too.

Our baby.

The simple pronoun convulsed within her.

A sob broke from her. 'Oh, Nikos, she is *ours*, isn't she?' It was an imprecation, a plea.

Her hand was seized. Crushed.

'For ever!'

Her other hand was seized, and then Nikos was sinking down on the bed, his eyes pouring into hers.

'Do you mean it? Do you truly mean it, Alys? *Can* you mean it, after the way I've treated you? I would give all the world to undo that!'

She let her hands be crushed in his, because their strength was hers now—all hers. Wonder filled her, and a joy so fierce she could barely bear it. But she knew it was a joy that she would bear all her life now.

'I fell in love with you at the villa, Nikos! And all I wanted, with all my heart, was to make a family with you—you and me and our baby.'

Her face convulsed.

'It hurt me so *much*, Nikos, when your father came! Ripping my hopes from me! Hating me so much—'

Tears were pouring down her face, and Nikos was bending forward to kiss them away.

'Don't weep, my dearest, sweetest love—don't weep! I cannot bear it if you weep!'

She only sobbed more, and then his hands were releasing hers and he was wrapping her in his arms, holding her close, so very close. As close as their hearts beat against each other.

Then, as her weeping ceased, she became dimly aware of another sound. A faint, displeased mewing. She drew back, her arms dropping from Nikos, twisting as she sat up to look down into the crib beside the bed.

In her cosy spot in the crib, their daughter's little face was screwed up, her mouth opening, and for a tiny human being her lungs were mighty! Her demand was peremptory and insistent.

Alys carefully scooped her up, peeling back her gown to expose her breast, already tingling on cue, carefully latching her on.

Nikos sat back, giving them space. But he lifted a hand, stretching out one tentative finger to stroke, with infinite gentleness, the cheek of his newborn daughter.

Then his eyes went to Alys. 'Is this really true?' he asked wonderingly. 'That we can go from hell to heaven like this?'

With her free hand she took hold of his, meshing her fingers with his. The joy that had burned with a furnace of fierceness was now the warm, cherishing glow of devotion.

'Wherever the three of us are, it will always be heaven for us, Nikos.'

Her eyes poured into his with all that she felt, all that she saw reflected in his own. And at her breast, their tiny daughter feasted, as much in a state of bliss as her parents, who were now leaning gently forward to kiss again and seal their love for ever.

EPILOGUE

'MY DEAR, MAY I really not pour some champagne for you? Just a little?'

The voice so like his own was as he had never heard it before, Nikos thought. Kindly, conciliatory—fatherly.

But this was a father such as he had never known before. Wonder filled him, and astonishment too—and above all gratitude.

He watched now as his father, still trying to tempt Alys to replace her innocuous elderflower spritzer with something alcoholic—vintage champagne from his own cellars in the opulent Drakis mansion in Kifissia, inside which they were all gathered—fussed over the woman he had once tried to separate from his son.

Nikos's expression changed. He knew full well what had wrought this extraordinary transformation. His gaze went to the woman he loved beyond life itself and to the baby she held on her lap, regally arrayed in a christening robe of such sumptuousness that Nikos could only profoundly hope that Alys had a muslin to hand in case of untoward posseting.

Love filled his eyes. Love—endless and eternal!—for Alys, who filled his heart and very being, and love—so fiercely, burningly protective and devoted—for the daughter they shared together.

The daughter who was a precious and most beloved granddaughter as well.

Again Nikos felt that wash of wonder and gratitude go through him. He suppressed a wry, private smile as he sipped his own champagne. In those desolate months when he'd been so desperately trying to find Alys, after she'd fled Greece, his father had finally come to realise just how much she meant to his son. And when Nikos had disclosed to his father Alys's devotion to her stricken mother, and the reason she had accumulated the debts she had, it had been all the confirmation his father had needed to know that Alys was nothing like the woman who had trapped him into marriage all those bitter years ago.

That and setting eyes on his granddaughter!

For when Nikos had brought Alys back to Greece, it had been to a reception warmer than he had dared hope for. His father had opened his arms to Alys, his apologies for what he had done so profuse and heartfelt that both Alys and Nikos had had finally to silence him.

They had been married in Yorkshire, as soon as it could be arranged, cosying down, while the necessary paperwork was completed, in the snug little cottage which they had decided to buy as their UK hideaway. Alys had donated her flat in Sheffield for the use of a charity that housed women fleeing domestic abuse.

But preventing his father fussing over and pampering both Alys and their daughter had been impossible—nor did he and Alys try.

'I have not been a good father, my boy—I let my bitterness poison me. Let me now strive to be a good father-in-law. And a good grandfather.'

Nikos felt his throat tighten as he remembered his father's apology. It tightened more as he heard again in his head his father's tentative request that one of their daughter's names be for Nikos's grandmother, who had died while his father was only a teenager himself.

Alys's face had lit up. *'Anatalia? Oh, but that's a beau-*

tiful name!' She'd given a little choke of emotion. *'And my own mother's name was Ann...'*

'Doubly perfect, then!' Nikos had said. *'Our wonderful daughter—named for two wonderful grandmothers!'*

As if she'd heard him thinking her name, their tiny daughter, Anatalia Nikola Alicia—*Ana, indeed*—opened her eyes and gave her little mewing cry, gazing fixedly up at her grandfather.

Nikos's wry smile deepened.

'Aha!' his father announced fondly. 'Now she wakes... our little princess!' He clapped a fatherly hand on Nikos's shoulder. 'We must raise a toast to her, my son, and to my new daughter!' He beamed at both of them.

They all duly raised their glasses as Nikos's father pronounced a traditional Greek blessing on his newly christened granddaughter. Soon, in a matter of weeks, he would be pronouncing another traditional Greek blessing—this time on newlyweds. For Nikos and Alys had conceded to his request that they add to their civil marriage one under Greek Orthodox rites.

All they had insisted on, though, was that they did not want a grand high-society event in Athens, however anxious Nikos's father was to make all the amends he could for his initial opposition to Alys.

So, instead, there was to be a small private wedding in the church in the *agora* in the harbour town on the island, and they would be married from the Villa Drakis, which was to be Nikos and Alys's home.

Nikos would continue to cut down on his workload, as he already had, minimising his globetrotting in favour of spending time with Alys and Ana, devoting more time to developing the island's economy—starting with investing in Spiros's cousin's winery, a bottle from which was already awaiting consumption over dinner, once Ana was abed for the night.

He heard his father give a sigh of pleasure and satisfaction. 'I am the happiest of men,' he said happily.

Nikos shook his head. 'That cannot be,' he contradicted smilingly. 'For *I* am the happiest of men!'

Alys looked up from discreetly latching Ana on beneath the muslin. 'And *we*,' she informed them, speaking on busy Ana's behalf, 'are the happiest of *women*.'

Her smile embraced them both—her beloved husband, and her doting father-in-law, who was lavishing upon her the fatherly affection she had never known.

Her smile deepened as her eyes focussed on Nikos, meeting his. And in them, as there always would be, was a blaze of radiant joy and love, whose warmth would be an unquenchable fire in his heart all his days, and all his nights, and for all eternity itself.

* * * * *

VOWS ON THE VIRGIN'S TERMS

CLARE CONNELLY

MILLS & BOON

This is a book for every girl who's ever been told she's 'bossy', but really just knows what she wants in life and isn't afraid to reach out and grab it.

CHAPTER ONE

If Olivia could have closed her eyes and disappeared to *anywhere* else in the world, then she absolutely would have done so. But, having tricked Luca Giovanardi's assistant into revealing that he would be attending this all-star event, spent money she could ill afford on a budget airfare to Italy, and actually turned up at the party on the banks of the Tiber, she knew she'd crossed the point of no return.

There was nothing for it.

Her eyes scanned the crowds, feasting on the unfamiliar elegance and sophistication, a churning in her gut reminding her, every second, that she didn't belong here. It was so removed from her normal life, so different from what she was used to.

The party was in full swing, the restaurant courtyard packed with affluent guests, the fragrance in the air a heady mix of night-flowering jasmine and cloying floral perfume. As she studied the swarming crowd of glitterati, a woman bustled past, bumping Olivia, so she offered a tight smile of apology automatically, despite having done nothing worse than stand like a statue, frozen to the spot, too afraid to move deeper into the crowd, despite the fact she'd come here for exactly this purpose.

Naturally, he was in the centre.

Not just of the party, but of a group of people—men and women—his obvious charisma keeping each in his thrall, so that as he spoke their eyes were glued to his chiselled symmetrical face.

Why did he have to be so handsome? This wouldn't be so difficult if he were ordinary looking. Or even just an ordinary man. But everything about Luca Giovanardi was quite famously extraordinary, from his family's fall from grace to his spectacular resurrection to the top of the world's financial elite. As for his personal life, Olivia had gleaned only what was absolutely necessary from the Internet—but it had been enough to know that he was the polar opposite of her in every way. Where she was a twenty-four-year-old virgin who'd never even been so much as *kissed* by a man before, Luca was every inch the red-blooded male, a bachelor ever since his brief, long-ago marriage ended, a bachelor who made no attempt to conceal the speed with which he churned through glamorous, sexy women.

Was she really aiming to be one of them?

Olivia licked her lips, her throat suddenly parched, and, despite the fact she was alone, she shook her head, needing to physically push the idea from her mind. She wasn't aiming to become his mistress; what she needed was to become his wife.

A drum seemed to beat inside her body, gentle at first, the same drum beat she'd been hearing for years, since she'd first learned of her father's will and the implications contained therein for her, and her life. But now, as she stared at Luca, the drum was growing louder, more intense, filling her body with a tempo that was both unnerving and compelling.

There must have been two hundred people, at least, in the courtyard, and yet, at the very moment she moved a single foot, with the intention of cutting a path through the crowd and getting his attention, his eyes lifted and speared hers, the directness of his stare forcing her lips apart as a shot of breath fired from her body, the searing heat of his appraising glance the last thing she'd expected. So much for making her way to him! Her legs were filled with cement suddenly, completely immovable.

She'd seen photographs of him—there were no shortage of images online—but they hadn't prepared her for the real, three-dimensional image of Luca, and the way his nearness would affect her. His eyes were dark—like the bark of the old elm that grew at the rear of Hughenwood House. But not in summer, so much as winter, after a heavy rain, when it glistened and shimmered. A tremble ran the length of her spine. Olivia blinked away, needing relief. But even as her eyes landed on the moonlit river that snaked through this ancient city, she could feel his eyes on her, warming her flesh, tracing the lines of her face and body in a way she'd never known before.

Almost as if they had their own free will, her eyes dragged back towards him, skating over the other guests, hoping to find someone—something—that would serve as a life raft. But there was nothing that could compare to the magnetism of Luca Giovanardi—and Olivia was sunk.

When her eyes met his, he smirked, as if to say 'knew you couldn't resist me', and then he turned back to his companions, resuming whatever story had held them in his thrall all along.

Olivia's heart sank to her toes.

This wouldn't work if she found her husband attractive. She wanted a businesslike marriage, ordained purely to free up her inheritance. There was to be no personal connection between them, nothing that could make their marriage messier than it already was.

And yet, how could she *not* find him appealing? Despite evidence to the contrary—a spectacularly uninteresting love life—Olivia was still a woman, and she recognised a drop-dead gorgeous guy when he was paraded right beneath her nose. Who wouldn't recognise how damned hot Luca Giovanardi was? From his chiselled features, swarthy complexion, hair that was thick and dark and rough on top as though he made a habit of dragging his fingers through it, to a physique that was half wild animal and half man, all sinew and lean muscular strength, a figure that was barely contained by his obviously bespoke suit. It fitted him like a glove physically, but his spirit was too primal for such elegant tailoring. He should be naked. The thought had her sitting up straighter, mouth dry, and before she could help herself an image of him *sans* clothes exploded into her mind—the details undoubtedly inaccurate for lack of personal experience with anything approaching a naked man, but it was still enough to bring colour to her pale cheeks.

One thing was certain: Luca was not the kind of man one simply propositioned out of nowhere. Even with the leverage she felt she'd found it was almost impossible to believe it would be enough. She was perfectly *au fait* with *her* reasons for needing this marriage, but why in the world would a man like Luca, who had the world eating out of the palm of his hands, accept what she was intending to suggest?

She forced her legs to move once more, but, rather than taking her towards Luca, they fed her away from the party, skirting the edges of it, until she arrived in a quiet spot near a table of empty glasses, with one solitary waiter sitting on an upturned milk crate, smoking a cigarette. Olivia pretended not to notice him as she made her way to the railing, curling her hands over it and staring down at the river, her stomach in a thousand knots.

Coward.

Are you really going to leave without even asking him?

Did you ever think you'd go through with this?

It wasn't as though she'd told Sienna or their mother, Angelica, what she'd planned, so they wouldn't hold the failure against her. Yet despite that, how could Olivia ever face them, knowing she had the power to fix their futures, and had simply balked at the first hurdle?

For the briefest moment, the threat of tears stung Olivia's

azure eyes, but it had been a long time since she'd cried, let alone run the risk of anyone *seeing* her cry, so she bit down on her lower lip until the urge passed, focusing on blotting her emotions completely, so that, a moment later, she was able to straighten her spine and turn around, ready to return to the party and once more weigh up her options—or torment herself with the path she knew she had to take, even when she was terrified to do so.

The waiter had disappeared, leaving the upended crate and a lingering odour of second-hand smoke that made Olivia's nose wrinkle as she passed. She turned her head to avoid the aroma, and as a result of not looking in the direction she was walking, stepped right into a rock-hard wall of a human's chest.

'Oh!' She tore her face back, apologising before she could make sense of what had happened, so even before she realised that the strong hands curling around her forearms to steady her belonged to Luca Giovanardi, she heard herself say, 'I'm so sorry, I didn't see you.'

'Now, we both know that is a lie,' he responded, his voice deep and gruff, and so much more sensual than she had ever known a voice could be. Her heart went into overdrive as she was confronted with, in many ways, her very worst nightmare.

Olivia sprang back from him, needing space urgently. She looked around, wishing now that the waiter were in evidence.

'Are you leaving?' Her question blurted out. His answering response, a slow-spreading grin, was like being bathed in warm caramel. Olivia tried not to feel the effects of it, but how could she resist? Nothing in her life had prepared her for this.

'No.'

'Oh.' Her relief was purely because that meant she hadn't lost her opportunity to do this. 'Good.'

When his eyes met hers, the speculation in them was

unmistakable. Oh, God. This was going from bad to worse. It was bad enough that she had imagined him naked, but that he might feel a similar curiosity about her…

'I take it you are not leaving, either?'

'I—no. Why?'

'This is the exit.' He nodded towards the garden.

'Oh.' She furrowed her brow. 'I didn't—no. I just needed space.'

He lifted a brow. 'And now, *bella*? Have you had enough space?'

Bella? Beautiful? A shudder ran through her. She was *not* beautiful. At least, she desperately didn't want to be. Not in the way any man might notice and praise her for. She was not going to be like her mother—praised for her looks, adored for them, and then resented for them and the power they wielded. It was one of the reasons she'd refused to dress up tonight, choosing to wear a pair of simple black pants and a cream linen blouse—nothing that could draw attention to her figure, nothing that could draw attention to *her* at all.

'Olivia,' she supplied quickly, stopping herself from revealing her surname by clamping her lips together.

'Luca.' He held out a hand, as if to shake hers, but when Olivia placed hers in Luca's grip, he lifted it to his lips, placing a delicate kiss across her knuckles. Delicate it might have been, but the effect of her central nervous system was cataclysmic. She jerked her hand away, her blood pressure surely reaching dangerous levels now.

'I know.' Her own voice was croaky; she cleared it. Don't be such a coward! Get this over with. 'Actually…' She dug her fingernails into her palms. 'You're the reason I'm here tonight.'

His expression didn't change, yet she was aware of a tightening in his frame, a tension radiating from him now that hadn't been there a moment ago.

'Am I?' There was dark scepticism in his words, and she wondered at that. 'And why is that?'

'I came to speak to you.'

'I see.'

Was that disappointment in the depths of his eyes? She'd been wrong before. They were nothing like bark. Nothing so ordinary. These were eyes that were as dark as the sky, as determined as iron, as fascinating as every book ever written. She was losing herself in their intricacies, committing each spec to memory when she should have been focusing on what she needed to say!

'Well?' he drawled, and now his cynicism was unmistakable. 'What would you like to discuss?'

Her heart stammered. *Say it.* But how in the world could Olivia Thornton-Rose stand there and propose marriage to Luca Giovanardi? It was so ridiculous that, out of nowhere, she laughed, a tremulous, eerie sound, underscored by a lifting of her fingers to her forehead. She ran them across her brow, searching for words.

'There are two reasons women generally approach me,' he said quietly. 'Either with an investment "opportunity"...' he formed air quote marks around the word '...or to suggest a more...personal arrangement. Why don't you say which it is you have come to discuss?'

She sucked in a jagged breath, his arrogance wholly unexpected. But somehow, it made things easier, because he reminded her, ever so slightly, of her father in that moment, and that in turn made her feel just a little bit of hate for him—a hate that helped her face the necessity of what she'd come to do.

'I suppose, if we have to place this conversation into one of those two categories, it would certainly be the former, and not the latter.'

His eyes probed hers for longer than was necessary, then swept down to her lips, blazing a line of fire and heat as he went. 'Shame,' he murmured. 'I am not interested in any further business opportunities at present. However, a personal connection would have been quite satisfying to explore.'

Her stomach rolled and tumbled and her breath seemed to burn inside her lungs, making breathing almost impossible. Stars danced behind her eyelids. 'Impossible,' she managed to squeak out, wishing for her trademark cool in that moment. 'I'm not interested in that, at all.'

His features showed that he knew that to be a lie. Was she so obvious? Of course she was. She had no experience. How could she conceal what she was feeling from someone like Luca? She was a lamb to slaughter.

'Then I cannot see what we have to discuss.'

Do it. Get it over with. What's the worst that can happen? That he'll say no?

'I know about the bank you're trying to buy.'

He straightened, regarding her with a new level of interest. She'd surprised him, the words the last thing he'd expected to hear from her.

'Everyone knows about the offer I have made,' he hedged with admirable restraint, as though it were no big deal.

'Yes.' She offered a small smile, trying to defuse the tension that was pulling between them, and failing miserably. 'Of course, it's not a secret.'

He didn't say anything in response, and his silence seemed to stretch between them.

'You want to buy a bank, one of the oldest in Europe, and the board won't sell because of your playboy reputation. They're conservative and you're…not.'

His features—briefly—glowered before he resumed an expression of non-concern. His control was impressive.

'In addition, your father—'

'My father is none of your business,' he bit out crisply, surprising her with his vehemence. So those wounds still smarted, then? Despite the passage of twelve years, it seemed

Luca hadn't recovered from the scandal that befell his father—his whole family—and the part he'd played in it.

'Actually, that's not exactly true.'

Luca's eyes narrowed. 'Ah. I see. Is this another debt of his? Money owed from him to you?' He frowned. 'But you are too young, so perhaps it is a debt to someone else, someone you love?'

Olivia's heart thumped. Someone she loved? Was there any such person? Sienna, of course, she thought of her younger sister with an ache in the region of her heart. But beyond Sienna, Olivia was alone in the world. There was no one else she loved. Her mother, she pitied, and felt a great deal of duty to care for, but loved? It was far too complicated to be described in that way, and impossible to express in such simplistic terms.

'It's not like that.'

Luca's nostrils flared. 'Then why do you not get to the point and tell me what it *is*, rather than what it is not?'

'I'm trying,' she promised from between clenched lips. 'But you're kind of intimidating, you know?'

Her honesty had surprised him. He took a step backwards, tilted his face away, drew in a deep enough breath to make his chest shift visibly, then expelled it slowly, before turning back to face her.

'I cannot help being who I am.'

'I know. But, just—bear with me. This isn't easy.'

He crossed his arms over his chest—hardly painting a picture of calm acceptance. She bit down on her lower lip then stopped when his eyes dropped to the gesture.

'Perhaps we should start with my father, not yours. I imagine you've heard of him. Thomas Thornton-Rose?'

Luca's demeanour shifted, his features changing, as he disappeared back in time. 'He was a friend to my father. During the trial, he supported him. There were not many who did.'

'They were very close friends,' Olivia agreed with a

murmur, wondering then if he knew about the will. There was no recognition in his features beyond that which was perfectly appropriate to an acquaintance of his father.

'He passed away shortly after my father went to prison. I remember reading a headline.'

'Yes.' Olivia blinked quickly, focusing on the Castel Sant'Angelo, a short distance away, glowing gold against the inky sky. 'It was very sudden.' Her brows knitted together. 'He hadn't been ill or anything. None of us expected—' She swallowed, ignoring the lump in her throat.

'I'm sorry.'

She brushed aside his condolences. 'That's not necessary.'

Her cool response had him arching a thick, dark brow. Olivia didn't notice.

'Shortly after he died, the terms of his will came to light. You would know that we're part of the British aristocracy, with much land and money held up in various investments?'

He lifted his shoulders in an indolent shrug. 'I do not know much more than we have already discussed. Should I?'

Another maniacal laugh erupted from her chest. He didn't know anything about this, and he didn't know anything about her? Panic was swallowing her whole. She'd counted on a degree of insight, but that had been foolish. After all, his father had been in prison a long time. She doubted they had regular tête-à-tête regarding thcir lives.

She would need to start from scratch. Careful to keep the anxiety from her voice, she began slowly. 'When my father died, it was discovered that his estate was carved up in a particularly unusual—' *cruel*, she mentally substituted '—way. My mother was to inherit nothing, and my sister and I would only inherit if we met very specific circumstances, by the time we turn twenty-five.'

His features gave nothing away. 'And what circumstances are these?'

Do it. Stop freaking out. He'll say no, and you can

go home again. And do what? Kick your mother out of the family home? Hand the keys over to horrid second cousin, Timothy?

'Well, it's very clear. You see, my father was very…' she searched for a word that was more socially acceptable than 'misogynistic' '…old-fashioned.'

He dipped his head forward. 'And this is a problem?'

She ignored his interjection. He'd understand, soon enough.

'He never believed women to be capable of managing their own financial affairs.' She couldn't look at Luca as she spoke, and so didn't see the expression of disgust that briefly marred his handsome features. And with good reason—since rebuilding his family empire, Luca had prided himself on employing a diverse workforce. His executive team was made up of more women than men. It had never occurred to him to discriminate based on gender.

'When my parents married, my mother signed over her life savings to him—she'd been an actress, quite successful here in Italy, and had earned well. But she was very young—only just twenty, whereas he was nineteen years older. She loved him.' Olivia's voice curled with a hint of disdain at the very idea of love, and Luca, who was an expert in nuance, responded to the subtle inflection by leaning infinitesimally closer. 'She trusted him.' It was impossible to flatten the emotion from her tone, but she didn't convey the depths of her anger—how her father had abused that trust, because young Angelica had made one mistake, had a silly youthful indiscretion, and for that she'd been punished every day for the rest of her life, no matter how hard she tried to fix things, no matter how often she apologised. Olivia turned to face him, her clear, blue eyes spiking through his black. 'My father managed everything, so that when he died, she had no idea how their affairs were arranged. She couldn't have known that he'd manipulated the estate to curtail everything away from her.'

'What reason could your father have had for doing this?'

His incredulity touched something in the pit of her stomach.

'He was angry with her,' she mouthed, clearing her throat, the barbarism of her father's final act something that had stung her for years. Olivia waved a hand through the air. 'It was ancient history by the time he died, a silly mistake my mother made, many years earlier. Clearly nothing can justify his decision.'

Luca compressed his lips, and her eyes fell to them, so something white hot radiated from low down in her abdomen, spreading through her body with fierce urgency, stealing her breath and weakening her knees. She wrenched her gaze away, unable to make sense of the emotions that were rioting through her. The truth was, the unmistakable rush of desire she felt for him made her want to turn tail and run, to hide from the things she was experiencing. Olivia considered herself to be an expert at hiding her feelings, but she was also used to her feelings making much more sense.

'He was never going to leave any part of the family fortune to our mother, nor to me and Sienna.'

'Nothing about that makes sense. Does he have other children? From an earlier relationship?'

'No.' An anguished smile tormented her beautiful face. 'If only it were that simple. There's only us. And in order to know that the money would be in safe hands, he had his will drafted to specify that Sienna and I must marry, by our twenty-fifth birthdays. Only then will our portion of inheritance become legally ours. Only then could he trust "his money" would be in safe hands.'

'And your mother?'

'She was granted a very small stipend. But it's been lessening every year and stops completely when we turn twenty-five. My birthday is next month.'

She caught the coarse swear word he issued from between clenched teeth. 'With respect, your father sounds like a jackass.'

Her eyes flew wide, and amusement bubbled through her. Were the situation not so very dire, she might have given into it and laughed, or even leaned forward and pressed her hand to his chest, to share the moment of agreement, but worry still dragged at her every breath.

'He was…very set in his ways,' she said, puzzling at the deep sense of loyalty that still ran through her. Even after all he'd done, after the nightmare he'd made all their lives, she felt driven to defend him.

Luca made a sound that suggested her description barely scratched the surface.

'I wouldn't be here if I weren't completely desperate.' Her voice snagged a little and she angled her face away, wondering why she was finding it so difficult to hold onto her usual reserve. 'When my father died, I was only twelve. I had no control of our finances, no insight into what my mother was spending. She continued to rack up enormous debts, maxing out all the credit cards she had, as well as a hefty line of credit set against the house. By the time I was old enough to see what was going on, things were dire. I have tried, Luca. I have tried to fix things, but there is never enough money to make even a dint in the debt. I have to work jobs close to home, and that limits my options, plus I'm not qualified for anything.' She shook her head, surprised at how much she was confessing to him. It was as though, having started, she couldn't put a lid on her feelings.

Drawing in a deep breath, Olivia tried again. 'We have lived on the breadline for years. I have scrimped and saved and done everything I can to get by, but it's no use. If it were just me, I would walk out of Hughenwood House and never look back. But I can't leave my mother saddled with hundreds of thousands of pounds in debt. I can't let my father do this to Mum and Sienna.' Not on top of everything else he'd already done. 'I won't let him do this to us.' The words were laced with a quiet, determined vehemence, but it was clear that they came from the very depths of her being.

'As I said, your father sounds like a jackass.' A hint of sympathy softened the words, surprising her and bringing an ache to her throat. 'But I cannot see why you have sought me out to tell me all this, unless you think my father has some control over the will?' He scanned her face, and she had the strangest sensation he was pulling her apart, piece by piece. 'If that is the case, I must disappoint you. I have no sway with my father. You would be better to approach him directly, believe me.'

'No, no, that's not it.' She fluttered a hand through the air then brought it to the bridge of her nose, pinching it between forefinger and thumb. 'If I don't get married soon, per the will, then the inheritance defaults to my second cousin. It's not just the money, but our *home*. Our family home.' To Olivia's chagrin, her voice cracked, and she tilted her chin defiantly, angered by the weak emotional display, and even more so by the fact the house still meant so much to her, despite the unhappiness they'd experienced within its walls. 'It's the only home my mother has, and it would kill her to have to leave.'

He crossed his arms over his chest. 'I'm not a matchmaker, *cara*. Besides, I find it hard to believe you would have any difficulty finding a man willing to play the part of your groom.'

As he offered the compliment, his eyes slid lower, to the outline of her breasts, barely revealed by the boxy linen shirt she wore. Despite that, heat simmered in her veins and, to her shame, her nipples puckered against the fabric of her bra, straining—but for what? Her eyes flew to his hands and she knew what she wanted, needed. For him to touch her. Intimately. All over.

She swallowed a groan and looked away, using every ounce of her determination to maintain a frigid expression.

'It cannot be *any* man.' Her voice took on a wooden quality. 'My father was explicit about that too.'

Silence hummed and crackled between them, anticipation stretching her nerves to breaking point. Did he know what was coming? She risked a glance at him but was none the wiser; she couldn't read what he was thinking.

'I have to marry *you*, Luca. No one else. You.'

CHAPTER TWO

IT WAS OBVIOUS just by looking at Luca that he was a man who prized his control and strength, but in that moment Olivia could have blown him over with a feather. It was, quite clearly, the last thing he'd expected her to say.

'You're saying—'

'That I need to marry you,' she confirmed, forcing herself to meet his eyes even when something sparked between them that set her blood racing at a million miles an hour. 'And that marrying me could be very good for you, too.'

'This makes no sense.'

'I know.' She bit down on her lip. 'I was really hoping you'd know about this whole thing.'

'My father and I are not exactly on speaking terms.'

She pulled a face, sympathy flooding her. But then, she knew more than enough about difficult family relationships.

'But they made the agreement so long ago. I just presumed, over the years…'

'It was never discussed with me.'

'Me either,' she promised. 'The first I heard about it was when the solicitors appeared at Hughenwood, grim-faced and stern.'

'How did you learn about the bank I am buying?'

'Trying to buy,' she corrected valiantly, because his desire to acquire the bank, and their determined rebuffing of his offers, was at the heart of her inducement. 'I read about it online. Why?'

'So you researched me, prior to coming here tonight?'

'Given that I came here intending to propose marriage to a man I'd never met, naturally I did some preparation.'

A curl of derision shifted the shape of his mouth. 'Then perhaps you also read that I have already been married once. It was, in every way, an unmitigated disaster. I have no intention of ever—' he leaned closer, so close that if she pushed up onto the tips of her toes, she could kiss him '—marrying again. *Capisce?*'

'This wouldn't be a normal marriage,' she said quietly, glad that years of living in the war zone that was her parents' relationship had left her with nerves of steel—or the appearance of them, at least. 'I don't want a husband any more than you want a wife.'

'I'm sorry, I thought you just asked me to marry you?'

'Yes,' she responded quickly. 'For the sake of satisfying a clause in my father's will. But our marriage would be a sham—nothing more than our names on a piece of paper.'

He stared down at her, his features inscrutable, so she had no idea what he was thinking. With a sense she was losing her argument, she clutched for the only straw she held in her possession. 'My family's name is well respected. Marriage to anyone would increase your chances with the bank's uber conservative board—but marriage to a Thornton-Rose, in particular, would improve your standing.' She had made her peace with this offer many weeks ago, but as she said it now, as she heard herself actually trading on her father's hated, hated surname, she wanted the world to open up and swallow her whole.

But freedom would be worth it. If she could just get him to agree, the money would be hers and she could finally fix everything her father broke—her mother would finally have some security and stability. And, most importantly, Olivia's beloved younger sister Sienna would be saved from having to make her own arcane match to inherit any part of the fortune—they simply wouldn't need the money.

'And you are suggesting I could use your ancient name to curry favour with a group of prejudiced snobs? That this is how I operate in business?' His sneer of derision warmed her to the centre of her being. She couldn't have said why, but his immediate rejection of that idea was a relief. 'I do not need your father's name to succeed, *bella*, just as I have never needed my own father's name.'

Admiration expanded inside her. He was right—everything he'd achieved had been off his own back. And yet, from what she'd read online, he wanted the bank more than anything else—and she was sure their marriage would help him achieve it. She narrowed her gaze, focusing on that salient detail. 'You want to buy the Azzuri Bank, and I believe our marriage would make that easier.'

'I don't do things the easy way.'

Her heart skipped a beat and she realised, all at once, that this wasn't going to be enough. She didn't hold enough of an incentive for Luca to agree to this. Why had she even allowed herself a glimmer of hope?

'Well, that's a lovely privilege to have.'

'Privilege,' he repeated with disbelief.

'Oh, yes, privilege.' She turned away from him, stalking back to the railing and staring out at the river. It had seen so much over the millennia, so many tragedies and heartbreaks, so much joy and delight. Her own emotions spilled towards it, adding to the multitude of experience. 'What must it be like to be able to turn down offers of help?'

'You said it yourself, you come from a very wealthy family. Do you really think you have any right to complain to me about privilege?'

'Wealthy, in theory, yes,' she responded, turning to look at him over her shoulder, only to realise he'd moved to stand right beside her and was staring at her in a way that made her feel as though she was completely naked—not in a physical sense, but right down to her soul. 'But not privileged. And not free. Do you have any idea—?' She bit back the words, shaking her head.

'Finish what you were going to say.'

'Why? There's no point, is there?' Her shimmering blue eyes caught his, scanning them, hunting them for answers. 'You've already made your decision.'

'My first decision, yes,' he agreed. 'I want no part of any marriage.' Was she imagining the slight hesitation to his voice? Yes. Of course she was. Men like Luca Giovanardi didn't hesitate about anything.

'Then I'll go,' she whispered, accepting her fate, numb to the future that lay before her.

'Not before you have explained some more,' he insisted, with a firmness to his tone that made it almost impossible to argue.

But Olivia was used to being dictated to, and had learned how to harden herself to another's commands. 'Is there any point if you've made up your mind?'

'We won't know unless you try.'

Hope beat wings inside her chest, but she refused to let it carry her away. He was offering her a chance, but it was very slim. She searched for words yet her brain refused to cooperate. She groaned, turning back to the river.

'Start with this,' he suggested, the gentleness of his voice making her stomach churn. She hadn't expected anything like that, from him. 'How exactly did you imagine this marriage would work?'

It was something—a way in. But was he simply trying to make her understand how stupid the whole idea had been? She sucked in a deep breath and forced her nerves to slow down.

'Well.' She spoke slowly. 'I thought a businesslike agreement would be best for the both of us.'

His brows shot up. 'A businesslike marriage? Isn't that a contradiction in terms?'

'Not for people like you and me?'

'And what exactly are we like, *bella*?'

'Please, don't call me that. My name is Olivia.'

He nodded, brushing aside her request.

'Both fundamentally opposed to marriage.' She returned to her original train of thought. 'You don't want a wife, and I don't want a husband. Therefore, we can dictate the terms of our marriage, making sure they suit us completely.'

'And what terms would you suggest?'

Something like danger prickled along her skin. Desires she had no business feeling, let alone voicing, spliced her in half. She did everything she could to ignore them. After all, desire was at the root of her mother's downfall. Love. Allowing herself to be swept up in a man's promises, a man's charisma, blinding her to reality, had led to Olivia's mother's life of misery—Olivia never intended to be so foolish.

'That's the beauty of what I'm offering,' she said quietly, trying to pick up the threads of the speech she'd prepared on the flight over. 'This would be a marriage in name only. I'd live in England, you'd live in Italy, and when a suitable amount of time had passed, we would quietly, simply file for divorce. After our wedding day, we'd never have to see one another again.'

He studied her in a way that sent little barbs running through her body. His eyes seemed to see everything, to perceive everything, so years of practice hiding her emotion no longer seemed to serve her. She struggled to maintain a mask of composure in the face of his obvious interest.

'I can see you've thought this through, but you've miscalculated. The promise of your name is not enough to induce me into marriage, with you, or anyone.'

She swept her eyes shut, failure inevitable now. 'I see.'

'You said that if you don't inherit, your portion of the family fortune goes to a cousin. Do you know this person?'

She shuddered involuntarily. 'Yes.'

'Is he the kind of person who would act in self-interest, to secure this inheritance?'

She bit into her lower lip. 'He would only stand to inherit *if* you and I don't get married.'

'Or...' he let the word hang between them '...if he challenged the validity of our marriage.'

She blinked up at him. 'But—could he do that?'

'It is my experience that people are capable of all sorts of things, when large sums of money are involved.'

She crossed her arms over her chest, then immediately wished she hadn't when his eyes lowered to the swell of roundness there. Anticipation ran like little waves across her skin. 'So what do you suggest?'

'I do not intend to make a suggestion, Olivia. Only to point out that the neat and tidy marriage you've imagined would never have worked.'

Of course, he was right. She should have seen all the angles. They were talking about a multimillion-pound inheritance. If they were going to fake a marriage, it had to be plausible. 'Then, what if we were to marry—' she thought quickly '—and live together, here in Rome, but only as housemates. Separate bedrooms, separate lives.'

His lips curled with a hint of derision. 'I cannot see what is in that for me.'

'Azzuri Bank—'

'I will acquire the bank, Olivia, on my own terms. Of that, I have no doubt.'

A shiver ran the length of her spine. His determination was borderline ruthless—she didn't doubt he'd succeed, and now felt a degree of foolishness for ever thinking a man like Luca Giovanardi could be tempted by something as flimsy as having her as a wife.

'If you want to tempt me to agree to this, you must think of something to offer beyond the bank.' A test? He was staring at her as if weighting her reaction.

Her cheeks went from paper white to rosy pink within

a second. 'Are you saying you would want our marriage to be—intimate? Because I have to tell you, I have no interest in becoming another notch on your very well-studded bedpost.'

A cynical smile changed his face completely. The smile whispered things into her soul. *Liar.* 'I'm not so desperate that I need to blackmail women into my bed.'

'No, of course not,' she dismissed quietly, wishing they were more like equals when it came to relationships. 'You probably have a line snaked around the block.'

His obsidian eyes narrowed. 'I was not referring to sex.'

'Then what did you mean?'

He scanned her face, and she wondered if he was going to dwell on the suggestion of a physical relationship. 'If we were to marry, there would be no advantage to either of us in maintaining separate lives, under the same roof. News of our marriage would inevitably break in the press, and then, public scrutiny would follow. A housekeeper could be bribed to provide details of our living arrangements. These things happen.'

'I hadn't thought of that,' she admitted.

'We would need to create the fiction of a passionate, whirlwind romance, for as long as it took to satisfy the terms of the will—I would imagine thirty days would be sufficient.' He lifted his shoulders in a charismatic, indolent shrug. 'To that end, we would need to share a bed.'

Her lips parted to form a perfect 'o'. How she wished she had more experience with men in that moment! 'Surely that's not necessary.'

'I have staff.'

'Couldn't they take a holiday for the duration of our marriage? A month isn't very long.' Except when you were sharing a bed with a man like this!

His lips twisted into a cynical smile. 'Don't worry, *cara*. I have no interest in sex becoming a part of our marriage. It would be purely for show.'

She stared at him, aghast. She wanted to demur, to fight him on this point, but something was shifting between them, and she no longer felt that failure was imminent. If anything, he was positioning himself to accept. She tilted her head, not quite a nod, but at least not a denial either.

'It is a big bed. You'll cope.'

She swallowed, her throat visibly knotting, then jerked her head once more, this time in agreement.

'Are you saying you'll agree to do this?'

He considered her for several long moments. Could he hear the rushing of her heart over the sound of the nearby party? Surely. It beat hard and fast, a fast-paced drum, hard against her ribs. He turned away from her abruptly, staring out at the river, his face in profile like something crafted from stone. She stared at him against her will, unable to draw her eyes away. He was captivating and magnetic, completely overpowering. It was not hard to understand how he had made such a success of himself and his life.

'There is something personal about me you would not have discovered on the Internet.'

She frowned, wondering at his tone, the darkness to his voice.

'My *nonna* is ill.'

The words were spoken quietly and yet they fell between them like rock boulders.

Olivia leaned closer, as if that might help her understand better.

'Not ill.' He turned to face her, the strength in his gaze sending a pulse radiating through her. 'She is dying.'

'I'm sorry to hear that.' Olivia's voice was gentle, sincere. 'Are you close?'

A grimace tightened his lips. 'Yes.' He paused, seeming to weigh his words. 'She has been my biggest support. I owe her a lot.'

'I'm sure she supported you out of love. Seeing you

make such a success of yourself is undoubtedly all she wants from you.'

His smile showed a hint of affection. 'She is still an Italian *nonna*, and cannot help meddling. She has expressed, on many occasions, a desire for me to marry.' The words wrapped around Olivia, steadier than steel. 'She worries about me.'

'Worries about *you*?' Olivia couldn't help remarking, the very idea of this man being the object of anyone's concern almost laughable.

He didn't look at her, nor did he respond.

'If we were to create the impression of a passionate, whirlwind love affair, it might go some of the way to easing her concerns.'

Olivia's eyes flared wide. 'You want to lie to her?'

'We would be legally married,' he pointed out. 'That is not a lie.'

'But a love affair,' she said with a soft shake of her head. 'No one would believe it.'

His eyes narrowed as he stared at her. 'They must. This marriage must convince your cousin, your father's probate solicitors and my grandmother. It must convince the world.'

Something twisted inside her. Surprise. Hope. It wasn't exactly an agreement, but, for a moment, he sounded as though he was seriously contemplating this. She might actually be getting somewhere—and that knowledge both excited and terrified her.

'If your grandmother wants you to get married, why haven't you done so before now?'

'Marriage is not a mistake I intend to make twice. Even for her.'

'But we're discussing marriage now.'

'A very different kind of marriage,' he pointed out. 'One with clear-cut rules and boundaries. One that precludes, by design, any emotion whatsoever.'

'Are you saying you'll agree to this?'

He stared at her long and hard, so long, so hard, that any pretence she might have liked to maintain that she felt nothing for him flew out of her soul and swam away on the crest of the Tiber. It was all physical—surely she could control that?

'I would have conditions of my own.'

Her heart skipped a beat. 'I see. Such as?'

He turned to face her now, looking just as he had the first moment they'd met, but with a hint of grief still stirring in the depths of his eyes, so Olivia was forced to re-evaluate her appraisal of him as a cold, ruthless tycoon. He clearly had a heart, and a large part of it, she suspected, belonged to his *nonna*. 'My grandmother would need to believe this is real.' He pressed a thumb to his middle finger on the opposing hand, counting off a list. 'There would need to be discretion and respect. No affairs for either of us.'

'Easier for me than you, I suspect,' she said, before she could stop herself. After all, the man's prowess as a bachelor was a well-established fact.

He let the barb sail by.

'This would be a marriage of practicality,' he continued with firm indifference, tapping another finger, not taking his eyes off her face. 'You'd get what you want, and I'd get what I want.' For a moment, his gaze dropped to her lips. 'This would not be a genuine relationship. We would not become friends. We would not have sex.'

A shiver ran down her spine as images of that sprang to mind before she could stop them, and, for the first time in her life, Olivia experienced a headlong rush of desire.

She kept her expression neutral with great effort. 'I'm not interested in your friendship. Or in having sex with you.'

He didn't smile. He didn't nod. He simply stared at her as though she were a mathematical equation he could understand, if only he looked long and hard enough.

'And what about love?'

It jolted her straight. She shook her head fiercely. 'No.'

His dark eyes narrowed speculatively.

'Absolutely not,' she rushed to reassure him, suppressing a shudder of sheer panic. It wasn't him, but the idea of submitting herself to any man, as her mother had her father, that sent arrows of terror down her spine. She wanted independence—true independence—and this she wouldn't find by falling in love.

'I'm not kidding. I will not run the risk of you fantasising about a relationship with me. It is something I never risk when I sleep with a woman.'

'But we won't be sleeping together.'

'No, we'll be married. That has the potential to be far more dangerous. You might start to think—'

'Believe me, I won't. If it weren't for this damned will, I'd never, ever say those vows. And the happiest day of my life will be when the ink dries on our divorce. Okay?'

'I'm curious,' he said slowly, so close the words breathed across her temple and she caught a hint of his masculine cologne. Goosebumps lifted on her skin.

'You are a beautiful, young woman. What happened to make you so opposed to marriage?'

'You don't hold the monopoly on disastrous marriages.'

'You've been married before?'

'No—I—didn't mean mine. My parents—' She shook her head, cleared her thoughts, and focused a steady, steel-like gaze on him. 'I was born with a brain,' she said after a beat. 'I don't see any reason to tie myself to a man. At least, not for real.'

'And do you promise me you will not change your mind? At no point in our marriage will you want more than I am willing to offer today?'

She tilted her face to his. 'Are you accepting my proposal?'

'Can you assure me that we can keep this businesslike?' he said thoughtfully.

'Absolutely.'

He considered that for several moments, and Olivia's pulse went into overdrive. So much hung in the balance for her. There was so much this marriage would achieve—not least, providing for her mother, securing their family home, and protecting Sienna. And yet it would come at a great personal cost for Olivia. To give into her father's misogynistic, sexist demands from beyond the grave rushed her skin like a rash, and anger speared her, despite the fact she'd made her peace with the necessity of this long ago.

'Fine.' He nodded once. 'Then we will marry.'

A shiver ran down her spine, even when he was giving her everything she'd wanted. Even when his acceptance was the first step on her pathway towards liberation. She forced her mouth into a smile, made her eyes hold his even when sparks of electricity seemed to be flying from Luca towards her, superheating her veins.

'Excellent,' she murmured, even when she had the strangest sense, for no reason she could grasp, that she was stepping right off the deep end with no idea how to swim.

After his divorce, Luca Giovanardi had destroyed almost every single piece of evidence that he had ever been married. There had been catharsis in that. He was only young—a boy, in many ways—and so the act of throwing his wedding back into the ruins of the Coliseum had felt immeasurably important, as though he were reclaiming a piece of himself. He had destroyed every photograph they'd had printed, and wiped almost all of them from his digital storage. He hadn't wanted to remember Jayne. He hadn't ever wanted to think of her again. Not of how much he'd loved her, nor how happy he'd thought they were. He didn't want to think about the way his world had come storming down around his ears and then she'd turned her back on him, leaving him for one of his most despised business rivals, a man who had swept in and triumphed as Luca's father's empire had come crumbling down around them.

Luca had learned two lessons that day—never to believe in the fantasy of love, and never to trust a woman.

So what the hell had he just agreed to?

He gripped his glass of whisky, eyes focused straight ahead, without seeing the view. Olivia Thornton-Rose filled his mind. *'I wouldn't be here if I weren't completely desperate.'*

Besides, there was no danger here. No risk. This was nothing like the emotional suicide he'd committed the day he'd agreed to share his life with Jayne. This was sensible. Safe. And short-term.

More importantly, it met both their needs. For months, he'd been wishing he could do something to calm his grandmother, to ease her as she approached the end of her life. Her repeated entreaties for him to find that 'one someone special', to 'give love another chance', were offered kindly from her vantage point of having had a long and very happy marriage, but marriage was not even remotely on Luca's to-do list.

Until now.

He reached for his phone and dialled his grandmother's number before he could change his mind. 'Nonna?' He took a drink of Macallan. 'There's something I want to tell you.'

CHAPTER THREE

It was like being in a dream, a dream from which she couldn't wake. But wasn't it better than the nightmare that had been life before this? At least some relief was on the horizon.

It had, however, been a mistake not to see him again before the ceremony itself. A mistake not to inure herself a little to the sight of Luca Giovanardi, dressed to the nines, in a black tuxedo with a grey tie, shiny black shoes, and hair slicked back from his face. She stood beside him in the unbelievably extravagant dress she'd been talked into buying at Harrods, after Luca's assistant had called to explain that he'd organised an appointment with the bridal team there. She was aware of his every breath, the husky tone to his voice, the magnetism of the man, and felt as if she wanted to turn tail and bolt for the door.

A wedding 'in name only' had seemed like a simple idea at the time, but, now that they'd come to the actual commitment, the reality of what they were doing bore down on her like a ton of cement. She glanced across at Luca, his sombre profile making her breath snatch in her throat, so she looked away again, panic drumming through her. She wished, more than anything, for Sienna to be with her. It would have meant the world to be able to reach out and hold her sister's hand, to see her smiling, kind eyes and know that this wasn't sheer madness. Only Sienna would *never* have approved. She wouldn't have smiled from the sidelines as Olivia committed herself to this farce—she'd have fought tooth and nail to get her to stop. Even if that meant losing their house. Even if that meant letting their father punish their mother one last, cruel, lasting time.

The priest said something, and Luca turned to face Olivia, dragging her back to this moment, in which it was just the two of them, and the lie they were weaving. He spoke his vows first, in English in deference to her, before slipping an enormous diamond ring onto her finger. The simple contact sent a thousand little lightning bolts through her; standing was almost impossible.

When it was Olivia's turn to say the vows, the priest spoke slowly, his accent thick, and Olivia stumbled on a few words. Nerves were playing havoc with her focus. She offered the priest an apologetic glance, before retrieving a simple gold band and pressing it to Luca's finger. Just like before, when he'd placed her ring on her finger, Olivia felt as though a marching band had started to run rampant through her veins. She pulled her hand away quickly, as though she'd been electrocuted, her eyes sliding to Luca's *nonna* without her intent. The happiness there was blatantly obvious—she had obviously bought the lie, hook, line and sinker. Olivia looked away again immediately, right into Luca's enormous dark eyes, their watchful intensity making her heart thunder.

'And that is it,' the priest said with a clap that completely undid the sombre nature of the ceremony. 'You may now kiss your bride.' He gestured to Olivia, and Olivia's heart seemed to grind to a halt. Oh, crap. How had she forgotten about this part?

Was it too late to back out? She stared at the priest with a sinking feeling, aware of Luca's *nonna*'s watchful gaze, then looked back up at the man who was now her husband.

Oh, God, oh, God, oh, God.

In name only. Except for right now.

Luca moved closer, one hand coming to rest on her hip, the other capturing her cheek, holding her face steady. His thumb padded over the flesh just beside her lip, low on her cheek, and goosebumps spread over her arms.

She wanted to tell him she couldn't do this, that she'd never even been kissed before, that too many people were watching, that she had no idea what she was doing, but then he was dropping his head, his mouth seeking hers as though it were the most natural thing in the world, and all she could do was surrender to the necessity of this. And the wonder.

Luca swore internally. His body had ignited, a flame of passion bursting through him the second their lips met. What had started as a perfunctory ceremonial requirement had blown way out of his control the second her lips parted beneath his and she made that husky little moan, pushing the sound deep into his throat. Screw ceremony. The hand that was on her hip slid around to her back, drawing her body hard against his, angling her slightly for privacy from his grandmother—not that he was capable of that degree of rational thought. Instincts had taken over completely. His mouth moved, deepening the kiss, his tongue flicking hers, and with every soft little moan she made he felt his control snapping, so within seconds he was fantasising about stripping the damned dress away and making love to her—not slowly and languidly, either, but hard and fast, as this passion bursting between them demanded.

Hell. This was a nightmare.

They had a deal, and at no point was he supposed to be attracted to his wife, of all people. At no point were they supposed to want each other like this. He wouldn't let this happen. Any other woman, fine. But not with his bride.

He wrenched his mouth from hers, and Olivia had to bite down on her lower lip to stop from crying out at the sudden withdrawal. Her eyes were heavy, drugged by desire, so that it took several seconds before she remembered where they were, and who they were surrounded by.

Mortification doused her sensual need. It had only been a kiss—albeit a passionate one—but in Olivia's innocent mind, they'd just done the first act of a live porno for Luca's grandmother and priest.

He was watching her in that intense way of his, eyes hooded and unreadable, his own face notably *normal*, not flushed and passion-filled, as she was sure hers must be. Of *course* he looked like normal. This was Luca Giovanardi. The man literally went through women as most men did underwear. Or bottles of milk, at least. She stifled a moan and blanked her face of emotions—but too late, she feared. He must have seen how affected she was by the kiss. He must know how completely he took her breath away. How *easily.*

She sucked in a deep breath, and another. *It's okay. It's over now. You never need to kiss him or touch him ever again.* The thought was supposed to be reassuring, but her heart did a strange, twisty reaction, painful and impossible to ignore.

The next moment, his hand reached down and linked with hers, fingers intertwined, so she jerked her gaze back to his face. He smiled at her, but the smile got nowhere near his eyes.

'Come and meet my grandmother. *Cara.*' He added the term of endearment as an afterthought. It brought a rush of warmth to her. She ignored it. This was all for show, for his grandmother's benefit. That was part of their deal, and, given what he was sacrificing for her, he deserved her to play along to the best of her ability.

'Yes, of course.' Her voice sounded, blessedly, normal.

Pietra Giovanardi was past her eightieth birthday but she stood straight and proud, silver hair pulled over one shoulder, slender body wrapped in couture and diamonds, yet somehow she managed to look approachable and down to earth. Her lips were quick to smile, her face well lined by time, by life, and her eyes sparkled as the couple approached. There was no hint of the terminal illness Luca had mentioned, beyond a body that was painfully slim.

'Ahh, Luca, Luca, Luca, this is the happiest day of *my* life,' she exclaimed, lifting a shaking hand and patting her grandson's cheek affectionately, tears dampening her eyes as she turned to look at Olivia. She smiled brightly, emulating a happy bride. That was, after all, their deal.

'Signora Giovanardi,' Olivia murmured, but the older woman batted a hand through the air then drew Olivia into a warm hug, enveloping her in a softly floral fragrance at the same time she dislodged her hand from Luca's, leaving a cool feeling of absence that Olivia wished she hadn't noticed. The older woman was painfully thin, her bones barely covered by fine, papery skin. Sympathy spread like wildfire through Olivia at this obvious indication of her illness.

'You must call me Pietra,' she insisted. 'Or Nonna.'

'Pietra,' Olivia rushed, softening her haste with a softer smile. 'It's a pleasure to meet you.'

'Ah, no, the pleasure is mine. I thought this would never happen, after...' Pietra's voice briefly stalled but she covered quickly, moving on. She hadn't needed to finish anyway; Olivia knew what the older woman had been going to say. After his first marriage. For the first time since they'd agreed to this sham, she wondered about his past, his ex, and why the marriage had left him so badly scarred. But Nonna was moving on, steering the conversation forward. 'And here he's been keeping you a secret all this time.' Pietra made a tsking sound. 'But it is no business of mine. I won't ask the details. I'm just glad it has come to this. Now, shall we have some Prosecco?'

Olivia blinked up at Luca, expecting him to demur—the sooner they concluded their 'wedding', the sooner they could be free of the need to act like a pair of besotted newly-weds, and the sooner their thirty days of captivity could start.

'*Sì*, I have arranged it.'

Olivia's eyes widened, but she couldn't argue with him, obviously.

'You would be welcome to stay at Villa Tramonto tonight, as well,' Pietra offered as they walked from the church.

'My grandmother's villa,' Luca explained to Olivia. 'Nestled above Positano. You would love it, *cara*.' He was so good at this! With effortless ease, he made it seem as though they shared a genuine connection. His voice was soft, romantic, so her skin pricked with goosebumps she was sure his dark eyes observed, before he turned to Pietra. 'Another time. It is our wedding night, after all.'

Heat bloomed inside Olivia at the implication of his words—at how they would be spending tonight if they were anything approaching a real couple. But they weren't, this was just make-believe. Soon they'd be alone again, and she'd be able to put some space between herself and this irresistibly charismatic man.

'Of course, of course. Will you return to Rome?'

'We will honeymoon in Venice for the weekend, actually.'

Olivia stopped walking, and for the briefest moment lost control of the vice-like grip she held on her cool exterior. Luca saw, and moved back to Olivia, putting an arm around her waist and drawing her close, so all she was conscious of was the hardness of his physique, the way her side melded to his perfectly.

'A weekend in Venice?' Pietra wrinkled her nose. 'In my day, honeymoons didn't count unless they lasted three months.'

'In your day, it took a month at least to get anywhere interesting.'

Pietra laughed affectionately. 'This is true.'

Olivia was struck by the natural banter between the two, and, despite the happiness of their mood, a chasm was forming in her chest, impossible to ignore. When she saw their easy affection, it was impossible not to dwell on how different her own upbringing had been, how tense and fraught with emotional complications. Only with Sienna could she be herself.

The afternoon light was blinding as they stepped out into the square, and a flock of pigeons flew past them, low to the ground, looking for treats left by the lunchtime crowd.

'Here?' Pietra gestured to a restaurant with tables and chairs lined up on the footpath, facing the square.

Luca turned to Olivia, surprising her with his consultation. 'Yes. I reserved a table. Are you happy to share a drink with Pietra before we leave, *mi amore*?'

My love. Her heart skittled. He was very, very good at this. What was he like in genuine relationships? she wondered as she nodded and they began to make their way to the venue. Undoubtedly, his affection shone as hot and bright as the sun, but, if the gossip blogs were to be believed, his attention wandered faster than you could say supernova.

Her gown was a sleek white silk, ruffled across one shoulder, and as she entered the restaurant the diners paused and then clapped, their excitement at seeing a couple on their wedding day, on the celebration of the great Italian tradition of love, something they couldn't contain. Luca lifted a hand in acknowledgement, and drew Olivia closer, pressing a kiss to the crown of her blonde hair. *It's all for show.*

But that didn't matter. Knowing it was fake didn't stop the very real chain reaction spreading through her—heat seemed to bloom from the middle of her soul, so she was warm and almost dizzy, and desire flickered through her, lazily at first, and then, as he pulled away, more urgently, so she wanted to lean close and kiss him properly, as they had in the church, but this time with no one watching.

He held out a chair for Pietra first, then another. *'Cara.'* He gestured towards it. She swallowed hard as she sat down, aware of his proximity, so sparks of lightning ignited when his hands brushed her bare shoulders. He took the seat opposite and their feet brushed beneath the table—an accident, surely.

Pietra was charming, intelligent, well read and politely inquisitive, asking just enough questions of Olivia without seeming as though she were prying, and the questions were all of a reasonably impersonal nature, so Olivia could answer without feeling that she had to speak to the nightmare that her home life had always been. Conversing with Pietra was a welcome distraction, allowing her to almost, but not quite, blot Luca from her mind. Except there was the subtle contact, beneath the table, his feet brushing hers whenever she moved, so wiping him from her consciousness completely was impossible. He sat back, watching the interplay, taking only two sips of his champagne and a forkful of cake, while Olivia enjoyed a full glass and then half of another, as well as her entire slice of cake. She smothered a hiccough as they stood, and Pietra embraced her again.

'You'll come to Tramonto soon? I would love to get to know you better.'

Guilt was now a full-blown stack of TNT in Olivia's belly, ignited and ready to explode in a confession. She clamped her lips together, trying to remember what was at stake, and that Luca's lie to his grandmother was none of her business. It was the only reason he'd agreed to this.

But misleading the beautiful, older woman felt like a noose around Olivia's neck suddenly. *She's dying.* Sadness dragged down Olivia's heart. There was so much vitality in the older woman, it was hard to believe she was so gravely ill.

'We'll come as soon as we are able,' Luca placated. 'Where is Mario?'

'Across the square.'

'We'll walk you to the car.'

'I can walk myself.' She batted the offer away with an affectionate shake of her head. 'I live alone and still he thinks I can't walk twenty paces without his help.'

'She has an army of servants, in fact,' Luca confided as they left the restaurant.

'I'd like to walk with you,' Olivia insisted gently, linking arms with Pietra.

Luca's eyes met hers and her stomach dropped to her feet. They were going to be alone together soon, husband and wife. She looked down at her wedding ring, diamonds sparkling back at her, and her pulse shifted, lifting, slowing, thready and strong at the same time.

Luca opened the rear door to a sleek black car and Pietra gave them both one last hug before slipping inside. An unknown man—the driver, Mario, Olivia presumed—started the engine and pulled into the light afternoon traffic.

Luca turned slowly to face Olivia and it was as though time were standing still. Her heart began to throb; nerves made her fingers tremble.

'Well, Signora Giovanardi,' he said. 'It's done.'

She grimaced. 'Yes.'

'You're not happy?'

'I'm—' She searched for the right words, words that wouldn't make him sound like a heartless bastard. 'Having met your grandmother, I feel pretty bad about lying to her.'

'Even when you saw how happy we made her?'

'But our divorce…'

'It is doubtful she will live to see it.'

Tears stung the backs of Olivia's eyelids, completely surprising her. She was a world-class expert at hiding her feelings. She looked away, shocked at the raw pain his words had evoked.

'And in the meantime, it's worth it to see the joy in her face.'

Olivia pushed aside her misgivings. 'She must have been very worried about the state of your life for you to have gone to these lengths.'

'I only took advantage of an opportunity that was offered,' he reminded Olivia. 'I would never have married a woman simply to fool my grandmother. But when you arrived, offering yourself to me on a silver platter, how could I say no?'

'I wouldn't put it that way,' she responded tautly. But it was too late. The vivid imagery of her sprawled out on a platter just for Luca's enjoyment filled her mind's eye, and her cheeks flushed bright red.

Luca had no idea what had caused her to react so vividly to his words, but it was clear he'd offended her. Anger glowed in her cheeks, and she didn't meet his eyes. It shouldn't have bothered him but, all of a sudden, all Luca wanted was for Olivia to look at him. Not simply to look. To touch. To lift her hand to his chest, as she'd done during their service, to grab his shirt and pull him closer, to part her lips and moan softly into his mouth.

But wanting his wife wasn't part of this deal. It *couldn't* be.

'This way.' He spoke more gruffly than he'd intended, gesturing toward the doors of a building, pressing a button for the elevator then standing a safe distance from his wife. Maybe it was the dress? Unlike their first meeting, when her outfit had offered only vague hints as to her figure, now he could actually *see* her body, her tantalising curves, could see every delectable ounce courtesy of the clinging silk fabric, so that even before their incendiary kiss he'd felt a jolt of need surge through his body.

The elevator doors pinged open, and they stepped inside, without realising that the elevator was incredibly small. He hadn't noticed when he'd travelled down, but being caged in here with a woman he was doing his damnedest to ignore on a physical level, having her so close their bodies were brushing, was the last thing he wanted.

'I thought you said we were going to Venice,' she enquired, but huskily, softly, and when he looked at her face, her eyes were trained on his lips, as though she couldn't look away. Oh, hell.

'We are.' His own voice was gruff in reply, frustration at their situation emerging in the force of his words. They were trapped by the agreement they'd made. Neither of them wanted this to get complicated, but damn it all to hell if he wanted to push her back against the wall and make love to her here and now.

She blinked, but didn't look away. 'Isn't Venice at sea level?' She swallowed, her throat shifting, and his groin strained against his pants. Hell.

'Sinking below it by the minute,' he managed to quip, despite the charged atmosphere.

'Then we'd better hurry.'

'That's my intention.'

'You're being serious?'

'What about?'

'A honeymoon in Venice?' She formed air quotation marks around the word honeymoon.

'Is that a problem?'

'Well, I mean, isn't a honeymoon sort of redundant?' Heat fizzed between her ears.

'Not if we want to convince the world—and particularly your cousin—that our marriage is genuine. I don't think anyone would believe me to be the kind of man to marry and not take my bride away for a time. We will go, take photographs as evidence. It may matter a great deal, if there is a legal challenge to your inheritance.'

Her lips formed a small 'o', because he was right. It was

a small, but likely important, detail, in terms of making their marriage look real.

'Va bene?'

Okay? She blinked up at him, wondering why she was fighting this, why she was dreading the idea of a honeymoon with this man in Venice, but unable to put her finger on it.

The doors pinged open but neither of them moved. It was as though their feet were bolted to the floor, as though there were something about the confines of the lift that required them to remain. Olivia felt as though she were about to move into a different realm, as though the moment she moved, everything would change and be different.

A steady, rhythmic whooshing sound broke through the spell, so they both turned in unison to regard the helicopter, with its rotor blades beginning to spin.

The luxury craft had a high enough body that there was no risk from the blades to either of them, no need to bend down as they approached. 'Are you ready?' he asked, not sure what the question referred to. The small frown on her lips showed she didn't either.

'I think so.'

And despite the fact they'd agreed to a hands-off marriage, it felt like the most natural thing in the world to reach down and take her hand in his, to guide her to the helicopter. The most natural thing in the world to hold her hand as she stepped up, only releasing it when she was seated, and then his own hand seemed to tingle, as if the ghost of her touch remained. Luca had conquered a lot in his thirty-three years, and desiring his wife was just another thing he would need to manage. But the strength of his desire was unexpected. For the first time in his life, Luca felt as though possessing a woman, this woman, was essential to his being. It had never been like this before, even with Jayne, even though he'd loved her. Perhaps, he rationalised as the helicopter lifted up into the sky, it was simply the temptation of forbidden fruit.

Yes, that was all he was dealing with—a simple case of pleasure denied. For a long time Luca had got everything he'd ever wanted in life. Not by accident, but through sheer hard work and grit. Having lost everything once, he'd made sure that would never happen again. As for women, he only had to show a hint of interest before they tumbled into his bed. He had never felt a rush of desire and known he couldn't act on it. Until now.

Understanding himself better, Luca was sure he could ignore the rampant throb of need twisting inside him. He was, after all, Luca Giovanardi, and he'd never failed at a single thing once he put his mind to it…

CHAPTER FOUR

'My assistant booked it,' he explained with a rueful expression on his face, as though this were no big deal. 'I specified the presidential suite, which has multiple bedrooms. She clearly misheard and arranged the honeymoon suite instead.' Both pairs of eyes settled on the enormous king-size bed in the middle of the sumptuous bedroom. Olivia's heart stampeded through her body. Everything since the wedding had taken on a surreal quality, as though with the saying of their vows she'd somehow morphed into someone else entirely.

'I see.'

All she seemed capable of was thinking about kissing Luca. Her lips tingled with the remembered sensations of their wedding kiss, and every second that passed in the same room as him, with neither of them touching, was like a form of torture, a string pulling tighter and tighter until she thought it might snap. But to share a bed? Olivia had never *slept* with anyone in her life. Not in the sexual way, and not in the space-sharing way. It was literally beyond her comprehension to even *imagine* what that would be like.

'I'll sleep on the sofa,' she said with a pragmatic nod. 'I'm shorter than you—by a mile. It makes sense.'

His laugh was dismissive. 'No one need sleep on the sofa, *cara*.' Not just for show, then. The term of endearment rolled off his tongue with practised ease—and that was exactly what it was. Practised. Luca Giovanardi always had a woman in his life, he was simply using the term that came to mind fastest. It wasn't impossible that he'd forgotten her name, she thought with a bitter smile. 'We are going to have to share a bed once we return to Rome. We might as well start practising early.' At her continued scepticism, he lifted his palms placatingly. 'I'm quite capable of sticking to one side, and to making sure my hands do the same.' He turned, taking a step towards her, so their bodies were only separated by an inch. 'I presume you can make the same promise?'

Was he teasing her? 'Of course,' Olivia muttered, heat exploding in her veins. Their eyes met and an electrical current, fierce and obliterating, arced between them. Olivia couldn't look away, but in the periphery of her vision, the enormous, sumptuous bed sat as an invitation, beckoning her—them—to join it.

'Good.' He didn't move. Nor did she. The air around them thickened, holding them still, trapping them, and Olivia couldn't muster an ounce of energy to care.

She badly wished she had more experience with men—but when and how would she have found the opportunity? She dropped her gaze to his lips, wondering how they'd moved so well over her mouth, wondering how he had the skill to evoke such a response in her.

'Olivia.' The word was a gruff command, so she frowned, forcing her eyes to abandon their exploration of his mouth.

'Yes?'

'We agreed to a platonic relationship, but if you continue to stare at my mouth in this fashion, I'm going to want to break that promise.'

'I'm not staring at your mouth,' she denied hotly, forcing her eyes to meet his gaze instead.

'Yes, you are. I am a man of my word, but still a man, nonetheless, with red blood thundering through my veins.

You are looking at my mouth as though you can will it to kiss yours, and you were doing the same thing in the elevator.'

'Was I?' Desire was so strong in her cells it left no room for embarrassment, even though she knew she'd feel it—in spades—later.

'Yes.'

'I'm sorry. I didn't mean—' But the words tapered off, the lie failing, because he'd called her out, accurately. It was exactly what she'd been thinking. A furrow crossed her brow. 'I just didn't expect—'

'No, nor did I.'

Her eyes flared wide, his confession surprising her. 'You didn't?'

'No.'

'When we kissed—'

He nodded.

'I didn't know it could be like that.' She lifted her fingers to her lips, as though she could wipe away the sensation. 'It was a charged moment. Our wedding, in front of a priest, saying our vows. It was probably just those factors that made the kiss seem so intense,' she mumbled. 'Right?'

'What else could it have been?' he asked, with a hint of mockery beneath the words.

She wished she knew. She had nowhere near enough experience to say with certainty.

He moved infinitesimally closer, his body swaying nearer to hers, so her eyes brushed closed as she surrendered to the moment completely. 'If it were not for our deal, I would suggest we test your theory,' he murmured. 'But that would be foolish.'

She hesitated, her eyes locking to his. He was right. Foolish. Stupid. Wrong. And yet… 'Surely, one kiss, on our wedding night, isn't such a big deal?'

His eyes flared and passion exploded between them. 'Are you asking me to kiss you again, Olivia?'

She wasn't capable of answering. Her lips parted and then she nodded, an uneven jerk of her head as she tried to reconcile what she wanted with what they'd agreed.

Luca moved closer, and her body ignited, burning white hot with a need to feel that same spark she'd experienced at their wedding. His fingers laced through her hair, dislodging it from the elegant wedding do she'd had styled, his body cleaved hard to hers before he claimed her mouth. It was only in that first instant that she realised how restrained he'd been in the church. That kiss had been passionate and consuming but nothing like this. Now, his mouth *ravaged* hers, his tongue tormenting, his lips mastering hers and disposing of any doubts, his body's proximity tantalising and insufficient. She wanted to feel him, to know him, to touch him, she wanted so much more than this alone.

The kiss stirred every bone in her body, sensuality she had no idea she possessed and was suddenly desperate to explore. He groaned into her mouth and pride exploded through Olivia, because he was every bit as lost to this as she was, as powerless to resist this passion as Olivia.

Her hands lifted to his jacket, pushing at it, sliding it from his shoulders and down to the floor and then her hands were forcing his shirt from his trousers, her fingertips connecting with the bare skin of his toned abdomen, warm and smooth, with a sharp electrical shock that pushed them apart. No, it didn't push them apart. Luca had stepped back as though burned, hands on hips, breath ragged.

'I think we have our answer,' he said, after a moment, the statement grim, as if it were the worst thing in the world that their experiment had failed. Olivia took her cue from him, but her veins were simmering, her mind at explosion point. She was a twenty-four-year-old virgin, she'd never explored this side of herself, never known it so much as existed, and suddenly desire was overtaking everything else. She blinked, turning away from him, needing space to process this, needing a chance to simmer down.

Wasn't a cold shower the legendary cure for frustrated desire?

She moved towards the bathroom with knees that were barely steady, closing herself in and sinking back against the door gratefully. After a moment, she met her reflection and wonderment stole through her. Passion was everywhere, from her swollen lips to dilated pupils, to cheeks that were flushed from the rapid flow of her blood in her veins. She stumbled forward and gripped the marble vanity, dipping her head forward and sucking in a sharp breath. Shower. Now.

She reached around to the back of her dress then groaned once more, this time with frustration. The gown had an intricate system of silk-covered buttons trailing down the back. The stylist had fastened her into it that morning and it hadn't occurred to Olivia to wonder how she'd get out of it again—nor had anyone offered advice, because the presumption had been made that Olivia would have her husband's help.

She tried several times to unfasten the buttons herself, attempted to push the gown over her head, and even briefly contemplated ripping it from her body—only the price tag was still emblazoned in her mind with an element of horror, the cost of the dress shocking to Olivia, who'd been robbing Peter to pay Paul for so long she couldn't imagine what it was like to have the kind of money to simply throw away on a dress like this, and no way would she do anything to damage said dress.

Balling up her courage, she opened the door, catching Luca unawares for several seconds, so she could observe him where he stood, now stripped down to his tuxedo trousers alone, feet bare, eyes trained on the view beyond the window. Flames licked through her. She'd *imagined* him naked more times than she could possibly admit—to herself or anyone—but seeing his bare torso was like a firework display right behind her eyes. She cleared her throat and he turned, as if coming from a long way away, his thoughts clearly distracted.

'I can't take off my dress,' she explained, mortification curling her toes.

'I see.' One corner of his lips lifted with self-deprecation. 'Another experiment?'

'No.' She'd learned her lesson. Hadn't she? 'Just a favour for a…friend,' she supplied awkwardly, because they weren't friends, they were strangers who'd just got married. The tangle she was in didn't escape Olivia, but remembering her destitution, her mother's situation, and most importantly the life Sienna deserved to live, propelled Olivia across to Luca with renewed determination. The ends of their marriage justified the means. She just had to keep a level head while waiting to divorce him. Only thirty sleeps to go… 'Definitely no more experimenting with kissing,' she said, for good measure.

'Turn around.' Oh, God. His voice was so sensual, his accent thick. She squeezed her eyes shut as she did exactly that, staring at the mirror opposite—except that was even worse, because the visage of Luca behind her was like catnip; she couldn't take her eyes away from the picture they made. She tried to focus on the most unsexy thoughts imaginable. She thought of the plumbing at Hughenwood House, she thought of the funeral they'd held for their nineteen-year-old cat, only two months ago, she thought of the day she'd had to leave school to transfer to the local comprehensive, but then Luca's fingers pressed to her back, finding the first delicate button, and all notions but the perfection of his touch evaporated from her mind. She bit down on her lower lip, to stem the tide of sensual need, but it did nothing, and the fact he was moving painstakingly slowly definitely didn't help matters. One button separated, and he moved on to the next, and Olivia held her breath, wanting it to be over at the same time she never wanted it to end. Once the third button was undone, the dress separated enough for her to feel the cool night air on her flesh, and then his warm breath, and goosebumps covered her skin. She was sure he'd noticed the telltale response, because his breath hissed out audibly from between clenched teeth.

'Cold?' he enquired, moving to the next button.

She shook her head. She was hot. Hotter than Hades, burning to a crisp. Their eyes met in the mirror and a tremble ran the length of her spine. She might not have any experience with men, but she recognised the emotion stirring in Luca's gaze, the heat of desire, because it was running rampant through her.

Whether he meant it or not, his body must have shifted, because his thighs brushed hers, and she had to catch a moan of her own. Her nipples strained against the lace of her delicate bra, painful and begging for touch. Surprise at her body's immediate response, at the strength of her reaction, had her lifting her arms, crossing them over her chest, as if to catch the dress as he unbuttoned it, when really she wanted to conceal the telltale response from him. She was too late though; when she lifted her face and looked to the mirror, his eyes were on her breasts, his cheeks slashed with dark colour, his shoulders shifting with the force of each breath.

Her stomach swooped to her feet and heat pooled between her legs, a rush of need she'd never known before. So she wanted him to touch her nipples, yes, but, more vitally, she wanted him to reach between her legs and stroke her there until the flames were extinguished. But what about their agreement?

Fifth button, and the dress began to droop at her shoulders. Sixth, and the ruffled shoulder slipped down completely, revealing the top of her lace bra. Her first instinct was to hold on tighter, but some feminine knowledge reverberated through her, so instead she dropped her hands to her sides, her gaze holding a challenge when she met his in the mirror.

The dress fell low enough to reveal her bra, and her engorged, sensitive nipples. He cursed from behind her ear, unfastening another two buttons then dropping his own hands to his sides.

'That's enough.' His voice held a strained quality.

Was it? Olivia wasn't so sure.

'I presume you can manage the rest?'

She didn't want him to stop. She wanted to say to him that, actually, help with her bra would be very useful, starting with cupping her breasts then moving to unclasp it, but the sheer strength of her desire was terrifying to Olivia, so she nodded jerkily and stepped forward. Only she hadn't countered on the dress's length, as it had fallen down her body, and she almost stumbled, but Luca was there, catching her with one strong arm, steadying her, holding her for a second too long before dropping his arms to his sides once more and stepping back.

'We'll go for dinner when you're ready.' He turned and strode towards the door, his voice and gait so normal that Olivia wondered if she'd completely imagined his responses to her, if perhaps she'd been imposing the strength of her needs on him. When he didn't turn to look back at her, she convinced herself that was the case—he walked away without a backward glance yet he was filling her mind, her soul, her thoughts and her needs. Thirty nights suddenly felt like a lifetime.

He dragged his eyes over the outfit with a glimmer of distaste and impatience. Having seen her half naked, and in the svelte wedding dress, he wasn't thrilled to have a return to the boxy, unflattering linen numbers, like the outfit she'd worn the night they'd met. But even with the average, oversized drab dress, there was no mistaking the natural beauty of Olivia. She shone like a diamond: stunning, elegant and irresistible.

He stood when she entered the room, noting that she barely met his eyes. Smart move, except her demure avoidance only made his desire increase ten-fold.

'Dinner,' he said with a sharp nod of his head, thinking that what they needed was to be surrounded by crowds, noise, bright lights.

'We don't have to eat out,' she offered. After all, this was a fake honeymoon for their fake marriage. Surely there were limits to how much play-acting he was willing to do?

'Yes, we do, and take photographs as evidence.'

'Right, of course.' He was very good at this, whereas Olivia had naively believed their marriage certificate would be enough to satisfy the terms of her father's will. Olivia moved to the glass doors that led to the balcony, rather than the door to their suite. The waters of Venice's grand canal glistened beneath her, the dusk light casting a shimmer over the surface, and the lights that had already come on in the buildings across the water gave the vista an almost magical look. 'Where shall we eat?'

'Do you have a preference?'

She wrinkled her nose as she tilted her face to his. 'I've never been to Venice.'

'No?'

She shook her head. 'In fact, I haven't been to Italy in a long time—fourteen years. But as a girl, I always loved it.'

'Where, in particular?'

'Florence. Rome.' She sighed, as memories tugged at her. It had been a different time of life. A better time, in some ways, and their occasional holiday abroad had been an escape from the doom and gloom and oppressive resentment that lived within the walls of Hughenwood.

'Did you buy other clothes, at Harrods?'

Her skin paled and he regretted having asked the question immediately. 'No. Why?' She looked down at the dress, and when she lifted her eyes to his face and he saw the shame lining her features, he could have kicked himself for being so insensitive.

'I know, my wardrobe isn't exactly…sophisticated. You're probably embarrassed to be seen with me.'

Idiot. He shook his head, moving towards her. 'No.' He pressed his finger to her chin, ignoring the blade of white heat that speared his side at the innocuous contact. 'I didn't mean that.' *Didn't you? What had you meant, then?* 'I intended for you to have new clothes because I presumed you'd like it. I gather your finances have been straitened in recent times, and that your wardrobe reflects that. The account was set up at Harrods for this purpose, not just for a wedding dress.'

'Oh, I see.' She swallowed, pulling free of his contact, looking beyond the windows, her delicate features concealing a storm of emotions he couldn't interpret. 'Shall we go?' The forced brightness in her tone made him want to eat his stupid question right back up, but instead, Luca nodded, gesturing towards the door.

Out in public was definitely better than here, alone. 'Yes. *Andiamo.*'

The hotel restaurant was beautiful, the food beyond compare, but instead Luca chose a small trattoria a five-minute speedboat ride away, and spent the entire trip trying to ignore the way Olivia's hair whipped her face and her hands flailed to catch it, tried to ignore the desire to reach out and help her, to offer to hold her hair for her, a fist wrapped around those silky blonde ends until the boat stopped and he could tilt her head to his, capturing her mouth once more…

Hell.

The trattoria was busy, just as he'd hoped, the lighting hardly what could be described as 'ambient'. The owner had run the same fluorescents for as long as Luca had been coming here, but the meals were exceptional, proper local cooking, hearty and plain. No fuss, no Instagram-worthy presentation or indoor plants, just good, old-fashioned food, wine and service. As a result, the tourist trade largely bypassed the trattoria, leaving a swell of locals, so the voices that reached his ears were unmistakably Italian. But as they were led to their table, Luca realised the error of his ways. The restaurant was so crowded that there was anonymity in every corner.

'This is nice.' Olivia sounded surprised, and amusement crested inside Luca.

'It's quite ordinary actually. Hardly a romantic honeymoon destination.'

'But this isn't a real honeymoon,' she rushed to remind him. 'Romance definitely isn't necessary. Just a few photos.'

'Of course.' Had he seriously forgotten? Or just been playing along?

The waiter appeared, brandishing two laminated menus and a wine list. Luca scanned the drinks and flicked a gaze at Olivia, who was determinedly staring at the menu. He wished she wouldn't do that. It made him want to resort to underhanded techniques for attracting her attention, like brushing his feet against her ankles as he had at the restaurant, right after their wedding. He took a perverse pleasure out of watching her responses to him, out of seeing the way her cheeks darkened or her eyes exploded with sensual curiosity. But it was playing with fire, and surely he was smarter than that? 'Wine? Champagne?'

'Bubbles, yes. That Prosecco this afternoon was lovely.'

Luca didn't tell her that the bottle had cost almost a thousand euros. He ordered another and handed the wine list back to the waiter, then gave the full force of his attention to his wife. The word shuddered through him like a sort of nightmare. But Olivia was nothing like Jayne, and their marriage was nothing like his first had been.

'Would you like help with the menu?'

She chewed on her lower lip and he wanted to reach across and wipe his thumb over her skin to stop the gesture—it was too sensual, too distracting. 'I should be able to read this better than I can. Even though mum's Italian, she rarely spoke her native language at home.'

'Why not?'

Because Dad didn't like it. She swallowed the acerbic response, reminding herself that their deal included not getting too personal. 'Just easier that way,' she said with a lift of her shoulders.

'Easier?'

'We lived in England,' she reminded him. 'We all spoke English.'

'I grew up bilingual despite the fact both my parents were Italian, and I was mostly raised in Italy.'

She dismissed him with a tight smile, but Luca didn't want to be dismissed. 'She didn't cook Italian food?'

'She didn't cook at all,' Olivia responded with a natural smile. 'We had staff for that, until…'

'Your father died?'

Turbulent emotions raged in her eyes. 'Yes.'

'And then what?'

Her eyes fluttered as she sought an answer. 'And then, my sister and I picked up the reins.'

'Of the household?'

'There was no one else to do it.'

'Your mother?'

Olivia laughed now, a bitter sound. 'My mother has many skills, but housework is not one of them.'

He frowned. 'You were, what, twelve years old?'

'Yes.'

'And your sister?'

'Eleven.'

'And at those tender ages, it was decided that you and she had more abilities around the house than your mother did?'

'You can't teach an old dog new tricks,' Olivia responded dryly, the words spoken as if by rote, leaving him in little doubt they'd been parroted to her often.

'And you juggled schoolwork as well?'

'Not particularly well,' Olivia said with obvious regret. 'My grades started to slip after Dad passed. I changed schools, so that didn't help—everything was new. But there was also a lot to do, which left little time for studying.'

'Or socialising,' he prompted thoughtfully.

She nodded her agreement.

'Anyway, that's ancient history.'

It was, quite clearly, designed to shut the conversation down.

'Have you eaten here before?'

'Whenever I'm in Venice.'

'Which is how often?'

'A few times a year.'

'Why?'

He lifted a brow.

'Do you have an office here?'

'No.'

'Then why Venice?'

'I like it.'

Her lips tugged to the side. 'I'm surprised you make time for leisure.'

'Are you?'

She considered him a long moment and then, as though she were forcing herself to go on, almost against her will, she spoke slowly, purposefully. 'I suppose the women you date expect a degree of attention.'

He relaxed back in his chair, despite the strange sense of unease stealing across him. Why did he want to obfuscate? To move conversation away from his previous lovers? The instinct caught him off guard and so he forced himself to confront it, by answering her question directly. 'Yes.'

She flicked a glance down at the menu, her features

shifting into a mask of something he didn't understand. Uncertainty? Embarrassment? He narrowed his gaze, as though that might be able to help him. 'So you bring them here?'

His original instincts surged back, stronger, more determined. 'I can't remember.' He brushed her enquiry aside, even though he knew he'd never brought a woman here before. 'Let me help you with the menu.'

She nodded, a cool, crisp acknowledgement that pulled at something in his chest. He didn't *like* cool and crisp. Not when he'd seen her eyes storm-ravaged by desire. He scraped his chair back, coming to stand behind her, breathing in her sweet fragrance before he could stop himself. His gut rolled; he ground his teeth together. The first moment he'd seen her at that party in Rome, he'd imagined her naked. He'd fantasised about making her his. Why the hell had he thought he could simply switch that desire off? Because he lived for control—and the harder it was to get, the more rewarding success was. He *would* control this.

'Here, there is fried calamari.' He pointed to the menu, his arm inadvertently brushing her breasts as he reached across, and he heard the smallest of gasps escape her lips, so any idea of control ran completely from his mind. He leaned closer, his cheek almost pressed to hers, his arm deliberately close to her now. 'Rice balls stuffed with cheese, spinach and cheese pasta.' He paused, finger pointing to the next item. 'Scallops carpaccio. Do you like scallops?' He turned to face her, his lips almost brushing her cheeks, and he waited.

Sure enough, as though the same invisible, magnetic force were operating on Olivia, she turned towards him. They were so close, he could see every fleck of colour in her magnificent blue eyes; he could see desire in them too, even when they shuttered slightly, her eyes dropping to his lips in that disarming and distracting way she had.

Kiss her.

Temptation hummed in his body. He was only an inch or so away. It would be so easy to brush their lips—but how easy to pull apart? On the two occasions they'd kissed, it had taken a Herculean effort to stop what was happening between them.

'I have to tell you something,' she said quietly, the words just a whisper against his cheek.

'I'm listening.' He couldn't help himself. Luca lifted his thumb and brushed it over her lower lip, so her eyes closed on a wave of anguish, fierce need like a cyclone around them.

'Luca.' God, his name on her lips was its own aphrodisiac. Her voice was husky, as though they'd just made love, as though she'd screamed herself hoarse. He dropped his hand, letting it rest on her shoulder. *Stop this. Control it.*

But was there really any harm in a kiss? It wasn't as if they would be having sex. It wasn't as if they'd be falling in love. If anything, it might actually work to their advantage, bursting the tension that was building between them.

Liar.

'Olivia.' He deliberately layered her name with his own sensual needs, watching as the drawled intonation flushed her cheeks pink.

'This isn't—'

He didn't want to hear what this wasn't. He knew their marriage wasn't real, and he was glad for that, but that didn't mean the passion could be ignored. Perhaps there was a compromise? After all, they were two sensible, consenting adults.

But hadn't he set the ground rules here? Hadn't he been the one to insist they'd never be more than spouses on paper? Could there be new rules?

'I know what our marriage isn't,' he said gruffly, bringing his face closer to hers. 'But I no longer think it makes sense to continue ignoring what it is.'

Her lips parted, and panic flared in her eyes, so he stayed where he was, thankfully with it enough to know that if they kissed now, it had to be her choice. He'd made it clear what he wanted. But would she be brave enough to admit what *she* wanted?

'I'm not ignoring that,' she whispered, her eyes like saucers as she leaned infinitesimally closer.

'Aren't you?' Her brows drew together.

She shook her head slightly, and with the movement, closed the distance the rest of the way. *Almost* the rest of the way, because her lips were still separated from his by a hair's breadth.

'But how—?'

'Do we really need to answer that?'

Her moan was the final straw. It was so quiet, only he could hear it, so sensual, he couldn't help imagining her in the throes of passion. Every cell in his body reverberated with fierce, undeniable need.

'Kiss me,' he commanded.

Another husky intake of breath.

'Now.'

Waiting was its own form of agony. He stayed where he was, even when he ached to claim her lips, to taste them, and this time he didn't want to stop, despite the fact they were in a busy restaurant.

'Our agreement—'

'We can make a new agreement.'

And then, thank God, she caved, mashing her mouth to his with all the urgency that was driving him crazy, moaning into his mouth now, so he swallowed the sound and ached for more. Her hands lifted up, catching his face, holding him there, as her tongue explored his mouth, as she took control of the kiss and he could do nothing but experience her greedy stake of ownership.

This was a terrible idea. He'd known he wouldn't want to stop what they were doing and he didn't. With every fibre of his being, he wanted to strip the clothes from her body and make her his, to hell with their agreement, their deal, their goddamned marriage of convenience. They could draw new boundaries, afterwards. They could do *anything*, after. For now, there was only this.

'Listen to me.' It was Olivia who broke the kiss this time, wrenching her lips away as if in desperate need of air, staring down at her lap. She withdrew her hands; they were shaking badly.

'Listen to me,' she said again, this time reaching for her Prosecco and taking a sip, as if that could erase the urgency of what they'd just shared.

He didn't—couldn't—speak, and so he waited, right where he was, body still close to hers, head bent, desire a tsunami in his veins.

'I've never done this before. I can't just—I don't know—what this feels like.'

He frowned, her words making no sense. He knew she'd never been married before. And he knew she'd never been to Venice before, nor to this restaurant. What was she trying to tell him?

'Are you trying to tell me you're a twenty-four-year-old virgin?' he joked, in an attempt to defuse the tension that was tightening her beautiful lips into a straight, flat line.

She pulled back from him as if he'd slapped her, cheeks glowing pink, eyes not meeting his. His own smile, already taut from the effort it took to dredge up past the storm of passion ravaging him, lost its will, and dropped from his face. He swore quietly, but they were close, so she heard it and flinched, took another sip of Prosecco then clasped the glass in her hands, at her lap.

'Yes.' It was so quiet he had to lean forward to hear the word, but by then he'd already guessed. He knew. He just didn't understand.

He jackknifed up, standing straight, staring out at the crowded restaurant without seeing anyone or anything. His mind was a whir of noise and movement, without the ability to comprehend.

'So when we kiss, I feel things, and I want things, but I have no idea how to—'

He lifted a hand, silencing her. He needed to get a grip on his own emotions. On the one hand, her revelation made him want to put a thousand acres of space between them, on another, it fascinated him, drawing him to her, making him want to teach her, to show her, to be her first.

He moved back to his seat, gripping the back of it, eyes on Olivia the whole time.

She was *so* beautiful. Literally, the sexiest, most stunning woman he'd seen in his life and, given his dating history, that was saying something. How was it possible she'd never been in a relationship before?

'You've never dated a guy?'

She stared at the table, shaking her head.

'You've never fooled around?'

Another head shake, more ignoring him, until she lifted her eyes, finally, pinning him to the spot. And there was cool and reserved Olivia once more—and for once, he was glad to see her. This was a conversation that called for level heads. He sat back down, assuming a relaxed pose he definitely didn't feel.

'Until our wedding, I'd never been kissed.'

He angled his face away, biting back the curse that filled his mouth.

'Why didn't you tell me this before we were married?'

'I didn't think it would be relevant. It's not supposed to be like this. I didn't even think we'd kiss at the wedding—my fault, that was naïve of me.'

'But you agreed to pose as my doting wife, for my grandmother's sake. Didn't you imagine we'd have to share some physical contact, at some point?'

Her eyes showed embarrassment and, inwardly, he winced, wishing he didn't sound so disbelieving.

'I don't know. I didn't—maybe. I guess I thought we might hold hands or something.'

'Hold hands,' he repeated incredulously. 'My God, Olivia, do you have any idea what I've been thinking about? What I thought about the minute I saw you?'

He ground his teeth together, trying to push away the memory of those thoughts, wishing his imagination weren't so damned vivid.

She shook her head, dropping it forward, shielding her face from his, so he wanted to reach across and lift her chin, to make her confront this head on.

But he couldn't.

There were some boundaries they could move. Incorporating a meaningless fling into their meaningless marriage-on-paper was one thing. But there was no way he was going to take her virginity. Not when sex would only ever be a physical act to him.

'I really don't,' she whispered softly. 'But I know what I've been thinking about...things I've never thought of before. My imagination has gone wild.'

'Don't tell me.' He compressed his lips, his jaw almost a perfect square. He didn't need to know that. There were other more pressing considerations. 'Tell me how this is possible.'

'Well, I simply forgot to have sex before,' she said with a tight smile, her joke falling flat, given that neither of them was in a laughing mood.

'You've never met someone who aroused your interest?'

She pleated her napkin over and over. The waiter appeared to take their order, and Luca could have cursed right in the man's face at the interruption. Instead, he rattled off a list of six dishes, hoping Olivia would like at least one of them, then waved his hand in an unmistakable gesture of dismissal.

'Go on,' he commanded.

She hesitated and he wondered if she was going to change subjects, or suggest they not talk about it. 'It's very complicated,' she said, eventually.

'We have time.'

Her lips twisted. 'It's not important. The details are—I can do a summation,' she said with a little shrug of her shoulders. 'My parents' marriage was a disaster. My mother and I don't have a straightforward relationship. She disapproved of men, dating, in fact, she basically disapproved of socialising, so Sienna and I had each other and pretty much no one else. Plus, I was running Hughenwood House from the time I was twelve years old. When would I have found the time to date? It's a miracle I managed to graduate high school.'

'So what? After that, you stayed home like some kind of modern-day Cinderella, with just your family and chores for company?'

'Don't mock me.'

'I'm not,' he said quickly, shaking his head. 'I'm only trying to understand.'

'I've been asked out before,' she admitted, with pink staining her cheeks. 'But my mother wouldn't have allowed me to accept. And I never liked the guys enough to fight with her about it.'

'And your sister?'

She hesitated, shaking her head. 'Sienna's life is her personal business. I'm not going to discuss it.'

'Fair enough.'

'So what do we do?' Her huge blue eyes blinked across at him, and the answer that sprang to mind was the exact answer he had to ignore.

'Do?' He reached for his own drink, draining it before

replacing the glass on the tabletop, then leaning forward, pinning her with the intensity of his gaze. 'That's very simple, Olivia. We do exactly what we said we would at the outset. We remember the boundaries we drew, we remember what this marriage is, and we keep our hands—and mouths—to ourselves. *Va bene?*'

CHAPTER FIVE

So much for being able to sleep in the same bed as Olivia without touching her. It was all he could think of. His whole body was on tenterhooks, wanting to reach out and touch her, wanting to feel her soft, supple skin, wanting to kiss her hollows, to taste her passion, wanting to make her his in every way.

He stared at the ornate ceiling, his pulse running wild in his system, as Olivia slept beside him. Thanks to the Prosecco, she'd fallen asleep as soon as her head hit the pillow, whereas Luca had ruminated on her revelation, on the fact she was completely innocent, until he was crazy with wanting.

But to sleep with a virgin…there was no way he could do it. She had no experience with men, with sex, with the euphoria that accompanied orgasms. How could they remain detached, as they needed to be, if they were sleeping together? He had to be able to walk away from this marriage in a month's time, and to do so guilt free—something he couldn't achieve if they complicated their arrangement with sex. And yet, for all that he'd wanted her before, knowing that she had no experience was an aphrodisiac he hadn't anticipated. He wanted to teach her. He wanted to show her body what she could feel, and he wanted to watch her as she felt her first orgasm, he wanted to go down on her until she could barely think, he wanted to lather her body in the shower then take her against the cold, wet tiles. He wanted…what he couldn't, wouldn't, have.

Ever since Jayne, he'd sworn off relationships. Sex was fine, anything more was where it got complicated. So? Couldn't this just be sex? A little voice pleaded with him, but he ignored it. They were trapped in the same house for the next month—there was no guarantee they could keep things casual. Particularly not given her lack of experience. He couldn't take the gamble that she'd be able to see sex as sex, and not start to want more. It was absolutely impossible.

Throwing off the covers, he stalked away from the bed, finally admitting defeat. He'd been wrong earlier. He couldn't lie with her and know he wouldn't touch. He was half afraid he'd reach for her in his sleep, without intending to, that he'd start kissing her without being aware of what he was doing, and that she'd kiss him back. Because, experienced or not, her body knew what to do, her body understood the chemistry that was flowing between them, and her body wanted to act on it.

Which was all the more reason he had to control this.

With one final look over his shoulder, regarding her sleeping frame with a surge of adrenaline, he left the room, opting instead for an uncomfortable, sleepless night on the sofa—where Olivia filled his dreams, if not his hands.

'What is this?'

Olivia stared in confusion, at first, and then horror, as a parade of not one, not two, but *six* hotel staff walked into their suite, each carrying armloads of clothing.

Luca nodded towards the master bedroom, and they filed in there, each returning with empty hands.

Olivia watched, bemused, confused, but also glad to have something to think about other than the confession she'd made the night before, other than the way she'd blurted out the fact she was a virgin. Certainly other than the way he'd immediately pulled away from her as though whatever he'd been thinking about a moment earlier was now a moot point.

Could she blame him for not wanting to sleep with a virgin? He was used to sophisticated, experienced women. What could Olivia offer him?

She watched as Luca tipped one of the staff, then pushed the door closed behind them, turning to face her, arms crossed.

'Luca?' It was then that she realised they'd barely spoken all day. He'd been working, she'd been pretending to read, anything to avoid the elephant in the room. How in the world was she going to get through the next month?

'You need new clothes.' He shrugged, as though it was nothing, when Olivia had seen the designer names emblazoned on the sides of the bags.

She groaned, shaking her head. 'I don't.'

'You do,' he insisted. 'We're going to have to attend events in Rome, we'll see my grandmother socially at some point. You cannot keep dressing as though you're a kindergartner.'

She flinched at his unwitting insult. He continued to stare at her, his eyes appraising.

'Was it your mother who insisted on this also?'

'On what?'

'Your clothes.'

Olivia looked down at her outfit—denim overalls and a pale yellow T-shirt—then lifted her shoulders softly.

'Partly,' she whispered, not meeting his eyes.

'Because she was jealous?'

'How did—?' She clamped a hand to her mouth. 'I don't know,' she said with a shake of her head. 'Let's not talk about my mother right now, please.'

'When she is at the root of so much of who you are?'

'I know, but…'

'Fine.' He lifted his hands in acceptance, trouble brewing in the dark depths of his eyes. 'Go and look at the outfits. We will have dinner in the restaurant tonight.'

She didn't need to have any experience to know she was being dismissed, but if there was any doubt, it evaporated as he turned away from her and strode towards the table he'd been using as a makeshift desk.

Fighting a dangerous urge to challenge him, she stalked out of the living room, into the bedroom, taking great pleasure in shutting the door as she went. Privacy. Oh, how she needed it!

It took almost an hour to remove everything from the bags. Stunning dresses, evening gowns, mini-dresses as well as casual clothes—designer jeans and jackets, simple blouses, but cut so they were the last word in flattering. She started with the bags on the left of the room, and worked to the right, so it was completely a coincidence that she left the lingerie to last. But as she opened a thick cardboard box, revealing a ribbon-wrapped, tissue-paper item inside, her heart did a funny little tremble.

It was unlike anything she'd ever seen before. Lacy knickers, ornate bras, and, my God, suspenders. She shoved them back in the box and stepped away, heat radiating through her whole body.

She couldn't wear them.

She couldn't wear half this stuff. It was too beautiful, too revealing, too…

But how could she resist?

Knowing that he'd chosen it for her? That he'd imagined her in it? As if that weren't temptation enough, there was a part of Olivia that had always loved pretty, feminine clothes, a part of her she'd been forced to hide, that she suddenly felt a compulsion to indulge.

Surrendering to temptation, she opened the lingerie again, withdrawing a particularly beautiful matching set, caramel and black silk. She kept an eye on the door as she changed, then glanced at her reflection, doing a double take at the woman who stared back at her.

And she *was* a woman. A flesh and blood, sensual woman. She took two steps towards her reflection, dragging her eyes over her body.

It was clear that he'd wanted her before she revealed the truth. Did he still want her?

Nothing had changed for Olivia.

She cast a glance over the bed, her eyes landing on one of the more outrageous dresses. It was a sure-fire way to get his attention…and suddenly that was what Olivia wanted most on earth. To hell with the consequences.

She slid the dress on—it hugged her like a second skin—then brushed her golden hair until it shone, pulling it over one shoulder. He'd bought her shoes too, and she slipped her feet into a pair with a red sole and a spiky black heel, pausing to admire the effect in the mirror. It was almost too much. The exact opposite of what she'd been raised to think she should be stared back at her, but Olivia fought the strong impulse to change into something less attention-grabbing.

You only lived once, right?

If he'd had any kind of heart condition, then Olivia's appearance would have tested it. She emerged from the bedroom like some kind of Venus, a transformation that completely took his breath away. He'd known she was beautiful—hell, she was stunning no matter what she wore—but when she was dressed like this, in heels that made her hips swagger, a dress that hid *nothing* from his appraising eyes, it was all he could do to stay in the kitchen with his hands by his sides.

'Will this do?'

He was drowning. *Would it do?* It would do for him to peel the dress right off her, not to take her out in public. He didn't want the rest of Venice to see her like this, he realised, even as, at the same time, he felt a purely masculine pride in the woman he'd married.

A muscle jerked in his jaw as he grappled with the contrasting emotions.

'Luca?' Her uncertainty confused him. Surely she knew how spectacular she was?

'You're perfect,' he growled, turning away from her on the pretext of grabbing a drink of water.

'There's something important I want to discuss at dinner.' Her cool voice was steady and calm—the exact opposite to how he felt. 'Do you think there'll be a private table at the restaurant?'

He dipped his head. Privacy was the devil—he had to avoid it. '*Forse.* Let's go.'

He didn't offer her his hand as they left, nor did he touch the small of her back to guide her towards the lift. In fact, he walked at least a metre away from her, and when the elevator doors pinged open he kept to his side of the small cube, mutinously staring ahead, refusing to look at her even when his eyes wanted to drink up the vision she made.

The restaurant was busy, filled with Venice's glitterati. Luca saw many people he knew, was recognised, heard the gossip, and also the change in tenor—the surprise at the woman on his arm. Was she being recognised? He doubted it. While her name might be well known, and well regarded, Olivia herself was somewhat of an anachronism. Unlike most people of her generation, she didn't have an enormous social-media footprint, or a paparazzi trail. It was further evidence, not that he needed it, that her life was every bit as confined as she'd indicated. That she'd been a virtual prisoner at Hughenwood House, a modern-day Cinderella, just as he'd charged the night before, left to do chores from dawn to dusk. Did that make him Prince Charming? Hardly. Nothing like it.

'This is perfect,' she said with satisfaction as the maître d' led them to a table at the front of the canal, set a little apart from the others. They were still visible, but their voices wouldn't carry, and that was foremost in Olivia's mind.

While he wanted to avoid being too close to her, Pietra had raised him with faultless manners, so he came to her chair and pulled it back, waiting for Olivia to settle before moving away swiftly, before he could do something stupid like brush his hands over her shoulders. But he did breathe her in, the same sweet, intoxicating fragrance wrapping around him, so he felt himself strain against his pants, as though he were some kind of inexperienced teenager, completely incapable of controlling his desire.

'You wanted to talk to me?' Please, let it be about something mundane and rudimentary. Let her bring up *anything* to take his mind off what he wanted them to share.

'When you agreed to marry me, we negotiated terms for our marriage that would suit us both.'

'I remember.'

'What if I want to change the terms?'

He sat very still. 'Which terms in particular?' But he knew what was coming. He braced for it, for the offer she was going to make, for the test that he was about to meet, no idea if he had the strength for it.

'The no sex thing.' She lifted her eyes to his, meeting his gaze with apparent calmness now. 'I want to lose my virginity, to you. Tonight.'

CHAPTER SIX

HE DIDN'T REACT, but inwardly his cells were reverberating with exquisite anticipation. 'No.' He tried to put a stop to the conversation before it went any further. 'Absolutely not.'

'Hear me out,' she murmured softly. 'Nothing else between us needs to change. I know what you want from me, and you know what I need from you. In twenty-nine nights, we'll separate and, as soon as legally viable, apply for a divorce. I know you were worried that being married might make me develop feelings for you, but I promise, Luca, that's not going to happen.'

'How do you know?' he demanded bullishly.

'Another time, remind me to ask you about the string of broken hearts you've clearly left behind.'

He ground his teeth together. 'I leave women before their hearts can become involved. I'm very strict about it. That is the point.'

'Because of your divorce?'

'Because of my first marriage. Because I have no interest in repeating that mistake,' he contradicted flatly.

'Don't you get it?' She breathed out excitedly. 'We're on the same page with this stuff. Marriage—a genuine marriage—is my idea of torture, one I saw enacted every single day with my parents, and I would rather die before getting involved in that, for real. Believe me when I tell you that the only thing I want in life is my independence. Falling in love would jeopardise that—I'm not stupid.'

His eyes narrowed at the logic of her argument. He knew there were still risks, but her sincerity was obvious. It was easy for Luca to be persuaded by her words. And yet…

'You don't know you'll still feel that way after we've slept together.'

A single finely shaped brow quirked in cynical amusement. 'You think you're so good in bed I won't ever want to leave you?'

He laughed. 'I've never had any complaints.'

'Good,' she responded enthusiastically. 'That's what I want. I'm a twenty-four-year-old virgin, Luca. I want my first experience of sex to be out of this world. Can you give me that?'

'Olivia.' He fought her suggestion with every fibre of his being, even when he definitely didn't want to fight her. He wanted to scrape his chair back and throw her over his shoulder, drag her right back upstairs and bolt the door shut for at least the next forty-eight hours. How many times since meeting her had he had that fantasy? And now she was serving herself up to him…

'This would still be a business deal,' she said after a beat. 'We're both laying our cards on the table, explaining our expectations. I promise, I won't ask you for anything else.'

He balled his hands into fists where they rested on his knees and absent-mindedly wondered what he'd done in a past life to deserve the experience of a woman like Olivia Giovanardi *begging* him to make love to her.

Still, he clung to sanity and reason, even when the alternative was so appealing. 'You can't say that with certainty.'

'Yes, I can.'

'How do you know?'

She toyed with the linen napkin to her right, then fixed him with a direct stare. 'Because my father was a complete bastard to my mother. Because I saw him eviscerate and humiliate her every day of my life. Because I saw her beg him to love her, and he delighted in withholding that. It is complete anathema to me to give a man that kind of power. To love someone so completely you will tolerate that behaviour—' Out of nowhere, the sting of tears swelled in her throat and behind her eyes, so she tilted her face away, looking towards the Grand Canal while she composed herself.

The waiter arrived at the table to take their order—which Luca placed, handing the menus back then waiting quietly, braced in his chair, eyes tracing the delicate outline of her face in profile. Finally, when Olivia's emotions were under control, she turned back to face him.

'I will never love you, or anyone, and I will never ask you to love me. I promise.'

He felt the honesty of her confession, and it reached right inside him, like a tentacle of ice. He'd never met anyone who'd spoken so calmly about love, and their aversion to it, but her words relaxed him, because it was exactly as Luca felt. Having loved once before, and then suffered through the devastation of that break-up, he had no intention of being so stupid ever again. Could he really trust this was a safe course of action?

'Why did your mother stay married to your father, if his actions were so terrible?'

Olivia's face blanched, in contrast to the fire in her eyes. 'Because she loved him.' The words were said with arctic disdain. 'We all did. It was only after his death that I began to see things with more perspective.'

'You were still just a girl. How were you to know that the way they lived wasn't normal?'

She pleated her napkin in her lap.

A strange sensation gripped Luca's gut, an unpleasant question formed in his mind and, at first, he resisted asking it. But he was Luca Giovanardi, afraid of nothing and no one, and he wanted all of the facts. 'Did he hit her?'

Olivia's eyes went round. She shook her head.

'Did he hit you?'

'No, no. He wasn't like that.' A tremulous smile tilted her lips for a brief moment before dropping away into a grimace. 'But I would still describe him, if I absolutely had to discuss him at all, as abusive. Financially abusive—he gave my mother an allowance while he lived, enough to maintain her to the physical standard he expected,' she said with withering disapproval, 'but not enough for anything more. She couldn't do anything without his permission—buy anything, travel anywhere. She was his virtual prisoner.'

The original hatred he'd felt for the unknown Thomas Thornton-Rose grew. 'And when he died, she was still kept under his thumb, by the restrictive conditions of his will.'

'Yes.' Olivia's lips twisted. 'I don't think my mother knew how to react to that. We've all carried on just as we did when he was alive, the same dysfunctional household, the same attitudes, the same restrictions.'

'On you?'

Her eyes met his, and he could see the battle being waged behind her eyes. 'On Sienna and me, yes.'

'Such as?'

She pleated the napkin more furiously now, her fingers working overtime even as her face held a determinedly placid expression—an expression she fought hard to keep in place, he suspected. 'Our father was—'

She broke off when the waiter appeared, brandishing a glass of Prosecco and a glass of red wine for Luca. When they were alone again, he nodded once, urging her to continue.

She hesitated, and he stayed very still, aware that she was sharing something she didn't relish speaking about, but also impatient to understand what her life was like.

'He was strict. I think he was worried we'd turn out like her, so he did everything he could to discourage that. Where he saw similarities, he belittled them.'

'And are either of you like your mother?'

'I'm her spitting image,' Olivia murmured softly, not meeting his eyes. 'If you were to see a photograph of her in her early twenties, you'd think it was me.'

'And so your father didn't approve.'

'He downplayed looks, generally, while at the same time expecting my mother to dress and look like a beauty queen at all times. It's so hard to explain. Someone like my father is very manipulative—a contradiction in many ways, and a total narcissist. That was his strength. We never knew where we stood with him, nor what would please him.'

She sipped her Prosecco then replaced the glass, running her finger over the condensation.

'For my twelfth birthday, I had a small party—just a few friends over to watch music videos, nothing particularly lavish. But I got dressed up. I did my hair and put on some of Mum's make-up. I'll never forget his reaction.'

She shivered, turning back towards the water, their vantage point affording an excellent view of the exquisite Basilica di Santa Maria della Salute. It shimmered gold, casting its reflection onto the Grand Canal.

'He was angry?'

'Coldly disapproving,' she corrected, 'but with an undertone of such venom, I've never forgotten it.' She pushed a smile to her lips, as if to change the subject. 'He didn't speak to me for days.'

'What about your sister?' He swerved the conversation sideways, instead, not ready to move on from the matter of her parents, but understanding Olivia needed a break from discussing herself and the ways in which she was parented.

'Sienna?'

'What were they like to her?'

'Sienna is—' Now her smile was genuine. 'She's the most darling person you'll ever meet. She's funny and kind, clumsy as anything, loyal to a fault. Have you ever met a person whose eyes literally sparkled? Sienna's like that.

It's as though a thousand stars have been crushed into dust that's been poured into her eyes. She glows with kindness. I love her to bits, Luca.' The intensity in her eyes reached out and took hold of him. '*She's* why I had to do this. Oh, I want my mother to finally be free of my father's oppression, and I want her to have the security of a home, but it's Sienna who just deserves so much better. For all my parents made my life a living hell, it was ten times worse for her.'

'In what way?'

Olivia sipped her drink once more, searching for the right words. 'Sienna and I are total opposites. I'm very like my mother, in looks and emotions, I think. Where my mother and I understood what my father was like, and how to keep our heads low and avoid conflict, Sienna was like… a puppy dog, always bouncing around, looking for affection. It drove him crazy. He came down on her like a tonne of bricks, trying to mould her, to change her.' She winced, hating how it had felt to see that, hating that Sienna could never learn to just stay out of their father's way. 'And so my mother, trying to keep the peace, would be very hard on Sienna, unnecessarily so, criticising her for everything, even things beyond her control, like the colour of her hair or when she gained a little puppy fat. And I—' She swallowed, and now tears did moisten her eyes, so a strange lurching sensation took hold of Luca. 'I'm embarrassed to say it, but I used to be *glad* sometimes that it was Sienna who was in trouble, because when it was her, it couldn't be me.' She screwed up her face. 'I can't believe I told you that. I've never confided that to another soul. You must think I'm a terrible person.'

'You? No, *cara*. I think you're a by-product of your home life, and that you developed the skills that were necessary to get by.' He hesitated a moment, but the moment warranted honesty. 'I think you're very brave.'

She blinked rapidly, to clear her tears, but one escaped regardless, making its way down her cheek. Luca reached over, catching it before it could drop to the table, smudging it over her soft, pale skin, then kept his hand where it was a moment, holding her face, and her gaze.

'No one deserves to live like that.'

Her expression softened for a moment, and then it was as if Olivia visibly pulled a shawl around herself, a cloak of cool distance. 'Lots of people have it much worse. He was never physically aggressive, and we grew up living a very privileged life, as you've pointed out. Hughenwood House, for all it's somewhat run-down these days, is still a stunning country home, with an impressive history.'

She needed to project this image to him, and so he nodded as though he believed her, even when he heard the heartbreak behind her carefully delivered lines. He sat back in his seat, dropping his hands into his lap, watching her with the full force of his concentration.

'I take it this general family dysfunction explains why you're still a virgin?'

Her eyes widened, showing how unexpected the question was. 'Yes.'

He waited for her to continue, probing her eyes thoughtfully.

'You said dating wasn't approved of. Why not?'

'This is really very boring, isn't it?'

'No.'

A plea filled her gaze, and Luca understood it, but he held to his resolve. 'You are asking to modify our agreement. I need more information before I make a decision.'

'I—' She closed her eyes a moment, sucking in a deep breath, and her free hand trembled slightly as she reached for her Prosecco. 'I didn't understand why my mother was so adamant about this. After all, she was married young, and my father wasn't her first lover. How come I couldn't date? But I think—' She paused, wincing, so he waited, curious as to what she might say. 'My mother is a very vain person, Luca. She was always very beautiful, and then my father seemed to value only her looks, so that became what she focused on for a very long time.'

Luca's lips formed a grim line. 'And as you got older, and turned from a child to an adolescent to a stunning young woman, she became jealous of you.'

Olivia's eyes grew wide. He was sure he was right, but some delicate sense of loyalty seemed to prevent Olivia from agreeing with him, so he continued.

'This is why your wardrobe is as it is?'

Heat coloured her cheeks. She didn't respond.

'And she kept you from dating because to see men pay attention to you, and not her, would wound her vanity.'

Olivia pulled a face before looking away. He took her silence as all the confirmation he needed, and suddenly what he wanted, more than anything, was to erase every bit of pain and dejection Olivia had ever felt. What he wanted was to give her *everything* she wanted, to make up for all she'd been denied.

'Are you hungry?'

She frowned. 'I'm—not really, why?'

He stood, extending a hand to her. 'Then let's order room service. Later.'

His final word landed between them and her eyes widened as his meaning became clear. Later might as well have been 'after', and they both knew what that meant.

It was as though she'd forgotten how to walk, her legs were that unstable beneath her, her stomach in a thousand knots, her blood thundering through her fragile veins so she could hear rushing akin to a waterfall with every step she took. At the elevator, he pressed the button without looking at her, and when Olivia risked a glance at Luca she saw only an implacable, inscrutable face, his eyes hooded, his features set in a mask of determination. A thrill ran the length of her spine even as nerves seemed to be hammering her from the inside out.

This was really going to happen.

Delight and euphoria clipped through her. She fidgeted her hands in front of her waist as she stepped into the elevator, holding her breath as Luca came to stand beside her. The doors pinged halfway shut only to open once more as another couple stepped in, joining them. Olivia stepped back, her bottom touching the metal of the lift wall, and Luca mirrored her step, staying right beside her. As the elevator began to ascend, his hand brushed hers, and she startled as a thousand lightning bolts flashed across her skin. She glanced at his face to find him still looking straight ahead, but this time there was the hint of a smile on his lips and her heart stammered in her chest.

The lift opened and the other couple departed. Olivia's breath sounds filled the cabin. Her skin was flushed from anticipation, her insides all contorted. Her body was wracked with a thousand and one emotions, none of them easy to interpret.

A moment later the doors pinged open to their floor. 'After you.' His words were deep and throaty, throbbing with the same emotions that were rolling through Olivia. She couldn't look at him, and jelly seemed to have replaced her knee joints. At the end of the corridor, he pushed open the door to the honeymoon suite and this time, when Olivia crossed the threshold, she felt as though something fundamental had changed between them. There was an equality to their pairing, an honesty and openness that hadn't been there at first. Inside the suite, she turned to face him, slowly, her eyes round, her lips parted. She'd focused so much of her energy on convincing him that they should do this that she hadn't actually prepared for what that would entail. Nerves began to bounce through her.

Luca held her gaze as he removed his dinner jacket, placing it over the back of a nearby chair, before unfastening the top two buttons of his shirt. He then turned his attention to his sleeves, which he rolled up to just below the elbow, revealing tanned, toned forearms that were, even on their own, erotic enough to make her heart go full pelt.

She reached for the zip of her dress, but a short jerk of his head forestalled her. 'I'll do it.'

Her stomach swooped; her hands fell to her sides. 'If we do this,' he said, something impossible to interpret darkening his features.

'If?' she interrupted with soft incredulity.

He dipped his head in silent agreement. 'I need you to promise you understand the limitations.'

'Haven't we already covered that?'

He seemed to impale her with the force of his stare. 'It's important.'

She suppressed a smile, because he couldn't have spelled things out more clearly if he'd grabbed a white board and started writing it down.

'Just sex. No love. I got it.'

His eyes narrowed. 'When we sleep together, it's simply a biological urge. There's no true intimacy between us, no matter how we make it look to the outside world. When thirty days expire, we will walk away from one another. No regrets.'

A challenge tilted her face. 'That's exactly what I want, Luca. And it's twenty-eight days, now.'

His eyes narrowed. 'And if you start to feel differently, at any point, you promise you will tell me.'

'I won't feel differently. It's not possible. I won't feel anything.'

He seemed to consider that for a moment and, finally, nodded.

'So? Can we do this now?'

He laughed quietly at her eagerness. 'No.'

'No?' She balked at the rejection. 'What the heck do you mean, "no"?'

'You've been drinking.'

She gaped. 'A single glass of Prosecco.'

He moved closer to her, so close their bodies were brushing, his eyes hooked to hers, before reaching behind her and slowly, painstakingly slowly, easing down the zip of her dress. 'When…' The zip reached the line of her bra; she shivered as he crossed it. 'Not if,' he placated, when the zip had gone all the way. He moved his hands to the off-the-shoulder sleeves of her dress and dropped them, his palms brushing her arms. The dress fell from her breasts and she shivered, her strapless bra a flimsy piece of lace and wire. 'You will be completely sober.'

'I am.' She trembled as the dress pooled to the floor and she stood before him in only a bra and panties.

'Completely.' And yet, despite his words, he leaned forward and drew her lower lip between his teeth, so she arched her back, the contact searing and sensational.

'But I want—'

'You want to learn about sex,' he said, reaching behind her and unfastening the bra, dropping it to the carpeted floor, beside her dress. She stepped out of the fabric, stiletto heels still in place, underpants just a scrap of fabric that could barely contain her heat and need.

'I want to *experience* sex,' she corrected.

'Ah, my mistake.' His eyes showed a glimmer of amusement when they met hers. 'But there is so much to learn before you experience,' he said gently.

'Such as?' Pique and disappointment crested through her.

His hands cupped her breasts when she wasn't expecting it, so her eyes widened and her gasp was involuntary.

'Are you aware you can be brought to orgasm through nipple stimulation alone?'

Olivia found it impossible to answer, but her eyes contained a plea, so Luca laughed under his breath. 'Would you like me to show you?'

'Are you really going to make me beg?' She huffed.

'Yes,' he said simply, moving his mouth to the sensitive flesh just beneath her jaw. 'I'm going to make you beg over, and over, and over again. And you're going to love it.'

His mouth moved from her jaw to her decolletage, pressing kisses along her collarbone before he moved lower, his stubble abrasive on the sensitive flesh of her breasts, in a way that she adored. A moment later, his mouth clasped over one of her nipples and she cried out as a thousand shock waves rolled through her, amounting to a massive tsunami of need. The pleasure was intense. She'd never known anything like it. He rolled her nipple with his tongue, flicking it, then intermittently pressing his teeth down so there was a heady rush of pleasure and pain, a mix of feelings that were hot and completely absorbing. His hand toyed with her other nipple, tweaking it between his forefinger and thumb until she was moaning, panting, barely capable of breathing, much less speaking. He moved faster, then swapped his mouth from one breast to the other, the sensation of his fingers on her moist nipple bringing her close to an edge she couldn't see, an edge she'd never before approached.

'I—I feel—' But the words were lodged in her brain, impossible to locate. How did one describe a feeling they'd never known before? 'Luca, I'm— Oh, Luca!'

He moved faster, and as he plucked and tweaked he brought a hand behind her back, holding her close to him, pressing her womanhood to his rock-hard arousal, so through the flimsy fabric of her underwear she could feel the intensity of his need, and knew that it matched her own. His arousal pressed to her most sensitive cluster of nerves, promising pleasure and delights she'd never known before. Olivia was spiralling out of control, with nothing and no one to hold onto. Except there was Luca, strong, clever, Luca; she gripped his shirt as her world began to change, moving beyond what she'd ever known, becoming fierce and fiery. She held him as she fell apart, sounds of her pleasure filling the luxury suite; her own hips began to writhe, seeking more, needing more, as wave after wave of pleasure wracked her body, redefining her until she knew that the experience had turned her into something, someone, she didn't know any more.

He pulled his head up, his own eyes heavy with arousal as he looked at her, scanning her face as if to reassure himself.

'I'm fine,' she promised. 'Better than fine.' Her hands moved to his belt, unsteady fingers moving to release it, but he stilled her with his touch, taking a step back.

'No.'

'No?' She pouted, still trembling from her first orgasm. 'But I want more. I want to see.'

His eyes sparked with hers, surprise obvious. 'We have a month. There's no harm going slowly, to make sure you don't regret this.'

She ground her teeth together. 'I'm not going to.'

'A few more days to be sure won't hurt.'

'You think?'

His smile lacked humour. 'Not too much, anyway.' He reached forward, brushing his hand over her sex, so briefly, but so perfectly, she whimpered at the subtle contact. 'Please…'

'Tomorrow,' he said, but with firm insistence. 'Tomorrow I'll go down on you until you see stars. *Bene?*'

He deserved a gold medal. A whole goddamned cabinet full of them. He had never wanted to sleep with a woman more than he had Olivia. Every sound she'd made, every whimper, every arch of her back, every press of her womanhood against his arousal had threatened to bring out his not-so-inner caveman, to hell with chivalry. If she weren't a virgin, it would have been a different story. If she hadn't grown up in such a vile atmosphere, been undermined at every turn, made to hide her beauty, made to feel ashamed of it, if she were meeting him as his true equal in terms of experience and confidence, then he wouldn't have let a single glass of Prosecco stop him from possessing her in all the ways they both wanted. But Olivia had lived through hell and the last thing she needed was another man disrespecting her wishes.

But hadn't he just done that? A part of him—his libido, Luca suspected—argued back, just as fervently. She'd clearly articulated what she wanted, and he'd refused to give it to her. No, not refused. Delayed. Besides, he meant what he'd said. There was more to sex than the actual act. She deserved to feel and experience all the things most people did as teenagers, when their hormones were just coming into play and they were exploring and experimenting.

And as she felt, and learned, he would be in control at all times. He would have to be. This wouldn't be like a normal affair, with the sorts of women he usually bedded. He would have to be particularly careful to keep Olivia at arm's length emotionally, to pleasure her by night, but maintain their boundaries anywhere and everywhere else.

Out of nowhere, Jayne breathed into his mind, her beautiful face, her lying eyes, the way she'd looked at him when his father's crimes had been revealed, when Luca had discovered that his once billion-dollar fortune was now worth nothing. And that was how she'd made him feel, too. Like nothing. Nobody. And he'd loved her so damned much, it had felt as if she were stabbing him, or slowly strangling him, the pain spreading through him, only worsening when he discovered she'd had an affair—that she'd used Luca as a stepping stone to climb to what she perceived to be a better marriage, a wealthier husband. And now?

Luca had the last laugh, because he was one of the richest men in the world, and he wouldn't touch Jayne with a ten-foot bargepole. Her legacy had changed his life—

he'd learned to keep all women at arm's length, and Olivia would be no different.

He bashed the pillow against the sofa, staring up at the ceiling with a hard-on that wouldn't quit, counting down the minutes until the morning, when her education could continue…

CHAPTER SEVEN

OLIVIA STRETCHED IN the enormous bed with a feeling of contentment that brought a smile to her lips even before she could recall why she felt so darned good. She arched her back and ran her hands over her body, but as her fingertips collided with her nipples, and remembered sensations came screaming back to her, she sat bolt upright, staring across the room at the large mirror.

Heat flushed her body.

Had she really propositioned her husband for sex? And had he really made her feel so incredible with his hands and mouth, and her breasts? Bemused, she stared at her reflection, wondering how she'd never known her body could be capable of such pleasure. His promise hung heavy in the air, driving her feet from the bed. *'Tomorrow, I'll go down on you until you see stars.'*

She could barely contain her excitement as she ran a brush through her hair and cleaned her teeth, then contemplated pulling on something more modest than the cream silk negligee Luca had bought for her, before realising how absurd that would be considering what she had planned for their morning…

With a heart that was thumping in her chest, she drew open the door to the lounge and stepped out, hoping he'd still be on the sofa.

He wasn't. Luca was, to her chagrin, fully dressed,

eating breakfast at the table with the spectacular view of the canal.

'Good morning.' His eyes lingered a little longer than was necessary on her face, scanning as if to see if she had any regrets.

She didn't, and so smiled with extra wattage, moving towards him slowly at first, a strange sense of nervousness that *he* might regret what she'd asked of him.

'Good morning,' she returned, husky-voiced, standing right in front of him.

Their eyes met and held, and electricity almost gave her a shock.

'How did you sleep?'

Really? He wanted to talk about sleep?

'Like a log,' she murmured.

'I'm glad.'

'You?' She arched a brow, unconsciously teasing him.

'I didn't.'

Her laugh was soft and spontaneous. 'No? Why ever not?'

He scowled at her before gesturing to the table, where an array of pastries and fruit was spread out. 'I think, even with your innocence, you know the answer to that. Have something to eat.'

'I'm not hungry.'

His body stiffened. 'No?'

She put a hand on his shoulder, drawing his gaze to her face. 'Not for breakfast.'

'You haven't changed your mind?'

She pulled a face. 'After your very effective demonstration last night? Not bloody likely.'

An arrogant smirk changed his features for the briefest moment and then he stood, towering over her. 'I haven't changed my mind either, Olivia. We take this slow.'

Oh, how she wanted to rail against that! How she wanted to scream that she was ready and to kindly stop telling her what to do and how she should feel, but even as she felt that surge of anger and frustration, she acknowledged the decency of his hesitation. She'd felt his arousal last night. She'd known he wanted her as badly as she did him, and yet he'd resisted. For her. To look after her. The realisation sent a strange wobble into her chest, and emotions of an entirely different sort threatened to overpower her so she tilted her jaw defiantly, employing all the skills she'd mastered in her life of concealing her thoughts and feelings from the outside world.

'So?' she challenged, eyes holding his.

'Ah, yes. I seem to remember I made you a promise last night.'

'Yes, you did.'

'Then I'd better make sure I don't break it. Are you ready?'

How could she ever be ready for such pleasure? How could she ever have prepared for the litany of sensations she'd experience as his mouth caressed her sex, his tongue alternately suckling and lashing, his stubble rough against her inner thighs, his kiss moving from firm and insistent to gentle and slow, until she was crying out, the torture of waiting causing sweat to bead on her brow as flames licked the soles of her feet and she wondered if anyone had ever had a heart attack from the intensity of this kind of passion? His hands held her thighs in place as his mouth drove her closer and closer to release, and as she began to soar into the heavens his hands cupped her breasts, tweaking her nipples as he had the night before, so shards of delight pierced her soul. His name spilled from her lips again and again, her nails scrambled to dig into the sheets first and then his shoulders, holding tight as she slipped off the edge of the world, into an abyss from which she wasn't sure she'd ever return.

Her breath tore into the room, rapidly at first, like a hurricane, and then slowing to a gale-force wind, until eventually she felt her pulse returning to something close to normal. He stood in the interim, turning his back on her, moving to the bathroom then returning a moment later, regarding her with an expression that gave nothing away.

'I'm starting to feel that this education is a little wanting,' she said, propping up on one elbow, uncaring, in that moment, for her nakedness.

'Oh? Is that a complaint?'

'Well…' she plucked at the sheet, heat spreading through her veins '…it does feel a little one sided.' Her eyes dropped, pointedly, to his trousers, which were still fastened, then returned to his face.

He stayed where he was, arms crossed over his broad chest. 'We have plenty of time.' He held out a hand, and she placed hers in it, so he could pull her to standing. 'Besides, we have plans this morning.'

'We do?'

He nodded slowly.

'What plans?'

'I thought we could tour Murano, seeing as you have not been to this part of Italy before. Their glass is incomparable.'

Her heart stammered for a different reason now, his thoughtfulness wholly unexpected. This wasn't a real honeymoon, and yet he was acting as though it were, and there was a part of Olivia—a large part—that was happy because of it.

Except it was all make-believe; she had to remember that. This was all a ruse, and she had to play her part. 'I've always wanted to see Murano,' she murmured.

'Then get dressed.' But he didn't relinquish his grip on her hand; instead, he squeezed it more tightly. 'Before I change my mind.'

'About that,' she said softly, allowing her own hand to brush his trousers, watching for his reaction. It didn't disappoint. His eyes lowered, his lips parting on a hiss of breath, and then he stepped backwards. 'Murano's been there for hundreds of years. Do you really think an extra hour will make any difference?'

'An hour?' He leaned closer, his eyes fighting with hers, his tone self-deprecating. 'Believe me, *cara*, if you touch me, nothing will take close to an hour.' A frisson of anticipation spread through her at the promise of his words. 'I'll be waiting.' He released her hand and left the room, with Olivia staring after him with a strange mix of arousal, satisfaction and frustration.

Murano defied every single one of her expectations. Brightly coloured buildings stood on either side of the canal, and the sun shone as their boat cruised along the water. Halfway, Luca asked that they stop, handing her from the boat and gesturing to one of the buildings.

'This is one of the oldest glass galleries in Murano. Come, see if anything takes your fancy.'

She walked beside him, happiness and contentment lifting her soul. It only intensified when they stepped inside the enormous ancient yet beautifully preserved building.

'Glass has been manufactured on Murano since the thirteenth century. The techniques haven't changed in all that time.' He gestured to large timber doors that led to a workshop. The area of creation was separate from the gallery. A handful of tourists was ahead of them, more entered behind, but as Olivia watched the workers below, crafting unique, individual, ethereal pieces, with Luca right by her side, she felt as though they were the only two people on earth.

'They're so skilled,' she commented in awe as they neared the end of the gallery, to a shop where various pieces were displayed, their price tags conspicuously absent.

'Yes. This is a family business. Each craftsman has been trained by their parents, the skills passed down from father and mother to child.' He reached out, lifting a delicate glass. 'It's fascinating how just a few elements can combine to make something so unique.'

She blinked, strangely overcome by the experience, and even more so by Luca's apparent reverence for the ancient skill. She offered him a tight smile then moved away, needing a moment to compose herself.

Shelves lined with glasses, bowls and little trinkets—statues and decorations—clamoured for her attention, so she circled the store several times, scanning the objects with growing admiration. But each time, her eyes lingered on one in particular—a brightly coloured bird with large wings. It stood on a glass base. The whole thing was about the size of Olivia's hand, but every time she passed it she felt a tingling sensation in her fingertips, as though she simply had to touch it. On the third time she passed it, she finally gave in, stopping and admiring it from every angle first, before reaching out and gingerly lifting the piece.

Something locked into place in her chest. Her eyes met Luca's and flames with all the intensity of those the glass blowers worked with flared between them.

'You would like this?'

She lifted it once more, looking for the price. None was visible. 'It's very beautiful,' she said, non-committally.

He reached out, taking it from her, then caught her hand, guiding her towards the cash register, where an older woman was working at the computer.

'Ah, this is one of my favourites,' she exclaimed, eyeing Olivia and Luca with approval.

'My wife chose it.'

My wife. The words were said so naturally, but they sparked a thousand and one feelings inside Olivia, feelings that she couldn't fathom. There was panic, fear, a sharp need to say 'no', because being some man's 'wife' was something she had always, always loathed the idea of. And yet, in the midst of that, there was surprise and warmth, pleasure at being marked as Luca's. Her nerves tangled, making it impossible to understand herself or her feelings.

'My son crafted this piece. It is a *fenice*.'

Olivia turned to Luca, frowning. His eyes, when they met hers, were appraising. 'A phoenix.'

'Do you know the symbolism of the *fenice*?' the older woman asked as she carefully surrounded the bird in bubble wrap.

'Something about rising from the ashes?' Olivia suggested.

'Yes. In many cultures, the world over, it is seen as a symbolism of rebirth, of hope, of newness.' She taped the bird, then placed it into a brown paper bag. 'He will be safe with you.'

A shiver ran through Olivia at the perfection of having gravitated towards such an ornament. Here she was, taking steps to begin her own new life, and she had unconsciously chosen a symbol of regeneration.

Luca handed over his credit card, a matte black with a silver centurion in the centre, before the shopkeeper could announce the price. Olivia decided she would do better not to ask.

'Thank you,' she said as they emerged back onto the sunlit street. They'd been in the glass factory for over an hour, and in that time the summer sun had warmed so it felt delightful against her bare arms.

They wandered the streets of Murano. The island was not big, and it did not take long, but as the temperature increased it was absolutely essential to stop and enjoy *gelati* from one of the street vendors. Olivia chose strawberry, and the sweetness filled her with a sense of completion.

'Thank you for this morning,' she said as she scraped the last of the *gelato* from the paper cup. 'I've actually really enjoyed our honeymoon.'

His short laugh sent tremors through her body. 'You are surprised?'

'Well, yes, frankly. Don't forget, when we married, I knew very little about you.'

For a moment, his smile dropped, and thunderclouds seemed to pass behind his eyes. 'Except what you read on the Internet.'

She frowned. That bothered him? 'That's right.'

'And still you chose to marry me?' he said as a joke, but she heard the caustic tension in his voice.

'I mean, I sort of had my arm up my back there,' she pointed out, then wished she hadn't when the mood changed completely. Oh, he still smiled at her, but she felt the change come over him, and couldn't quite pinpoint why.

'I thought we'd fly directly to Rome. Unless you have any objections?' he prompted as an afterthought.

The suggestion made her head spin. She was just starting to settle into her honeymoon and now he was suggesting a change? Except, this wasn't really unexpected. He'd said their honeymoon would last for two nights, and it had been that. It was time to go home now. Not to a real home—at least, not for Olivia—but to the place she'd live in for the rest of her very short, very necessary marriage.

'Luca, may I ask you something?'

He regarded her from the back of the limousine with a look that might have scared anyone else off, but Olivia had lived with fear and intimidation all her life, and Luca simply wasn't capable of causing her to feel either. He was nothing like her father. Nothing like she feared all men might be.

'You don't have to answer,' she offered.

'Believe me, if I do not wish to, I won't.'

She *did* believe it. Luca wasn't capable of doing anything *but* calling the shots. She nodded her acceptance of that, flicking her gaze to the window for a moment. Rome whizzed past, the early afternoon light shimmering with that Mediterranean clarity. Ancient buildings stood sentinel to their journey, grey and magnificent, so Olivia wanted to stop the car and go and explore them now, to trail her hands over each, one by one, until she felt their secrets bury deep into her soul.

'Earlier today, you seemed annoyed to think I'd read up on you.'

He was quiet for a long time. She turned to face him, arching a brow.

'I'm sorry, was that a question?'

She could feel his impatience, and something else. A hesitation born of an emotion she didn't understand. 'Yes. *Why* does that annoy you?'

'On the contrary, I think it's a wise precaution. You asked a virtual stranger to marry you. I'd think you stupid not to do a bit of research.'

'Sure, fine, but it still annoys you.'

He drummed his fingers into his knee, his eyes not leaving her face.

'You're not going to answer me, are you?'

He compressed his lips, and she felt a battle raging in his mind, a choice being made. Before she could determine who was the victor, the car drew to a halt. She could just make out a street sign, an old mosaic attached to the building at the corner. Via Giulia, it said. She didn't need to know anything about the street to know that it was expensive real estate. The buildings here were very old, beautifully maintained, with abundant greenery and splashes of colour bursting from gardens that were concealed by high walls.

He waited for her to step from the limousine, before gesturing to a dark wooden door, arched, nestled within a pale pink rendered wall.

'This is Palazzo Centro,' he said, pinning a series of numbers into a discreet electric pad. The door sprang open. He held it wide to allow Olivia to pass. Frustrated at having her question unanswered, she passed without looking at him, and was quickly overwhelmed by the sheer beauty of this place. She had expected something elegant, of course, but not rich with history like this. It felt as though it should have been a museum, and not a home.

'You live here?'

'When I'm in Rome, *sì*.'

'Which is how often?'

The garden was very old, if the size of the trees was any indication. A water feature was set against one wall, creating the delightful sound of rain falling, and in the centre there was a bird bath, with little balls of moss floating on top. A marble path cut through the garden, towards a front door that was timber, with gold detail.

'Most of the time. Perhaps three weeks out of four.'

'And the rest of the time?'

'Wherever I need to be.' He didn't need to push the door open. A housekeeper appeared, dressed in black, her hair worn in a low grey bun. 'Signora Marazzi, this is my wife, Signora Giovanardi.'

The housekeeper did a double take. 'Your wife?' she clarified in Italian.

Luca nodded. 'Please make her feel welcome when I am not home.'

'Certo, certo.' The housekeeper stared at Luca and then gave the full force of her attention to Olivia, who was, by now, feeling a little self-conscious. The housekeeper's scrutiny didn't help. 'But you are so beautiful.' She clapped her hands together. 'Like a Caravaggio figure with your porcelain skin and luminescent eyes.'

Olivia squirmed under the extravagant praise, a lifetime of criticism impossible to shake off.

Luca reached for her hand. 'We were married only two days ago and will want privacy. Would you see that the fridge is stocked before you leave, and ask the other staff to give us space?'

It seemed to call the housekeeper back to her duties.

She blinked, smiling. '*Certo.* I will come back tomorrow afternoon, to see if *la signora* needs anything.'

Luca jerked his head by way of thanks, and Olivia watched the interaction with amusement.

'You know, that bordered on rude.'

He laughed. 'Believe me, Signora Marazzi will be almost as pleased as my grandmother that I've remarried—even if it does prove to be temporary.'

She ignored the tightening in her stomach as his words foreshadowed the end to their ruse.

He guided her through the entrance hall with its vaulted ceilings and chandeliers to a lounge room that was surprisingly modern.

'An electrical fire destroyed most of the house's interior and the owners could not afford the repair. I bought it for a steal, salvaged what I could, but, for the most part, a total reconstruction was required.'

'Oh, what a terrible shame,' she murmured. And yet, as she looked around the room, the juxtaposition of the ancient stone walls and modern interior had a sort of magical property, as though the house was bridging the gap between new and old. 'It's very striking,' she said sincerely.

'It works.'

'It reminds me of the *fenice*,' she said, with a small smile. 'A phoenix, risen from the ashes.'

He cocked a brow. 'I suppose you are right. I have not thought of it like this before.' His hands caught her hips, holding her still, his eyes probing, asking questions, wondering. She stared back, an open book.

'There are many things written about me on the Internet. It doesn't generally bother me. What strangers choose to opine about me or my family is more a reflection of them than me. And yet, the idea of *you* having read them, of you believing them, is strangely disconcerting.'

Her heart slammed into her ribs. 'I didn't say that I believe what I read.'

His lips formed a grimace. 'Some of them are true.'

'Such as you being a womaniser?'

He hesitated a moment before confirming that with a nod. Jealousy fired through her, fierce and debilitating. She pushed it aside.

'So? Do you think that matters to me? This isn't a real marriage, remember?'

'And if it were?'

She considered that. Would his philandering have had an impact on how she felt about him?

'It's not,' she dodged the question. 'As for your father, do you really think I'm in any position to hold the sins of one man against his child?'

Luca let his hands fall away, turning away from Olivia's penetrating gaze.

'And my first marriage?'

Olivia frowned. 'There was surprisingly very little about that,' she admitted, because she *had* looked. Curiosity had fired her fingers; she'd wanted to understand it—and him.

'No.'

'It wasn't amicable?'

He made a sound rich with disbelief. 'It was far from it.' He turned to face her, speaking mechanically. 'My wife left me for someone she viewed to be far wealthier, far more powerful. I don't know how long it had been going on, but when my father went to prison, she walked out on our marriage. Jayne wasn't prepared to slum it with me.'

Olivia's lips parted with surprise, and anger. How could his first wife have been so callous? To leave him when he was already suffering so much because of his father?

'She didn't love you.' She answered her own question.

'No.' His lips formed a grim line. 'I came to that conclusion eventually, but it took a long time.' He seemed to rouse himself. 'Her husband did everything he could to rewrite their relationship, to avoid a scandal developing. I had no interest in dragging her name through the mud, so allowed the narrative to play out. There was very little tabloid interest, given the way it appeared on the surface.'

Sympathy softened her features. 'It must have been very hard for you—going through what you did with your father, and then Jayne.'

A muscle jerked in his jaw. 'But I had Nonna,' he said quietly. 'Without her, I cannot say with any certainty that I would have survived.'

But Luca didn't want to talk about his past. He never did, not with anyone, but he felt a particular distaste in discussing it with Olivia. He told himself it had nothing to do with making him look like a failure in her eyes, and everything to do with the vow he'd made himself, to keep her at a distance from him. There had to be some boundaries in their marriage.

But there were others they could disregard. Others they could tear down. Turning to face her, with eyes that glittered with dark speculation, he lifted a single finger, beckoning her towards him.

She dug her teeth into her lower lip as she moved, half gliding across the room, until she stood right in front of him.

Deliberately, with as little passion as he could display, he lifted his hands to her shirt, finding one of the buttons that lined the silken seam. Her eyes clung to his face as he flicked it apart, then moved to the next. Calm, in control, just as he promised himself he'd be with her.

'It's time for another lesson.'

He felt the shiver that sparked through her blood. 'I thought you'd never ask.'

CHAPTER EIGHT

'YOU KNOW, TECHNICALLY that's a revision, not a lesson,' she pointed out, pushing up on one elbow when her breathing had returned to normal. He grinned from between her legs, before pulling himself up the bed, his body over hers, his arms braced on either side of her head as his full weight pressed her into the mattress.

'Complaining?'

'Not at all,' she assured him huskily. 'Just eager for advancement.'

'An A-plus student,' he murmured, nibbling her ear lobe. Olivia held him right where he was, his body so heavenly against hers, his proximity launching a kaleidoscope of butterflies in her abdomen. She could feel his arousal and yet she had no experience, no knowledge, and so, despite his obvious physical awareness of her, worry permeated her fog of pleasure, so her eyes flickered away from his, filled with uncertainty.

'What is it?'

She glanced back at him with a start. Was she so easy to read?

'Yes,' he responded to her unasked question. 'I can tell when something is bothering you. Your face is very expressive.'

'I know.' She expelled a soft sigh. 'I've tried to change that.'

'It's your eyes. They give everything away.'

She grimaced. 'Perhaps a pair of very dark sunglasses,' she suggested thoughtfully.

'Or, you could tell me what's on your mind.'

'Well,' she pressed her palms flat to his chest. 'Actually, that would be you.'

Triumph shaped his features. 'I'm pleased to hear it.'

'Not in a good way.'

'I see.'

'I just...'

He waited, and when she didn't continue, prompted her gently. 'Yes?'

'Is there something wrong with me?' she blurted out, then pulled her hands from his chest purely to cover her face and the eyes he'd just said he could read like open books.

'Wrong with you? What the hell do you mean?'

'It's just, you seem to be able to touch me and kiss me and make me feel a thousand and one things, then walk away again. Don't you...*want* me?'

He swore in Italian, his eyes boring into hers. 'Look at me, Olivia. Look at my face. Do you not see the tension there? Do you not realise that it is taking every ounce of my willpower to take this slowly, to make your first time what it ought to be?'

Her heart stammered. 'But it's just sex,' she whispered.

'No, it is your *first time* having sex. After me, you may make love to whomever you want, and at whatever speed you want. With them, it will be "just sex". But with me, and for your first time, it is different. Special. Even when we have both agreed it means nothing, it means *something* because you have not done this before. If this were about what I wanted, and what I wanted only, I would have made love to you in the elevator in Positano.'

Her breath squeezed from her lungs. 'Seriously?'

'You think I didn't want you even then?'

He dropped his head, kissing her lips gently. 'You think I didn't want you the second I saw you at that damned party? I watched you and wanted you, even before I knew you were looking for me, *cara*.'

She lowered her gaze.

'So do not think for even one moment that I am simply walking away from you. I am torturing myself by waiting.'

'Torturing us both,' she promised throatily.

'And if I promise the wait will be worth it?'

'How long a wait?'

He laughed before moving his mouth to her breast. 'Not long.' He flicked her nipple lazily, sending arrows of pleasure barbing through her body.

'Do you realise I haven't even seen you naked?'

Heat slashed his cheeks with dark colour and then he pushed to standing, his eyes on hers the whole time. Their eyes locked as he moved his hands to his belt buckle and unfastened it, as he slid his trousers down, as her eyes saw his naked arousal for the first time. Olivia sat up a little straighter, fascinated, compelled, and utterly turned on.

'I—' She was at a loss for words. Helplessly, her eyes drifted to his and stayed locked there as he finished undressing, then stood, stark naked, like an incredibly sculpted statue, a Roman deity, all muscled and mouth-watering. Her eyes flickered lower, across his broadly muscled chest, to his tapered waist, taut thighs, manhood, and lower to his shapely calves. Her heart was in her throat when she dragged her gaze back to his face.

'And now you have seen me naked,' he growled, heat simmering in his eyes, pooling between them. She swallowed past a constricted throat then stood, matching his body language, slowly removing the last of her clothing, until she was also naked in this palatial bedroom with panoramic views over Rome.

The air around them crackled with a challenge, an invitation, and she felt Luca's tension as he decided what to do. Finally, he held out a hand to her. 'Come. Let me show you something.'

He led her from the bedroom, down the corridor, both as naked as the day they were born.

'What about Signora Marazzi?'

'What about her?'

'What if she sees—?'

'I suspect she left almost immediately.'

'I suppose she's used to your philandering habits.' Olivia giggled softly, wondering why the sound was oddly forced to her own ears.

He threw a glance over his shoulder. 'This way.'

She noticed he didn't respond to her statement. Well, so? What could he say? They both knew the lie of the land—he was a bachelor, through and through. Nothing about this was new for him, except the whole 'marriage' part, and even then, he'd been married before. Something rolled through her, something dark and fierce, surprising her. It was a mix of curiosity and something else, something fiercer, compelling her to understand about his first marriage, about his life before her, about the experiences that had shaped him. But that was none of her business. Per their agreement, she had no right to ask, and certainly, no expectation that he'd answer.

The hallway opened onto a landing and a narrow set of stairs. She followed behind his naked form, admiring the muscled firmness of his rear as he moved up two flights then pushed a modern steel door open. They burst onto a rooftop terrace, shielded from view by hedges that grew in large terracotta pots. At the centre of the paved terrace was a pool, submerged, and the most striking turquoise colour Olivia could imagine. The afternoon sun bounced off it tantalisingly, invitingly, so she glided towards it on autopilot.

'How stunning,' she murmured, not realising that Luca had followed. He placed his hands on her hips, drawing her back against him, so his arousal pressed between her buttocks. She closed her eyes on a rushed gasp, her pleasure only increasing when he brought one hand around to her breasts, lazily stroking her nipples before moving his mouth to the crook of her neck, whispering and tasting her there until she was moaning softly into the afternoon sun.

'Swim with me,' he suggested.

She wanted to do so much more than swim with him, but when he released her and dived into the water, she stood there, watching his lithe athleticism, spellbound by his masculine beauty, before she did the same, splashing into the water with a heady sense of euphoria. Her wedding ring glinted as she swam, catching her eye, the diamonds so clear and sparkling.

It was a sign of possession she'd always railed against, but on this day, in this minute, wearing this man's ring, Olivia couldn't say she minded, at all.

'That was incredibly delicious.' She dabbed her lips with the linen napkin, then placed it in her lap.

'Signora Marazzi is an exceptional cook,' he agreed.

'Does she make all your meals?'

'Or I eat out.' He shrugged.

'You never cook for yourself?'

'No. I never learned.'

'It's not rocket science.'

'Perhaps. But there's no need.'

'What about during your marriage? Don't tell me your wife was chained to the kitchen?'

'Hardly,' he drawled, without elaborating further. The same curiosity that had burst through Olivia earlier that day flooded her again.

She leaned forward. 'You don't have to answer if you don't want to.' It was a silly precursor to say—naturally Luca wouldn't do *anything* he didn't want to. 'When your wife left you, you went to live with your grandmother?'

'That is no secret,' he said, quietly though, warily, as though he was bracing for an even worse question.

'She wasn't affected by the bankruptcy?'

'He's her son.' Luca's voice was strained. She reached over and pressed her hand to his. 'Of course, she was affected.'

'I meant in a financial sense.'

His smile held a rejection. 'My grandmother owns her own house, and her own business. When my father inherited from my grandfather, it was always on the basis that Nonna's assets would be held separate. There was no threat to her.'

'What a wise precaution that turned out to be.'

'My grandfather insisted. Nonna came from nothing, and he always joked that it was the only way he could be sure she really loved him. He made her a very wealthy woman even before he proposed, so he knew there was no financial incentive in her accepting the proposal.'

'He was a cynic?'

'Or a realist. He was worth a small fortune.'

'She obviously loved him.'

'She did. But even once they were married, her fortune was kept aside, all in her name, all her own. So when my father was charged, and everything he owned was taken away, Nonna lost nothing.'

'Except her son,' Olivia murmured sadly.

'And her good name,' he added. 'Thanks to my father, Giovanardi now means "mud" in Italian.'

Olivia winced. 'You don't deserve that.'

'Don't I?'

She pulled her lips to the side, shaking her head a little. 'Of course you don't. None of it was your fault.'

He placed his knife and fork on his plate, glaring at them. 'I wish things had turned out differently.'

'Do you speak to him?'

'No.'

'Your choice or his?'

'Mutual.'

'You haven't forgiven him?'

'Not really. And I know he'll never forgive me.'

'Why? What did you do that was so terrible?'

Luca's eyes met hers, almost as though he was challenging her to think as badly of him as he did himself. 'I caused it all, *cara*. It's my fault.'

'What are you talking about?'

'I discovered what he'd done. I couldn't fathom how he'd dug such a deep hole, and so I confronted him, hoping for a simple explanation. Only the one he gave made no sense. I could see there was never going to be a way to pay off all the investors. It was a Ponzi scheme, an enormous house of cards, ready to tumble at the slightest breeze.'

She grimaced. 'It must have been terrible for you to realise that.'

'He preyed on our friends, the parents of my school friends, men he'd known all his life. He was unscrupulous and greedy. When I went to the police, it was in the hopes some of the money could be recovered, but the scheme collapsed and everyone lost everything.'

'You most of all,' she said quietly.

He ran a hand through his hair. 'We were very wealthy, but it wasn't enough for him. He wanted more, always more.'

Olivia couldn't offer any words to comfort him, so she did the only thing she could, moving around the table and settling herself on his lap, arms hooked behind his neck.

'That isn't your fault.'

He met her eyes, and she saw the trauma in them, the regret, the fervent wish that things had been different. How she ached for him!

'Not your father's actions, nor your wife's betrayal. You didn't deserve any of it.'

He kept his gaze averted from hers, a muscle throbbing low in his squared jaw, so she lifted a finger to it, feeling his pulse, fascinated by the tightness there as he clenched his teeth together.

'How did you do all this?' She shifted the subject a little, waving a hand around her to the palatial lounge that opened onto the back garden. 'You rebuilt an empire from nothing.'

'Not nothing,' he corrected with a bitter smile. 'There was Nonna's business.'

'She handed it to you,' Olivia guessed.

'Yes.' His expression was defiant. 'She trusted me, and I desperately wanted to make her proud, to prove her right. I worked around the clock for two years, growing her small chain of accommodation into a global force of exclusive, boutique hotels, before branching out into transport logistics, and then airlines. It wasn't easy. None of the major banks in Italy would, initially, lend to me.' A cynical smile tilted his lips. 'Including Azzuri—the bank I plan to acquire.' The rejection had been one of many he'd experienced at the time, but it had cut him deep, representing what he'd thought to be the end of the road. The humiliation he'd felt, at having to go in there to beg, in the first instance, and having his proposal tossed out as though it were worthless junk. He'd never forgotten that humiliation.

'Even with your grandmother's wealth?' Olivia stroked his cheek gently.

'Even then.' Luca brought himself back to the present. 'Giovanardi means mud, remember?'

'What did you do?'

'Sold two of her hotels to raise capital.'

She shook her head. 'You must have been so scared.'

His lips twisted in a mocking smile. 'Angry, actually.'

She laughed softly. 'Yes, that too.'

'I hated the banks, all of them. And particularly Azzuri,' he was surprised to hear himself admit. 'It was when I expanded into new tech that things really improved. I was able to pay back my father's debts—every last one of them—and to create an empire my grandfather would have been proud of.'

She heard his drive and determination, and the dark forces that had compelled him to work so hard for so long, and felt a surge of pity. Would he ever feel that he'd done enough?

'Pietra must have been impressed.'

His smile was just a hint. 'Yes.' He lifted a hand to Olivia's cheek, tucking her hair behind her ear. 'She'd lost so much. My grandfather, then the family reputation, the business. I knew that I couldn't fail her.'

'You didn't.'

He dipped his head in acknowledgement. 'And yet,' he said quietly, 'it doesn't matter how much I am worth, or how much business succeeds, there is always a question hanging over my head. Did I cheat to get here? Am I like my father? Can people trust me? His shadow has dogged me my entire adult life.'

She shook her head a little. 'And yet, look at my father—a man whose ancient name earned him a seat at any table, who was thought of so highly, and yet, he was—as you said—a total jackass.' She leaned closer, her gaze intense. 'What does a name matter, Luca? It's the man that counts, the man you are, the deeds that you do. That's what people should care about.'

She ran her finger around his lips, tracing the outline there. 'And I think you are a good man, who's done great deeds. In fact, I think you're very noble.'

'Because I married you?' he prompted, his voice lightly teasing.

'Absolutely,' she responded in kind, only half joking, then sobered. 'You saved me. I mean that seriously.' Tears threatened so she forced a bright smile. Things were getting too serious between them, too intense. Neither of them wanted that. 'And because you paid back the money your father stole, when you didn't have to.'

'Not legally, but morally. Ethically.'

She brushed her lips over his. 'See? You're undoubtedly decent.'

He expelled a short sound of amusement. 'I don't think you'd say that if you knew the decidedly indecent thoughts I've been having about you.'

Pleasure warmed her. 'Tell me,' she invited, moving her bottom a little from side to side, watching as his eyes darkened with the unmistakable rush of desire. 'Or better yet…' She moved her mouth to his, kissing him gently at the corner. 'Show me,' she invited, pushing his shirt up his body, revealing his taut abdomen, her fingers brushing his wall of abdominals then discarding the shirt on the floor. He didn't fight her and she was so glad; she didn't realise *how* sure she'd been that he would fight her until he didn't and relief flooded her body. Relief, and a rush of desire.

She shifted on the seat, needing more purchase, more of him, so she lifted up and straddled him, allowing her head to drop to his chest, her tongue to tease his nipples, as he'd done to her on so many occasions. He shuddered beneath her touch, pleasure radiating through him, so power surged in her veins.

'Are you sure you want to do this?' he asked, and hope was an explosion in the centre of her chest.

'Do what?' she prompted with mock innocence, blinking her blue eyes at him.

He groaned, bringing his hands to cup her buttocks, drawing her right onto the hardness she could feel through his trousers. The smile dropped from her mouth as urgency overtook her.

'I'm sure,' she agreed. 'Did you think I'd change my mind?'

'I don't know.' His smile was taut. 'You only get one chance to lose your virginity.'

'Do you think I want to wait until I'm thirty?'

'I think you might want to wait until you meet someone you're in an actual relationship with.'

'We've discussed that.' She shook her head resolutely. 'I'm no more interested in an actual relationship than you are.' Saying those words felt good. Important. Because they also felt very wrong, and she couldn't understand why, but she needed to hold onto their agreement, the pledge they'd made to one another. 'I'm only after meaningless sex, remember?'

She moved back to kissing him, need propelling anything else from her mind. It was the same for Luca. Having held off for days despite the temptation, he felt, finally, as though he were about to be unleashed and his impatience knew no bounds. He undressed Olivia as quickly as he could, not wanting to move her from his lap but needing better access to lower her pants. God, if it weren't her first time, he'd have loved to make love to her right here, like this, with her on his lap at the dining table, God help him, it would be perfection. But not for her first time.

He stood, lifting her easily, wrapping her legs around his waist as he carried her through the house, up the stairs to his bedroom, his fingers kneading her buttocks.

'I can walk,' she said on a tremulous laugh, her voice brushing his throat.

'And then I would not get to hold you like this.'

His bedroom felt like a thousand miles away. Finally, he shouldered his way through the door and placed her on the bed, bringing his body over hers, not pausing to draw breath, just needing to kiss her properly now that he could. Her hands roamed his naked torso, feeling, touching, exploring, familiarising herself with him completely; he'd never known something as simple as touch to be so incendiary. He stepped out of his pants with urgency, needing to be naked and close to her, needing her with a fire-like intensity.

Her fingers glided down his arms, latching with his, so he held her arms at her sides as he kissed her, devouring her, passionately possessing her until he pushed her back onto the bed and they fell, a tangle of limbs, legs entwined and writhing as they sought the ultimate closeness. His need for her cracked through him, contorting him, so he had to focus to remember her innocence, to hold himself back, to stop from taking her as he wanted.

But at every step, Olivia met him as an equal, so that despite her innocence she was his match, her enthusiasm giving her confidence. But it was more than that. Holding back, waiting for this, exploring each other day after day, had built to a crescendo. They'd been engaged in a torturous form of foreplay for days and nights, desire building until it reached a zenith. Her touch drove him wild, driving all ability to think from his mind. She wrapped her legs around his waist, drawing him closer, and the tip of his arousal nudged between her legs, so he groaned, long and low, aching to push into her, to feel her muscles spasm around his hard length. But caution was ingrained in Luca, so even now, while incapable of stringing two words together, he knew enough to pull up and take a moment, to stare down at her, before reaching to his bedside table and removing a condom. His eyes latched to hers as he opened the packet, then slid it over his length—an act Olivia's own gaze devoured in a way that made desire spear him from the inside out. 'Do you have any idea what you're doing to me?'

'Me?' She purred.

He laughed gruffly. 'Oh, you know *exactly* how you make me feel.'

She reached up, grabbing him by the shoulders so she could pull him back on top of her. 'Maybe a fraction of how *you* make *me* feel?'

'Is that a fact?'

'I think it might be.'

'And what about this?' He pressed himself inside her, just enough for Olivia to gasp, her eyes widening, so confused wonder crossed her features.

'Are you okay?'

She nodded, her features tense.

'Breathe,' he said gently, lowering his mouth to hers, brushing their lips as he pushed into her completely, slowly at first, giving her time to adjust to the invasion of his arousal.

Olivia tensed as pain gripped her, unexpected, immediate, but searing, like a flash of lightning in the sky, and then it was gone, giving way to slight discomfort at first, and then a warm glow of pleasure as he began to move, his arousal so deep inside her that she felt a pleasure she'd never known possible. He kissed her in time to his movements and she scratched her fingers down his back as euphoria threatened to overtake everything else.

Only the sound of her rushing blood filled Olivia's ears. She would never have said pleasure could be excruciating but, to her, that was what it felt like, as each thrust of Luca's arousal seemed to bring her both pleasure and impatience all at once. Stars formed behind her eyelids and then, out of nowhere, she was bursting apart at the seams, pleasure no longer excruciating but almost too exquisite to bear. She rolled back her head and squeezed her eyes shut as she rode the wave of release, his name on her lips, filling the silence of the room, adding to the cacophony of her own body's pleasure.

He pushed up on one elbow, scanning her eyes as if seeking reassurance, and when Olivia's breath slowed, she smiled at him, wonder and joy in her features.

But it was only a temporary reprieve and then Luca was moving again, and now his possession was hard and fast, showing Olivia how gentle he'd been the first time, how deferential to her inexperience. Pleasure had built quickly, but it was nothing compared to this. As he thrust into her again, and again, hard and fast, a primal, animalistic need spread like wildfire, so she was pushing up and rolling over, needing to be on top, to take more of him, all of him.

He growled, a low, husky sound, as he grabbed her hips,

holding her deep on his length for a moment, then letting go, so Olivia controlled the rhythm, bucking and rolling hard and fast at first then moaning softly as she slowed down. His hand brushed her sex, his fingers pressing her there until the combination of his possession and his touch was too much, and she was tumbling again, over the edge of reality, into a field of utter heaven. But this time, she wasn't alone. Luca lifted his hips, taking control once more, and then he was joining her, exploding as he said her name, then pulled her down towards him, kissing her as his body was wracked with his exploding pleasure, kissing her as both morphed into something beyond what they could recognise.

'So, that's sex, huh?' She pushed up a little, to see into his eyes. Pleasure still throbbed between her legs, and she was glad he stayed inside her; she wasn't ready to lose that intimacy yet.

'Pretty much,' he responded in kind, light-hearted, both somehow understanding that they needed to contrast the intensity of what they'd just shared with the casual nature of their relationship.

'Well, I'm not sure I see what all the fuss is about,' she said with obvious sarcasm, her body still trembling with the force of her release.

He laughed softly, caught her wrists then rolled them, pinning Olivia on her back beneath him, pulling out of her so she moaned, wanting him back more than anything. 'Then perhaps you need another demonstration?'

She batted her eyelids, pretending to consider it. 'That could be useful,' she said after a lengthy pause.

'Minx.' But he laughed for as long as he was able, before taking one of her nipples in his mouth and biting down on it, hard enough to make her moan. Olivia lifted her hips, surrendering to the hedonism of this, and in the back of her mind, in the small part of her brain capable of rational thought, she was aware of how fortunate she was. She'd married a man who was teaching her the pleasure her body was capable of feeling, and in a few weeks, they'd walk away from one another—no hard feelings. It was everything she hadn't known she'd wanted, until she'd married Luca Giovanardi.

CHAPTER NINE

'HANG ON. WHAT are you wearing?'

He turned to face her, a sardonic look of enquiry on his face that made her simmer with desire. 'Brioni, I believe.'

'A suit? But whatever for?' After all, in the week since their first time together, Olivia and Luca had barely left bed, except to eat or swim, and even then they'd been naked.

'I have a meeting and I'm pretty sure, though not one hundred per cent, that nudity would be frowned upon.'

'A meeting? With other people?' She reached out a hand, drawing him to her, her eyes an invitation Luca couldn't resist.

'With the chairman of Azzuri Bank, in fact.'

Olivia tilted her head to the side, considering that. He'd only mentioned it briefly, but she hadn't forgotten the fierce look of determination that had gripped him as he'd referred to the bank that had refused to lend money to him when he'd been starting over in life. She knew what this meeting would mean for him.

'I've been out of the office way longer than intended,' he continued, conversationally. Calm. In control. Just like always.

'I'll take that as a compliment.'

'As it was intended.' He pressed a kiss to the tip of her nose, aware that if he didn't pull away from her, he'd start undressing, adding a delay to his schedule he couldn't afford. 'You have no need to do anything so horrible as pull on clothing. In fact, I'd suggest you don't.'

A smile tipped her lips. 'Oh? What shall I do all day, then, Luca?'

'Lie naked in bed and wait for me.' He grabbed her hand, pressing it to her sex. 'Think of me. Miss me.'

Her heart stumbled and pleasure burst through her, but it was quickly followed by a surge of panic so fierce it took all her energy to conceal any display of it. Wait for him? Think of him? *Miss him?* What happened to the independence she was fiercely chasing? To never wanting to be like her mother, so stupidly loyal and in love she forgave Thomas anything and everything?

Olivia angled her face away on the pretence of scoping out the weather. 'It's sunny again today. I might go and explore. I fear clothes will be necessary for me, too.'

'My driver can take you anywhere,' he offered, after a slight pause.

'I'd prefer to walk.'

He lifted his shoulders in a shrug then straightened. She didn't fight his departure—she'd had a wake-up call and it had been a vital, timely reminder. Do *not* depend on him. Do *not* ask him for more.

'Suit yourself. Don't get lost.'

He moved to the door, all casual, breezy, non-committal, so she felt silly for having experienced a sense of panic. They were nothing like her parents. This was nothing like their marriage. Olivia would *never* be beholden to another person as Angelica had been Thomas.

And yet, a powerful need to underscore that drove through her, so she called to him, when he was almost out of the door. 'Only three weeks to go, Luca. Let's make the most of them.'

It was the affirmation she needed, words that were a balm to her soul, even when they pulled at something in her chest, leaving her scrambling, a little, to draw sufficient breath. Life after Luca loomed, and she no longer knew exactly what shape it would take.

It was precisely because he was thinking of Olivia almost constantly that Luca remained at his desk until after seven, that evening. He was getting close to securing the deal of the century. It wasn't final yet, but he finally had the support of the chairman of the Azzuri Bank. It had taken years of delicate negotiations, but he'd done it, and there was vindication in his success. Revenge, too. Because they kicked him while he was down, and he'd sworn he'd never forget it.

He hadn't.

And now the bank would be all his; he was sure of it.

It should have been all he could think of, the success of his day's meetings monopolising his thoughts, but instead, Luca found his mind wandering to Olivia, obsessing over his memories of her in his bed, of the way she'd looked when he'd left, so beautiful, so distracting.

While it was true that he had mountains of work to catch up on after his spontaneous wedding, honeymoon and protracted post-honeymoon holiday here in Rome, and that his time was therefore very well spent in the office, it was far more accurate that he was challenging himself to resist her. Or, proving to himself that, after a week spent almost exclusively in bed, she had no greater hold on him now than she had on the first day they'd met. That was to say, she was a woman he found desirable, that he enjoyed sleeping with, who he'd walk away from without a backwards glance when the time came. And the time would come—more surely than in any previous tryst—because they'd agreed on that. Three more weeks of Olivia, and then she'd be gone from his life, just as they both wanted.

Having worked late, Luca had every expectation that Olivia would be at home when he returned. He was so sure of it that he'd already started fantasising about how it would feel to pull her into his arms and strip the clothes from her body, to kiss her until she was a puddle of desire, begging him to make love to her. He stormed into the palazzo, already hard, wanting her with a strength that should have terrified him. But it didn't, because this was simple and clear-cut—they both knew what they needed from this relationship.

Only, Olivia wasn't home, and the frustration that gripped him was dark and intense. He stopped walking, having inspected the house thoroughly, a frown on his handsome face. He contemplated heating himself some dinner, going for a solo swim, just as he would have in his pre-Olivia life, but her parting words still rang in his ears.

'Only three weeks to go, Luca. Let's make the most of them.'

He reached into his pocket and drew out his cell phone, dialling her number then pressing the speakerphone button, so he could begin removing his work clothes as the phone rang. She answered on the fourth ring.

'Luca, hi.'

Her voice wrapped around him like tendrils from the deep sea, threatening to drag him under. He pressed his hand to the wall, emulating a nonchalant pose.

'Where are you?'

The sound of laughter filled the phone, distant and remote.

'Out at dinner.'

'With whom?'

'Myself.'

'Why?'

'You weren't home. I presumed you were busy, and I was hungry.'

'The freezer's full.'

'When in Rome, do as the Romans do. And I took that to mean, eat out,' she said, so he could just picture her slender shoulders shrugging with casual indifference. Hunger flicked through him.

'I haven't ordered yet. Why don't you join me?'

He jerked his head once in silent agreement. 'Text me the name of the restaurant. I'll see you soon.'

She might not know the city, but Olivia had exceptional taste. She'd opted for one of the most adored restaurants in Rome. Not the fanciest, nor the predilection of the glitterati, but a place where true Romans who loved good food, wine and conversation chose to eat. And because the owner Francesco understood the value of placing beautiful patrons in the windows, Olivia had been afforded a prominent table in the centre of the glass that framed the front of the venue.

Luca approached slowly, his eyes picking her from a distance, and, owing to the fact he was coming from across the street, he had several moments to observe her while she studied the menu, a small frown on her stunning face.

She wore a black dress, simple yet elegant, with cap sleeves and a neckline that was low enough to show the smallest hint of cleavage. The dress was fitted to her waist then flared a little, to just above her knees. Her blonde hair was left out, slightly curled, and she'd applied a coat of red lipstick, completing the look of femme fatale. She was beyond beautiful; she was exquisite, a completely unique woman who was impossible to ignore. Indeed, as he moved closer, he was aware of the table behind her—a group of four men on what looked to be a business dinner—casting lingering glances in her direction, appreciating her in a way that made Luca's blood boil.

But he stamped out that reaction before it could take hold.

He had no right envying her that kind of attention. Theirs was not a real marriage, and whatever they were sharing was a very temporary state of affairs. Sleeping together didn't equate to anything more serious—they both knew that—and he was glad. If anything, it was useful to observe her like this, to see her from outside the restaurant. The symbolism didn't escape him. A physical barrier stood between them, and in a few weeks that physical barrier would be a whole other country, and then, something more significant—a divorce. Soon, they'd be strangers, just memories to one another.

As that thought hardened in his mind and heart, she looked up, her eyes landing on him, widening, before a smile curved her perfect, pouting lips.

'Hello,' she mouthed.

His own grin was slow, and felt a little discordant, but she didn't appear to notice. With a graceful shift of her hand, she indicated the chair opposite, wordlessly inviting him inside, to join her. His gut tightened with something like anticipation and then he nodded, pushing into the restaurant. *Let's make the most of this.*

'Buonasera,' she greeted him as he approached her table.

He dipped towards her, pressing a kiss on her cheek, lingering there longer than necessary so he could breathe her in and placate nerve endings that were firing wildly, desperate for her, for more, for everything.

'Ciao.'

He slid into the seat opposite, grateful that the table was small and intimate, that their knees brushed and that neither shifted to break that connection. But why would they? They'd been far more intimate than that, and yet the small contact sent a thousand flares through his body.

'How was your day?'

He'd been floating on air after leaving the office, the success of his meeting with the Azzuri chairman puffing out his chest. But there was a light behind Olivia's eyes, a thousand lights that made her whole face shimmer, that pushed his own thoughts of his day from his mind completely. 'Fine.' He brushed it aside as though it meant nothing. 'Yours?'

'Actually, it was pretty wonderful.'

His gut rolled. 'Oh?'

A waiter appeared to take their drinks order. Olivia met his gaze, smiled, and in halting Italian proceeded to order the bottle of Prosecco she enjoyed so much.

'Bene, signorina.' The waiter's eyes lit up.

Luca resisted the impulse to inform the waiter that Olivia was, in fact, a *signora*. What did it matter? She was his wife, they both knew it; nothing else mattered.

He focused his attention back on her face. 'You were saying?'

'My day.' She nodded, pleating her napkin into her lap, searching for the right words. 'I went sightseeing, and I had a revelation.' She paused, and before he could prompt her to continue, the over-zealous, over-attentive waiter appeared, brandishing the Prosecco for *'signorina'*, asking in slow Italian if she would like to taste the bottle. She turned to Luca, lost, and he shook his head, delighting in taking over the conversation.

Was he seriously jealous of a waiter she didn't even know?

He blamed his naturally possessive instincts. It wasn't Olivia he was asserting a claim over, so much as their temporary, meaningless relationship.

'The bottle will suffice,' he said in his native tongue. 'Leave it; I can pour.'

The waiter disappeared with a disgruntled expression.

'What did you say to him? He seemed cross.'

Luca flattened his lips. 'It's not important. You were saying something about a revelation?'

Her eyes chased the waiter with obvious sympathy, but then she blinked back to him, watching as Luca poured a generous measure of bubbles into her flute.

'I didn't go to university, you know. I couldn't have left home. Mum depended on me, and there was too much to do anyway. We couldn't afford any help, and the house was massive.' She pulled her lips to the side, her expression one of timelessness, as though she were back in the past. 'And somewhere along the way, I suppose I've lost sight of—'

The waiter reappeared, notepad in one hand, and a pen in the other.

Luca cursed under his breath. 'Bring us whatever the chef recommends,' he bit out curtly, then, as an afterthought, to Olivia, 'Is that okay?'

Olivia looked bemused. 'Yes. I'm sure that will be fine.' She turned a megawatt smile on the waiter, and, as a result, he left somewhat mollified compared to his previous retreat.

'You're cranky.'

'I've never known a waiter to interrupt so often.'

Her eyes widened with surprise. 'I'm fairly sure that's an ordinary amount, actually.'

'It doesn't matter. You were saying?'

'Yes.' She nodded slowly, then laughed. 'What exactly was I saying?'

'Somewhere along the way, you've lost sight of something.'

'Right.' She sipped her Prosecco, closing her eyes for a brief moment, to savour the ice-cold explosion of flavour. 'I have no idea who I am.' She delivered the words with complete calm, but there was a tempest in her pale blue eyes, so he knew what a momentous pronouncement that was. 'I don't even remember what I used to want to do with my life, before my father died and everything changed. I suppose the sorts of things every child fantasises about—to become a ballerina, an astronaut, prime minister.' She wrinkled her nose and, out of nowhere, he felt as if he'd been punched, hard. He leaned closer without realising it. 'But then, as a teenager, I never really developed any other goals. I suppose I knew it would be fruitless, that I'd never be free to pursue them. I didn't plan to go to university, I simply accepted that it wouldn't be my fate. And then today,

I went to Il Vaticano, and as I toured the rooms, one by one, I remembered something I buried a long, long time ago.'

He leaned forward slightly. 'Which is?'

'I love art. As a child, I used to relish creating paintings, sculptures out of clay, craft from the garden. I adored the ancient paintings that adorned the walls of Hughenwood House, many of which we've had to lease to cover the running costs,' she said with a grimace of regret. 'But it wasn't until today that it occurred to me I could actually pursue art as a career. Or *any* kind of career. Once we divorce, I'll be free for the first time in my adult life. There'll be money to go towards the maintenance of the house, even to restore it to its former glory. I can take a flat in London and go to university, albeit as a mature age student. I can have a real life, Luca.'

His frown was instinctive. 'You do not need to wait until we are divorced—'

'I know,' she interrupted, taking another sip of her drink, her enthusiasm almost as effervescent as the drink. 'I was thinking that, too. And so I decided I'd go to the Vatican every day while you're at the office, and see every bit of art, taking notes on what I like and don't like, then expand to other galleries. I'm in one of the art hubs of the world—what a place to discover myself, and work out exactly what it is I want to do with my life.'

As she spoke, her cheeks grew pink and the sparkle in her eyes took on a stellar quality.

'You're right.' He reached for his own drink, holding the stem in his hands, watching as the bubbles fizzed.

'Anyway, the point is, I'm excited. It's like I'm just realising the horizons that are opening up for me, and it's all thanks to you.'

'Not thanks to me,' he said with a shake of his head.

'Without this marriage, none of it would be possible.'

His brow furrowed as he contemplated her father's will,

the barbaric terms that had seen her penalised, infantilised, punished, for no reason other than her gender.

'A regrettable circumstance.'

She tilted her head to the side, studying him for a moment before a shy smile spread over her lips. 'I don't regret it though, Luca. I really don't.'

Strangely, nor did Luca.

CHAPTER TEN

LUCA PICKED UP his phone with the totally foreign sensation that he was floating on air, calling Olivia without a moment's thought. She answered on the third ring.

'How's *il Papa* today?'

'I haven't seen him, yet,' she responded, quick as a whip. 'But if I do, I'll tell him you said hi.'

'Careful, he probably thinks I dance with the devil as much as the rest of Italy does.'

'Then I'll disabuse him of that mistaken belief, and tell him that you're actually a bit of a guardian angel.'

What was that grinding sensation in the pit of his stomach? 'Hardly,' he demurred, but a smile crossed his face.

'Are you home?' Her simple question took on a breathy quality.

'No.' He flicked a glance at his Montblanc watch. 'I'm calling to see if you can join me for a thing tonight.'

'A "thing"?' she repeated with obvious amusement.

'My offer for Azzuri Bank has been formally accepted by the board. The announcement went out this morning, and to celebrate the news, and encourage a smooth transition, the previous owners and I will be hosting a party this evening. It's going to be quite an event—high profile, lots of celebrities and, therefore, lots of paparazzi.'

'And it would be helpful for you to have a wife on hand?'

she murmured. Was that strain in her voice? He wished he weren't so attuned to her, so aware of her every mood.

'Frankly, yes.'

She was quiet for a beat too long, but when she spoke, her voice was light-hearted enough. But was it sincere? Or forced, for his sake? 'Then of course I'll come. Where?'

'I'll pick you up from home.' He didn't give it a second thought, relief whooshing through him. 'Can you be ready by eight?'

The amusement crept back into her words. 'It's two o'clock. How long do you think I'll need?'

'About thirty-seven seconds,' he agreed. 'You could pull on a hessian sack and outshine anyone else in attendance.'

The throwaway remark seemed to spark something in Olivia though. 'Hmm, but there will be a heap of people, right?'

'About two hundred.'

She let out a low whistle. 'And you said celebrities?'

'*Sì.* Clients of the bank—old Italian money, celebrities, you know the sort.'

'So the dress code is—what?'

'Conservative black tie.'

'A ball gown?'

'A dress of some sort,' he responded. 'Ideally something that will not be too complicated to remove as soon as we are home again.'

Olivia was quiet, and he hated that he couldn't see her face, because he had no idea what that silence represented. She didn't laugh at his quip.

'Okay, I'll see you at eight.'

A Cinderella moment might have been a fantasy for many women but, for Olivia, the longer she spent being transformed into a society wife, the more ice flooded her veins, until eventually, a little before eight that night, she met her reflection with sheer trepidation. Look back at her from the full-length mirror in the bedroom was a younger version of her mother.

She'd turned into what she'd always run from, what she'd been made to run from. At first, she'd planned to do her own hair and make-up, but it wasn't as though she had much experience with either, so on a whim she'd asked Signora Marazzi to book her into a salon. The chic stylist assigned to her had spoken enough English to understand what Olivia had wanted, but somehow the instructions for 'understated' had still resulted in, frankly, a work of art. It was to the stylist's credit, not Olivia's, that her face was exquisitely made up. She wore barely any foundation—*'Because your skin is so glowing, we not want to cover it, eh?'* But her eyes had been made to look like a tiger's, with delicate eyeliner slashing out at the corner, and mascara applied liberally to her naturally long lashes, so she felt as though she were a film star from the sixties. A hint of bronzer on her cheeks, and cherry red on her lips, a complete diversion from her usual, natural colour. Her blonde hair had been styled into voluptuous curls and pinned over one shoulder, the perfect complement to the dress she wore—one of the gowns that he'd given her in Venice.

Their honeymoon hadn't been that long ago, and yet, she felt as though she were a different person. Luca was so new to her then, so unknown. So much had changed—between them, and within her. She was now an entirely different person, almost unrecognisable to herself.

When she'd tried on the gown—a silk slip dress that fell to the floor, with delicate ribbons for sleeves and a neckline that revealed just a hint of cleavage, in a colour that was silver, like wet sand in the moonlight—she had wondered if she'd ever wear it. It made a little too much of her assets, showing off her rounded breasts, her neat waist and gently swollen hips, her rounded bottom. She hadn't thought she'd *ever* want to draw attention to herself, the kind of attention a dress like this demanded. And she still didn't want attention. At least, not from the crowds, not from random strangers. But from her husband?

Heat took over the ice in her body as she imagined Luca's response to the dress. For him, this was worth it.

She slid her feet into heels, the red soles just visible as she walked, grabbed a clutch purse from her dressing table and checked it for the essentials—phone, credit card, lipstick—then made her way to the top of the stairs. Purely by happenstance, the front door opened as she reached the landing, so she had a moment to observe Luca without his knowledge. He'd changed at the office, into a jet-black tuxedo and snowy white shirt, a black bow tie at his neck. It was a completely appropriate outfit and yet his primal, raw energy made a mockery of the formality of his tuxedo. Even the suit couldn't hide the fact that he had a latent energy just waiting to be expelled. Her heart leaped in instant recognition, moving from its position in her chest and somehow taking up almost all the space within her body, so its rapid beating was all she was conscious of.

She placed her hand on the railing to steady herself, her wedding ring glinting in the evening light. She stared at it for a moment—for courage?—then began to move down the stairs.

Since when had her wedding ring become an object of strength? Initially she'd viewed it as a mark of possession, something she'd resented almost as much as the necessity of this marriage, and now she took comfort from it? Olivia didn't want to analyse that—she could barely acknowledge it to herself—as though she knew danger lurked somewhere behind the realisation, a danger she didn't want to face.

Luca placed his wallet and phone on the hall stand when a slight movement caught his eye and he turned, chasing it down before anticipating that it might be Olivia. One look at her and the world stopped spinning, all the breath in his body burst from him, and his eyes seemed incapable of leaving her.

She was—there was no way to describe her. 'Beautiful' was a word he'd used before, to describe other women at other times, so there was no way he could apply it to Olivia now, because she was more magnificent, breathtaking and overwhelmingly stunning than he'd ever known a woman could be. Her eyes held his as she moved down the stairs, and with each step she took it was as though an invisible cord formed between them, knotting, putting them together inexorably, unavoidably, until she reached the bottom of the stairs and then they were both moving, his strides long and determined to her elegant.

They stopped a few feet apart. *He* stopped, because he wanted to be able to see her properly, and she stopped because she hesitated. Her eyes clouded with something like uncertainty. As though she sought reassurance. Surely not. Olivia had to know that she was the most spectacular woman who'd ever walked the earth.

'What do you think?' she asked after a moment, her eyes almost pleading with him to reassure her.

A frown pulled at Luca's mouth. What was he missing? Her hand lifted, self-consciously running over her hair, and he remembered her disclosure about the time she'd applied make-up and done her hair, for her twelfth birthday party, and her mother had overreacted. She'd never dressed up again.

Not until now.

His gut twisted at his insensitivity, at the momentousness of this night, and he ached to reassure her and comfort her, but his own body was still in a sense of shock at the sight of Olivia, so it took him a few moments longer than he would have liked.

'I wasn't sure if it was appropriate.' She dug her teeth into her perfect, bright red lower lip and every part of him tightened. He wanted to cancel the whole damned night. He wanted to throw her over his shoulder and take her back upstairs to bed, to strip the dress from her body and destroy her perfectly curled hair, to run his fingers through it until the curls were untidy and her make-up was smudged from passion. He wanted…but that was precisely the lack of control he wouldn't allow into this marriage. It was the reason he'd been forcing himself to stick to his regular work schedule, to limit their time together. It would be so easy to forget the terms of their marriage, to allow himself to want *more* of Olivia, and he would never put himself in that position again. He established the boundaries of his life. He relied on no one. He loved *no one*. Jayne had taught him well there, and it was a lesson he never intended to forget.

'You are perfect,' he said, the word coming to him out of nowhere. But it was the right way to describe her. He reached out, running the back of his hand over her hair. She swept her eyes shut, impossibly long lashes forming half-crescents against her cheeks.

'Not too much?'

'Perfect,' he said again.

'I wasn't sure.'

Her insecurity made him simultaneously sorry for her and furious on her behalf. How could a twenty-four-year-old woman be so unsure of herself? Her mother had failed Olivia completely. She'd been denied all opportunities to experiment socially and to explore herself, so that she might know who and what she was. And yet, somehow, Olivia had come out of it as socially adept and fascinating as anyone he'd ever known. It was only her looks that made Olivia uncomfortable, as though by dressing to attract attention she was stepping into an unknown arena, one she'd prefer not to occupy.

'You will be the most beautiful woman in the room tonight.' *And every night*, he silently added.

Ambivalence flared inside Olivia. There was pleasure at his praise, his obvious admiration, but there was also a deep sense of guilt, as though she were betraying her mother. She offered a tight smile, then looked to the door. 'Should we go?'

His eyes held hers for a beat too long. '*Sì.* And we will stay only as long as is absolutely necessary.'

There was promise in those words and it fired heat deep within her, pushing everything else aside.

Olivia was aware of Luca on a cell-deep level in every minute that passed, from the moment they exited the house until they arrived at a restaurant across from the gold-lit Coliseum, the ancient stadium taking Olivia's breath away for a moment. She wasn't aware of the photographers standing in a roped-off area to the side of the doors—she was, briefly, not even fully aware of Luca, as she stood and gaped at the sight, surrounded by the hum of evening traffic, so stately and terrific, her heart trembling as she imagined the scenes of terror that had been played out, while simultaneously admiring the craftsmanship of creating such an epic space.

'Have you ever toured it?' His breath fanned her cheek, bringing her back to the moment with a rush.

She shook her head. 'We didn't have time when I came as a child.'

'And this week you have been far too busy with the Pope,' Luca teased, reaching down and weaving their fingers together. It was such a natural gesture, Olivia had to remind herself it was all completely for show.

'That's right. Though perhaps next week,' she said, and then, with a small frown furrowing her brows, 'Definitely before I leave Rome.'

It was like the setting of a stopwatch, or perhaps simply reminding them of the incessant ticking of time in the background of their lives.

They were halfway into this marriage of theirs. Two weeks down, two weeks to go. She glanced up at him but his expression gave nothing away.

Whatever she'd been about to say flew from her mind as a photographer's bulb flashed close by and instinctively Olivia flinched closer to Luca.

'Smile through it,' he advised, squeezing her hand as they began to walk towards the doors. Questions were flung at him as they went, in Italian, so she could only pick out certain words. Corporate. Purchase. Record-breaking. Scandal. Tradition. Outcry.

It was enough to draw her gaze to his face once more, but he was implacable, as though he hadn't heard a single question.

They moved through the doors, into a restaurant that was far more charming than Olivia had expected. The tables and chairs she imagined usually filled the restaurant had been removed, leaving only a tiled floor covered in the expensive shoes of Italy's wealthiest personalities. She recognised very few of those in attendance and was glad—there were none of the nerves one might have felt when rubbing shoulders with celebrities you knew and admired.

'The usual.' But his voice was gruff, sparking questions inside her.

'Is there a scandal because you've bought the bank?'

'They are alluding to the scandal of my past.'

'Your father's scandal?'

'Italian society has a long memory,' he said with a smile that didn't reach his eyes. 'Let us find you a drink.'

The first hour passed in a whir of introductions, and, despite the fact Luca insisted on speaking English for Olivia's benefit, conversation switched back and forth, from Italian to English, at breakneck speed, so she found it almost impossible to keep up. He didn't leave her side, nor did he drop her hand, so despite the fact she felt completely off the deep end, she was also enjoying herself, the spectacle, the vibe, the noise, the joy of life. It was the sort of event she'd never attended—something she'd read about online or seen in movies, but to actually attend, and with the star of the show, was actually surprisingly fun. When the room was so full she could barely move, he turned to her.

'I have to make a speech.' He pressed a kiss to the soft flesh just beneath her ear, sending a thousand sparks into her bloodstream. 'It will be in Italian, but you'll get the gist. Excuse me.'

Olivia watched as he made his way through the crowd, his dark head inches above most, his shoulders broad, his stride somehow cutting through the gathering of people with ease.

At the front of the restaurant, a microphone had been set up, and even before Luca approached it, the crowd grew quiet.

When he spoke, it was as though Olivia were being pressed back against a wall. She saw him as he appeared to the rest of the world, as he'd appeared to her, the first time they'd met. He was no longer Luca, the man she'd come to know so well, but a powerful, self-made tycoon with more strength, arrogance and ambition than anyone that had ever lived. The crowd was completely captivated by him, the effect of his words inspiring laughter, then nods of agreement.

She was in awe.

'You are here with Luca?' The question was unwelcome, an intrusion on a private moment between Olivia and Luca—despite the fact hundreds of people surrounded them. She blinked away from him, annoyed, meeting the eyes of a beautiful dark-haired woman.

'Yes.' She smiled crisply then turned back to her husband.

'I wondered why I had not heard from him. Have you been together long?'

'Only a couple of weeks,' Olivia said, before remembering they were supposed to be playing the part of a happily married couple.

'Then I'm sure it's almost at an end. He never strays for long.'

Hairs on the back of Olivia's neck stood on end. 'Oh?' The other woman smiled banally, but her claws were out. Olivia felt them trying to find purchase in her back.

'He will get bored of you soon enough, and then he'll be back in my bed.'

Olivia's heart slammed into her ribs. This vile, beautiful woman was right. When their marriage ended, Luca would return to his normal life, and resume his normal activities, which, Olivia gathered, included this woman. It was the expectation Olivia had come into this marriage with, and nothing had changed to affect that. So why did her throat now feel filled with sawdust?

'Perhaps.' Olivia tilted her head to the side, affecting a look of nonchalance. If there was one thing she was glad of, it was that her upbringing had equipped her with all the skills to hide how she was feeling. To an onlooker, she appeared as zen as one could get. 'That's really up to Luca.'

The reply surprised the other woman, taking the wind out of her sails completely. She left without another word. But all of the enjoyment of the night had faded for Olivia, and she couldn't say precisely why. After all, nothing had changed. She'd married Luca knowing it was fake, and temporary. They had agreed to sleep together on the basis that sex wouldn't change the cold terms of their marriage. He would go back to his life, as it had been before her, and that shouldn't bother her. So why did it? Why did Olivia suddenly feel as though she were falling into the depths of the ocean? Why did it feel as though she were drowning?

'You are very quiet.'

Olivia blinked up at Luca, annoyed at herself for not having been able to fool him into thinking everything was fine. After all, it was fine, wasn't it?

'Perhaps I'm tired,' she offered.

Luca's eyes skimmed the room. The crowd had thinned a little, but, at almost midnight, the party was still in full swing, the voices growing louder as the alcohol intake grew.

'We'll leave.'

'We don't have to,' she demurred with a shake of her head.

He leaned closer, breathing into her ear. 'I want to. We've stayed far longer than I intended. Let's go home.'

It was such a simple, oft-repeated phrase. It meant nothing. But when Luca referred to 'home', a hole formed right in the middle of Olivia's heart, because his wonderful property in the heart of Rome was not, and never would be, her home. That was in England, the dreaded Hughenwood House, and soon Olivia would have to return there. Not for long, but initially, to sort out their business affairs and launch herself into a new life. Uncertainty made her stomach off-kilter. It was the future she'd longed for, the future she'd fought damned hard for, even marrying a total stranger to achieve, so why did it stand before her like a pit of lava she was now obliged to cross?

CHAPTER ELEVEN

'DID YOU ENJOY yourself last night?'

Olivia flipped her face on the pillows, eyeing Luca with a sardonic expression. 'Are you taking a victory lap, Signor Giovanardi?'

He frowned.

'I should have thought my enjoyment—on multiple occasions—was self-evident.'

He roared with laughter, lifting a hand and pressing it to his forehead. 'That is, naturally, very gratifying, but actually, I was asking about the party.'

'Oh.'

He will get bored of you soon enough.

She covered the glut of displeasure and the strange taste that filled her mouth with a steady smile. She hadn't been able to push the other woman from her mind, not for long, anyway.

'It was…fascinating.'

He grinned, lifting onto one elbow and regarding her thoughtfully. 'Fascinating? What exactly does this mean?'

'Oh, just unlike anything I've ever experienced.'

'Surely you've been to parties?'

She studied the ceiling, lost in thought. 'Not a lot, actually. As a teenager, a few casual things, but after that, not really.'

'You really have lived the life of a recluse.'

'Yes.'

'And after this?'

She turned to look at him, then wished she hadn't. Her heart clutched, echoing the worst indigestion she'd ever known. She'd been trying so hard not to think about 'after'. Why did he have to bring it up? 'What do you mean?'

'What will your life be like?'

She really didn't want to think about it. 'I don't know.' She inched closer, her body craving him despite the hours they'd spent exploring one another the night before. In the back of her brain, she imagined nights without Luca, and wondered how she'd cope, how her body would cope, without him.

'Is this normal?' She blurted the question out before she could second-guess the wisdom of asking him something so telling.

'Our life here?'

Our life. Pain sheared her chest. She blinked away, focusing beyond him. 'No, I mean…' She swallowed past a lump of embarrassment.

'Sì?'

'Erm…sex. The way it is with us…is it always like this?'

He reached out, pressing a finger to her chin, drawing her gaze back to his face. 'No.'

Something shifted inside her. She bit down on her lower lip.

'At least, not in my experience.'

'How is it different?'

'Now who's taking a victory lap?'

'Is that what I'm doing?' she murmured. 'I wouldn't know. I have zero experience.'

'That's true.' He moved closer, so their hips met, his arousal pressing to her, and fierce heat flashed in her body.

'He bores easily.'

The question shaped in her mouth, but she found it almost impossible to ask. Shyness stole through her, even as they lay together, naked, far from strangers, so she couldn't simply ask him about the other woman, about what their relationship was. Or was it that Olivia didn't want to hear the answer? Was it that she couldn't bear to hear the answer? And if so, why was that? Where was the cold dispassion she'd been banking on? When was the last time she'd been with Luca and not felt as though a part of her were burning alive? And why did she suddenly want to grab hold of him with both hands and never let go?

Stricken, she could only stare at him, as her brain kept throwing questions at her, forcing her to face reality, to answer them, to acknowledge that what was supposed to be a straightforward marriage agreement was suddenly so much more complex.

A buzzing pierced the room, so Olivia glanced at Luca's bedside table first, where his phone sat with a dark screen, then over her shoulder to her own bedside table. Her sister's face filled the front of the device. She reached for it gratefully. Saved by the bell.

'It's Sienna,' she said crisply. 'If it were anyone else, I'd leave it…'

His eyes sparked as though filing away that piece of information, but Olivia was already rolling away, disappointment curdling inside of her at the distance between them.

'Hey, Sisi.'

'Libby! What the heck is going on?'

Familiarity was a new kind of warmth, running over Olivia, at the sound of her childhood nickname. 'What do you mean?'

'Are you actually engaged to Luca Giovanardi?'

Olivia sat upright, her eyes bolting to Luca's.

'Why do you ask?'

'Because it's in the papers. Mum's beside herself, which, I have to say, is actually kind of funny, but then, you did look ridiculously beautiful in the photos and you know she hates that.'

'What photos?'

'Have you not been online today?'

'No, I—' She glanced at the time and pulled a face. It was later than she'd realised. 'Haven't had a chance.'

'Well, there are enough gossip pieces about you and Luca Giovanardi to keep you busy a while. Speculation that you're engaged—even married.' Sienna's voice lowered to a hushed, earnest tone. 'I know about dad's stupid will, Libby. You really did it, didn't you?'

What else could I have done? She didn't ask it, because the answer was simple. Leave them living in destitution. Leave her mother paying the price of her father's cruelty for the rest of her life? Or worst of all, leave it to Sienna to get married before the deadline and improve their fortunes? None of those options were possible. This marriage was all Olivia could do, and yet she didn't resent it. She sure as hell didn't regret it.

'What else are the papers saying?'

'Let me see.' Olivia could imagine Sienna clicking open her iPad. 'There's a ton of pictures, all very nice. A bit of background on Luca, some scandal with his father a long time ago, his very, very varied dating past, including photos of—phwoar, did you know he used to date Elizabeth Mason?'

Olivia tried not to conjure images of the stunning American actress—and failed, so all she could see was Luca and Elizabeth, and what a beautiful pair they'd make. Jealousy gripped her, hard.

'There's a close-up of your hand—nice ring, by the way. And— Oh. This is a new article.'

Olivia tensed. 'What is it?'

'"In response to fierce speculation that one of Italy's most eligible bachelors has been removed from the market for good, Luca Giovanardi's grandmother Pietra has released a short statement confirming the marriage. 'My grandson has finally found happiness, and with a

woman who is quite his perfect match. I am very pleased for them both.'"'

All the air whooshed out of Olivia.

'You *are* married?' Sienna squeaked. 'Tell me this isn't true?'

Olivia scrunched up her face, aware that Luca was watching her intently. 'It's true.'

'Oh, Libby. Darling, you didn't have to do this.'

'Didn't I?' She turned to face Luca and her heart jolted in her chest. *Didn't I?*

He reached out, putting his hand on her knee, a question in his eyes. She looked away. Questions were all she could feel now, questions about her choices, her feelings, and, most importantly, her desires. Because knowing their marriage was coming to an end felt like the slow dropping of an executioner's blade, and she desperately wanted to slow it, or to stop it altogether. She could barely breathe.

'No! This is for the money, isn't it? Oh, Libby. Why didn't you talk to me about this? We could have worked something out.'

Olivia compressed her lips. She'd shielded Sienna from the worst of their financial situation, protecting her sister from the truth of just how bad things had been for them, but the truth was they'd have been ruined if she hadn't gone through with this.

'Let's discuss it when I'm home.'

'And when will that be?'

'Two weeks. A little less.' Her heart splintered, her lungs burned.

'And will your *husband* be coming?' She layered the word with cynical disapproval and the bite of disapproval from kind-hearted Sienna hurt like hell—almost as much as the realisation that Luca wouldn't be joining her on that trip, or any other, once their brief arranged marriage was at an end.

'No. I'll come alone.' Her voice cracked a little. She

swallowed to clear the hoarse feeling in her throat. 'I'll talk to you later, Sisi.'

She disconnected the call and pasted a determinedly bright smile on her face. 'Well, that went about as well as could be expected.'

'You didn't tell her about any of this?'

'No.'

'Why not?'

'Because I didn't think she would approve, and if anyone can talk me out of anything, it's my sister.'

Olivia placed the phone down and stared straight ahead, at the wall across the room.

'And were you right? Does she not approve?'

'It doesn't sound like it.' She pleated the sheet between her forefinger and thumb. 'Sienna is the kindest person you'll ever meet, but I've tried very hard to keep her from understanding the ins and outs of our family's financial predicament.'

'So you alone have borne this worry?'

Olivia tilted him a steady look. 'I'm the oldest.'

Disapproval marred his features. 'Your parents have failed you.'

She pulled a face. 'Look who's talking.'

'Perhaps that's why I can recognise the signs so easily.' He reached out, drawing her down to him then bringing his body over hers. 'You deserved so much better, Olivia.'

Their eyes met and understanding passed between them, a fierce sense of agreement, and then his head lowered, his mouth seeking hers, gently at first, as if to reassure her through his kiss, and then with urgency, passion overtaking them. Already naked, he simply pushed aside the sheet between them, and drove into her, so Olivia cried out with pleasure at his immediate, urgent possession, his arousal filling her, moving fast, deep, his rhythm demanding, explicit, exactly what she needed.

'It is not always like this,' he promised against her

mouth, reminding her of their earlier conversation. 'I find I cannot get enough of you.'

Pleasure curled through her as his words mixed with the physical sensations he was arousing with such need, until she was incandescent with heat and fever, building to an unavoidable release, perfectly coinciding with his own explosion.

'I can't get enough of you either,' she admitted, when their breathing had slowed and he'd rolled onto his back, bringing her with him, so her head lay on his chest. His heart thumped heavily beneath her. *I can't get enough of you, but, eventually, this will have to be enough.* Their marriage would come to an end, and, while she was regretting that, there was a part of Olivia that was also glad. There was a danger here she hadn't appreciated at first, a danger of wanting so much more from Luca than she'd originally anticipated—and he was just the kind of man who would swallow her whole.

Olivia knew that love was a very dangerous force, and she'd always sworn she would avoid it, rather than turn into the kind of woman her mother had become, in the service of love. She just hadn't appreciated that love was a force all of its own, that it could chase after you when you had no intention of being caught, that it could bombard you and threaten to wrap around you unless you were ever, ever vigilant. And being vigilant while in the arms and bed of Luca Giovanardi was proving almost impossible.

Soon, it would be over, and she'd be able to breathe again. Wouldn't she?

'My grandmother has asked us to visit her for a night or two. Do you have any objections?'

Olivia met Luca's questioning gaze as she stepped out of the shower. He stood draped against the bathroom door jamb, his presence not an invasion so much as a sign of the intimacy she'd begun to accept as totally normal. In the back of her mind, a warning bell was almost constantly sounding, the small incursions something she knew she should fight back against. After all, she'd always sworn she'd maintain her independence and autonomy, but with Luca all her barriers were being eroded—and she didn't seem to mind. But there was no threat here. No danger. They knew when and how their relationship would end. She would never turn into her mother, no matter how much she surrendered to him, and this.

Ever-hungry, her gaze feasted upon his physique, her mouth drying as it always did when she allowed herself to drool.

'Olivia? Eyes up here.'

Guilt flushed her cheeks. 'Of course not. It's one of the main reasons we married.' She answered his question with a hint of embarrassment at having been caught out. But he laughed and prowled towards her, whipping the towel from her body.

'My turn.' He stepped back, and his own inspection of her was so much slower, his gaze travelling from the tip of her head to her toes and back again, lingering on her curves, her most intimate body parts, until her breath was coming in pants.

'Luca.' The word burst from her.

'I know.' His eyes flashed with an emotion she didn't understand and then he drew her into his arms, kissing her soundly. A kiss was never enough, though. It was the flicking of a switch, the lighting of a torch that had to be burned down completely before it could be released. She kissed him back with full comprehension of that, her body cleaved to his, naked, hungry, yearning, as his hands reached behind her back and pressed her to him. She ground her hips to him, and heard the sharp expulsion of air, and then he was pulling apart, fire in his eyes as he glared down at her, heat in his cheeks.

He dropped to his knees and she groaned, because at

first she thought he was ending what they shared, but then he separated her legs and brought his mouth to her sex, kissing her and whipping her into a frenzy, so she had to brace her palms on the marble counter, head tilted backwards, vaguely aware of what a wanton sight she must make—and not giving even half a damn. How could she care about anything but pleasure when there was pleasure such as this?

'Signora Giovanardi, thank you for coming.'

'My husband's message said it was important?'

The assistant nodded. 'Signor Giovanardi is just concluding a meeting and has asked you to wait in his office. This way, please.' The deference with which Olivia's assistants treated her brought a smile to Olivia's lips, but she was aware, all the time, of how temporary this was. When she wanted to savour every moment of their marriage, instead it was rushing towards its conclusion, seconds passing in a blur, days flicking by, so that she knew there was barely any time left.

She fell into step beside the receptionist, and, at the door to Luca's office, dredged up something like a smile. 'Thank you.'

'Would you like anything to drink? Tea? Coffee? Wine?'

Olivia suppressed a smile at the Italian indulgence for a lunchtime *aperitivo*. 'A mineral water would be lovely, thank you. It's warm out there today.'

'Indeed. Summers in Rome are unbearably humid.'

Olivia thought of the dark, dank hall at Hughenwood House, contrasting it to the sun-filled streets she'd traversed on the walk to Luca's office. 'I think it's lovely,' she murmured as the assistant left the room.

When she was alone, curiosity got the better of her, and she wandered towards his desk first, admiring the spotless work environment. No clutter, no personal effects, no photographs, just a laptop, and a Manilla folder with the word

'Singapore' on the side. She ran a finger over the top then eyed the boardroom table. Several more folders sat here. She moved to them out of idle curiosity and pulled up short when she saw her name on the side of one.

THORNTON-ROSE

Another folder, beside it.

HUGHENWOOD HOUSE

And another.

PORTFOLIO

Heart thumping, she was torn. It was abundantly obvious that these folders pertained to her, and her business, and yet she felt like a snoop to open them and look inside. Torn, she prevaricated and a moment later the door opened. She looked up, expecting to see his assistant, only to be met by the appearance of Luca, striding in with sheer, obvious impatience, his shirt unbuttoned at the collar, his hair tousled as though he'd been driving his fingers through it all morning.

He stopped short when their eyes met, a grim line on his lips before he changed direction and closed the distance. The door opened once more, and the receptionist followed with a tray—two coffees, a bottle of mineral water, and a plate of biscotti.

'Thank you,' Luca dismissed, without looking in his assistant's direction.

Once they were alone again, he lifted a coffee cup and extended it to Olivia. Their fingers brushed and sparks shot through her, sparks she might have imagined would have faded by now, but which had, instead, intensified, overtaking her completely. She took the coffee on autopilot, staring at the golden liquid a moment. She hadn't wanted a coffee, but now that it was in her hands, she took a sip, relishing the strong, bitter flavour.

'You left a message for me to meet you here,' Olivia reminded him, wondering at the strange sense of hesitation—an emotion she hadn't felt a moment ago. But seeing the folders had unsettled her—it was as if her old life was slipping into the room with them, reminding her forcibly of why they'd married. It was a reminder she resented.

'Yes.' He looked awkward. Her heart went into overdrive. Was she here to discuss their marriage? They still had a little over a week left. Surely they didn't have to talk about the end just yet? She knew she was living in a fantasy land but Olivia wasn't ready to face the practicalities of leaving him—yet. When the time came, she would. She'd be strong, just as she had been at every other time in her life where strength was required, but for the moment she wanted to blot out the path ahead. Unless...what if he wanted to change the terms of their agreement? What if he wanted to extend things? Hope was an unstoppable force, exploding in her chest. She dug her fingernails into her palms, waiting, wishing, wondering...

'I'd like to discuss your finances,' he said with quiet control. 'Or rather, their ongoing management.'

Olivia could have been knocked over with a feather. 'Oh.' *Was that all?*

'I'm sorry to say, yet not surprised, I admit, that the lawyers handling your father's estate are as misogynistic as he evidently was. I was contacted earlier in the week and advised that I could collect this information on your behalf, now that we are legally married.'

'They've been ignoring my calls,' she said with a sigh. 'Bastards.'

'You're angry?'

'Aren't you?'

'Well, yes, of course.'

'I cannot see any God-given reason you should require your husband to collect your own financial documents,' he responded curtly, his anger obviously not directed at her.

Olivia's heart skipped a beat. His support was something she hadn't known she needed.

'I know financial independence is your goal and I'm sorry I've had to be involved in obtaining this information—however, these files contain everything you'll need to know about your family's business affairs. The money that is now yours, how it is invested, as well as other investments that will pass to you.'

Olivia blinked, her stomach twisting.

'There is also information pertaining to your sister's inheritance.'

'Thank you.'

His eyes narrowed, darkening. 'Don't thank me, Olivia. You should never have needed me, for any of this.'

Her heart swelled. 'But it's not your fault that I did. And I am grateful to you, Luca.'

His mood didn't improve and warmth spread through her. It was a sign of his decency and loyalty that he was so incensed.

'Please, have a look.' He gestured to the files. 'I will be working over here, and am happy to answer any questions you have. Alternatively, I have the name of an excellent financial advisor, and can put you in touch. Just let me know.'

He nodded curtly, all business, so she wanted to start removing her clothing, piece by piece, to jolt him back to the intimacy they shared, the heat that exploded between them. And yet, how could she overlook this gesture? He was making everything as easy as possible for her. Right down to offering help without presuming she'd need it.

He wasn't mansplaining things to her, but rather allowing her to find her own feet, waiting until she asked for assistance, but letting her know it would be freely given. It was the perfect gesture, and she was touched, right to the centre of her core; even, she feared, to the centre of her heart.

CHAPTER TWELVE

'HOW COME YOU didn't tell me?'

He paused, carrying her holdall over one shoulder as though it weighed nothing. 'Tell you what?'

Olivia wrinkled her nose. 'Well, that this place would be so—'

They looked around the entrance with its turquoise walls just visible behind dozens of paintings, each showing a different landscape or still life. The floor was large, marble tiles, and in the centre of the ceiling, a chandelier hung, ornate and—Olivia guessed—original to the history of the house. The exterior walls were a washed pink, and the garden was every bit as bright as the home suggested—exotic splashes of colour every which way.

'Extra? Over the top? Garish?'

'Perfect,' Olivia said on a sigh.

'I knew I liked you.' Nonna appeared from behind them, unseen and unannounced, her slender frame elegant in black trousers and a lemon-yellow blouse. Her hair was coiffed into a bun, high on her head, and a daisy pin that sparkled with, Olivia presumed, real diamonds gave the hairstyle some fun and glamour. 'Don't pay my grandson any attention. He's all about bland, modern aesthetic, whereas I prefer—' She swept a manicured hand around the entrance.

'Psychedelic vomit?' Luca drawled with a grin, so Olivia suspected this sort of sparring was the norm for them.

'Evidence of a life well lived.' Pietra winked at Olivia then embraced her, kissing both cheeks. 'I'm so happy you could join me. Come, I'll give you a tour.' She fixed Luca with a glare that was mock irritated. '*You* can put the bags in the room.'

He did a navy salute and Olivia couldn't help chuckling to herself as she was led away by Pietra. The entranceway was really just a hint of the bright, joyous décor throughout. Each room boasted a bright colour scheme, cheerful and somehow cohesive. Despite the fact there could be, in some rooms, blue walls and green curtains, there was always an element that drew it together, such as a sofa with matching cushions that picked up the colour scheme across the entire room, so it was far less chaotic and more harmoniously happy.

'It is a beautiful home.' Olivia sighed as they finished the tour on a balcony with black wrought iron and an abundance of red geraniums, which tumbled from their terracotta pots towards the pool below.

'Thank you. I am pleased you like it. In fact, may I make a confession?'

Olivia nodded slowly.

'I was nervous this morning.'

'Nervous?' Olivia's smile spread over her face. 'Whatever for?'

'That you might, perhaps, not like my home. That you might not want to come.' Nonna's eyes sailed across the countryside, fixing on Positano, sprawled beneath them. 'You see, Luca's all I have, and I couldn't bear it if you and I were anything other than friends. There is not so long left for me, and I want to enjoy the time I have—'

Emotions burst through Olivia, chief amongst them grief that none of this was real. Nonna was offering genuine friendship and Olivia knew it would never really come to pass. Her fake marriage was almost over. After this weekend, Olivia was quite sure she and Pietra would never see one another again. She blinked back a rush of tears and focused on saying what Nonna obviously needed to hear.

'I don't think my marriage would survive if I did anything to alienate you. I know how much you mean to Luca.' She couldn't acknowledge the older woman's reference to her mortality.

'And he to me.' Pietra reached out, tapping a hand on Olivia's. 'And you, *carina*. I never thought, after Jayne, that he would allow himself to love. It was such a bad time in his life, such a hard time for him all round, let alone dealing with her awful treatment. He pushed everyone away, even me, for a long time. I honestly believed I was going to lose him.'

Olivia regarded the older woman thoughtfully. 'Was it really so bad?'

'Oh, worse than you can even imagine. Every friend deserted him. My son swindled them all, you see. No, not every friend. There was one—Alejandro—who stuck by Luca. A man worth his weight in gold. But everyone else, including Jayne, turned their backs on him.' She waved a hand in the air, as if to dispel the recollection of such an unhappy time. 'And now, with you, he is happy. He is himself. Thank you.'

Olivia was overwhelmed—with emotions at the compliment, with guilt because it wasn't real, and then with sadness because she wanted, more than anything, for all of this to be true. The thought struck her like a lightning bolt, but it didn't come completely out of the blue. No, there had been precipitation and storm clouds building for days, suggesting that nothing was as it had first appeared, that everything had changed since their fateful wedding. There was also a jealousy—unmistakable now—for Luca's first wife. A woman he'd once loved, loved enough to have been destroyed by. Loved enough to have sworn off love and relationships evermore.

'And you are happy,' Nonna continued, then winced. 'Or you were, until I started to meddle.'

'Not meddle.' Olivia shook her head. 'I'm just... touched...that you have such faith in us.'

'Who that has seen you together could fail to have faith? And I must believe, you see, because soon I will be gone, and I do not want him to be alone.' Her voice cracked. 'Luca acts so tough, as though he doesn't need anyone, but when I look at my grandson, I still see the little boy I used to bounce on my knee. I want the best for him, *carina*.' Nonna's voice was a little wobbly and she pulled away with a determined effort to laugh. 'But enough of this. I am being too maudlin; Luca would not approve.' She straightened, making an obvious attempt to appear relaxed. 'You must go and explore the town while it is daylight.' She waved a hand towards the exceptional view of Positano. 'Dinner is served at six—I am afraid I eat unfashionably early these days; my medication makes me tired.' Before Olivia could offer a comment of condolence, Pietra pushed on, 'But it leaves you free to do something wonderful tonight, afterwards, no?'

Positano defied every single one of Olivia's expectations. It was prettier than a postcard, with the buildings carved into the cliff-face, a tumbling mix of colourful houses, terracotta roofs and the backdrop of greenery that grew beyond it. She walked beside Luca as he traced the well-worn path he'd traipsed as a child and teenager, pointing out interesting titbits as they went, until finally they began to descend, steep steps carrying them towards the beach and the busy main street that ran parallel to it. Cafes spilled out with tables and umbrellas playing host to a mix of elegant locals and happy, loud tourists. The boutiques boasted beautiful clothes and homewares, so Olivia scanned each with growing interest as they walked.

'Hungry?'

She only realised, as he asked the question, that she hadn't eaten all day. Never a big breakfaster, she'd woken with butterflies in her tummy at the prospect of travelling to Nonna's home, and the idea of remaining for an entire weekend. Of course, she shouldn't have worried, and now that she'd met Pietra again, the nerves had abated, and her hunger had returned.

'Actually, yes. Shall we grab something light? Nonna said dinner is served at six.'

He pulled a face so Olivia laughed softly. 'She also said that eating early leaves us free to do something wonderful after dinner…'

His expression relaxed immediately, speculation darkening his eyes. 'She's very clever.' He pulled Olivia against him, kissing her right there in the middle of the street, where tourists milled about them and the sun beat down, warm and golden.

Breathless, Olivia pulled away, something like hope trembling in her mind. This marriage was nothing like they'd planned for. 'Where do you suggest?'

'I know just the place.'

She smiled. 'Of course you do.'

In Positano, Luca was treated like royalty. He knew many of the shopkeepers, who came out to shake his hand as he passed, and each of the restaurant owners gestured towards tables, inviting them in, but he smiled, offered a kind word, a promise for 'next time', then continued onwards, until they arrived at a quaint trattoria—little more than a hole in the wall, with a green awning, a narrow door and six small tables set up inside. Each table had a round-based wine bottle with a candle in its top, the legs of wax running down towards the table.

'Gianni, *ciao*,' Luca greeted.

Olivia smiled through the introductions, tried to keep up with the Italian and then took the seat that was offered—affording a beautiful view, not of the beach, but of a small garden at the back of the restaurant, where a single bougainvillea had grown up to form a canopy of explosive purple flowers. Beneath it, there was a pot with a lemon tree, and as she watched a woman walked out, round and dimpled all over, wearing a dark blue apron, and plucked two lemons from the tree. When she turned around and saw Olivia watching, she winked, smiled so dimples dug into her rounded cheeks, then disappeared into a timber door with peeling red paint.

'Oh, Luca.' She turned to look at him, emotions welling in her chest. 'This is all so beautiful.'

He looked around, as though that had never really occurred to him. 'It's very traditional.'

'I love it.'

'I'm glad.'

The waiter appeared with some menus, and Luca explained the dishes to Olivia, translating the words and phrases directly.

'Tortellini—called this because they are like little cakes—torta—filled with cheese and spinach.' He moved his finger down the menu. 'Chicken with lemon and asparagus.'

She selected something light and sat back in her chair, watching him thoughtfully.

'Yes?' He lifted a thick, dark brow, continuing to study her.

Guilt flushed her face. 'What do you mean? I didn't say anything.'

'You have your "question" eyes in.'

'My "question" eyes?'

'How you look at me when something is on your mind. So? Out with it.'

She wanted to laugh, but also nerves were thickening her veins, making it hard to think straight. 'You—'

Gianni reappeared, brandishing two glasses of Prosecco, and two glasses of mineral water.

'Thank you,' she murmured.

When they were alone, Luca continued to stare at her, waiting, one brow cocked.

She flattened her lips. 'You don't have to answer this,' she said gently. 'I know we agreed that neither of us has to share our life story.'

'We did.' He inclined his head in silent agreement of that.

'Only, Pietra mentioned something about Jayne.'

He scowled. 'Did she?'

'Don't be cross with her.'

'I'm not. But I told you she meddles, no?'

'Yes, but only because she loves you so much.'

'And you have a question about my first wife?'

She knew him well enough to know he hated the idea of talking about her, but he stared straight at Olivia, holding her gaze. Fearless. Determined. In control.

'It's not really a question.' She furrowed her brow. 'Only...you must have loved her very much.'

He gripped the stem of his Prosecco flute until his knuckles glowed white. 'Why do you say that?'

'Am I wrong?'

He glared at her, and she knew he wanted to avoid the question, but this was Luca. He didn't shy away from difficult conversations. With a small exhalation of breath, he shifted in his seat, his pose a study in relaxation. Only Olivia could see beyond it, to the tension radiating from his frame.

'I was young and idealistic.'

'So you didn't love her?'

His nostrils flared. 'I would have died for her. I loved her with all that I was, Olivia. But I think, at that age, love felt like a rite of passage. I can't say that I would feel that way for her if we met now.'

Something like danger prickled along Olivia's spine. 'Or for anyone?'

He dipped his head in agreement, without hesitation, and it was that lack of pause that cut her to the quick. If he felt anything for her, she would have seen it then.

'And you believed she loved you?'

Cynicism curled his lips. *'Naturalmente.'* The word dripped with sarcasm. 'It never occurred to me that she was using me for money.'

Indignation flared in Olivia's gut. 'I can't imagine anyone fooling you.'

'I'm not the same man now that I was then.'

'Because of her?'

'Because of life.'

'But Jayne is the reason you've sworn off relationships.'

'I have relationships. You've seen the pictures on the Internet, remember?'

Pain lashed her heart. She forced herself to be brave. 'That's sex. I'm talking about emotion. I'm talking about connection.'

There was a storm raging in his eyes but he didn't look away. 'Sex is the only kind of relationship I'm interested in.'

'Doesn't that get lonely?'

His lips curled into an approximation of a smile, but it spread like ice through her veins. 'Are you lonely, *cara*?'

Beneath the table, his fingers sought her knee first, then higher, to her thigh, shifting the fabric of her skirt with ease so he could touch his skin to hers. She bit back a soft moan.

'What we have is just sex, and yet it suits us both perfectly, no?'

No. She wanted to scream her answer. She wanted to scream it at him as she punched his chest, but how could she? He hadn't said anything wrong. It was perfectly in line with what they'd agreed.

'And after this, you'll find someone else to have "just sex" with?'

It was like laying down a gauntlet, forcing them both to face a reality that Olivia personally wanted to hide from.

Her blood began to hammer inside her, and she could hardly breathe. She waited, and she waited, and agony invaded her every cell, until finally, he shrugged indolently. 'As, I imagine, will you.'

Olivia focused on the view beyond the window, doing everything she could not to react, not to recoil, when the truth was the idea of another man ever making love to her was like setting herself alight. She couldn't fathom it, and she knew, in that moment, that he was wrong. Luca Giovanardi would likely be the only man she ever slept with.

The water rippled against Olivia's breasts, the Lycra of her bathing suit turning an almost copper colour in the pale moonlight. Positano was a patchwork of lights beneath them, the view of the city and, beyond it, the ocean quite mesmerising. Luca came to rest beside her, standing easily against the pool's tiled bottom.

He cast her a smile and the moonlight met his face, bathing it in silver, so he was breathtakingly beautiful. It was an almost perfect moment. Almost, because Olivia couldn't blot out their conversation over lunch. She couldn't ignore the ease with which he faced the prospect of their separation, while she was aware, all the time, of the beating of a drum in the back of her mind, a constant, rhythmic motion, propelling her through time, almost against her will.

In less than a week, she'd leave Italy, and Luca. She had to. It was what they'd agreed. It was what he still wanted. *And what do you want?*

She wanted, with all her heart, to stay. It terrified Olivia to admit that to herself, but she wasn't an idiot. She knew what had been happening the last few weeks. Every look, every touch, every moment they shared had been drumming deep into her soul, making him a part of her in a way she'd sworn she'd never allow any man to be.

That was why she had to leave in a week.

Marriage to a man like Luca was too dangerous. He was too much—too easy to love, and she knew what love did. Her parents had shown her again and again. It was the most powerfully destructive force in the universe, capable of wreaking so much havoc and anger. She'd never allow that to happen to them. It would hurt like hell to leave Luca but at least she could leave while things were still great between them, and carry with her cherished memories of their time together. That was so much better than waiting for their love to turn to hate. She couldn't bear that.

'I came to live with my grandmother, after my divorce. I used to love this view.'

'Used to?'

'Still do,' he murmured, and her heart lurched in her chest.

'What was it like, living here?'

'It was exactly what I needed,' he said, after a beat, and she understood his hesitation—that he was contemplating pushing her to share what was on her mind. She was relieved he didn't.

'In what way?'

'Here, I was able to immerse myself in nature for a time, to strip everything away and focus on simply existing. I would walk to Positano almost every day, take out an old timber boat, catch fish that Pietra and I would eat for lunch, right here on this terrace. I would free dive for scallops, and swim through the caves at the edge of Positano. I walked until my skin burned from the sun, and until my legs were like jelly. I did everything I could to silence my brain, my thoughts, to blot out the real world.'

'What about your friends?'

A snarl curled the corner of his mouth. 'My father's actions affected almost everyone I knew.'

Anger pulsed in her veins. 'So they took it out on you?'

A muscle jerked in his jaw. 'Many lost their fortunes.'

'But you repaid them.'

He lifted his shoulders.

'Your grandmother mentioned one friend who stood by you. I can't remember—'

'Alejandro.'

'You're still friends?'

'More like brothers,' Luca agreed. 'He was the only one. I will always be grateful to him, for standing with me.' He turned away from her, his eyes roaming the horizon. She followed his gaze, the beauty stinging now. It was the last time she'd see it.

'Thank you for bringing me here.' Her voice was hoarse; she cleared her throat. 'I like your grandmother, a lot. I'm sorry I won't get to know her better.'

The air between them grew taut. She heard the unspoken implication of that sentence. The inevitable was coming.

'She would have liked to get to know you, too.'

'When will you tell her about our divorce?'

His features gave nothing away, but he turned towards her slowly, his eyes probing hers, as if to read something in her question, something she couldn't see or say.

'When I have to.'

'You'll continue the charade?'

He frowned. 'It's not exactly a charade.'

'You know what I mean. You'll pretend I'm still here, even when I'm back in England?'

'I simply won't tell her anything at all,' he corrected, then made an effort to soften his words. 'She'll be okay, *cara*. She is used to my short attention span with women.' His smile was barely a flicker of his lips, and the coldness of it turned her core to ice. Not because of Luca, but because of her father, and his supreme control of his emotions, because of the way he could turn on a dime.

He was wrong about Pietra. He clearly didn't understand

how relieved the older woman was that Luca had, apparently, fallen in love. He didn't know what their marriage meant to her. The peace she would get on her deathbed, of believing that he was no longer such a determined loner.

Olivia shivered, despite the balmy warmth of the night. Everything about their surroundings was perfect, but she was cold to the core. 'I think I'll go inside, Luca. I'm tired.'

He watched her swim away, fighting a desire to follow her, to draw her back into the water or to follow her inside. They'd been spending too much time together, despite his best efforts to guard against that. She was putting space between them—and that was wise. The smartest thing to do was to go along with it. After all, in less than a week they'd be living different lives in different countries.

CHAPTER THIRTEEN

As a child, Luca had never counted the sleeps until Christmas, or birthdays, or any life event, and yet he was aware, every minute of the day, of the nights remaining with Olivia, and he resented her that power, he resented their marriage for how easily it had become a part of him. For a man used to living alone, having Olivia at his side was strangely perfect.

Because she was undemanding.

Because she was temporary.

Because there was no risk that she would want more than he could give, that he might come to love her or she might come to love him. The black-and-white agreement they'd made offered protection, and in that protected space he'd come to *enjoy* her company.

His phone began to ring and he glared at it sharply. He wasn't in the mood for interruptions. He ignored it, standing up and striding to his windows, looking down on Rome.

Three more nights. And then what?

And then what? He berated himself angrily. And then, life would continue as it had before. She'd leave, he'd be alone, but he'd be fine—alone was a state he was perfectly used to.

'I've let my assistant know you'll need to use the jet over the weekend.'

Midway through lifting a fork to her mouth, Olivia paused, replacing the bite in her bowl. 'Oh?'

'For your return to the UK. That was the date we agreed, yes?'

Her heart skittered around her chest cavity like an ice skater out of control. She focused on her plate extra hard, staring at the pasta dish until the noodles began to swirl before her eyes. *Don't cry. Don't emote. Don't express anything.* Suddenly she was eight years old again, caught between her father and her mother, in the midst of one of their terrible arguments. She tried to fade into the background then took in a deep breath and pushed a smile to her lips, forcing her eyes to meet his. 'Yes, that's right. But I don't need a jet. I booked a commercial flight ages ago, before we were even married.'

Was she imagining the way he expelled a rushed breath? Was it a sigh of relief? Or of something else?

'I see.' He took a drink of wine, then replaced the glass quietly on the table. 'You can cancel it.'

Her eyes widened. Hope danced.

'My jet is at your disposal.'

'That's completely unnecessary.'

He shrugged, nonchalant, unconcerned. Her throat felt as though it were lined with acid. 'As you wish.'

I don't wish! She blinked rapidly as she lifted some spaghetti to her mouth, silencing herself before she could make the protestation. This was best—for both of them. It was what they had agreed to, and she needed to go through with it.

Two nights to go. Luca was impatient and unsettled. He couldn't focus. He sat through meeting after meeting, glowering, so his staff assumed a permanently worried air—and he didn't notice. His mind was absorbed by another issue.

Olivia's departure.

A month had seemed like an interminable period of time when they'd first agreed to it. It was longer than he'd spent with any woman, since Jayne. He'd thought it would drag, and that he'd be glad to see her go, but he wasn't an idiot. He couldn't ignore the fact that he was looking forward to her departure in the same way a man might look forward to chopping off his own arm.

So, what to do?

He stood abruptly, and the meeting grew silent. He scanned the room, fixed his glance on his vice president and nodded. 'Take it from here.'

He needed to be alone; he needed to think.

Olivia packed carefully, each item she folded neatly reminding her of their honeymoon, when Luca had surprised her with bag after bag of couture—of a trip she'd had no expectations of, but that had quickly morphed into something way beyond her wildest dreams. In fact, that basically summed up their entire marriage. Nothing was what she'd expected, it had all been so much more.

She heard the closing of the downstairs door and her pulse went into overdrive.

Luca.

She continued folding, one dress after another, her heart stammering in her chest, until she felt him behind her and turned slowly, a practised smile on her face. 'Hello. How was your day?'

She heard the stilted, formal question, so at odds with the relationship they'd developed, and winced.

He stood against the door jamb, casually reclined, as though he had not a care in the world, but there was something in his face, a mask of concentration, that made a mockery of his pose.

'Why are you packing? You don't leave for two nights.'

Two days. The words were like thunderclaps in her chest.

'I like to be organized,' she offered with a tight smile.

He said nothing for some time, simply watched her, and then, finally, his words broke the silence that was tightening the air in the room.

'I've been thinking.'

She continued with what she was doing, but her actions were stilted, because she was having to concentrate hard on such a simple task. Everything felt unnatural.

'Well, that's good, I suppose.' She aimed for levity, even when her cells were reverberating with a desperate need to know *what* he'd been thinking.

'When we agreed to get married, it was for a very specific purpose. Each of us benefited, and we made sure the marriage would work for us both—by having clear-cut rules in place.'

She arched a brow, her smile a quirk of her lips. 'I remember.' She cleared her throat, reaching for another dress. He pushed up off the door jamb, coming into the room, hands in pockets.

'When we agreed to sleep together, it was the same thing—we made an arrangement, we drew out the terms of what we were doing, to make sure we were on the same page.'

She nodded once, placing the dress in her suitcase, her fingers shaking a little.

'One of the terms was that our marriage would end after a month.'

She reached for a blouse. 'I'm familiar with what we agreed.' Her response was sharper than she'd intended.

His eyes narrowed. 'And what if we were to renegotiate the terms of our marriage?'

Her heart leaped without her consent. 'Which terms, in particular?'

'The term in which you leave.'

The world stopped spinning. She stared at Luca, trying not to react, trying not to feel, but her heart was exploding with something terrifyingly like joy.

'Hear me out.' He lifted a hand placatingly, perhaps misreading her expression. 'This marriage is obviously different—better—than either of us thought it would be. Why walk away from it after only a month?'

Her breath burned in her lungs.

'Why stay?' she asked instead, because she knew the answer she would give, but what was Luca's? Everything hung on his response. She stood there, waiting, and hating, because in that moment she became a child again, waiting for approval, waiting for more than it was possible to be given—by the man in front of her, at least. But Luca wasn't her father. What if she was wrong? What if?

'Because this works,' he said quickly, with no idea of how those words fell like the executioner's blade. 'We're good together, and a marriage like this—a marriage that's logical and sensible—suits us both.'

She bit down on her lower lip, rather than contradicting him.

'You saw your parents' disastrous marriage and swore it would never be for you. But what I'm offering is so different. I'm not suggesting we stay married because we're in love, nor because we're emotionally involved. I'm suggesting it because we're neither of those things. I like being around you, I like spending time together, I love sleeping with you. We make a good team. Isn't that worth staying for? Worth fighting for?'

Her heart was racing far too fast. A thousand things flashed into her mind, but she wasn't sure if she was brave enough to say them. He talked about fighting for their marriage, but she couldn't. She couldn't fight for what she'd never get—her mother had spent a lifetime doing that, fighting for the love of her husband, and it was withheld, cruelly, callously. Luca wouldn't ever intentionally hurt Olivia, but the effect would be the same regardless, because he'd never love her.

She stood straighter as the thought struck her like a lightning bolt, acceptance right behind. Of course, she loved him. The thought sank her like a lead balloon.

She *loved* him. She loved her husband. Her eyes were as wide as saucers as she looked at him, shock reverberating through her.

'I know your experience with marriage was traumatic. The way your parents were with each other, the way your father treated your mother.' He moved closer to her and she flinched, because her heart was too raw for him to touch her. 'The love they shared turned to hate.' He lifted a hand to her cheek and her eyes swept shut, the contact sending shock waves through her body. 'That would never happen with us. A marriage that's built on respect and friendship, a partnership rather than a romance, protects us both.'

'But can't you hear how cold it is?'

His eyes flared. 'There is *nothing* cold between us.'

She bit down on her lip. 'I don't mean sex. I mean—emotionally. I don't want what you're describing.'

His eyes darkened. 'You don't want more of what we've shared this last month?'

Of course she did. She yearned for that.

'You don't want to depend on anyone,' he said gently. 'You want independence, at all costs. I'm not asking you to sacrifice that. I'm not asking you to share more of yourself than you're willing to share. That's why this works so well. Without love, we can be calm and dispassionate, we can meet each other's needs, we can be friends who see the world together, who live side by side. Hell, we can even share a family of our own one day, without any risk of getting hurt. Can't you see how right that is?'

No, it was all wrong. So much of what he was offering made her heart swell, because it was what she wanted—to see the world with him, to have a family with him, but without love? Even when she had seen the dark side of love, and was terrified by its power, she knew she couldn't stay with Luca, loving him as she did. It was better to leave, to nurse a broken heart, than to stay and yearn for what he'd never give.

'It's not what I want,' she whispered gently.

So gently he had to lean closer to hear her words properly.

'I have a life back in England, Luca.'

'Do you? Because it never sounds like much of a life, when you talk about it.'

Her eyes dipped between them. He was right; he knew her too well. She swallowed past a lump in her throat, and then his finger was lifting her chin, tilting her face to his.

'I have responsibilities.'

'So we'll go back for the weekend,' he said with a nonchalant shrug. 'It's a couple of hours in a plane.'

'No.' Now that she understood her feelings, she couldn't pretend any longer. The time they had left was going to be a minefield. She fidgeted her hands in front of her, then lifted one to his chest. 'We had a deal.'

Disbelief was etched in the lines of his face. 'And that deal originally included no sex. Then we realised we were attracted to one another and we changed the deal. Why can't we do that again?'

She dipped her head forward.

'Try it for three months. If this isn't working, we can both walk away then.'

But she wouldn't be able to walk away. If she was already finding the prospect to be a form of torture, how hard would it be in twelve weeks' time?

'I don't want to change our agreement.'

Something shifted in his features. Rejection? Her heart ached. She was hurting him. And he was hurting her. It was exactly what they'd sworn they wouldn't do.

'I see.'

'No, you don't,' she said with a small shake of her head.

He lifted a finger to her lips, silencing her. 'It's okay. It was just an idea, *cara*.'

She opened her mouth to explain, then slammed it shut. Just an idea. No big deal. He didn't care. It didn't matter. None of this did. When she left he'd replace her because, ultimately, she meant nothing to him. She was a convenient wife, just as she'd always been a convenient daughter, flying beneath the radar. Olivia's heart was on the line, Luca was simply trying to manoeuvre a beneficial relationship into lasting a bit longer. She'd said 'no', and now he was brushing it aside. 'Shall we eat out?'

She barely slept. Their strange conversation played over and over in her mind, tormenting her, making her doubt the wisdom of her response, so she wondered why she hadn't just accepted his suggestion. It would mean more time with him. Wasn't that what she wanted?

But at what cost?

Dawn light filtered into his room and, beside her, Luca woke, pushing out of bed and striding into the en suite bathroom. Olivia rolled over and pretended to sleep, pretended not to care that it was the first morning in weeks they hadn't made love. Her heart was splintering into a thousand little shards.

The house felt like a mausoleum suddenly. Olivia couldn't find peace, couldn't get comfortable. She didn't want to go out—she was too tired from a sleepless night—and she was finished packing. There was nothing left to occupy her, which left her mind with too much time to fret, to obsess, to panic.

Olivia caught a reflection of herself as she moved from one room to the next and stopped in her tracks. Her face was drawn, her lips turned downwards, her eyes dull, devoid of spark. She looked like her mother often had. Miserable.

Was this what heartache felt like? How had her mother lived with it for so many years?

And suddenly, Olivia knew she couldn't stay any longer. One more night sounded simple enough, but it would be a torment beyond what she could manage. She was turning into her mother, allowing herself to be hurt, and Olivia knew one thing: she wanted better than that. She pulled her phone from her back pocket and began arranging the logistics, bringing her flight forward and booking a car.

It felt surreal to coordinate this, and wrong to do so without Luca's knowledge, but wasn't her independence something she valued? They were two strangers, really, regardless of what had happened in the last month. She'd fought hard—not for their marriage in the end, but for her own life, for her independence—and now she could step into it and enjoy the fruits of her labour. She could go home and see Sisi, and know that her sister would never have to make the kind of pragmatic marriage Olivia had.

She told herself it was relief she was experiencing as the cab driver loaded her suitcase into the boot, the engine idling. She gave one last look at his exquisite home, then slid into the back seat of the car, dark glasses in place.

It was only once she'd checked in her suitcase at the buzzing Fiumicino airport that she dared to call Luca. She'd contemplated leaving a note at his house, but that had felt wrong. And she'd known she couldn't see him again, couldn't say what she needed to say face to face. It was cowardly, but self-preservation instincts were in overdrive.

He answered after one ring. 'Olivia.'

God, she would miss hearing him say her name. 'Luca.'

'How are you?'

She squeezed her eyes shut as tears filled her gaze. 'I'm fine,' she lied, shaking her head a little. 'Look, there was so much I didn't say last night, because I couldn't find the words at the time, and I was scared to admit what I wanted, when you were offering something so reasonable and sensible, something I might have jumped at, in another life.'

Each of his breaths was audible as he waited for her to continue.

'The thing is, the way my father treated my mother, it's just like you said—love turned to hate. They did love each other at one time, and they were happy, and then things went wrong, he never forgave her, and she was miserable. She's still miserable. There's nothing quite so awful as being married to someone you love, who doesn't love you back.' The words hung between them like little blades.

'But what I was offering cut that concern out of the equation.'

Her smile was bitter. 'For you, perhaps, but not for me.'

'I don't understand.'

'I know that.' Despite her efforts, a sob caught in her throat, punctuating the final word.

'Olivia, what is it? You're upset.'

'No.' She blinked around the terminal, the fluorescent light too bright, even with her dark sunglasses. A voice came over the speakers, muffled by static. She stood, pulling her handbag strap over her shoulder.

'Where are you?'

'I'm at the airport.' She sniffed.

'The airport? What the hell? Your flight's tomorrow.'

'I moved it forward.'

'Why?'

'What's the point in drawing this out? We want different things.'

'Because I asked you to stay another three months?'

'Because you asked me to stay *only* another three months.'

'To begin with,' he insisted, muffled noise in the background. 'You were the one who balked at the idea of a real marriage—'

'But that's not what you were offering.'

'You know what I mean—a lasting marriage, like we have now, but ongoing. I thought three months would reassure you that there was an escape clause.'

'I don't want an escape clause.'

'Then why are you at the airport?'

She groaned, tilting her head back to stare at the ceiling. 'I realised something, last night. When you were offering a perfectly reasonable loveless relationship, a marriage founded, in fact, on the absence of love, I came to understand that it's the exact opposite of what I want. I love you, Luca. Somehow, I fell in love with you, despite having sworn I'd never love anyone. And if I stay here in Rome, with you, I'll start to hope you'll love me back, and the hoping will make me miserable, just like my mother was.'

'What did you just say?'

She moved towards the boarding gate, tears streaming down her cheeks now.

'My worst fear is being married to someone I love, who doesn't love me back. I know what that can do to a person, and I can't do it to myself—even for one more night. Now that I understand how I feel about you, I have no choice but to leave.'

'Olivia—'

'It's okay,' she interrupted. 'I've thought about this from every angle. I just wish I was brave enough to have said this to your face, so that you could see the genuine gratitude in my eyes when I thank you for what you did for me.'

He groaned almost inaudibly. 'Stay. Spend tonight with me.' His voice was deep and throaty. 'Come home.'

'But this isn't my home,' she said with finality. 'And you're not really my husband. You never were. A marriage isn't a marriage without love, we both know that.' She waited for him to disagree, bracing for it, and then, after a long pause, shook her head. 'Goodbye, Luca.'

CHAPTER FOURTEEN

'OH, COME ON,' she groaned, slapping her forehead as the announcement came over the PA.

'Owing to a technical issue with the landing wheel, Aster Airline flight 251 to London Heathrow has been delayed. We apologise for the inconvenience. Another update will be provided in thirty minutes. Thank you for your patience.'

Olivia ground her teeth together, scanning the departures board, hoping a different airline might be making the same trip to London, so she could book another seat, but there were no other flights for the next two hours.

Resigning herself to her fate, she strode towards the newsagent's, browsing magazines, looking for something, anything, to distract herself with. But a sense of claustrophobia was clawing at her. Having decided she wanted to leave Rome, that she needed to leave Rome, she found the delay completely unacceptable.

She chose two magazines at random, paid for them without looking at the covers, then found a seat apart from most of the crowd. Rather than reading the magazines, she stared out of the large, heavily tinted windows, at the concourse, watching as passengers disembarked planes directly onto the runway, from skinny staircases, walking in organised lines towards the building. Planes took off, others landed, but after thirty minutes another announcement was made: their plane would be delayed at least another hour.

It was tempting to go to the information desk and ask for more information, but the queue snaked halfway through their seating area, and the staff member there was already looking harried and stressed. Olivia had no interest in adding to her load.

She continued to watch the happenings of the airport, the piercing blue of Rome's sky making a mockery of her mood.

In her peripheral vision, she was aware of another traveller approaching and she bristled, wanting company like she wanted a hole in the head. She kept her gaze resolutely focused on the window, staring at the sky, actively discouraging any attempt at communication.

'Do you need a lift, *cara*?'

Her heart went into overdrive and her head turned towards him in complete shock, his voice jolting something inside her to life. She was too overcome to pretend calm. How grateful she was that her dark glasses were still in place!

'Luca! What are you doing here?'

'Did you think I would not move heaven and earth to finish our conversation?'

She stood up to meet his eyes, not liking the height disadvantage of her seated position.

'We did finish our conversation.'

'Too abruptly.'

'What else is there to say?'

He looked around, and in that moment she allowed herself the brief weakness of drinking him in, all suit-clad, six and a half feet of him. The power of his physique took her breath away, as it almost always did.

'More than I'd care to discuss here,' he said with a shake of his head, holding out his hand. 'Come with me.'

She looked at his hand as though it were a bundle of snakes.

'My jet is fuelled up. I'll fly you to London. We can speak on the way.'

Her lips parted. The offer of the flight was tempting—but to have her escape route shared with the very man she was running away from?

His eyes darkened as her hesitation became obvious.

'Fine,' he ground out. 'You can take the flight without me.' He lifted one finger to the air. 'On one condition.'

'Another deal?'

'Yes.'

'What is it?'

'Give me ten minutes first. To talk. Privately.'

Privately. A shiver ran down her spine, desire sparking in her belly. She looked away. 'Okay, that's fair enough.' Had she really thought she could avoid this? 'Where?'

But he took her hand, drawing her with him, away from the crowds, the disgruntled voices, and right back out of the terminal, towards a central concourse, and then across it. Neither of them spoke—not even when he gestured for her to enter a set of timber doors ahead of him.

A first-class lounge, so exclusive it wasn't even badged, awaited them. Luca was clearly known here by name. Here, it was easy to find a private corner—there were only half a dozen or so other travellers, and the room was enormous.

At a table in the distant corner, he pulled out a seat. She eyed it sceptically, nervously, then eased herself into it.

'Thank you.'

He took the seat opposite, and the table seemed to shrink about three sizes. She toyed with her hands in her lap, then forced herself to stop, to meet his gaze. To be strong enough to do this.

'What would you like to discuss?'

His laugh was a short, sharp sound, totally lacking amusement. 'What you said on the phone, for one.'

'Which part?'

His eyes narrowed. 'Which part do you think?'

She compressed her lips, the answer obvious. 'Why?'

'Olivia, you told me you *never* wanted to fall in love. When we agreed to this marriage—'

'I know that. I'm sorry.'

'You're sorry?'

'We had a deal. I broke it. I never meant to. I didn't *want* to love you.'

'How do you know it's love?'

She frowned, the question totally surprising her. 'How do I know the sky is blue or the earth is round?'

'Science?'

She smiled despite the heaviness in her heart. 'Fact. And this is fact. Not scientific, perhaps, but no less real.'

'Since when?'

Another question she hadn't expected. 'I can't say. Probably the moment you heard me out. I half expected you to get me thrown out of that party in Rome. That you didn't, that you listened and agreed to my crazy proposal, showed me what a decent guy you were. And every day since—'

'And every night?'

'Yes, every night.' She swallowed. 'But this isn't just about sex. I mean, that's a part of what I love, but it's so much more than that.'

He stood up, scraping his chair backwards, pacing towards the windows, gazing for a moment at the aeroplanes lined up on the tarmac, their tails forming a perfect line, then turning, staring at her as if pulling her apart piece by piece. 'The thing is, Olivia, I need to know that you know, beyond a shadow of a doubt. Because I thought I was in love, once, and I believed my wife loved me, but it was the worst mistake of my life. And yet, the impact of Jayne's breaking up with me is nothing compared to this.' He returned to the table, bracing his palms on the edge. 'With her, my pride was hurt. I was blindsided. But losing you—'

She held her breath, her features contorted by confusion.

'I can't have you say that you love me, if you are then going to decide you don't. I can't let this be a real marriage, in every way, unless you promise me that's what you want. Don't you see, Olivia? I suggested a continuation of what we had because it was safe. What you're offering, what you're asking for, is filled with risks.'

'Yes.' She nodded, her heart soaring at what he was unintentionally revealing. Or was he? Her own feelings burned so brightly, she feared she'd lost the ability to comprehend his. 'I'm aware of that. Like the risk that you might not love me back. Or that your love for me might turn to hate, just as my father's did for my mother.'

'I know enough about love turning to hate. I had a masterclass in it with Jayne. But that doesn't mean I would ever hurt you. Not like your father hurt your mother.' His eyes probed hers. 'Ask yourself if I could ever be capable of the things he did, or if you could ever act as Jayne did. You know the answer to that.'

She bit back a sob.

'I love you because you're nothing like him,' she whispered, dipping her head forward. 'But that doesn't mean you won't hurt me. That you're not hurting me now.'

He crouched down in front of her face, reaching out and removing her glasses, placing them on the table softly. At the sight of her tear-reddened eyes, he cursed softly. 'I don't want you to go.'

'I know that.' Anguish tore through her. 'But I can't stay.'

'Even for love?'

'My loving you isn't enough. You know that.'

'What about the fact I love you, too? What about the fact I am terrified of what that means, but I'm here, saying it anyway, because I know one thing for certain—if I lose you, I will regret it for the rest of my life.'

Her lips parted in surprise.

He lifted up, curling a hand around her cheek. 'I didn't realise, until you called me an hour ago, and told me you loved me, that the reason I can't bear the thought of you leaving our marriage as agreed is because I don't want you to leave—ever.'

'You said that last night,' she groaned. 'But it's not enough to want me to stay. That's *not* love, it's convenience.'

He pressed a finger to her lips. 'I asked you to stay, not because I want to continue our convenient arrangement, but because I don't want to live without you. Because you have given meaning to my life, because you have made me smile again, *cara*, and because with you, not only do I feel complete, I *feel*, in here, after years of nothing.' He tapped a hand to his heart. 'Is there any part of you that wants to walk away from this?'

She squeezed her eyes shut, everything she'd ever known to be true in her life like an enormous impediment. 'No,' she whispered, finally. 'But I'm scared.'

'And I am terrified,' he countered. 'I thought I had been through the pits of hell when Jayne left me. I thought that was as bad as it got. But now, I imagine a life without you, I imagine you waking up and deciding you no longer want me in your life, and I know that it would be ten thousand times worse.'

She blinked, his passion obvious.

'Yet, I am kneeling here now, asking you to stay with me regardless because, whatever I fear, a life with you is worth the risk.'

Her throat was too thick with unshed tears for Olivia to speak coherently. A muffled sob escaped.

'I do not want you simply to stay,' he said, after a moment. 'I want you to marry me, for real. This time, in front of family, friends, the world. I want everyone to join in the celebration of our love, to witness our commitment, to understand that I am pledging myself to you, for the rest of my life. Love is a leap of faith, but what is the alternative, Olivia? To both run from our past, to keep ourselves closed off?' He lifted closer to her, so their mouths were separated by only an inch. 'To lose one another? This? For me to live each day without you, without what we share? Is there anything worse than that?'

Anguish tortured her, but it was pierced by hope and joy. She shook her head, tears rolling down her cheeks. 'There is nothing worse than losing you,' she confirmed.

'And so you never shall,' he promised. 'Olivia, the last time we discussed marrying, it was with very carefully worded conditions in place. Now, I ask you this: Will you marry me? With no condition, no caution, no limitation on our joy, our future? Marry me, stand beside me—your own person, as independent as you seek to be—but with my companionship, my love, and always, always, my support.'

A smile cracked her face. She closed the rest of the distance between them, kissing him, and into the kiss, into his soul, she said the word 'yes', over and over and over again, because she felt it in every fibre of her being, every part of her own soul. She loved him, and always would. While it was true that love was a gamble, a leap of faith, the strength of their love had given them both wings to catch them, should they fall. She trusted Luca, and knew her heart to be safe with him—there was nothing she wanted more than to return to their life, as his wife, and to truly start living.

'Luca?'

'Mmm?'

'Let's go home.'

His eyes widened, the meaning of her statement not lost on him.

'*Sì, cara.* Let's go home.'

Luca loved his wife, and he loved her in a way that had expanded his soul, had expanded everything he knew about life. He'd learned that the fear he'd felt was actually excitement, that stepping into a life with Olivia gave him an adrenaline rush every day. A month after their airport reunion, they were married, and only one week later Olivia realised the reason for her changeable appetite and sudden aversion to cured meats and alcohol. A honeymoon baby, or close to, conceived during their first week together in Rome, when they had been making love and falling in love all at the same time. So that now, eight months after Olivia had told Luca she loved him, and he'd realised how he felt about her, he stared down at a little infant wrapped in pink, a new kind of love stealing through him, happiness making him feel as though he could take on the world.

'She is perfect, *cara*. How clever you are.'

'I think we can both take credit for her,' Olivia said with a smile, head pressed back against the crisp white hospital pillow. Luca had never loved her more.

'That is very kind of you.'

'Would you hand her to me?' Olivia asked, tired, but arms aching to once again hold their hours-old daughter.

'Certo.' He picked up their newborn, cradling her to his chest a moment before snuggling her into Olivia's arms, and watching as their baby nestled against her. Completion wrapped around him. Everything in his life was perfect.

The sound of wheels on linoleum woke Olivia, and a moment later Luca appeared, pushing Pietra into the hospital room. Three days after giving birth, and Olivia was feeling somewhat normal, except for breasts that suddenly felt so enormous she wasn't sure how she could stand without toppling over.

'Ah, Nonna.' Olivia smiled, pushing up to standing and wincing slightly.

'Stay, stay,' Pietra insisted, so much frailer than the last time they'd seen each other, but with eyes still sparkling with intelligence and wit, and a ready smile softening her slender face. Her continued wellness was, doctors kept saying, a 'miracle', but Olivia knew better. Pietra wasn't finished yet—from the moment she'd learned of Olivia's pregnancy, it had seemed to give her a new lease on life, a determination to stave off the ravages of her disease, or perhaps it was fate, being as kind to Pietra as it had been to Luca and Olivia, when it had delivered them into one another's arms. 'You do not need to get up.'

'I want to bring the baby to you,' Olivia demurred, love in her eyes as they met Luca's.

'Thank you,' he mouthed.

She moved to the plastic-sided crib and removed the swaddle, then lifted her daughter out. She placed her carefully in Pietra's arms, aware that Luca was there, waiting, ready to intervene if Pietra's strength failed her.

'She is so lovely.' A tear slid down Pietra's cheek. 'So much like you, Olivia.'

Olivia stroked their baby's head. 'I see a fair bit of Giovanardi in her as well.'

'Do you?' Pride touched Pietra's face.

'Oh, yes. She has your eyes.'

The baby grabbed Pietra's finger, curling her tiny fingers around its frail length.

'Does she have a name yet?'

'Actually, that is something we wanted to discuss with you,' Luca said, nodding, gently prompting Olivia to continue.

'We were wondering how you would feel about us calling her Pietra.'

Pietra's lips parted in surprise. 'I would be touched, of course. Are you sure?'

'It's the only name we considered,' Olivia promised. 'To us, she's already Pietra.'

'Luca, look!'

'What is it, *cara*?' On the eve of their tenth wedding anniversary, Luca emerged from the kitchen, apron tied around his waist, looking impossibly sexy. She loved him in myriad ways, but his determination to learn to cook for her and their children, and to be a present, hands-on father and husband, made her fall in love with him more and more each day.

'Look what I found!' She carried the item, wrapped carefully in bubble wrap, to Luca, triumph in her features.

'A toy? I don't know. What is it? The children's teeth?'

Olivia laughed, lifting a finger to her lips. 'You know the *fatina dei denti* takes those away.' She held the bubble wrap out to him. 'I was looking for my wedding dress, on a whim. Pietra was asking about it.'

'I am not surprised it was our daughter, rather than the twins.' He laughed with paternal indulgence.

'Rafaello and Fiero are busy with their soccer match, of course.' She rolled her eyes, because it seemed to be all their seven-year-old sons cared for at present. 'Anyway, I was looking in the box of wedding things, and found this.'

He peeled the tab of the sticky tape, casting his wife a rueful glance as she hopped from foot to foot, until eventually he revealed what was within: the Murano *fenice*. He looked from the bird to Olivia, shaking his head. 'I had quite forgotten about this.'

'Yes, me too. It's exquisite. Do you remember the day we chose him?'

'I do.'

'How did we ever forget?'

'Life,' he said with a warm smile. 'We have been busy living.'

Happiness spread through Olivia. 'Well, now I don't feel quite so bad. Where shall we put it?'

'Somewhere prominent,' Luca said, and then, as an afterthought, 'But far from the boys' football kicks.'

She laughed, sashaying through the living room, placing the bird atop the grand piano little Pietra was obsessed with playing each night.

'Perfect. And here it will stand to remind us that, from the ashes, good things really can rise,' Luca murmured, wrapping his arms around his wife, pressing his chin to her shoulder. They stared at the bird, content, and grateful, all at once.

'What time is Sienna arriving?'

Olivia glanced at her wristwatch. 'Their flight should land any minute.'

'Then I had better get back to the kitchen.' He kissed her cheek, then spun her in the circle of his arms, seeking her lips, never able to pass up an opportunity to taste his beloved wife.

'Are you sure you don't have any spare time?' she asked silkily, wrapping her arms behind his back, just as the twins burst into the room, speaking in rapid-fire Italian about alleged on-field grievances, so Olivia and Luca shared a glance of amusement and pulled slightly apart.

'Come into the kitchen and tell me about it, *terramotti*,' Luca said, then, leaning closer and whispering, purely for Olivia's benefit, 'Tonight, *mi amore*. Tonight.'

It was a promise he intended to keep—for that night, and every night for the rest of their lives.

* * * * *

MILLS & BOON

Coming next month

DESERT PRINCE'S DEFIANT BRIDE
Julieanne Howells

Lily watched as Khaled came closer, all smouldering masculine intent. Seconds ago she'd been in a snit. Now she couldn't remember why. By the time he reached her she was boneless and unresisting, letting him gather her hand and lift it to his lips.

'*Habiba*, you are beautiful,' he purred.

Beautiful? Her breath fluttered out. Dear Lord, she'd sighed. She'd actually just *sighed*.

He dipped his head. He was going to kiss her. She shivered as warm lips brushed the tender skin of her ear. A delicious, scintillating caress.

But not a kiss.

He was whispering to her.

'Something has come up. Follow my lead.' Louder, for the benefit of the others, he said, 'Mother, ladies, our apologies. An urgent matter needs our attention and we must go.'

Okay. It was part of the act.

'Can I leave you to gather everything Miss Marchant will need for her stay? You have her sizes?' The assistants nodded vigorously. 'And please send a selection of everything you think appropriate.' He turned to gaze adoringly at her. 'Don't stint.'

As if they would. They were staring at him as if he were a god come down to earth, imagining all their commission.

His long fingers curled through hers, warm, strong and wonderfully comforting—drat the man. And then he set off for the private lift they'd arrived in.

Focus, Lily.

He'd said something had come up. Perhaps there was news on Nate?

The lift doors closed. 'What's so…?' Where had that husky note come from? She tried again. 'What's so urgent that we needed to leave?'

'This.' He gathered her close and pressed his mouth to hers.

She should have pushed him away—there was no audience here—but his mouth slanted over hers in a kiss so tantalisingly gentle she leant in. He began a delicate exploration of her jaw, her throat, and found a tender spot beneath her ear, teasing it with a slow swirl of his tongue.

Her fingers sank into his biceps.

When he nudged a thigh between her legs she instinctively rubbed against it, seeking contact where she needed it most.

'Come,' he said.

Yes, oh, yes…

Wait…no. What?

He was walking. He meant her to go with him. He was leaving the lift.

She teetered in her new heels and he drew her protectively against his side. Together, eyes locked, they crossed the foyer and stepped outside into the now familiar intense heat and something else—something new.

With the dazzle of sunshine came camera flashes. A cacophony of voices. Crowding figures.

'Your Highness? Sir? When's the wedding?'

'Lily? Has he bought you a ring yet? When did you know it was love?'

She blinked as the lights exploded, over and over. With a jolt she realised he'd walked them into a press pack—and he knew enough about those for it not to be an accident.

Continue reading

DESERT PRINCE'S DEFIANT BRIDE

Julieanne Howells

Available next month

www.millsandboon.co.uk

JOIN US ON SOCIAL MEDIA!

Stay up to date with our latest releases, author news and gossip, special offers and discounts, and all the behind-the-scenes action from Mills & Boon...

millsandboon

millsandboonuk

millsandboon

It might just be true love...